HELEN FORRESTER

MOURNING DOVES

LONDON NEW YORK SYDNEY TORONTO

This edition published 1996
by BCA
by arrangement with HarperCollins*Publishers*

Second reprint 1997

CN 2598

Printed in England by Clays Ltd, St Ives plc

To Stephen and Lauren, with love

This is a novel and its characters are products of my imagination, its situations likewise. Whatever similarity there may be of name, no reference is intended to any person living or dead.

I gratefully acknowledge information and advice regarding the Hoylake and District War Memorial from Mr J.T. O'Neil of Hoylake, Mr R. Jones of West Kirby, and Mr K. Burnley of Irby; help regarding costume from Mr Richard Brown, Victoria Public Library, Westminster, London; and information regarding flora of the area from Mr J.T. O'Neil of Hoylake and Miss Jemma Samuels of Wallasey. The background information which they supplied was invaluable, and I thank them all.

PROLOGUE

11 November 1995

The cenotaph stood on its great concrete plinth at the top of Grange Hill. To reach it meant a long climb for aged veterans and decrepit widows. Nevertheless, in this fiftieth anniversary year, a larger number than usual had turned out for the Remembrance Day service. Now the last wreath had been laid, and the parade had been formed up and was marching slowly down to the village.

As the voices faded away, Celia sat in her wheelchair, waiting with Rosemary, her West Indian carer, and her godson, Flight Lieutenant Timothy George Woodcock, DFC, until the narrow path down to the road was clear of people, and the wheelchair could be manoeuvred down.

Coming straight off the distant snow-topped mountains of North Wales and the estuary of the River Dee, the wind was cold, and, despite the blanket Rosemary had tucked round her, Celia was shivering.

She did not weep. Crying never helped anybody, she would say tartly. She had, however, a keen sense of inward loneliness, and she remembered suddenly her sister, Edna, friend and partner in so much of her life – ever since 1920.

What a year that had been. A year of final realisation that the men killed in the First World War would never come back, and neither would the safe, predictable life of 1914. Millions of ignorant, untrained women had had to remake their lives and find work to maintain themselves. I was one of them, considered Celia, as she sat patiently in her wheelchair and looked out across the misty landscape of the Wirral. And I suppose that, in some ways, I was lucky.

1

She was, she knew, the oldest person to attend the service, one hundred years next week; and she was probably the only person in the district with truly clear memories of the First World War, of life before it began and of its aftermath.

Her luck had not held. The names of five members of her family were listed on the cenotaph, and every year she made the effort to come to lay a family wreath, gorgeous with huge plastic poppies and black satin ribbons, at the foot of the memorial. From the wreath dangled an old-fashioned black-edged card, which said,

IN TENDER MEMORY OF MY SONS, PETER, PAUL AND BERTRAM TREMAINE, KILLED IN ACTION IN WORLD WAR II, AND OF MY GRANDSONS, MICHAEL AND DAVID TREMAINE, LIKEWISE KILLED IN ACTION IN THE FALKLANDS WAR. NEVER FORGOTTEN.

As they waited, Timothy George also felt the cold and longed for a warm fire and a whisky and soda. A pity Bertram's wife could not be here, he thought; but, after her sons, Michael and David, had been killed, there was nothing to keep her in the Wirral, and she had gone south to live with her own mother in Devon.

Celia had remained, alone, in the red-brick Edwardian house which she and Alec had bought on their marriage.

It was strange to realise, Timothy ruminated, that, to most of the parishioners, both the First and the Second World Wars were forgotten wars, forgotten sacrifices. Except in special anniversary years such as this one, the crowds around the cenotaph grew smaller each year.

The flight lieutenant sighed. He supposed that Celia and he were, by now, simply walking history, not that Celia could walk very far; she was quite frail. This would probably be the last Poppy Day for her – and probably the last for many of the men like himself, some in uniform and some in shabby macintoshes, all with glittering collections of medals pinned to their breasts – and for the pitiful little bunch of widows and elderly spinsters, each with a red poppy in her buttonhole.

As he had glanced at the huddled old women, he had felt

uneasily that even today there were some elderly women who were still not very good at managing life alone.

Their husbands, sons and lovers had died in the Second World War. Theirs was the second generation of women to be widowed by war or left without hope of marriage.

His own brother's name and also the names of Celia's brothers were on the Roll of Honour in the glass case on the cenotaph in Liverpool Cathedral. His brother, Eric, had been shot down by a sniper in Normandy during the Second World War, leaving a pregnant wife. His little nephew, he considered, had been fortunate to have been brought up by a kindly stepfather, considerably younger than his mother.

The wars had created a dreadful double generation gap, he thought grimly, and judging by the mismanagement in the country, the gap had not yet been closed.

He had for years held the notion that nobody had been able to fill the empty spaces left by the fathers and grandfathers who had died – or had been so wounded or exhausted that they were too weary to do anything much, once they had returned to civilian life. He remembered how tired he had been himself; it had been an enormous effort to start again after he had been demobbed.

Rosemary shook his arm, and said, 'I think we can go down now.'

He jumped, and then grinned agreement. In the comparative silence now surrounding them, the cold wind whined and the artificial foliage of the wreaths rustled faintly in reply, like distant voices calling.

Before they moved her, Celia turned to glance once more at the wreaths and then upwards to the bronze soldier in battledress who stared out over the sands of the estuary.

She remembered three little boys who had built a sand castle on the seashore, and how they had squabbled about who should place a paper Union Jack on its summit. She felt a sudden terrible pain go through her. Years later, they had followed that Union Jack and had gone gaily off to war and never come back. And in the Falklands War her two grandsons had done the same, for reasons that she could never understand.

3

'Goodbye, my dears,' she whispered, as the wheelchair began to move. 'See you soon.'

She took out a paper handkerchief and firmly blew her nose. One must never give in. Edna and I certainly never did.

Chapter One

✦

March 1920

Was it really as small as that? Had that weed-covered quarter-acre ever held a formal flower garden, a lawn at the side of the house and a vegetable garden?

Louise Gilmore glanced up in despair at the house itself, one of a semi-detached pair. Sharp shards of glass stood upright in the frame of the broken hall bedroom window. She remembered how Gracie, her father's housemaid, used to shake her dust mop out of that window – regardless of who might be standing below on the front step. When the family came to spend their holidays in the house, one of the maids had always come with them; it was usually Gracie, who hated the isolation of the place, the steady boom of waves on the sea wall, and the sand which constantly sifted in from the surrounding dunes.

Now, Louise noted hopelessly, damp brick beneath the windowsill indicated that rain had soaked into the wall. The front sitting-room window had had a piece of board nailed over it, and the front door had lost most of its shiny black enamel; what remained was bubbled from the heat of many summers.

There was no garden gate. Only the wooden gateposts remained, and the encroaching front hedge had nearly obliterated them, too.

As a result of the death of her husband the previous Saturday, Louise had been terrified by the dire warnings of his executor, Cousin Albert, and of his lawyer, Mr Barnett. She had, they said, been left almost destitute and must, in order to raise some money on which to live, sell their beautiful Liverpool mansion immediately.

It was essential that she find speedily some other place to live in, so she had, that morning – only the day after her husband's funeral – dragged herself out of her bed and, with her younger daughter, Celia, made the tiring journey by train out to Meols, a small village on the Wirral Peninsula.

They had come to inspect a small – small from her perspective – summer cottage which had been in the family for years and had been rented out for most of the time. Cousin Albert had suggested that it would make a suitable retirement home for her, into which she could move almost at once.

She lifted her mourning veil from her face and flung it back over her black bonnet, then stepped on to the path leading to the front of the house. One of its dull red tiles had heaved and she tripped on it and nearly fell. She shivered, her breath coming in sobbing gulps.

'Be careful, Mother!' admonished her twenty-four-year-old spinster daughter, Celia, who was following closely behind her. 'Hold your dress up. You'll get it all muddy round the hem.'

Equally as scared as her mother, Celia was more snappish than usual. She herself was clutching her wide-brimmed black hat with one hand and holding down her own ankle-length skirt against the buffeting sea wind. She had sand in one eye and it was running tearfully from the painful irritation. She looked worn out.

Louise's lips tightened. She did not reply to Celia, as she lifted her black satin dress and petticoat an inch so that they did not draggle in the damp puddles on the dirty path.

Sometimes Celia could be very trying. Wasn't it enough that, only yesterday, they had stood by the grave of dear Timothy, her husband, who had shared her bed for thirty years? What was a bit of mud on the hem of one's skirt compared to losing him?

To add to her misery, Cousin Albert Gilmore, sole executor of her husband's will, had told her, upon his arrival, that Timothy had left heavy business debts, an announcement which had sent a frightening chill down her back. He had said that to keep up her fashionable home in the village of West Derby on the outskirts of Liverpool on what remained of her dowry would be impossible.

Cousin Albert had been completely heartless, she felt, not to give her some time to mourn, before unloading such cruel facts upon her.

Cousin Albert himself had, at first, not known what to do. He had, on Sunday, been telephoned by Mr Barnett, and he had arrived from his home in Nottingham on Monday. He had gone straight from Lime Street Station to see Mr Barnett in his office, and, warned by him, had gone on to Timothy's office to interview his chief clerk and to look at his files and account books.

What he had found was a financial disaster, which would, he thought in quiet rage, take him weeks to sort out. He berated himself for ever agreeing to be his cousin's trustee. He was, therefore, not in a very good temper and, when he arrived at Louise's house, he was, in addition, rumpled and hungry from his journey.

He had paid off the taxi at the driveway entrance and, carrying his suitcase, had puffed his way up a slight slope round a fine bed of laurel bushes to the imposing front steps. He pulled a huge brass bell handle and fidgeted fretfully until the door was opened by a frightened-looking parlourmaid.

Close behind the maid came Celia, wringing her hands helplessly, and whispering, 'Oh, Cousin Albert, I'm so glad you've come!'

'Yes, yes, my dear, I've come.'

He plonked down his small suitcase, and took off his black bowler hat to reveal a tumble of snow-white curls. He handed the hat to the maid and then peeled off his heavy black overcoat and pushed that on to her, too. He gave Celia a light peck on one cheek, and asked abruptly, 'Where's Louise?'

'In bed.'

'And your father?'

'He's laid out in the downstairs front sitting room.' Her voice quivered, and she added with evident anxiety, as she pointed to a closed, white-enamelled door, 'Mother wanted him buried from home, so I sent for the undertaker in West Derby. The undertaker thought that that room would be most convenient for visitors to come into, so I agreed.'

'Quite right, child. Quite right. When's the funeral?'

He looked around the hall. Seeing a door open, he remembered the family breakfast room and made straight for it, hoping to find a fire where he could warm himself. Celia fluttered after him.

'Tomorrow – at ten o'clock,' she told him, as he thankfully turned his back to a good coal fire and let the heat flood over him.

He had no feelings about the loss of his cousin, only a sense of irritation. He knew that it would be his duty to deal quickly with the affairs of a pair of tear-sodden women, who must change their way of life immediately. He also knew that he must make sure that grasping creditors could not lay hold on Louise's own modest assets. Timothy's clerk had assured him that she had not jointly signed with Timothy anything in connection with the business, which was a relief. At least she had, according to what Timothy had once told him, her dowry in the shape of the rents from six working-class houses in Birkenhead, for what little they were worth, and, in addition, this very fine house.

But he had been a lawyer himself, and he knew from bitter experience that moneylenders could be quite ruthless and, occasionally, dishonest in their seizing of assets. Like any good Victorian gentleman, he was aware of his duty to any of his family, and nobody was going to strip his cousin's widow of her assets, if he had anything to do with it.

This rectitude did not prevent his being judged by Celia and her mother as inhumanly abrupt and callous with them, when, the next morning, Louise was persuaded to get up very early and get dressed in order that she might receive the many callers who would come to pay their respects to the dead before the funeral.

On the day of his arrival, since he felt that time was of the essence, she had also had to face, after a late lunch, the sad truths discovered earlier by her husband's trustee.

'You will need money from somewhere on which to live,' he had announced baldly. 'You will certainly have to sell this Liverpool house, and do it very quickly.' He sighed when he saw her shocked expression, but went on firmly, 'Whatever you get for

8

it can be invested in an annuity to give you a modest income on which to live.'

Albert had gazed reflectively at the lovely embossed ceiling of her large upstairs drawing room, normally used only for big parties, and added, 'It's a valuable property in a good district – so close to the countryside – so it should fetch a good price.'

In his opinion, it was little less than a miracle that Timothy had long ago had enough sense to put the house in her name, so that it could never be seized to settle his business debts. Timothy had always taken the most appalling financial chances, he reflected. Of course, he had made a lot of money, though his luck, it seemed, was running out just before he died.

Albert had, therefore, very early the next morning, while Louise dealt with her visitors, been to see an estate agent and arranged for the house to be put on the market immediately; because she owned it, there was no need to wait for Timothy's will to be probated before doing this. With the money it fetched, he had decided, he would buy the annuity for her from a reputable insurance company, which should just produce enough to keep her and young Celia in genteel poverty. In the meantime, they would just have to manage on the rental money from her Birkenhead houses – or take a small loan from the bank, which could be repaid from the money received for her home. Though he was not her trustee, he assumed that Louise would expect him, as the only man in the family, to undertake these financial arrangements on her behalf. Women were, in his opinion, quite helpless; he would present his very sensible plans for her future to her and, undoubtedly, she would accept them.

Before Timothy's sad demise, Louise had had no idea that she bore the burden of owning the Liverpool house, and the information had increased her bewilderment and her terror of being left alone. Timothy had always done everything, as a good husband should; all she had had to do was balance the housekeeping accounts, entertain his guests charmingly and be kind to him in bed.

It had been scant comfort to her when Cousin Albert, when talking to her on his arrival, had warned, 'My dear, you will

9

probably have to manage without a servant. However, since there will be only you and Celia, a very small house will be quite appropriate, and I am sure you are an excellent housekeeper.' He had smiled at her with as much benignity as he could muster.

Louise moaned into her black handkerchief. Did he not realise that he was tearing her whole life apart? It was too much to endure.

He had watched her weep for a few moments, and then had leaned forward to pat her hand and remind her, as Mr Barnett, the solicitor, had earlier reminded him, that she also owned a little house, really a cottage, on the other side of the Mersey River. 'Your father's summer home – by the sea – in Meols, near Hoylake,' he had encouraged. 'When your sister Felicity died, she left it to you. Remember?

'Mr Barnett tells me that he recollects that it was let for years. I understand, however, from the agent, Mr Billings, whom I phoned today from Mr Barnett's office, that there is no one living in it at present.'

He heard Celia take a quick intake of breath, and he glanced over to her. Pale-blue eyes stared back at him from a dead-white face. She looked scared to death.

He continued in a more cheerful tone of voice, addressing himself partly towards her. 'After being let for so long, it will almost certainly require renovation – but that is soon arranged. You've probably seen it, Celia?'

'No, I haven't,' she muttered.

He stopped, wishing heartily that he had not been left the unpleasant task of telling these stupid women what they must do; he felt too old and tired to be bothered with them. He went on heavily, 'When Mr Barnett told me about it, I had thought of selling the cottage on your behalf, instead of this house. But it would not fetch much – I hope, however, that it won't need too much to make it a very comfortable home for you – and you must have an income from somewhere to live on, which only funds from this big house can provide.' He reminded himself that, after the funeral the following morning, he should make a quick trip out to Meols to check that the cottage was indeed habitable.

Louise had temporarily forgotten the cottage; she had not seen it since Felicity had died ten years before. Though the day-to-day care of her property was done through Mr Billings, dear Timothy had always kept an eye on it for her, including that which had been settled on her by her father at the signing of her marriage contract. The thought made her weep ever more heavily into her black handkerchief.

Now, as she looked at the cottage, she despaired. What would happen to her in this awful place? How could she bear it? And to add to her distress, her scandalous elder sister, Felicity, did not seem to have done much to keep the building up during her ownership of it. She remembered that, when the property had passed to her, Timothy had insisted on letting it, because, he said, it was too shabby for family use. Perhaps it was the tenants who had left it in such a mess.

How devout churchman Timothy had condemned Felicity's way of life. He would not hear of Louise having anything more to do with her. All because Felicity had dared to live in the cottage with handsome Colonel Featherstone, a scarred veteran of the Matabele and Boer Wars – without marrying him. As a result, Timothy had always insisted that she might have a bad influence on the children. He had even frowned when Louise bestirred herself enough to say defiantly that she must occasionally write to her only sister, no matter what she had done. And Timothy must have known very well that, if she married a second husband, Felicity would automatically lose the army pension left her by her first husband, dear Angus, killed at Rorke's Drift during the Zulu Wars. But Timothy had always insisted that shortage of money was no excuse for Sin.

Only her father had understood Felicity, she thought, as she sniffed into her handkerchief. Felicity had died childless, but, sometimes, when her own elder daughter, Edna, had grown up, she had seen in her some of Felicity's sprightliness and brave defiance of convention.

She would have been glad to have Edna with her now, but the girl was married and far away in Brazil.

When, before setting out for the cottage, cold dread of a future without a father or brother or son to care for her had consumed her soul, Louise had at breakfast wept openly in front of fat, elderly Cousin Albert.

Harassed Celia, at twenty-four far too old for marriage, had pressed a glass of sherry on her. Mother was so set in her ways, so difficult to deal with if her normal routine was upset, that Celia knew that if any action had to be taken, it would be she who must, somehow, take it.

She felt despairingly that she had no idea of business matters; Papa had always kept such information in his own hands. In consequence, she had become numb with fear as Cousin Albert explained to her her late father's financial circumstances.

The loss of her father, however unloving, had reopened her grief over the loss of her brothers, Tom and George, during the war, and her stomach muscles were clenched as she did her best to keep calm.

The more she considered her mother's and her own circumstances, the more terrified of the future she became. With no male to protect them or earn a living for them, what would happen to them? And still worse, what would happen to her when her mother died? She had nothing of her own; she had been her mother's obedient companion-help ever since she was fourteen. She was totally dependent upon her.

She also felt a profound unease about Cousin Albert himself. Was he altogether trustworthy? She did not know him well, but he struck her as a manipulative man, a man with little idea of kindness or humanity – though her father must have had some faith in him to make him his executor.

Immediately after the funeral was over, Albert had had a private discussion with Timothy's solicitor and old friend, Mr Barnett of Barnett and Sons.

Elderly Mr Barnett was himself trembling with fatigue and

grief, because the AND SONS of his practice no longer existed; one had died while a prisoner of war and the other had succumbed to trench fever in the horrors of 1916. With difficulty, the old man had single-handedly kept the practice going for his sons while they were at war. Now, he knew he would never enjoy a peaceful retirement; to keep himself, his wife and three daughters, he must continue his practice until he dropped. It was no wonder that he found it hard to concentrate on what the pompous Mr Albert Gilmore was saying, and that he agreed to everything suggested in connection with Mrs Louise Gilmore's affairs.

After lunch, Albert took out his gold hunter watch and announced that he would go again to Timothy's office to do some more work, would stay one more night and then, the next morning, catch an early train back to his Nottingham home. 'Mr Barnett will have the will probated and will do a further check in case there are any, as yet, undiscovered assets,' he told Celia.

'My dear Louise,' he continued paternalistically to the tear-soaked widow, 'I shall be in constant touch with Mr Barnett – fortunately, I have a telephone – and, in a few days' time, I'll be in touch with you again by mail. In the meantime, you should go out to Meols – that is the nearest railway station – to look at your cottage there.' He tucked his watch back into his waistcoat pocket. 'Mr Barnett will oversee the paperwork regarding the house for you. An estate agent may come tomorrow to evaluate it.'

He carefully did not mention to her that, since her present home and its contents already belonged to her, she had the right to refuse to sell it. Nor did he tell her that that afternoon he would pay a quick visit to the cottage to check that it looked repairable. She must face reality herself, he felt defensively.

Albert did not want any argument about the sale either. He dreaded dealing with women – they were so volatile and so lacking in common sense, and physically they revolted him. Better by far to persuade Louise to sign a quick agreement with Mr Barnett that he should arrange paperwork of the sale.

That evening, after Cousin Albert and Mr Barnett had dined

with her, she had signed the agreement to sell without even reading it.

It never occurred to her that she was signing away her own property, that she was free to make her own decisions. She was certain that men always knew best.

Terrified, white-faced Celia's instinct that something was wrong was, therefore, correct. Albert Gilmore's intentions were, however, of the best. He was simply convinced that women were totally incapable of running their own lives, a belief certainly shared by his late cousin, Timothy. With money coming in every month from an annuity and with Celia to care for her, he could comfortably forget Louise.

Now, buffeted by a brisk sea breeze, Celia and her mother stood in front of a dwelling which looked as shabby as a house could look without actually falling down.

'Built in 1821,' Celia said without hope. 'See! There's the date above the front door. No wonder it's shabby – it will be a hundred years old next year.'

A wave of pure panic began to envelop the younger woman, as her mother sniffed into her handkerchief, and wailed, 'What are we going to do, Celia? We can't possibly live here. What is Albert thinking about, suggesting such a thing? Couldn't we buy another house?'

Her daughter shivered, and tried to muster some common sense. She replied, 'Well, probably this is the cheapest roof we'll ever find, Mama, even if we have to have it repaired. Mostly, I suspect that Cousin Albert wants us resettled quickly, because he doesn't want us to live with him.'

Her mother turned back towards her, and with a sigh, inquired, 'What did you say, dear?'

Celia had bent down to pick up two hairpins which had fallen out of her untidy ash-blonde bun. Her voice was muffled, as she replied, 'I think he may wish us to begin a new life together without delay. He may fear that we expect him to invite us to live with him – he has a big house – I remember our going to visit him once, when I was little.' She straightened up and pushed the pins into her handbag. 'But he hasn't offered us a home, Mother – and I don't think he should have to. It is not as if he were your brother – then he'd have a duty towards us.'

Her mother responded with unexpected acerbity. 'Well, he is your father's trustee until the estate is settled. He might at least have stayed long enough to help us, instead of leaving us in the hands of a solicitor – and an estate agent who has had the insensitivity to come in the day after the funeral, and run around our home – with a tape measure!'

'The estate agent is concerned only with selling our house, Mother. He came to see it this morning only because Cousin Albert wants it sold quickly. He did apologise for intruding on us, remember. And the house is enormous, Mother, with seven bedrooms and three servants' rooms. Too much for just two of us.'

Her mother's puffed eyelids made her eyes look like slits in her plump face, as she replied pitifully, 'I don't want to sell it, Celia. It's our home. And, what's more, I don't like the agent – so officious and totally lacking in delicacy or compassion.'

Celia wanted badly to cry herself, but she put her arm round her mother's waist, and said gently, 'Try not to grieve, Mama. This little house is yours, too, remember – you can do anything you like with it. We can probably make it very pretty.'

Celia gestured towards the shabby front door facing them. 'I suppose Cousin Albert imagines we can arrange for the renovations ourselves?' She paused, as she tried to think clearly.

Louise continued to cry. At Celia's remarks, however, her petulant little mouth dropped open. She could do anything she liked with this miserable cottage? What rubbish! Men always looked after property.

'How can I get it done up? I have no idea how to proceed, and where would we get the money to do it?' she wailed.

Celia had to admit that she did not know either. She responded firmly, however, by saying, 'Perhaps we can find someone in the village, a builder, who could at least advise us about what it would cost.'

Then another frightening thought struck her, and she asked, 'Did Cousin Albert say what we were to do about money until the house is sold? We would have to pay workmen, wouldn't we?'

Albert had not mentioned immediate financial needs, except to say that he had himself advanced the money for dear Timothy's funeral.

Her mother closed her eyes. She had no idea what, if any, money she had to draw on for the time being. It was all too much. She was trembling with fatigue and bewilderment at the sudden upheaval in her life. She wished heartily that she could follow Timothy – and simply die.

It really was most inconvenient that Timothy should have a heart attack before he had even reached his fiftieth birthday – and die in his office. What a fuss that had caused!

As if she could bear anything more, when they had already lost both their sons, George – her baby – in the dreadful sinking of the *Hampshire* in 1916. Drowned with Lord Kitchener, she had been told; as if that made it any the less painful to her. And big, strong Tom, her eldest and the pride of her soul, killed on the Somme.

Her terrible frustration at their youthful deaths still haunted her. There was nothing she could do to express her love of them. She could not give them beautiful funerals to mark the family's grief at their passing. They had left no wives or children to be comforted. They did not even have graves which she could tend in memory of them. All she could do was weep for them.

And her own two brothers, who could have been so much help to her in the present crisis? Both long dead, Peter from yellow fever while serving as an administrator on the Gold Coast, and Donald, a major in the 43rd, killed in a skirmish in the Khyber Pass just before the war broke out. The Empire had cost an awful lot of men, she thought, with sudden resentment against governments as well as against poor Timothy.

Celia patiently repeated her question about money, and her mother mopped her eyes and responded mechanically, 'I suppose he thinks I'll find it out of my own small income – my dot. There may be a little money in the bank which is mine, and I still have most of my March housekeeping.'

'Do you have any idea how much is in your banking account?' Celia knew that her grandfather had settled on her mother a dowry – a dot, as such a settlement was popularly called – of rental housing in Birkenhead. It was doubtful whether the income from their small rents would be enough to tide them over, never mind pay for extensive repairs to this dismal house.

'I don't know how much. I will have to ask the bank manager – and Mr Billings.'

'The agent who collected the rent for this cottage and manages your Birkenhead property?'

'Yes, dear. Cousin Albert says I am lucky that, when I married, your grandfather made quite sure that that property always remained mine.'

At the mention of Mr Billings, some of Celia's fear receded. Mr Billings would surely know how to deal with house repairs. He might know how they could obtain credit so that they did not have to pay immediately.

As she searched in her leather handbag for the key to the house, handed to her by Cousin Albert, who had found it, neatly labelled, in Timothy's key cupboard in his office, she said with false cheerfulness to her mother, 'Let's go inside. It may not be so dreadful as we think. Then, instead of going directly back home to Liverpool, we could pause long enough in Birkenhead to see Mr Billings; he'll know something about house repairs, I'm sure. We can take a later train back to Liverpool.'

'Well, I suppose,' Louise whispered wearily, 'since we are here, we might as well look at the inside.'

As Celia slowly turned the big iron key in the rusty lock, Louise paused to look round what had been the front garden, and sighed deeply at the sight of the foot-high weeds. She sobbed again into her large, black mourning handkerchief, one of the same set of handkerchiefs she had used when crying for her lost boys.

Celia's hand was trembling as she put the big key back into

her handbag, before pushing hard on the stiff door to open it. What will become of us? she fretted. What shall we do?

Nineteen twenty was supposed to be a year when, two years after the war, things would settle down and life return to normal. Mourning was supposed to be over, your black dresses put away. But you can't bury grief as quickly as you can bury men, she thought bitterly.

At best, life was proving to be totally different from that of 1914, when during a gloriously hot August, Europe was plunged into war, and life's main preoccupation became the casualty lists.

Added to the death of her sons, her poor mother now had this burden of comparatively early widowhood, a penurious one, and the loss of her superbly furnished home.

As she pushed hard at the reluctant door, she thought for a moment of herself, and she saw no hope of a decent future anywhere.

Chapter Two

❧

As the door swung open to reveal a tiny vestibule, decayed autumn leaves rustled across a dusty tiled floor. Facing them was an inner door, its upper panels consisting of a stained-glass window with an elaborate pattern of morning glory flowers.

In an effort to cheer her mother up a little, Celia exclaimed, 'Wouldn't that be pretty if it were cleaned?'

'Mother loved it,' Louise said abruptly. Because her nose was so swollen from weeping, she sounded as if she had a heavy cold.

Using the same key, Celia unlocked the pretty door and hesitantly opened it. She had never been in the cottage before, and did not know exactly what to expect.

A very narrow, gloomy hall was revealed. It was poorly lit by a window at the top of a steep staircase to her right. To the left of her, two doors led off the hall. At the back was a third door. The lower half of all the walls was painted brown; the upper half looked as if it had once been cream. It was, however, very dirty; every corner was hung with cobwebs, and dust clung to them. Dust lay thickly on the wooden banister of the stairs, on the bare wooden treads, and on the ridges of the door panels. Under their feet fine sand, blown in from the dunes at the back of the house, crunched faintly on reddish tiles.

Celia quickly flung open the two doors and they glanced in at tiny rooms which looked equally dirty and depressing, their fireplaces choked with ashes, the bare wooden floors grimy and littered with bits of yellowed newspaper. The light from the windows, filtering through gaps in the boards hammered over their exterior, did little to lift the general air of dinginess.

Determined to be brave, Celia said to her mother, again steeped in melancholy, 'They've both got fireplaces – and quite big windows.'

Louise did not reply. She was past caring.

She did, however, follow Celia, as the younger woman approached the door at the end of the hallway, which she presumed correctly would lead into some sort of a kitchen.

A very rusty range had been built into one wall. With a long-handled water pump at one end, a sandstone sink was set below a filthy casement window positioned high in the house's end wall. Through the window Celia caught a glimpse of the straggling tops of hedges which she supposed marked the edge of the property.

Cautiously she pressed down the pump handle. It gave a fearsome squeak, but no water came out.

Her mother stared at it, and then said heavily, 'It has to be primed and it's probably rusted inside.' After a pause while she dabbed at her reddened nose, she added, 'There's a well at the bottom of the garden.'

Celia was appalled. The kitchen was awful, filthy beyond anything she had ever seen before. How on earth could one ever get such a neglected house clean – without a couple of skilled charwomen? But Cousin Albert had said no servants.

She realised with real shock that, if they did come to live in it, she herself would have to clean it. Her mother would not dream of doing an unpleasant job while she had a daughter to push it on to, and Celia had no idea even how to start.

She swallowed, and opened another door. 'This must be the pantry,' she said. 'Phew! How it smells!'

Because there was a sudden scuffle of tiny feet in its confined space, she hastily slammed the door shut again. 'Ugh!'

'Mice!' her mother burst out. 'Oh, Celia!' She hastily gathered her skirts up to her knees, as if expecting an immediate invasion of her petticoats by the tiny intruders. Tears ran down her face.

'It's all right, Mother. It's all right! I don't think any came out.' Celia turned back to the hallway, and suggested heavily, 'We'd better have a look upstairs.'

There were three small bedrooms, and, in addition, a very tiny room at the front, over the hallway, which Louise said, with an effort, had been her elder sister's bedroom when they were children. It was in the latter that the window had been broken. Rain had got in and damaged the plaster. Under their feet brown linoleum squelched as they trod on it, indicating that there was water under it.

'Pooh!' exclaimed Celia. 'This room reeks of damp.'

Her mother blew her nose, and said very wearily, 'The floorboards have probably rotted.'

Celia nodded. She wondered, with a shiver, if they would ever have enough money, never mind enough strength, to put this tiny house into some sort of order. Cousin Albert must believe that it was possible, she decided.

In fact, Albert Gilmore had not thought the matter through very well. His main goal was to avoid having to take the two bereaved women into his own home in Nottingham, where he dwelled very happily with an obliging manservant. He did not want them there even temporarily – they might be hard to dislodge.

He hoped that they would agree to settle in the cottage, or, alternatively, go to live with Louise's elder, married daughter, Edna, and her husband, Paul Fellowes, something he had not yet suggested to either lady – he felt that the latter idea must come from Paul and Edna, and was, in his opinion, a decision of last resort. In the meantime, he had pressed on Louise the idea of the cottage as a suitable home.

Paul was an electrical engineer, a director in his family firm which had grown hugely during the war, because of the international reputation of its engineers and their innovative approach to new problems. He had just completed managing a lucrative seven-year contract for the wiring of an entire city in Brazil. He and Edna would, according to Louise, sail for home this month. Once he was resettled in England, considered Cousin Albert, Paul Fellowes would certainly be able to afford to take in a couple of women, who would probably make themselves useful in his house, as such women always did.

On the other hand, he pondered, if they would agree to live in the cottage and were very careful, they should be able to manage on the rents from Louise's six houses in Birkenhead. The rents, in addition to the annuity which he proposed to buy for them from the proceeds of the sale of the West Derby house, should be enough for two women to live on.

He knew from his talks with Mr Barnett and with Timothy's chief clerk that there would, almost certainly, be nothing left of Timothy's estate. The man owed money everywhere, probably because much of his basic income had come from investment in railways, which, now that the war was over, were not doing very well. Had he lived, he might have been able to pull through a difficult period, but now there was no hope. His few assets must be liquidated to meet his debts.

He trusted that Paul Fellowes would, when he returned to England, help him with the paperwork necessary to wind everything up. Paul should soon receive his letter, sent to Salvador, Brazil, informing him of his father-in-law's death and asking him to break the news to his wife.

It was possible that the couple had already sailed for England before the letter's arrival. In that case they would receive the news from a telegram, which he had dispatched to Paul's father at their company head office in Southampton. Edna's last letter to her mother had mentioned that they expected to dock in Southampton and spend a few days with Paul's parents before coming north to visit her own parents.

As Louise and Celia struggled round the overgrown garden of the cottage by the sand dunes, Louise mentioned how relieved she would be to see Paul and Edna.

Celia agreed. She had almost forgotten what the couple looked like. She had never had a great deal to do with her elder sister, and she had met Paul only three times, so she was not particularly hopeful of being comforted. Their presence would, however, add a sense of stability to Louise in her shattered state, for which she would be grateful.

If Paul returned quickly enough, thought Celia, he would, at least, be someone to consult about the cottage – if he had any time; she had always understood from her father that businessmen never did have much time to spare for the affairs of women.

Standing in the cottage garden after the stuffiness of the house, it was a relief to Celia to breathe clean, salt-laden air, and, despite its total neglect, there was a healthy smell of damp earth and growing things.

At the bottom of the garden, they inspected an earth lavatory.

'It's utterly disgusting!' Celia exclaimed. 'Did you really use it?'

'Yes,' Louise admitted. 'It wasn't something we looked forward to. It was your father's main objection to continuing to come here for holidays.' She began to whimper, as she recalled with anguish the handsome water closet which Timothy had had installed in their West Derby home.

'Perhaps we could get a proper bathroom put in here,' Celia suggested doubtfully, as she shut the door firmly on the obnoxious little hut. Though she had long since learned that, to survive, she must bow her head and do whatever her parents decided, even her broken spirit had, on inspecting such primitive sanitary arrangements, begun to feel a sense of revolt.

After several days of being confined indoors, the fresh air was reviving Louise, and she looked around her, and sighed. She replied quite coherently, 'I don't think we could put in a water closet, without piped water and drains.' Then she exclaimed with something of her normal impatience, 'What a mess! I can't imagine what kind of a tenant must've been living here. Mr Billings must have been very careless about his selection of one.'

Celia contemplated the jungle of weeds and sprawling bushes round her. 'Did he pay the rent? The tenant, I mean,' she asked practically.

Her mother shrugged. 'I don't know. Your father took care of these things.'

Celia turned to stare at the back of the house. The roof looked all right, no slate tiles missing and the chimneys were all intact, as far as she could judge. Her eyes followed the ridge of the roof, and she remembered suddenly that there was another house attached to theirs.

'Do you own the house next door, Mother? I can see that the other side of the hedge has been trimmed, and there are curtains in the bedroom windows – and smoke is coming from the chimney. Someone must live there.'

Her mother looked up. 'No, I don't own it. My father bought this house simply as a summer cottage, rather than as an investment, and when he died he left it to your Aunt Felicity.'

Anxious to encourage her mother to take an interest in anything, Celia asked, 'Who does own it?'

'A Mr and Mrs Lytham bought the other side. I used to play with their children.' Louise's expression softened, and she added wistfully, 'We had some lovely times, playing in the sand dunes and paddling in the sea. I wonder what happened to them?'

Celia forced a smile. 'How nice that must have been.' Then she looked at her brooch watch. 'Perhaps we had better lock up, Mother, and go to have a talk with Mr Billings. He could advise us about repairs.'

Her mother nodded and they retraced their steps to the house, ruefully brushing down their long skirts. Even Celia's ankle-length, tailored skirt had caught in the undergrowth and had burrs and bits of leaves and seeds clinging to it.

Celia locked the back door and they walked slowly and dismally through the house, leaving muddy tracks behind them.

While Celia turned to secure the inner front door, Louise proceeded slowly down the front steps. She suddenly let out a frightened little cry, 'Oh!'

Celia spun round.

Standing in the middle of the red-tiled path was a tall thin man. As the women stared at him, he raised his cap and bowed. 'Good afternoon,' he greeted them politely.

Chapter Three

❧

Confronted by a man, both women were suddenly acutely aware of how isolated the cottage was.

Walking down the lane to it, they had passed only one other cottage, a squat little dwelling with a thatched roof. It had, Louise told Celia, been lived in for centuries by a family of fishermen. Now, they stared uneasily at someone who seemed to have sprung from nowhere.

'Good afternoon,' responded Celia nervously, while her mother stiffened, as she catalogued the man as no gentleman, despite his courteous greeting. The lanky man's grey hair was roughly cut and framed a lined, weather-beaten face. He wore a striped union shirt without a collar; a red and white cotton handkerchief was tied round his neck. His wrinkled, old-fashioned moleskin trousers, held up by a worn leather belt, were stained with dried mud.

As he looked down at her, Louise's silence did not seem to disconcert him in the least. His faded blue eyes held the hint of a smile, as he said, 'You must be Mrs Gilmore. The gentleman as was here to take a quick look at the cottage for you said as you would be coming. He come out late Tuesday. Nearly dark, it was.'

A quiet rage against Cousin Albert rose in Louise, blotting out all sense of fear or grief. So, during his stay with her, he had not spent all his time in Timothy's office checking over with the clerk just exactly what the financial situation was; he had also been out here, planning to condemn her to live in this awful place. He knew precisely what it was like.

With sudden understanding she realised how she had been

manipulated. Albert and Mr Barnett had made her sign away her present home.

It was so unfair. They should have explained to her what she was about to do. Consulted her. The fact that the outcome would probably have been the same did not make any difference. She had not been asked what she felt about moving out here.

Could she not have sold this horrible cottage and bought another tiny house in a decent, civilised Liverpool street?

No time had been allowed her to recover from her bereavement, she raged; there had been no understanding that she was distraught with grief.

She was healthily furious, not only with Albert and Mr Barnett, but also with Timothy.

Timothy might have had enough sense to tell her that she owned their home, when he had originally transferred it.

Unless he had not trusted her? What a dreadful thought!

That was it. He must have felt, like Cousin Albert, that she was not capable of dealing with the ownership of such a valuable property; in transferring the ownership to her he must simply have been ensuring that no creditor of his could ever seize his home.

Men were like that, she felt with sudden, bitter understanding of the helplessness imposed on women.

She drew herself up to her full height, and replied frigidly to the stranger. 'Yes, I am Mrs Timothy Gilmore.'

'And the young lady?'

'My daughter, Miss Celia Gilmore.'

The man smiled down at the tiny younger woman. Framed by untidy blonde hair, her face had the whiteness of skin never exposed to sunlight. Her loose, black-belted jacket and full skirt were relieved only by a white blouse. A tiny gold cross and chain glittered on a blue-white throat. A wide-brimmed black hat, worn squarely on her head, did nothing to improve her looks. A proper little mouse, her mam's companion-help, he judged her, but probably amiable enough to be a good neighbour. 'Nice to know yez, luv,' he said warmly.

Celia smiled nervously in return. She sensed that the old man

26

approved of her. It felt nice; she rarely got approval from anybody. As her mother's patient shadow, she was usually barely noticed.

Their visitor pointed an arthritic finger at the house next door, and, as if taking it for granted that the ladies would be moving into the cottage they had just inspected, he said, 'I'm your neighbour. Me name's Eddie Fairbanks. Was head gardener to the earl till he sold the family home to be a nursing home for wounded soldiers. Proper kind to me, he was. Served him forty years I did, ever since I were a lad of ten, so I was close to retirement, anyway. He give me the cottage rent free for me lifetime and me wife's lifetime – 'cos, he said, I designed one of the best rose gardens in the north for him, and he loved roses. He hoped the servicemen would enjoy the garden. He lives in London now.' He paused to take a breath, while the two women stared at him. Since they did not say anything, he went on, 'My Alice passed away six years ago, so I manage by meself.' He paused again, as if expecting some response from Louise, but when there was none, he asked, 'Would you like a cuppa tea? The kettle's already hot. That house must've been cold when you went in – with the wind, and all.'

'No, thank you,' Louise replied stiffly. Tea with a gardener? What was she coming to?

Celia, however, caught her arm and, smiling unexpectedly prettily at the old man, she said, 'Mother! It would be so nice to get acquainted with Mr Fairbanks. He might be able to tell us more than Mr Billings would.'

'Ha! Old Billings?' interjected Mr Fairbanks. 'In Birkenhead, eh? He hasn't taken much care of the place for you, has he?'

Celia replied ruefully, 'No, not by the look of it.' She turned her head to smile up at her mother. 'A cup of tea would be lovely, Mother.' She gave Louise's arm a warning little tug. In their desperate situation, a male neighbour could be very helpful.

Louise was still inwardly steaming with rage, but out of courtesy she reluctantly agreed. She said to Mr Fairbanks, 'Very well. It is very kind of you.'

She made herself smile at the man, and he said, obviously pleased, 'That's better, Ma'am. This way, if you please.'

He led them down the path and round the wild, ragged front

hedge. At the halfway mark, it suddenly became a neatly trimmed privet, and he led them into a front garden boasting a few daffodils and other small spring blooms. Near the house wall, sheltered from the cold wind, a blaze of red tulips stood tall and straight as an honour guard. The front window was neatly draped with lace curtains, and the front door stood open, giving a glimpse of a flowered stair carpet.

They entered through a lobby similar to the other one next door, though it lacked the stained-glass window in the inner door and the tiles were covered by a large doormat.

They carefully wiped their feet as they went in, and looked down the passageway with some curiosity.

It had the same brown paint with cream upperworks as the house they had just been in. It was, however, spotlessly clean, and the hall runner was thick cream wool with a lively Turkish pattern in dark reds and greens. Celia looked at it and hesitated to step on it.

'My shoes must still be muddy from the garden,' she said doubtfully to the old man.

'Don't worry, luv. The carpet cleans up fairly easy.' He smiled at her and at her mother behind her, and gestured towards the colourful stair carpet. 'Alice and me, we hooked all the carpets in the house. Pure wool, they are. They sponge clean something wonderful.'

Murmuring polite amazement at such industry, the ladies were ushered into the back room, where a good coal fire glowed. 'Come in, come in and warm yourselves.'

He eased a rather bewildered Louise into a battered rocking chair, and told Celia to take the chair opposite, which was a low nursing chair with a padded seat and back, its velveteen worn with age.

As she sat down, she wondered how many babies Alice had fed while seated in the armless chair. She spread her skirt comfortably round her, and, a little sadly, thought how good it must feel to have a baby at the breast and be cosy with it by the fire. Then, as Mr Fairbanks hurried to get his best, flowered cups and saucers out of a corner cupboard and set them on a table in the centre of the little room, she almost blushed at her wickedness at harbouring such an idea.

Her duty was to her mother; she had been taught that in childhood, and, anyway, at aged twenty-four she was on the shelf – too old to think of marriage and babies.

Edna had been the pretty one, who had been groomed for marriage and had gone triumphantly to the altar with Paul Fellowes, a good solid match. Her father had, however, been worried when a besotted Edna had insisted on following her husband out to Brazil, though she was pregnant with their first child. Her daughter had survived being born in a hot climate, only to die of dysentery at the age of two. There had been no other children, and Celia often wondered why. Her friend, Phyllis Woodcock, had told her ruefully that babies arrived every year.

Edna was lucky that Paul was still alive. Had it not been for the contract in Brazil, he would surely have volunteered for the army at the beginning of the war, and it would have been remarkable if he had managed to survive until the conflict ended. She wondered if he had felt any regret at not being able to come home and fight – or had he thankfully made the business contract with Brazil, an allied country, an excuse not to have to sacrifice himself for king and country?

The latter was such an ignoble thought that she immediately turned her attention back to her mother.

Louise was sitting silently, her eyes half-closed, as the fire warmed her frozen feet. Her sudden spate of rage was draining away, and she felt dreadfully tired. She longed to lie down in the cosseting safety of her own bed.

After a few minutes, she roused herself sufficiently to take off her gloves and allow the heat to warm her hands. While Mr Fairbanks bustled into the kitchen to fill the kettle, Celia whispered to her, 'When do you think Paul and Edna will dock?'

Before replying, Louise waited for Mr Fairbanks to push between them to place the kettle on the hob, and turn it over the fire. It soon began to sing, and Mr Fairbanks said cheerfully, 'It won't be long, Ma'am.'

Louise acknowledged his remark with a condescending nod, and then, as he vanished in search of milk and sugar, replied to Celia, 'I really don't know. Albert thought it would be within two weeks. He thought it very likely that they had sailed a day or two before ... before ...' Her lower lip began to tremble.

Celia's voice was very gentle, as she suggested, 'So that it is possible that they will not receive his letter – or your letter to Edna?'

'Yes, dear.'

'That's what he said to me. In any case, once they get word in Southampton, I am sure they will take the first train up here.'

'Yes, dear.'

It was Celia's turn to sigh. 'I wish they were here. Paul would know what to do about everything.' She felt like adding, 'And he would know how to deal with Cousin Albert, so that at least we would know more exactly what our financial situation really is.' She restrained herself, however, because she could see that her mother was crying silently to herself.

Louise's tears had not gone unnoticed by Mr Fairbanks. It was clear that Albert had told him the reason for Louise's coming to the cottage, because he said soothingly to her, as he rescued the puffing kettle and took it over to the table to fill the large earthenware teapot, 'Don't grieve, Ma'am. A good cup of tea'll set you up.'

He stirred the pot briskly, put an ancient knitted tea cosy over it, and asked, 'How much sugar, Ma'am?'

'Two, please.'

'And you, Miss Celia?'

'The same, please.' Really, he was being immensely kind, Celia thought, just like a grandfather would be. Both sets of her grandparents had died when she was small, and she had little recollection of them, except of veined wrinkled hands producing bonbons and popping them into her mouth, and being hugged and kissed. Her mother might not be getting much comfort from their encounter with Mr Fairbanks, but she herself was.

Before giving them their tea, Mr Fairbanks went back to his corner cupboard and produced a largish bottle.

'Would you be liking a drop of rum in your tea, Ma'am? It might help you a bit, like . . .'

Louise glanced up at him. For a moment she was shocked out of her misery. 'Oh, no, thank you. I couldn't possibly!' A gentlewoman drinking rum like a common sailor's wife? Brandy, perhaps, but not rum!

Celia, however, saw the sense of his suggestion, and she said, 'Have a tiny bit, Mother. It would give you strength. And we have yet to get to Birkenhead, to see Mr Billings – and then go home – it will take all your strength.'

Louise faltered. The remaining part of the afternoon stretched before her like a long staircase hard to climb, and she was so tired, so dreadfully tired.

Mr Fairbanks smiled at her encouragingly, 'It won't do you no harm, Ma'am.'

She was persuaded, and she did cheer up, though she drank her two cups of tea with her nose wrinkling up in distaste at the odour of the rum.

Eddie Fairbanks did not offer rum to Celia. As a single lady she shouldn't be drinking anything but wine, and he didn't have anything like that in the house.

Warmed and comforted and a little drunk, Louise relaxed enough to ask the old man if he knew what had happened to her childhood playmates, the Lytham family, who used to live in his house.

He did not know where the family was, he said. He knew only that the leasehold of both cottages had run out, and that the Lythams had not renewed theirs, but that Celia's grandfather had come to an agreement with the earl to renew his for another hundred years. 'Because the houses are very well built, and your granddad probably wanted to keep his in the family for holidays.'

It was obvious from Louise's expression that she had no idea what was meant by leasehold, so Celia asked, 'What exactly does that mean? I've always wondered.'

Mr Fairbanks picked up his cup of tea, and took a sip. 'Well, you see, luv, nobody round these parts owns much land. Nearly all of it has belonged to the earl since time began. If you want to build on land round here – or farm it – you can persuade the earl to give you a long lease on it – these cottages had one for fifty years – and then you can build on it. However, at the end of the lease, you have to pay the earl to renew it; otherwise the land – and the buildings that you have built on it – revert to him, and he can rent them to somebody or pull them down.' He put his cup down neatly in its saucer, and then added, 'And what's more, you'll probably find that Mr Billings 'as been paying a ground rent to his lordship's agent each year on your behalf.'

Louise asked, 'Can we sell the cottage, if we want to?'

'Oh, yes, Ma'am, if someone is prepared to buy the lease from you. But you'd have difficulty getting a good price for it – they're a bit isolated – it's a fair walk to Meols railway station, and your cottage has bin proper neglected, if I may say so. And in winter the wind comes in from the sea something awful. The gentleman that came to look at it brought Mr Parry, the estate agent from Hoylake, along with him – and that's what he said. Neither house is worth a great deal.'

Louise felt a little comforted. At least Albert had considered selling the cottage, before he had condemned her to it.

For her part, Celia swallowed hard. Pay an earl for the right to live in a house that belonged to you, but you probably could not sell? What other money problems that they knew nothing about lurked amid the present turmoil of their lives? What other financial demands could they expect? She felt faint with fear, unreasonable fear that Cousin Albert might have deserted them, leaving them penniless. He had made it clear that the price of their Liverpool home would be used as the foundation of their income, and certainly not to buy another house. Once he had sold it for them, would he be honest and hand over the money? Celia felt sick with apprehension.

Her mother must have had similar vague fears, because she said rather desperately to her daughter, 'Perhaps we should go to see Mr Billings now, Celia.' She rose carefully, to hand her cup to their host, and thank him quite sweetly for his hospitality. He was a mere working man – but he was male and he knew things that she did not. Like Celia, Louise began to view him as a possible pillar of support, like a good butler would have been, had she been fortunate enough to have one in her employ, instead of a giggling fool of a parlourmaid.

Chapter Four

❦

Eddie Fairbanks insisted on walking with the ladies down the sandy lane to Meols Station, and waiting with them until the steam train chugged in. He recommended that, instead of changing to the electric train at Birkenhead Park Station, they should get a cab from that station to Mr Billings' office. 'Being as it's getting late, and his office is nearer to Park than it is to Birkenhead Central.'

They took his advice, and were fortunate in catching small, rotund Mr Billings just as he was putting on his overcoat ready to go home.

As the ladies were ushered in, after being announced by his fourteen-year-old office boy, he resignedly took off his bowler hat again and hung it on the coat stand, then went to sit at his desk. As the women entered, he half rose in his chair and smiled politely at them.

The office boy sullenly pulled out chairs for the forlorn couple. Because of their late arrival, he would be late home and his mother would scold him. He returned to the outer office to sit on his high stool and depressedly contemplate the beckoning spring sunshine which lit the untidy builder's yard outside.

Louise had retired behind her mourning veil, and Mr Billings eyed her with some trepidation: widows could be very tiresome, particularly a real lady like this Gilmore woman; they never understood what you told them. Since she showed no indication of an ability to speak, he turned his eyes upon her companion, a thin sickly-looking woman, dressed in mourning black. She must be the daughter. He smiled again.

'Good afternoon, ladies. How can I help you?' he inquired

politely of Celia. Then, before Celia could respond, he added, 'May I express my condolences at your sad loss. Very sad, indeed.'

There was a murmur of thanks from behind Louise's veil, and Celia blinked back tears. They were not only tears because of the loss of her autocratic father, but tears for herself because she had little idea of how to deal with business matters – and Mr Billings represented a solid weight of them.

With what patience he could muster after a long, trying day, Mr Billings waited for one of them to speak, and, after a few moments, Celia nervously wetted her lips, and explained about the need to get the cottage at Meols into liveable shape.

While he considered this, Mr Billings brushed his moustache with one stout red finger and then twisted the waxed points at each end of it. He said slowly, 'Oh, aye, it needs a bit of doing up if you're going to live in it yourselves. It was rented for a good many years to a Miss Hornby after your auntie died; she was crippled and she never did aught about aught. When she died, Mr Gilmore saw no point in doing repairs on a place he didn't use – and the rent wasn't much. So I had the ground-floor windows boarded up – they being expensive to replace if they were broken by vandals. And that's how it's been for a couple of years now.'

He clasped his hands over his waistcoat and leaned back in his chair.

Celia told him about the broken bedroom window and asked if he could recommend a builder who could repair it quickly, and anything else that needed doing, like new floorboards in the hall bedroom.

He immediately wrote out on the back of one of his business cards the name and address of a Hoylake man, Ben Aspen, who, he assured Celia, was as honest as the day. 'I'll get my own man to put a new windowpane in for you tomorrow – I got a handyman I keep to do small repairs. Later on, you can tell Ben Aspen what else you want doing.'

She was greatly relieved and thanked him, as she carefully put the card into her handbag.

'Don't mention it, Miss,' he replied, as he turned to her mother, to address the daunting veil. 'Seeing as how you're here, Ma'am, I'd like to speak to you about your property in Birkenhead.'

Louise sniffed back her tears and lifted her veil sufficiently to apply a black handkerchief to mop up under it. 'Yes?' she fluttered nervously.

She jumped as Mr Billings shouted to his young clerk, still fidgeting in the outer office, 'George, bring the Gilmore file.'

Muttering maledictions under his breath, the youngster got down the file and brought it in and laid it in front of Mr Billings. When he was dismissed he bowed obsequiously to the ladies as he passed them.

They ignored him.

'Now, let me see.' Mr Billings rustled through an inordinate number of pieces of paper, while Celia watched anxiously.

'Humph.' He leaned back in his chair again, and addressed Louise. 'Now, yesterday afternoon a Mr Albert Gilmore come in. Said he was your trustee – when he said it, I thought for a second that you was passed on as well as Mr Gilmore. Anyway, he says that I'm to send the cheque for your rents to him, like I always sent them to Mr Timothy Gilmore – prompt each quarter day.'

Celia drew in her breath sharply, and opened her mouth to protest, but, seeing her expression, Mr Billings continued, 'Yes, Miss. That was my reaction, too. Them houses belong to you, Mrs Gilmore – according to my notes, they're your dowry, and, therefore, they aren't part of Mr Gilmore's estate; and so I tell him – and he was really put out. But I said to him as it is one thing to send the rents to your hubby, Ma'am, for which I have had your written permission these many years – in fact, my father had it before me – but another to hand them over to a stranger I don't know.'

He straightened up and looked at Louise, rightly proud of his personal rectitude.

Both Louise and Celia gasped at this information, and Celia felt sick, because it tended to confirm her poor opinion of Cousin Albert. It did not occur to her that Albert merely wanted to check that Mr Billings handed over the correct sum each month.

Louise was so shaken that she actually threw back her veil, to reveal a plump, blotched face, which might have still been pretty in happier circumstances. 'But he has no right,' she faltered.

'Precisely, Ma'am.'

Mr Billings smiled knowingly at her. 'But it so happened, Ma'am, that I was a trifle late making up me books this quarter and didn't do your account till this morning. One tenant, Mrs Halloran, being late with her rent – she owed five shillings – I held back to give her a chance to get up to date before I reported to Mr Gilmore that she was in arrears. I read your sad news in the obituary column, Ma'am – and I'm proper sorry about it, Ma'am – so I held the cheque back until I heard from you. I'd have written to you in a few days, if you hadn't come in.'

He fumbled in his waistcoat pocket and brought out a key ring. Then, selecting a key, he got up and went to a small safe at the back of the room. He took out an envelope and handed it to Louise.

'There you are, Ma'am. A cheque for three months' rents in total. Mrs H. paid up, and there was no repairs this quarter – it's less me commission, of course. All rents up to and including last Saturday, payable to you today, Lady Day, as per usual, Ma'am.'

Louise looked up at him with real gratitude. She was not sure how to cash a cheque, but she did know that it represented welcome money. In her cash box at home, she had a month's house-keeping in five-pound notes, which Timothy had given her, as he usually did on the first of each month; beyond that she had no idea what she was supposed to do about money. Behind her expressions of woe a deeper fear of destitution had haunted her as well as Celia.

Her thanks were echoed by Celia, who hastily added that they would, as soon as the cottage was habitable, be leaving their home in West Derby, Liverpool – it was already up for sale – and that she or her mother would let him know, before the next quarter day, which would be Midsummer's Day, exactly where he should send the next cheque.

He was a kindly man, and, as he gently clasped Louise's hand when they took their departure, he felt some pity for her. Women were so helpless without menfolk – and there were so many of them bereaved by the war. They had the brains of chickens – and it appeared to him that these two already might have a fox in the coop.

He said impulsively, 'If I can be of help, dear ladies, don't hesitate to call on me.'

Though Louise only nodded acceptance of this offer, Celia, whose stomach had been clenched with fear ever since her father's clerk had come running up the front steps with the terrible news of Timothy's sudden death, felt herself relax a little. She longed to put her head on the little man's stout shoulder and weep out her terror at being so alone. Instead, she held out her hand a little primly to have it shaken by him and apologised for keeping him late at his office.

Exactly how does one cash a cheque, she worried inwardly, and she wished passionately that Paul and Edna were in England to advise her.

Chapter Five

❧

They were exhausted by the time they returned home, and were further alarmed by the notice hooked on to their front gate. It announced that This Desirable Property was For Sale. The estate agent, in response to Cousin Albert's instructions that he wanted a quick sale, had not wasted any time.

Louise immediately broke into loud cries of distress, and it was with difficulty that Celia and Dorothy, the house-parlourmaid, got her into the sitting room. The pretty, formal room, ordinarily used for teas and at homes, still smelled faintly of hyacinths and lilies, despite having been carefully aired after the funeral, and Celia felt slightly sick from it.

While Dorothy fled upstairs to her mistress's bedroom to get a fresh container of smelling salts, Celia laid Louise on the settee. She carefully removed her bonnet and put cushions under her head.

Then she kneeled down by her and curved her arm round her. 'Try not to cry, Mother. Everything will be all right in the end. Please, Mother.'

Louise shrieked at her, 'Nothing's going to bring your father back – or my boys! Nothing! Nothing!' She turned her back on Celia, and continued to wail loudly. 'My boys! My boys!

'She'd be better in bed, Miss.'

Startled, Celia looked up. Winnie, the cook, had heard the impassioned cries, and had run up from her basement kitchen to see what was happening. Now, she leaned over the two women, her pasty face full of compassion.

'This isn't the right room to have her in, Miss. What with the Master having been laid out here, like.'

Celia herself, frightened by the faint odour of death, would have been thankful to run upstairs to her own bedroom, shut herself in and have a good cry. Instead, she rose heavily to her feet.

'You're quite right, Winnie. Will you help me get her upstairs?'

'For sure, Miss.' She turned towards a breathless Dorothy, who dumbly held out the smelling salts to her.

Winnie took the salts and said above the sound of Louise's cries, 'Now, our Dorothy, you go and fill a hot water bottle and put it in the Mistress's bed. And put her nightgown on top of it to warm.'

Dorothy's face looked almost rabbitlike as her nose quivered with apprehension. She turned to obey the instructions, but paused when the cook said sharply, 'And you'd better put a fire up there. It's chilly. You can take a shovelful of hot coals from me kitchen fire to get it started quick.'

The maid nodded, took a big breath as if she were about to run a marathon, and shot away down the stairs to fetch the hot water bottle and the coals.

As Celia and Winnie half carried Louise up the wide staircase with its newel post crowned by a finely carved hawk, the widow's cries became heavy, heart-rending sobs.

'She'll feel better after this,' Winnie assured Celia. 'A good cry gets it out of you.'

Dorothy stood at the bottom of the staircase, hot water bottle under one arm, in her hands a big shovel full of glowing coals, and waited for the other women to reach the top. The shovel was heavy and she dreaded setting the stair carpet alight by dropping a burning coal on it.

Have a good cry? And what had she in her fancy house to cry about? Her old man had probably left her thousands, and not much love lost between them. And here she was howling her head off and the house up for sale, and never a word to her maids as to what was happening. Proper cruel, she was.

Would she turn Winnie and Ethel and herself off as soon as

the house was sold? And, if not, where would they be going to live?

As her coals cooled, Dorothy's temper grew. She plodded up the stairs after the other women, handed the hot water bottle to Winnie, and then skilfully built the bedroom fire, while Winnie and Celia partially undressed the sobbing Louise, removed her corsets and eased her huge Victorian nightgown over her head.

Behind the blank expression on Dorothy's pinched, thin face, anger seethed. Winnie must ask the Mistress what was to happen to them. She must! If they had to find new situations, they should start now. Although there was a demand for good domestic help, the big mansions in the country were being closed down in favour of London apartments, and their domestic staffs dismissed; in consequence, a lot of competition faced a middle-aged house-parlourmaid like herself. And it was always difficult to find a considerate employer. She sighed. She had not felt that Timothy and Louise were particularly considerate, but she had become accustomed to them. Ethel, the maid-of-all-work, was young enough to try for a factory job, but she herself was in her forties – getting really old – and Winnie must be nearing fifty – it would be hard for her to get another job of any kind.

She took fresh lumps of coal from the fireside coal hod and laid them on top of those she had brought up. She ensured that they had caught and that the fire was beginning to blaze and then swept the hearth. Then she got slowly to her feet, and picked up the shovel.

As she contemplated her future, she began to feel sick. She berated herself that she had not saved some of the good wages she had earned in an ordnance factory during the war years. She had spent like a king until the factory closed down at the end of the war, and then she had come to work as a house-parlourmaid for the Gilmores, because domestic work was all she was skilled at.

She turned from the fireplace and paused to stare at the scene before her.

Seated on the side of the bed beside her mother, Celia held a small glass of brandy to Louise's lips and encouraged her to sip it between sobs. Winnie had folded back the bedclothes ready for the sufferer to lie down.

Nice woman, Miss Celia – but that useless, you'd never believe it. No spirit. Never had any fun, the Master being so difficult to please, especially so, Winnie said, since he lost his son with that Lord Kitchener, and then Mr Tom in France, poor lad.

Her own father had been a bit of a cross, she remembered, and not past beating her if she did something he didn't like – but when he had work, even if he was fair wore out by the end of the day, he could make the family laugh and they'd have a neighbour or two in and do some singing, with a drop of ale to drink by the fire. Old Gilmore had done nothing but complain, complain – and order you around as if you were muck.

She wondered if Celia's sister, Edna, was like her. She had never seen her, but she had heard she was a real beauty, and at least, it seemed, she had had enough sense to get out from under her old man by getting married.

Winnie impatiently glanced back over her shoulder and said, 'Get downstairs, Dot, and look to the soup for me. Give it a stir. I'll be down in a minute.'

Dorothy nodded, and went sulkily down to the basement kitchen, carrying her shovel carefully so that she did not drop a bit of ash on the stair carpet, which, every morning, she had to brush, from cellar to attic.

Louise finally cried herself to sleep, and an exhausted Celia was persuaded by Winnie to put her feet up on the old chaise longue in the breakfast room at the back of the house, while the cook put together a dinner tray for her.

'The Mistress didn't tell me what to make for dinner, so I made this nice thick soup, but I've got some cold beef, if you feel like something more. And the bread come out of the oven only a couple of hours ago.'

Celia nodded wearily, and said that the soup sounded lovely. When it was brought to her, she drank it slowly while Winnie stood and watched her anxiously.

When Celia's bowl was finally empty, Winnie removed it, and

then hesitantly inquired if Celia could tell her what was going to happen to them all. 'Seeing the For Sale sign was a proper shock, Miss,' she explained. 'And Dorothy and Ethel is all upset. They're asking me what they should do.'

'You should all start looking for new situations,' Celia answered her frankly, though she did her best to hide her own sense of despair. 'I know Mother will be glad to keep all of you on for a week or two, while we sort out the house, and decide what to take with us – we are going to live in a cottage in Meols, which Mother owns.' She paused, and then said rather helplessly, 'We have no choice but to sell this place quickly, Winnie. And we shan't be able to afford servants.' She looked up at the shocked elder woman. 'I shall, personally, miss you terribly, Winnie, after all the years you've been with us, especially through the war.'

Winnie took a big breath, as she tried to control her own sense of panic. She inquired, 'Things must be very bad, Miss?'

'In a way they are, Winnie, though not as bad as they might be. Mother's lucky that my Aunt Felicity left her this cottage by the sea.' She sighed and fiddled with the fringe of the woollen shawl that Winnie had put across her legs to keep them warm. Then she said in explanation, 'Father had heavy business debts. We can't afford a servant – I'm hoping that we shall be able to have a daily cleaning woman – because I don't think I shall be very good at keeping house!'

She smiled faintly at the stricken cook, who, despite her own sense of despair, noted that poor Miss Celia was taking it for granted that she would have to run the house – and she probably would have to. And she so small and sickly-looking.

'How long do you think we've got, Miss?'

'Well, I haven't consulted Mother yet. Mr Albert Gilmore, who was here for the funeral, told us that the estate agent felt he would have no trouble selling this house. When it is sold, I suppose that we shall have to set a final date when we have to leave it – to suit the new owner. But we will have to let you go very soon.' She looked up imploringly at her old friend, as if to ask forgiveness.

Winnie's stout chest heaved, but she replied woodenly, 'I understand, Miss.'

'The other house has to have a few essential repairs done – and we have to get it cleaned – it's filthy at present.' She bit her lower lip, and then added quickly, 'I think that Mother can pay you all for this week – and, I hope, for another week. Tomorrow I'll talk to her, and we'll try to make a timetable of some sort, to help you.'

'It's good of you to be so honest with me, Miss. Can I tell the others?'

'Of course. There is so little time. You should all start looking for other situations immediately.' She stopped to consider the appalling upheaval facing her, and then added heavily, 'I'll ask Mother to write references for you tomorrow – and if one of you wants to go for an interview on a day other than your half-day, will you arrange it as best you can between yourselves?'

'We will, Miss. Thank you, Miss.'

Winnie bent and picked up the tray.

To Celia, her perceptions heightened by her own fears, the cook looked suddenly old as she turned slowly and went out of the room. She watched Winnie quietly close the door after her, and then she began to shake helplessly.

She clasped her arms tightly round her breast, and rolled herself over, so that her face was buried in the feather cushions which had propped her up. She began to sweat and her teeth chattered uncontrollably, as her fear of the scary world she was having to face and her sense of having betrayed an old friend overwhelmed her.

'Oh, God,' she whispered in desperation. 'What's going to happen to us? Heaven help us.'

She rolled again, to curl herself up in sheer terror into a tight foetal ball.

With what was left of her sanity she begged to die.

But she knew from experience of these attacks of panic that death did not oblige so easily. So in the unnatural silence of the home she was about to lose, she lay as still as she could, and prayed incoherently for release from the blind fear that engulfed her.

After a little while, her breathing became more normal, and she began to mutter very slowly, as she always did, '"The Lord is my Shepherd; I shall not want."' She hoped that, if she could concentrate well enough to recite the psalm right through to the end and was comforted by King David's immortal words, the seizure would ease.

It had always worked before when she was terrified, even when she was a child and had first realised that she was being brought up differently from her sister.

Because of her parents' special interest in Edna's wellbeing, she had always believed that their neglect of herself indicated that there must be something wrong with her. Had she some deficiency in her which they were hiding from her? Something weird which would one day spring out and send her mad – or, at least, make her a useless invalid, like a neighbour's daughter who had been confined for years to a wheelchair by an attack of infantile paralysis?

This childhood dread, implanted by careless, selfish parents, had fed upon itself until, in her confused, early teenage years, it became an overwhelming terror, which periodically swept over her like some mighty wave whenever she felt threatened.

Frightened themselves by these seizures, her parents had firmly put them down to that popular female complaint, hysteria. It was the height of vulgarity, an effort to draw attention to herself, they said. They had slapped and beaten her at such times, then locked her in her bedroom, until she saw sense, as they put it.

The panic would eventually wear itself out, and, exhausted, she would drag herself out of her bed and knock on her bedroom door to plead tearfully to be let out. She invariably promised that it would not happen again, but, sooner or later, it invariably did.

Now, in adulthood, she had slowly realised that she was probably quite normal. But Church and custom reinforced her parents' declaration that it was her duty as a good churchwoman and

45

devoted daughter to care for them when they grew old. They had often made it clear to her that she was too stupid to be capable of doing anything else.

Sundry aged aunts and cousins at various times nodded their grey heads sadly over her and agreed that, since she was so plain and lacking in vivacity, she could not hope to marry. It was better she be the companion of her own dear mother than be faced with the horrors of having to earn a living at something dreadful, like being a companion-help in a strange household.

She had been devastated as it slowly dawned on her that she had simply been kept single and poorly educated for Timothy's and Louise's own convenience, not because they loved her and wanted to keep her by them. Her plaintive request during the war that, like many other women, she be allowed to nurse was met by a threat from Timothy to leave her penniless; nurses didn't earn anything, he assured her. With two servants deserting the family in favour of working in ordnance factories, Timothy was not about to allow a useful daughter to desert as well. Such was the class distinction that it never once occurred to Celia that she could do precisely what the servants were doing – earn in a war factory.

Though hopelessly cowed by her parents, she carried under her subservience a terrible bitterness. This week it had been added to by the realisation that, at his death, her father had indeed left her nothing. She was now entirely dependent upon her mother's whims.

Once she had understood that she was sane and not particularly unhealthy, she had not had a terror attack again. Like many other middle-class women, she sadly accepted that there was no escape from home. As a result of the war, marriage must now, in any case, be discounted – there were barely any men left for pretty girls to marry, never mind plain ones; they had died, like George and Tom, for the sake of their country; their names would be inscribed on one of the new war memorials going up all over a country which was already finding the wounded survivors an expensive nuisance.

'You can't marry a name on a war memorial,' she had complained pitifully to her only woman friend, Phyllis Woodcock, whose husband had proved to be too delicate for call-up.

Phyllis, who was not very enamoured of the married state, muttered agreement. Like Celia, she had been warned in her youth that, for a single woman who left home, there was no way for her to earn a living except by being a governess or, if one was uneducated, face a fate worse than death by joining the crowds of ladies of the evening all over the city. These sinful hussies were there for even the most innocent, honest women to observe, and it was whispered that they died of horrifying diseases. Just what ladies of the evening did to come to such untimely ends, neither Celia nor Phyllis were quite certain, but both of them were sufficiently scared not to want to try it.

Once when he came home on leave, George had told her cheerfully that someone had to keep the home fires burning while the men were away, and this had been a small comfort. The walls of the West Derby house became to her at least some sort of defence against the unknown.

She bowed her head and, with her mother and a group of elderly females, rolled bandages and knitted socks and Balaclava helmets for the troops. Her mother did a lot of organising of sales of work and big balls at the Adelphi Hotel to raise money for the Red Cross, which, for Celia, meant endless writing of letters and running hither and yon on small errands for her mother. She became accustomed to the invisible walls of her prison and to being her mother's obedient shadow.

Now, however, the sudden crumbling of the relative safety of her imprisoning walls had frightened her so much that panic had set in again; that open gates might lead to greater freedom for her to do something for herself did not occur to her; long-term prisoners do not always try to escape when the opportunity offers – and Celia was no exception.

'"... and I will dwell in the house of the Lord for ever."'

The muttering ceased, and she lay still. If she remained very quiet, she comforted herself, God would give her strength. He had to, because there was nobody but herself to look after Mother until Paul and Edna arrived to help her.

Chapter Six

Soon after six o'clock the next morning, young Ethel, sleepy and irritable, clumped into the breakfast room. She swung a heavy coal scuttle into the hearth and followed it with a clanking empty bucket in which to carry downstairs yesterday's cold ashes from the fireplace. The room was dark, except for a faint glimmer of dawn through a crack between the heavy window curtains.

Suddenly awakened, a bewildered Celia sat up on the chaise longue.

At the sight of her, Ethel screamed and clutched her breast dramatically. 'Oh, Miss! You give me a proper fright! Haven't you been to bed?'

Celia swallowed, and pushed back her long tangled fair hair, from which all the hairpins seemed to be missing. She laughed weakly as she swung her feet to the floor. 'No,' she told the little fifteen-year-old. 'I was so tired that I fell asleep here on the sofa.'

Rubbing her hands on her sackcloth apron, Ethel came over to stare at her. She thanked goodness that it was only Miss Celia there, not the Missus. She had not bothered to put on her morning mobcap to cover her own untidy locks, and the Missus would have been furious to see her without a cap.

'Are you all right, Miss?'

'Yes, thank you, Ethel. Would you light one of the gaslights? I think it will still be too dark to draw back the curtains.'

'I were just about to do it, Miss, when I seen you.' Ethel drew a box of matches out of her pocket, and went to the fireplace. After striking a match, she stood on tiptoe to turn on one of the gaslights above the mahogany mantelpiece.

There was a plop as the gas ignited and the room was flooded with clear white light. Dead match in hand, Ethel turned, for a moment, to stare at her young mistress, before beginning to clear out the ashes. In her opinion, Miss Celia was taking her father's death proper hard and looked real ill with it.

She began to hurry her cleaning, so that she could return to the kitchen to gossip with Dorothy about it.

Celia sat on the edge of the chaise longue, absently poking around the cushions in search of some of her hairpins, while her eyes adjusted to the bright light.

As she rose unsteadily to her feet, she noticed the silver card plate from the hall lying on the table in the centre of the room. It held a number of visiting cards. Dorothy must have brought it in the previous evening, and it had lain neglected because of Louise's collapse. Now Celia quickly sifted through the cards.

They indicated that the vicar's wife and two of Louise's women friends had called. In addition, there was a card left by her own friend, Phyllis Woodcock, who had been too far advanced in her fourth pregnancy to come to the funeral. She had scribbled a note to Celia on the back of her card to say that she would try to visit again tomorrow, after the midwife had been to check on her state of health.

Dear Phyllis! Childhood playmate and still her friend, despite her brood of awful children and her whining husband.

Tomorrow is today, thought Celia. God, I must hurry. See to poor Mother, talk some sense into her – about the maids, about the cottage, about what furniture we should take with us, what we should sell. How did one sell superfluous pieces of furniture? Go to Hoylake to see Ben Aspen, the builder recommended by Mr Billings – would he need money down or would he send a bill later on? Go to see Mr Carruthers, the bank manager, about what one did to cash the cheque from Mr Billings. Did Mother know how to cash a cheque?

After she had done all that, Celia remembered, there was the enormous task of writing letters of thanks for masses of flowers and in response to black-edged missives of condolence. Her father had been a well-known businessman and churchman, but, nevertheless, the interest engendered by his unexpected death had amazed Celia.

'He must have known everyone in the city!' Celia had exclaimed to her exhausted mother, who, on the day before the funeral, sat with that morning's mail, still unopened, in her lap, while Dorothy added yet another floral tribute to the pile surrounding her father's body in the sitting room, and Cousin Albert greeted the vicar and his wife at the door.

Louise responded wearily, 'He did. We did a lot of entertaining.'

'We did,' Celia agreed, remembering the long and boring dinners, which involved so much work. She herself often helped Winnie and Dorothy on such occasions, by doing the complicated laying of the table and overseeing, from the kitchen, that the right dishes for each course were lined up, ready for Dorothy to carry upstairs. She herself rarely appeared at the parties.

Now, with her father safely in his grave and Cousin Albert back at his own home, she stood, for a moment, balancing herself against the table and looked shakily at the visiting cards. Through her tired mind rolled unusual words, like dowry, annuity, bankruptcy, land ownership. How could she deal coolly and calmly with visitors, when her tiny world was in such chaos?

Paul! Edna! Please, dears – please come soon, she prayed. She feared she might sink again into her panic of the previous night.

But Ethel was making a great dust as she cleared the ashes from the fireplace, and Dorothy was pushing the door open with her backside, as she carried in her box of brushes and dusters and her Bissell carpet sweeper. 'Mornin', Miss,' she said mechanically, as she saw Celia.

To calm herself, Celia took in a big breath of dusty air and replied gravely, 'Good morning, Dorothy.'

She went slowly out of the room and up the stairs. Her legs dragged, and she could not make herself hurry. Better leave Mother to sleep and then give her breakfast in bed, she considered. Before she wakes, I could make a list of things we must do, and, after breakfast, get her going on the more urgent ones – like seeing the bank manager.

Upstairs, she shivered as she stripped off her clothes still damp from the perspiration of the previous night. She hung up her black skirt to air, and left the rest in a pile on her undisturbed bed for Dorothy to take away to be washed.

Looking down at the smelly garments, she realised dully that she did not know how to wash clothes properly, and she wondered if they would be able to employ a washerwoman. Even during the war, when they had had to manage the house with only Winnie living in, they had been able to find women to do the washing and clean the house; they were usually army privates' wives, living on very small army pay, who had children whom they did not want to leave alone for long. They had been thankful to come in by the day to earn an extra few shillings.

As she washed herself in the sink of the jewel of her mother's house, the bathroom, which glittered with white porcelain and highly polished mahogany, she remembered the earth lavatory of the cottage. Such primitive sanitary arrangements meant that they must take with them the old-fashioned washstands with their attendant china basins, jugs, buckets and chamber pots; she recollected that three rooms in their present home were still equipped with these pieces of furniture. And there was a tin bath in the cellar – they would need that, with all the work that it implied – heating and carrying jugs of hot water upstairs to a bedroom, and afterwards bringing down the dirty water, not to speak of the dragging up and down of the bath itself, all chores that she herself would probably have to attend to.

While she brushed her hair and then tied it into a neat knot to be pinned at the back of her neck, she wondered resentfully whether, in addition to all the usual jobs her mother expected her to do, she was going to spend her whole future trying to deal with the domestic problems of the cottage.

Later, when she was dressed, the last button of a clean black blouse done up and a black bow tied under her chin, she paused to look at herself in the mirror, and made a wry face. She looked pinched and old. She was drained by the fears besetting her, acutely aware of her own ignorance. Even Ethel, struggling to make the fire go in the breakfast room, was not as helpless as she was. At least Ethel could make a fire and could probably cook a meal on it if she had to.

Why haven't I learned to cook? she asked herself dully. Or even watched Mrs Walls, when she comes in on Mondays to do the washing? Or looked to see in what order Dorothy does the rooms, so that she doesn't redistribute the dust? And as for making the cottage garden look decent, I don't know how to begin.

The answer was clear to her. As a single, upper middle-class lady, she was not expected to know. Her job was to run after her mother, be her patient companion, carry her parcels, find her glasses, help her choose library books in the Argosy Library, make a fourth player at cards if no one else was available, write invitations and thank-you notes – and be careful always to be pleasant and never give offence to men, particularly to her father. And when her parents were gone, she would probably do the same for Edna – tolerated in her brother-in-law's house, either because Edna had begged a roof for her or, on Paul's part, from a faint sense of duty to a penniless woman.

'I wish I were dead,' she hissed tearfully at the reflection in the wardrobe mirror, and went down to the breakfast room to find a pencil and make a list.

Chapter Seven

❧

While Dorothy and Ethel finished cleaning the breakfast room, Celia, list in hand, went down to the basement to talk to Winnie.

On seeing her young mistress, the cook hastily rose from eating her own breakfast at the kitchen table. With the corner of her white apron, she surreptitiously dabbed the corners of her mouth.

'Don't get up, Winnie. Finish your breakfast. I just thought I'd have a word with you, before Mother rings for her tray.'

Winnie sank slowly back into her chair and picked up her fork again. She looked cautiously at Celia, who had walked over to the kitchen dresser and taken down a cup and saucer. The girl looked as if she were on the point of collapse.

'Would you be liking a cup of tea, Miss?'

Celia laid the cup and saucer down in front of the cook, and then pulled out another kitchen chair to sit down on. 'Yes, please, if you can spare it from your pot.'

'To be sure, Miss.'

While Celia slowly sipped a very strong cup of tea and Winnie finished up her egg and fried bread, both women basked in the warmth of the big fire in the kitchen range. Ethel had made it ready in anticipation of Winnie's beginning the serious cooking of the day as soon as she had finished her own meal.

The heat was very comforting, and some of Celia's jitteriness left her. 'I was wondering, Winnie,' she began, 'if one of you could come out to the Meols cottage with me and help me clean it. I think it will take more than one day. Could two of you manage, here, to look after Mother? I think I may have to be quick about making arrangements, and we can't move anything from this house until the other one is clean. Mr Billings, the agent, will be going out there today to make sure it is watertight.'

At the reminder of the impending demise of the household, poor Winnie's breast heaved under her blue and white striped dress. Her response, however, showed no resentment. She said helpfully, 'Oh, aye, Miss. Our Dorothy would be the best one to take – and you'd need to get the chimneys swept, no doubt.' She paused and ran her tongue round her teeth, to rid them of bits of egg, while she considered the situation. 'Anybody living nearby will put you on to a sweep, I'm sure. And you'd have to take brooms and brushes – and dusters and polish with you, wouldn't you?'

In twenty minutes, Winnie had a cleaning campaign worked out. She inquired whether the water in the house was turned on.

Feeling a little ashamed at how low they had sunk, Celia admitted that there was only a pump that did not work and a well of uncertain cleanliness. She said hopefully, 'I think Mr Fairbanks from next door would let us take water from his pump for a day or two. He's very nice.'

'Would he? That would be proper kind. A friendly neighbour's worth a lot.' Winnie heaved herself out of her chair and began to clear the table. 'You'd better get a plumber to fix the pump, hadn't you? You could ask him what to do about the well. He'll know – and I'll put together some lunch for you.'

Celia began to feel that her life was regaining some sense of order, and she looked gratefully at the cook. 'You're wonderful, Winnie,' she said with feeling, as she took her empty teacup to the kitchen sink ready for Ethel when she came down to the basement kitchen to do the washing up.

At that moment, Dorothy, carrying her brooms, bucket, dustpan and brush, and carpet sweeper, pushed open the kitchen door. She was bent on snatching her breakfast before she had to serve Louise and Celia their meal. Winnie told her immediately that she would be spending the next day in Meols, cleaning Miss Celia's new home.

Dorothy opened her mouth to protest, and then decided that it might be a bit of a change. She nodded assent, and said, 'Yes,

Miss,' to Celia very primly, as if being whisked out to Meols was something that happened regularly to her. Then she hung up her dustpan and brush in a cupboard, and picked up the carpet sweeper again to take it outside to empty it into the dustbin. She unlocked the heavy back door and trotted into the brick-lined area outside.

As she opened the flaps of the carpet sweeper and shook out the dust, she could hear, very distantly, Ethel singing 'The Roses of Picardy', as she scrubbed the front steps, and she began to regret her agreement to go out to Meols. Out there, it would likely be scrubbing, scrubbing all the way, she considered sourly, as she clicked the sweeper shut. Why hadn't she suggested that Miss should take Ethel instead?

Before leaving the kitchen, Celia turned and gave the cook a quick hug. 'I don't know what we're going to do without you,' she said.

Winnie forced a smile, and wondered what she was going to do without the Gilmore family, whom she had served for over fifteen years. All through the war, I stayed with them, she considered dolefully, when I could have earned much more in a munitions factory – I was proper stupid. I could have saved something to help me now.

A bell in the corner of the kitchen rang, and she turned to see which one it was. 'Your mam's awake,' she shouted after Celia, who was running up the kitchen stairs. 'Will you tell me when she's ready for her breakfast?'

'I will.'

As Celia went up the second staircase to her mother's bedroom, she smiled slightly. Things were already changing. Winnie would never have referred to her mother as 'your mam' if her father had been alive; and, at the sound of the bell, Dorothy would have had to climb the two staircases to inquire directly what it was that Madam required.

Considering her flood of tears the previous night, Louise managed a remarkably solid breakfast. Celia, who did not want any, sat on the bed beside her, patiently wondering how to discuss their problems with her without causing yet another collapse into tears.

Finally, Louise laid her empty cup down on its saucer, and sighed. 'Put the tray on the side table for me, dear,' she ordered.

Celia did as she was bidden, while Louise crossed her hands over her stomach and stared disconsolately out of the window at a fine March day. She took no notice when Celia pulled out of her skirt pocket the list she had made earlier.

'Mother,' she said tentatively, 'because Cousin Albert thinks we may have to move quickly from here, I've made a rough list of what I think we must do at once.'

Her mother turned to look at her, her pale, slightly protruding blue eyes showing no sign of tears. There was, however, a total absence of expression in them, and Celia wondered if her mother was feeling the same sense of unreality that she was, as if she were a long way off from what was happening, that this wasn't her life at all; she was merely watching a play.

'Yes, dear?' Louise's voice was quite calm, though she sounded weary.

Celia gathered her wandering thoughts, and began by saying, 'I thought we'd better see, first, how much money we have access to.' She paused, feeling that it was vulgar to consider money when they had just been bereaved. But they had to live until the house was sold, so she added firmly, 'I suppose that dear Papa gave you the housekeeping at the beginning of the month?'

Louise gave a sobbing sigh, and said, 'Yes, dear. I hope I can make it last through the first week in April.'

'Then there's the cheque Mr Billings gave you yesterday. How do we get money for it? Do you know?'

'Your dear father always paid it into my bank account, and when I wanted to pay for a special dress, or something, for either you or me – or gifts – personal things, I wrote a cheque. I'm sure Mr Carruthers would show us how to put Mr Billings' cheque into my account.'

'Is there anything in the account at present?'

'I don't think so, dear. Your dear father got me to write a cheque on it for him about three months ago. It was a loan.'

Celia felt an uncomfortable qualm in her stomach at this disclosure. She wondered what else her father might have done, which would further imperil their limited finances. She suggested that if Louise felt strong enough they should pay a call on the bank that afternoon, to which Louise agreed.

'Did Papa have a solicitor for his affairs, Mama?'

'Well, he had Mr Barnett, of course, who came to the funeral, dear. As far as I know, he did any legal work in connection with your father's business. He's supposed to be supervising the sale of this house, remember?' Louise moved restlessly in her bed. 'But Father didn't use his services very much, because he was expensive. He even wrote his will himself; but Cousin Albert says that it is perfectly valid. He said it was witnessed by Andy McDougall and his chief clerk.'

Celia knew of old Mr McDougall. When he had attended the funeral, he had looked as ferocious as his reputation held him to be, and with him there had been another old gentleman, who could well have been his chief clerk. She recollected vaguely that he was a corn merchant and had a small office, similar to her father's, in the same building. She had noticed Cousin Albert talking with them after the funeral, probably because, as Albert had told her, he needed, first, to satisfy himself of the authenticity of the witnesses' signatures to the will.

'Do we need a solicitor, Celia?' The question held a hint of anxiety in it.

Celia chewed her lower lip. 'I don't really know, Mama,' she confessed. 'But this house belongs to you – and it's a handsome house – it must be worth quite a lot.' How could she say that she did not trust her father's cousin very much – she had no real reason to feel like this, except that he was being very domineering and he had apparently tried to collect the rents which Mr Billings had refused to hand over to him.

She said slowly, 'I think that you should have a legal man to make sure that you receive what is yours.'

Her mother gave a small shocked gasp, and Celia hastily added, 'Well, laws are funny things, and it is difficult for us to know what we are signing – we can read it – but understanding is something different. Did you understand the papers that you signed for Mr Barnett and the estate agent the other day?'

Louise was frightened. 'Not really; they both said they gave them permission to sell the house and for the agent to charge me a commission for doing it. Should I have had a solicitor of my own? Albert said I should sign – and he was once a solicitor himself.' She looked helplessly up at Celia.

'Try not to worry, Mama. The papers probably are all right.' How could she say to her mother that it was Albert Gilmore himself about whom she felt doubtful? She finally replied carefully, 'I know he was a solicitor. But he's looking after the will – which is Father's affair. You don't have anybody. Perhaps there should be someone who is interested only in your affairs.'

'Yes, dear. I see.' Louise was trembling with apprehension as she began slowly to get out of bed. Her huge, lace-trimmed cotton nightgown caught in the bedclothes, and momentarily a fine pair of snow-white legs were exposed to the spring sunlight pouring through the windows.

She hastily hitched her gown more modestly round her, but not before Celia had the sudden realisation that, though her mother always appeared old to her and her face petulant, she was extremely well preserved, with a perfect skin and luxuriant hair.

She might marry again. And, if she did, where would I be? she asked herself fearfully.

She swallowed hard. She had enough to worry about without anything else.

She said carefully, as she moved out of Louise's way, 'Perhaps Mr Carruthers at the bank could recommend a solicitor to us. We could ask him.'

As Louise nodded agreement, they both heard the front door bell faintly tinkling in the kitchen.

'I think that will be Phyllis. She left her card yesterday when we were out, and said she would come again today. There are some cards on the tray for you, too. Will you be all right, Mother, if I go down? We could walk round to the bank this afternoon. Phyllis won't stay long.'

Louise was already on her way to the bathroom and in the distance they could hear Dorothy running across the hall to answer the front door. Over her shoulder, Louise agreed resignedly, and then said in a more normal voice, 'Really, Phyllis should not be walking out in her condition.'

'Times have changed, Mother. Ladies-in-waiting go about a lot more than they used to do.'

'A true gentlewoman would not!' The remark sounded so much more like her mother's usual disapproval of Phyllis that Celia was quite relieved. Louise had disapproved of Phyllis ever since she had first appeared at the front door, when she was nine years old, to ask if Celia could come out to play hopscotch. In Louise's opinion, the daughter of a carriage builder – a tradesman – was no companion for the granddaughter of a baronet and daughter of a prominent businessman in commerce. The girls had, however, clung to each other. Both were lonely and shy, great bookworms, and were over-protected – Phyllis because she was a precious only child and Celia because she was to be kept at home as a companion-help. Neither was allowed to mix very much with other children.

Celia let her mother cross the passage to the bathroom, and then ran lightly down the stairs, to be enveloped – as far as was possible – in her friend's arms.

Chapter Eight

With a toddler clinging to her hand, Phyllis greeted her friend tenderly. 'I'm so sad for you and for Mrs Gilmore. It must be terrible for you.'

'Thank you, dear. How are you?'

The inquiry did not need a reply. Phyllis was her usual untidy self. Her hair below her wide-brimmed beige hat was threatening to fall down her back at any minute, and her face was drained of colour, except for black rings round her tired eyes. Her long black skirt, which had dog hairs on it, half-covered her swollen ankles. To disguise her pregnancy, she wore an out-of-fashion cheviot cape of her mother's which barely met across her swollen stomach.

Phyllis simply grimaced in response to Celia's mechanical inquiry, and then shrugged as if to convey that her wellbeing was of no consequence.

Celia went down on her knees to ask the toddler, 'And how's little Eric today?'

Eric turned away from her and buried his grubby, marmalade-smeared face in his mother's skirt. Celia smiled and patted his flaxen head as she got up again.

'Come into the breakfast room. There's a good fire there. Dorothy hasn't done the sitting room yet.'

Phyllis sighed with relief as she sank into Louise's favourite chair. It was upholstered in faded green velveteen and was armless, which allowed space for the stout or pregnant to spread their skirts comfortably around them. She remarked with feeling, 'I shall be thankful when my little burden arrives.'

'It can't be long now, can it?' Celia asked. Though Phyllis had explained to her how dreadfully vulgar were the things a husband did to you which led to having a baby, Celia had never liked to inquire how long it took the baby to grow.

'Any time now, the midwife thinks. This morning she advised that I should stay close to home.' She shifted uneasily in her chair, and then went on, 'You always get hours of warning, though, so I thought I should squeeze in a visit to you. You and Mrs Gilmore must be absolutely devastated.'

Celia nodded. She did not know how to explain what she was feeling, because after her little talk with Winnie in the basement kitchen she had sensed in herself a stirring of relief.

She had realised suddenly that she was not grieving for her father so much as she was upset at her own lack of competence in dealing with the disarray he had left behind him. He had been very hard to live with; and she had to admit that she had not, in the past week, missed his hectoring voice criticising some alleged fault in her behaviour.

To cover her confusion at Phyllis's remark, she glanced round to check on little Eric.

She saw that he had discovered one of the household cats asleep on what had been Timothy Gilmore's chair. He was nuzzling into the animal's long black fur. It seemed to be tolerating him quite well, so she asked Phyllis if she was comfortable in the chair in which she was sitting. Having been assured ruefully that she was – as far as it was possible to be comfortable in her situation – Celia asked, 'How many babies do you want to have, Phyllis?'

Phyllis laughed. She said cynically. 'I don't have any say in the matter. They simply come.'

'Does it hurt?'

'Yes – and it makes you so tired afterwards and you want to cry a lot. And husbands don't like that, of course.' Phyllis winced under her breath and straightened her back.

Celia drew a stool towards the fire, so that she could sit close to her friend. 'Perhaps, when Mr Woodcock progresses in his career, you will be able to have a nanny as well as your maid?' she suggested. She leaned forward to tug at the bell pull hanging beside the fireplace, to call Dorothy and ask her to bring some coffee.

Phyllis slowly drew off her black gloves, as she replied, 'I hope so.'

Long ago, she had, when Celia had asked her, told her frankly the basic facts of sexual intercourse and that it was a right of a man to demand it of his wife. Poor Phyllis had gone into her marriage totally ignorant of what it implied, and had been so shocked and her husband so clumsy that she had never enjoyed it. She endured it as best she could – and the babies came, and her husband grew ever more irritable and hard to live with. Neither she nor Celia, therefore, had any idea that intercourse could be pleasurable. It was popular to coo over babies and forget what went beforehand.

Celia did not know the details of Phyllis's marriage, but she did understand that her friend was worn out and unhappy, and she had long since begun to think that marriage was not quite the happy state that girls were told it was.

If one had an income of one's own, she had considered, it would be pleasanter to remain single – except that one could not have a baby, and she herself would love to have just one, like little Eric.

Phyllis returned to the reason for her visit. 'How is Mrs Gilmore?' she asked.

'She seems more herself this morning, a little less exhausted.'

'I was horrified to see the For Sale notice on your gate. Does Mrs Gilmore really want to move?'

Even to Phyllis, Celia did not feel able to talk of financial problems; it was not the thing. So she said abruptly that the house was far too big and that they were going to renovate a summer cottage that they owned, in Meols. 'The sea air, you know – Mother thinks it will be good for both of us. My Aunt Felicity left the place to Mother. Father didn't like it, so it has been let for a number of years. It's vacant now.'

Phyllis's dejected expression lifted a little. 'How lovely to be able to live by the sea,' she responded longingly.

'You'll have to bring the family to visit us, once we're settled in,' Celia replied with a sudden glint of enthusiasm. 'Sea air would do you a world of good.' She suddenly saw an advantage to living in Meols. She could really give some relief to Phyllis by inviting her out for the day, with the children.

A sullen Dorothy arrived in response to the bell, and Celia told her to bring a pot of coffee and some biscuits and a glass of milk for Eric.

Celia's ring had interrupted an anxious conning by Winnie and Dorothy of the Situations Vacant column in *The Lady*, a magazine devoted to the interests of middle-class families, which included a constant search for competent, cheap domestics.

Back in the kitchen, while she assembled the tray, Winnie glumly closed the magazine. 'All the best jobs is in the south. Nothin' up in the north here at all. We'd better look in the evening paper when it comes.'

'Oh, aye,' Dorothy agreed, as she quickly measured coffee beans into the grinder and turned the handle vigorously. 'I were thinking I might try for a waitress's job. You get tips then.'

'That's all right if you've got a home to go to. If you haven't, you've got to find a room somewhere – and that'll cost you.'

'I suppose.' Dorothy whisked the ground coffee into a pot and poured boiling water over it from the kettle kept simmering on the hob. She stirred the coffee and clapped the lid on the pot. Then, as she paused to let the grounds settle, she asked, 'Do you know where the Missus is? I want to do her bedroom.'

'Lying in her nice warm bath, I'll be bound – and no hot water left for washing the tiles in the hall. You take the tray up, and I'll put the big kettle on the fire again.'

'Ta ever so.'

As Dorothy moved a small side table closer to Celia and then set the tray down on it, she took a quick look at Phyllis's face. Very close to her time, she reckoned knowingly, and this was confirmed by Phyllis's face suddenly puckering up as the ache in her back became sharper.

If I were her, Dorothy thought, I wouldn't be sitting here

drinking coffee; I'd be on my way home, I would. It was not her business, however, so she withdrew discreetly, to descend again to the kitchen and share her thoughts with Winnie.

Chapter Nine

As Ethel clumped through the hall on her way to the kitchen to get a bucket of clean hot water with which to wash the tiles of the front hall, she heard a high shriek from the breakfast room, followed by the sound of someone bursting into tears. She paused uncertainly, wondering if the Missus and Miss Celia were having a row. Then she remembered that Mrs Woodcock had come on a visit while she had been wiping down the front railings and she wondered if the lady had, perhaps, fallen over the Old Fella's footstool – and her expecting.

She put down her bucket, wiped her hands on her sackcloth apron and ran across to the breakfast-room door. Clearly through it, she heard Miss Celia's agitated voice say, 'You mean it's coming?'

Mrs Woodcock replied tearfully, 'Yes, dear. The water's broken. Could you ask Mrs Gilmore to come – quickly? Please!'

In response to this urgent request, the bell in the kitchen jangled distantly. Ethel tentatively opened the door, to peep round it.

Mrs Woodcock was writhing and whimpering in the Mistress's chair. She was gasping, 'I'm so sorry, Celia. I'm so sorry.'

In order to remove her visitor's wide-brimmed hat, Miss Celia was trying to take out Mrs Woodcock's hatpins, which were pulling at the poor lady's hair as she turned and twisted.

Thumb in mouth, Eric was staring at his mother. Then he let out a frightened yell and ran to her, to clutch at her skirt and try to climb on to her knee.

Dorothy came running through the green baize door at the back of the hall. She inquired of Ethel in a low voice, 'What's up?'

She crowded close to the little kitchen maid, her nose twitching nervously as she peered at the breakfast-room door.

Ethel stepped back from the door and turned to her eagerly. 'I think Mrs Woodcock's baby's coming,' she replied in an excited whisper. 'Shall I run up and tell the Mistress?'

Dorothy paused for a moment, her hand on the brass doorknob. 'Holy Mary! Are you sure?'

'Sounds like it.' Ethel pointed a thumb at the half-open door. They could both hear Phyllis's frightened little gasps and Miss Celia's ineffectual reassurances.

'Oh, aye. Go and tell the Mistress – quick.' Dorothy pushed the girl aside and, feeling a little scared, entered the room. She nearly tripped over a cat which shot out and across the hall.

Celia was bent over her friend. She looked up and exclaimed through white lips, 'Oh, Dorothy! Thank goodness you're here. Ask the Mistress to come down. Mrs Woodcock is in great distress.'

Eric, pushed away by his mother, was sitting on the hearth rug. At the sight of another strange woman, he began to shriek in good earnest.

Over his noisy protest, Dorothy replied calmly, 'Ethel's gone for her, Miss. Here, let me take the little boy.' She bent down and swept the child up into her arms. ''Ere, now. You just be quiet – and your mam'll be fine.' She spun round and picked up a Marie biscuit from the coffee tray, then walked him over to the window. She pointed out a couple of pigeons roosting on the back wall and gave him the biscuit to eat. In thirty seconds, she had reduced his howls to small sobs.

She wiped away his tears with her apron and told him he was a good, brave little boy, and, in a minute or two, his Auntie Dorothy would take him down to see the tom cat in the kitchen.

Over her struggling friend's head, Celia looked at Dorothy with amazement; she had never seen her before as anything but an automaton who cleaned rooms and waited at table, and said dully and mechanically, 'Yes, Miss,' or 'No, Miss,' in response to whatever was said to her.

Wrapped in a camelhair dressing gown, knitted slippers on her feet, Louise came running into the room, twisting her wet hair into a knot as she came. 'That fool of a girl said . . .' Then, as she saw the little tableau by the fireplace, she realised that the message Ethel had blurted out was true.

She had been feeling helpless and deserted as she lay crying in the cooling water of her bath. But when Ethel had knocked frantically at the bathroom door and poured out her message, she had instinctively responded to the call for help.

Now, faced with Phyllis's obvious desperate need and the necessity of saving her fine old Turkish hearth rug from being ruined by having a baby born on it, she entirely forgot her grief.

She said calmly to Celia, 'Find Ethel and send her for Dr Hollis.'
Celia fled.

Phyllis lifted a woebegone face, flushed with shame, to Louise. 'I'm so sorry – oh – I've ruined your chair – the water's broken.' She gave another little moan. 'I'm having a midwife, Mrs Fox from Green Lane – if I could get home, I could send for her.'

There was a tartness in Louise's voice, as she responded, 'I don't have a carriage to send you home in, my dear. Timothy would never have a carriage – said they were more nuisance than help.' As she spoke, she was pulling back the stool on which Celia had been seated, to clear a path to the door, so that they could move Phyllis upstairs.

'To order a cab would take precious time,' she went on. 'I don't think we should chance it. But don't worry.'

The tearing, familiar ache which enclasped Phyllis's waist eased for the moment and she protested quite coherently, 'The pains don't seem to be coming very fast yet. Surely I could reach home all right, couldn't I?'

For reasons which Louise could not analyse herself, she was reluctant to let Phyllis go.

The sudden crisis had jolted her out of her own grief, diverted her mind. She was loath to face again a long day which, she knew, would otherwise become filled with problems which she did not know how to deal with. Childbirth was familiar – at least she knew from experience how to deal with that, she told herself.

With a sense of power and new-found energy, she said gently,

'Don't chance it, Phyllis. The baby might be damaged, if you gave birth in a cab. We'll try to get you upstairs and on to a bed.'

With all her normal authority, she turned to Dorothy, who was jigging round and round to make the child in her arms laugh and was having some success with him. 'Take the little boy down to the kitchen – Eric, is it? And ask Winnie to come up, please.'

Making a great game of Eric riding a horse, Dorothy galloped out of the room. Before Louise turned back to her stricken guest, she actually smiled briefly at such an amusing display from her parlourmaid.

Celia had already found Ethel in the kitchen, placidly emptying more hot water from the kettle into her bucket. She hastily instructed the young girl to take off her apron and run – run – for Dr Hollis. Then, a little breathlessly, she explained to a startled Winnie what was happening.

'Well, I never!' Winnie exclaimed with interest. She wiped her hands on the towel tucked into her waistband, and then stood with arms akimbo, as she considered the situation. 'Do you think it'll be born here?'

'I don't know, Winnie – I don't know much about these things. Mrs Woodcock seems in great pain.'

'Well, of course, you don't know, Miss Celia. You being a single lady, like. I'll put the kettle on in case.' She seized her largest kettle and went to the sink to fill it.

'Mrs Woodcock is all wet, Winnie – and the hearth rug and the chair are soaked.'

'Oh, dear.' The cook looked knowingly at her young mistress, as she hung the kettle on a hook over the roaring fire. She was about to say something more, when Dorothy clattered down the stairs, with a giggling Eric bumping on her shoulder.

'Missus wants you – now. There's a right to-do up there.' She jerked her head towards the staircase. 'And this young man wants to see Tommy Atkins, don't you, pet?'

Tommy Atkins, long, thin and black, was curled up on Winnie's rocking chair. At the sound of his name, he pricked up one ear and half opened a green eye, perhaps suspicious that he was about to be dumped in the cellars to deal with a mouse.

Winnie was already taking off her blue and white striped kitchen apron, to reveal a spotlessly white one underneath. She looked a little grim, as she said, 'Oh, aye. Miss Celia just told me.'

Feeling that Eric was better left with Dorothy, who had obviously captivated him, she said to Celia, 'If you don't mind, Miss, you'd better come up as well. If we got to move Mrs Woodcock, like . . .' She stumped up the stairs and Celia followed her, her thin white hands folded tightly against her stomach, as she tried to quell the panic within her. She dreaded to think what might be happening to Phyllis – and yet the situation held a morbid fascination for her. Could a baby really arrive like Phyllis had told her they did?

When they hurried into the breakfast room, Phyllis was still sitting in the ruined chair. To Celia's relief, she did not appear to be in pain.

Louise was patting the pregnant woman's shoulder comfortingly, as she said briskly to Winnie, 'Celia will have told you of Mrs Woodcock's condition. Do you have an old oilcloth tablecloth downstairs?'

To Celia's surprise, Winnie did not seem particularly mystified by the question. 'Er . . . Yes, Ma'am. There's one on the table I keep the bread bin on. I could wipe it down for you.'

'Good. Open up the spare room bed and lay it on the mattress. Then get some of the old sheets from the sewing room and put them over it – in a pad, if you understand what I mean. Tuck them in well.'

Winnie smiled widely, showing a gap where a front tooth was missing. 'Yes, Ma'am. We'll have Mrs Woodcock comfortable in no time.'

'There's one basin on the washstand – better get a couple of tin ones from the kitchen as well. And tell Ethel or Dorothy to make a fire in the bedroom – it'll be too cold for a newborn baby.'

Showing a surprising turn of speed, Winnie went to do as

she was told, while Phyllis wailed, 'I'm putting you to so much trouble!'

'No, no, my dear. You can't help it.' Louise sounded calmer than she had at any time since her husband's demise, and Celia realised with astonishment that all the women were thrilled with what was happening, including the usually lethargic Ethel, who had not even stopped to take off her sackcloth apron before sprinting off to get the doctor.

With infuriating leisureliness, the doctor's wife received Ethel's breathless message, panted out in her dark hallway.

'Doctor's still doing his morning surgery,' she told the little maid, and, as if to confirm her words, an elderly lady accompanied by a young girl came out of a back room, followed by the cheerful voice of Dr Hollis. 'Now, remember, three times a day – and plenty of rest.'

The old lady smiled faintly, but did not respond, and Ethel and Mrs Hollis made space for her to get to the front door. 'Goodbye, Mrs Formby,' Mrs Hollis said courteously to the patient, as she closed the front door after her.

She turned back to a fidgeting Ethel. 'Do you know how fast Mrs Woodcock's pains are coming?' she inquired, and before Ethel could reply, she continued, 'I don't think Mrs Woodcock is one of our patients, is she?'

Ethel was sharp enough to realise the inference of the last remark. It meant, who will pay the doctor's fee? She liked Mrs Woodcock, who was always polite to her, so she answered stoutly, 'I don't know about the pains, Ma'am. But she's a real friend of Miss Celia, and it were Mrs Gilmore herself what sent me here.'

'I see.' The reply appeared acceptable, because Mrs Hollis said she would ask the doctor to step round immediately surgery was over. In about an hour, he should be there.

'Thank you, Ma'am.'

Full of excitement, her need to find another job completely forgotten, Ethel opened the doctor's front door and sped down the steps.

70

Chapter Ten

❧

Immediately upon her return, Ethel was entrusted with the job of taking Eric home. At first, Eric objected strongly to being taken from Dorothy and the comfortable security of the Gilmore basement kitchen. He remembered that his mother was upstairs and he shrieked that he wanted her. Fortunately, from the distant confines of the spare bedroom Phyllis could not hear him. If she thought about him at all, it was with the confident expectation that he would be properly cared for in her friend's house, and would soon be delivered safely back to Lily.

Ethel carried with her a note from Louise to Lily, Phyllis's cook-general, explaining what was happening, and asking her to feed the children their lunch and tea, and to make sure that Mr Woodcock's dinner was ready for him when he came home from work. It was possible, Louise advised her, that Mrs Woodcock would not be home for a couple of days. She added that she would arrange for Mr Woodcock to be informed, at his office, of his wife's predicament.

While Louise hastily scribbled a note to Arthur Woodcock, Phyllis sat on the edge of the wooden chair in the spare bedroom. Winnie helped to divest her of her sodden clothes and then slipped one of Celia's huge cotton nightgowns over the young mother's head.

'Arthur's going to be awfully cross,' Phyllis whimpered to Celia. She gave a small shivering sigh, and then winced as a roll of pain commenced.

Startled, Celia looked up at her. 'Why?' she asked. 'It's his baby, too!' She had been inspecting the soft pad of old sheets Winnie had contrived in the middle of the bed, and now she

71

shook out and spread over it another clean sheet and a light blanket to keep her friend warm. She was surprised at Phyllis's remark; it contradicted all that she had learned from the many romances she had read. Didn't men love their wives for producing their children?

Phyllis gritted her teeth and waited for a spasm to pass before she said hopelessly, 'Oh, he'll be cross about everything. For my being such an idiot as to get caught like this – and having to help Lily care for the other little ones. He always gets angry if his routine is upset, and Lily will have her work cut out with three children and the house to look after.'

Winnie interrupted the exchange, to get Phyllis into bed before the pain increased. She smiled benignly down. 'Don't you worry about your hubby, Ma'am. You just concentrate on the baby, and relax as much as you can between your pains. You'd be surprised how men can manage, if they have to.'

But Phyllis knew her husband too well to hope for anything other than constant complaints and weak bursts of sudden rage, and she closed her eyes to try to stop the tears rolling down her cheeks.

Celia gently folded the bedclothes over her friend, and bent to kiss her. When she saw that Phyllis was crying, she took her handkerchief out of her sleeve and wiped the tears away. Then she hesitantly kissed her again. Though she was quite frightened at being so close to a birthing mother, she said cheerfully, 'Winnie's right. Mother will talk to Arthur, I'm sure. She's just gone downstairs to write a note to him – Ethel will take it to his office – and she can write today to your mother, if you'll give her the address, to ask her to come like she did for the other children. If we post a letter soon, she'll get it by tomorrow afternoon's post.'

Phyllis conjured up a small smile. Her mother would certainly come and would run the family like a general conducting a battle – and Arthur would hate her more than ever. And take it out on Phyllis the day her mother left.

Winnie had gone to look at the old clock on the mantelpiece to check the timing of the recurrence of Phyllis's pangs of pain.

As Louise bustled back into the room after dispatching Ethel, Winnie said to her, 'The baby will be a while yet, Ma'am. Shall I make some tea? Miss Celia could sit with Mrs Woodcock while I do it; and you could get dressed before the doctor comes.'

Louise had forgotten her own bedraggled state. She glanced down at her dressing gown, and laughed. 'Yes, indeed, I must, mustn't I?' She hastened off to her own bedroom, saying to Phyllis as she went that she would send Ethel to Arthur's office as soon as she returned from delivering Eric to Lily.

The laugh surprised and pleased Celia. Though childbirth was not a normal thing to her, it obviously was to her mother; and a sense of normality was what they all needed. As Winnie pushed the bedroom chair towards her, so that she could sit by the patient, she took Phyllis's hand and squeezed it.

'Is there anything I need to do for Mrs Woodcock?' she asked Winnie, hoping that she herself would not faint if the baby came while the other two women were out of the room.

'If the pains are sharp, you just hold Mrs Woodcock to comfort her until they pass. If they start to come close together, pull the bell immediately and I'll run up. But she'll know, won't you, Ma'am?'

Phyllis nodded. She knew only too well from experience, and, in her despair, she wondered how she could endure being racked by childbirth almost every year of her life.

As it happened, Celia was not left alone with Phyllis, because Dorothy came up with buckets of coal and wood chips and yesterday's newspaper tucked under her arm, to make a fire to warm the room for the arrival of the new infant. She had reluctantly relinquished Eric to a buoyant Ethel, who was undeterred by Eric's howls and flying little fists. She picked him up and held him firmly against her shoulder, as she ran down the front steps.

As Dorothy expertly built the fire, she realised that she was enjoying the unusual morning. 'Young Eric went off quite happy with Ethel, Ma'am,' she told Phyllis. She paused while she screwed up the newspaper and laid loose balls of it in the fire grate. 'She comes from a family of thirteen, so she's fine with children. Lovely little fella, he is,' she added.

Phyllis nodded, and then gave a long, slow moan. God help me if I have to go through this thirteen times, she thought.

Celia leaned over and put an arm round her. Phyllis's face was contorted; then, to Celia's relief, she relaxed, and said in her usual soft tones, 'Thank you, Dorothy, for managing him so well.'

'It were nothin', Ma'am.' Dorothy was acquainted with Mrs Woodcock's Lily and knew all about Arthur Woodcock's relations with his wife. Both maids had lost sweethearts in France and had little hope of marrying. They were agreed, however, that it was better to be single than have a nit-picking husband like him. She picked up a pair of bellows lying in the hearth and blew the struggling fire until the coals had caught thoroughly.

As she tidied up the hearth, and with a polite bob towards the bed, went slowly down the stairs to the kitchen, her mood changed. If her Andy had survived the second battle of the Marne and come home last year, she could have been hoping for a baby now, even though she was middle-aged. Andy would have made a great dad, like the old man who was his dad, she thought wistfully. Pity they'd waited so long, though seven years' engagement wasn't that long. After all, you were supposed to save before you could marry. Not that she had saved when she had been working in the ordnance factory. Easy come, easy go.

As she washed the coal dust off her hands in the pannikin in the kitchen sink, she smiled and shrugged her shoulders at the memory of the good times she and Andy had had when he had come home on leave.

Forget it, she told herself. You could have been stranded now, with a young baby to bring up alone. It was going to be hard enough to find a new, decent place without a child. With one, she wouldn't have a hope.

A bell on its spring near the kitchen ceiling rang suddenly.

She grinned wryly to herself as she dried her hands on the kitchen roller towel. Miss Celia getting into a panic, no doubt.

Winnie was busy pouring hot water into a big breakfast teapot. As she laid the pot on the tray she had prepared, she chuckled. A similar thought had occurred to her. As Dorothy quickly took off her enshrouding sacking apron which she used for rough work, the cook said, 'It won't hurt Miss Celia to see a birth – it's probably the only chance she'll get! And any woman ought to know what to do. Here, take the tray up to them.'

Dorothy's small mouth quirked into a smile of agreement. 'Oh, aye, if she does, she's going to be proper shocked. She don't know nothin' about nothin'. I'd bet on it.'

Years later, after another war, looking back on that day, Celia had smiled. She had been terrified. But in a few hours, she had learned so much about women, she considered; that they could organise in a crisis, work through it together, be brave under suffering. And, further, that you did not know what friendship meant until you had faced crises together.

It changed for ever her ideas of what women could do, without men to tell them what incompetent fools they were. They had, of course, sent for the doctor – male – but, unlike her father, he had actually approved of their efforts on Phyllis's behalf.

Chapter Eleven

ↄ⌒ৄ৶

Because she had no idea at what point in the proceedings the baby would arrive, Celia had rung the bell when a much sharper pang had struck Phyllis; instead of a moan, she had suddenly cried out.

By the time Dorothy had navigated two flights of stairs with the tea tray, Phyllis was more relaxed and was whispering an apology to Celia for being such a coward.

Dorothy put down the tray on the dressing table, and inquired if Madam would like a cup of tea.

Facing for the moment only an awful ache round her waist, Madam said with a sigh that she would, so Celia propped her up a little with an extra pillow and held the cup while she sipped. Dorothy filled another cup and set it down on the bedside table near Celia.

Since Phyllis did not seem threatened by another immediate spasm and Celia's face was an unearthly white, the maid tried to reassure Celia by saying, 'Don't fret, Miss. You drink your tea, too. It'll be a bit yet afore the baby comes. The pains come quick when baby is actually on its way. Winnie's got the kettle on for when the doctor comes, and she's going to make a bit of lunch for everyone.'

The reminder that the doctor would be coming was a comfort, and Celia felt a little better. In fact, Louise had only just finished her toilet, when he arrived.

While Celia and her mother retired to a corner of the room, he did a quick examination of his patient, then pulled down her nightgown and neatly replaced the sheet and blanket over her. He assured the struggling mother that the baby appeared to be positioned correctly and that he did not expect the delivery to be difficult.

Phyllis told him that she had arranged for Mrs Fox, the midwife, to help with the delivery, but that she had been caught unexpectedly in dear Mrs Gilmore's house, and that Mrs Gilmore had sent for him.

'Excellent. Excellent woman, Mrs Fox,' he said, as he picked up his hat. 'She has a telephone by which she can be reached – the chemist next door to her is very obliging in this respect. I'll phone her as soon as I get back to the surgery.' He patted Phyllis's hand, and when Louise came forward, he told her, 'I doubt if Mrs Woodcock will need my services, but I expect you have someone you could send for me, if Mrs Fox feels it necessary?'

All the women were reassured by the doctor's visit, and, when warm, friendly Mrs Fox rolled quietly into the bedroom, her tiny slippered feet making no sound on the carpet, despite her vast bulk, Phyllis greeted her with pleasure before suddenly arching her back and emitting a sharp scream.

Shocked, Celia spilled some of Phyllis's second cup of tea as she hastily put the cup down on the bedside table. She looked imploringly at Mrs Fox as she straightened herself up. Phyllis's eyes were closed, and she was taking small, quivering breaths.

'Don't leave me, Seelee,' Phyllis breathed and sought for Celia's hand, which she clutched tightly. Only Celia understood how fretful and awkward Arthur was. She would understand how Phyllis was dreading going home to face his constant nagging, when she would be at her weakest after the ordeal of childbirth; the presence of Celia in his home had never deterred Arthur from humiliating his wife by picking at her whenever he was annoyed. Even if Celia did not understand the root causes of it, her friend had seen enough to understand her terrible underlying unhappiness.

At the use of her childhood nickname, Celia was almost moved to tears. She gulped and said, 'Of course, I won't, dear.'

Mrs Fox approached the bed and glanced down at Celia's left hand. No wedding ring. No wonder the woman was looking as scared as a mouse before a cat. Probably hadn't got the faintest idea of what was happening. She leaned forward and wiped the thin perspiration off Phyllis's forehead and her closed eyelids. The lids were not crunched tight with pain, so she said, 'That's right, Ma'am. Rest yourself in betweens. I'm just going to take a look to see how things are. Just lift your knees up and apart a bit.'

As the bedclothes were lifted back and Phyllis's nightgown flipped up, Celia politely turned her eyes away and concentrated them on Phyllis's face. Phyllis opened her eyes and smiled wryly up at her, while the midwife probed and pressed with her hands, and then carefully sponged her with surgical spirit. The midwife said quietly to Louise. 'Her time's too close to give her an enema to empty her bowels.'

'Stay with me!' Phyllis begged her friend again. 'It's not as bad as it sounds. I'll make an awful noise, but if you'll hold on to me, it'll feel easier.'

With her face as white as a newly donkey-stoned doorstep, Celia assured her that she would never leave her.

Louise intervened with a protest that it was not suitable for a single woman to remain in a birthing room. 'My dear Phyllis, it simply isn't the thing at all.'

Phyllis looked at her with wide uncomprehending eyes, and Louise turned to her daughter. 'Celia, you must leave!'

Winnie, peering over Louise's shoulder, her expression genuinely concerned, added, 'You may faint, luv – and we'll be too busy to deal with you.'

Celia cringed, and then as Phyllis's grasp of her hand tightened, she found the courage to say coldly, 'I shall be quite all right, Mother – Mrs Fox.'

Mrs Fox did not rise to the appeal in Celia's voice. It did not matter to her who was present, as long as they kept out of her way.

Celia faltered, and then, as Phyllis groaned, she said quietly, 'No. I want to be with Phyllis.'

Louise's voice was frigid, as she said sharply, 'Celia. You are being most disobedient. Please, leave the room.'

Outraged at being ordered about like a child, in front of a

servant and the midwife, Celia said, 'I won't.' She loosened her friend's hand, turned her back on Louise and very carefully slipped her arm under Phyllis's shoulders. Phyllis put an arm round Celia's neck and clung to her.

Louise was red with anger; Celia had never defied her like this; she would not have dared, if her father had been alive. She took a step forward, as if she might pull her daughter away, and Mrs Fox, for the sake of her patient, put a restraining hand on her arm. 'Let them be, Ma'am. Let them be, if it helps Mrs Woodcock.'

Breathing hard, Louise stared at the midwife. 'It's most improper,' she protested.

'It may be, Ma'am, but this is not the moment to argue. Will you be so kind as to step back, so that I can deal with Mrs Woodcock.'

Rebuked, Louise stepped back, and Winnie persuaded her into an easy chair by the fire. 'Best to leave it, Ma'am,' she advised.

'It's scandalous, Winnie!'

'Nobody will know, Ma'am, if you don't say nothin'.'

Sitting rigidly in the chair, Louise closed her eyes. Suddenly she turned her head into the curve of the chair's padded back and began to cry softly into her black handkerchief.

Frightened to death by what she had done, nevertheless Celia stood by her promise. She would not shift. Phyllis became rapidly far too absorbed in her own struggle to take much notice of any argument. With Celia, she concentrated on Mrs Fox's instructions, both of them shifting position as needed.

With a groan so deep that Celia had never heard anything like it before, a tiny, perfect person was finally expelled and the cord was cut and tied. And, to Celia's astonishment, the baby immediately cried out.

Phyllis relaxed in Celia's arms. Her smile was so triumphant that it was as if she had not gone through what was, to Celia, an appalling operation.

The baby was quickly bundled up in a warm towel, while water to wash it was poured into a bowl by a smiling Winnie, and Celia glanced down to see what was happening.

Phyllis's legs were still spread. Mrs Fox had pushed sheets of newspaper under her buttocks and, with a tin bowl in her hands, seemed to be waiting. In fact, except for hearty yells from the baby, everyone was very quiet.

Phyllis's tired body heaved suddenly. It seemed to Celia that there was an awful lot of blood as the placenta came clear. She had never heard of an afterbirth. She believed that something dreadful was happening to Phyllis and that she was bleeding to death.

In a blaze of fear for her friend's life, she fainted.

Chapter Twelve

❦

Celia came round to find herself sitting on the floor, leaning against Phyllis's bed. Winnie was kneeling by her, one plump arm round her. She was chuckling at her, as she wiped Celia's face with a cold, clammy face flannel.

At the same time, Louise was standing by her and scolding her. 'It's disgraceful. I told you to leave the room,' she was saying. 'Birth is not a pretty sight. Single women are not supposed to watch it – it's like a guttersnipe gaping at a street accident.'

Winnie squeezed Celia gently, and said to Louise, 'Now, don't take on so, Ma'am. Miss Celia's a brave little lady, and Mrs Woodcock is her dearest friend. Of course she wanted to help – and I think she did.'

'Indeed, she did help,' came Phyllis's voice from above her head. 'Are you all right, Seelee?'

The sound of her friend's voice, clear, though a little weak and sleepy, was a great relief. Whatever she had witnessed was evidently something quite normal. The women round her were calm and undisturbed; in fact, as she gazed at them it was astonishing how happy everyone looked; even her mother's scolding voice did not sound as acidic as she had expected it would be.

'Come and see the baby,' urged Winnie as she helped Celia up. As she staggered to her feet, however, Celia's first thought was for Phyllis.

The young mother lay with eyes closed, great black rings round them in marked contrast to an ashen face. Mrs Fox was bathing her and there was a strong smell of disinfectant from the bowl of water she was using. As she sponged, she threw each piece of rag that she used into another bowl. Mrs Fox had never yet lost a patient to childbed fever and she was taking no risks with this one. The precipitous arrival of the baby had not given her time to assemble boiled sheets, boric lint, and so on. Disinfectant and her own well-scoured person had to be the barrier against infection.

Celia laid a shaky hand on Phyllis's narrow wrist. 'Are you all right?' she asked.

Phyllis slowly opened her tired eyes. She smiled. 'Yes,' she said, and then, with more animation, 'A little boy!'

'Congratulations,' Celia said mechanically. 'I'm sure Arthur will be pleased.'

A shadow passed over Phyllis's face. 'I hope so. Do have a look at him.'

Winnie had turned and picked up the new infant out of the drawer, which, with a bolster pillow in it, had been pressed into service as a temporary cradle.

'Isn't he loovely!' she exclaimed, her plain face transformed into beauty as she looked down at the tiny baby. 'Here, luv, you hold him for a minute.' He was thrust into Celia's arms.

He was so light! So tiny! So helpless! She automatically closed her arms tightly round him, and felt a surge of protective love for him. She was aware of no one else, simply this tiny scrap of humanity and herself. It was the beginning of a lifelong devotion to her godson.

'Bring him to me,' whispered Phyllis.

With a sudden sense of guilt, Celia turned and reluctantly laid the little bundle on his mother's chest.

'What are you going to call him?' she asked.

Phyllis's eyes turned towards Louise, who was handing a clean nightgown for the patient to Mrs Fox. 'Well, if Mrs Gilmore doesn't mind, I'd like to call him Timothy George. I'll have to ask Arthur if it is all right, of course. When I asked him the other day about names, he said let's wait to see if it's a boy or a girl.' She did not add that he had seemed unable to face the advent of another child.

Her father's and her dead younger brother's names.

Celia saw her mother's face soften. 'How very sweet of you,

my dear,' Louise said, and bent to kiss the weary mother. She sighed. 'Since Edna lost little Rosemary, I have begun to doubt if I shall ever have any grandchildren. I must say that it would be so nice to have the names perpetuated.'

Phyllis gripped her hand. 'You and Seelee have been so good. I can never repay you.'

Mrs Fox came forward to help Phyllis into the clean nightgown.

She muttered a little anxiously that Phyllis must rest now. She took Timothy George away from his mother and then slipped the starched nightie over her patient's head. In the distance the front doorbell rang.

'I wonder if that is Arthur?' Phyllis's muffled voice came through the fine cotton.

Chapter Thirteen

❧

The women waited expectantly. Mrs Fox fussed around her patient. She told her she should sleep for a little while and then have some hot soup. Winnie smiled down at Phyllis and said she had a pan of soup simmering on the kitchen fire.

But Phyllis ignored them, as she watched the door eagerly, and her face fell as only the dragging footsteps of Dorothy were heard along the passage. Arthur was obviously not going to ask the bank manager, under whom he worked as accountant, if he could leave a little earlier, so that he could come to see her. She supposed, despondently, that he would come when his day's work was finished rather than break his perfect record of never having taken time off, except for statutory holidays. She began to cry weakly and noiselessly; it had been the same with the arrival of all her children.

When Dorothy opened the bedroom door, after knocking politely and being told by an impatient Louise that she could enter, the reason for her slowness and for the whiteness of her face was immediately apparent.

On the small silver tray that she carried lay two telegrams.

She proffered them to Louise. 'The boy's waiting on a reply, Ma'am. I asked him into the hall.'

After a war in which a telegram almost always announced a death or, at best, someone missing in action, the very sight of a small orange envelope was terrifying; two of them at the same time was enough to paralyse Louise. She could not make herself take them off the tray.

Mrs Fox was the first to recover. She moved a chair swiftly under Louise, and said gently, 'Sit down, Ma'am.'

Staring at the tray as if it were a cobra about to bite her, Louise mechanically did as she was told.

Already very shaky, Celia was fighting against fainting again. She made herself move towards her mother and put a protective hand on her shoulder. 'It really can't be anything very much, Mother,' she half whispered. 'The war's over.'

Winnie broke in. 'Maybe Miss Edna and Mr Paul has landed,' she suggested.

'Of course,' responded Louise with immediate relief. She took the envelopes off the tray, and said, 'Thank you, Dorothy.'

While she slit the first envelope, the others relaxed and muttered about being so silly over telegrams.

She read the missive aloud.

> 'Darling Mother stop so sad about Father stop meet me Lime Street Station London train arriving 1.30 pm Friday stop all my love Edna stop'

Louise laughed in relief. 'Quite right, Winnie,' she told her beaming cook.

As she opened the second envelope, Celia queried, 'I wonder where Paul is. Edna sent the telegram.'

The answer to her question was in the second telegram, sent by Edna's father-in-law, Simon Fellowes.

Louise's voice faltered as she read it out.

> 'Regret to report passing of my son, Paul, from influenza stop died aboard ship stop buried at sea stop devastated stop our condolences to you in your loss stop letter already in the mail stop'

'My God!' Louise let the telegram flutter into her lap. 'I thought the flu epidemic was finished.'

'I seen one or two cases recently.' It was Mrs Fox's cool voice as she read the telegram over Louise's shoulder. 'It's lucky your daughter didn't get it, Ma'am. When it strikes it tends to take everybody in the prime of life.'

Louise nodded agreement. Edna alive – but widowed – and still so young – it was too awful to contemplate. 'It's too much!' she cried. 'I can't bear it.' She began to rock herself backwards and forwards like a demented child.

'Don't, Mama. Please, Mama.' In tears herself, Celia clasped her mother to her.

Gone was the woman who had so efficiently organised the baby's birth – Louise was again wrapped in her own grief, crying with a depth of despair which had not occurred even when her husband's body had been brought home.

'Let her cry, Miss. She'll be better afterwards,' Winnie whispered.

'Poor Mrs Gilmore! Poor Edna!' Propped up on one elbow, Phyllis was staring at the stricken group of women at the foot of the bed. She stretched out her hand towards them. She turned her gaze towards Celia. 'Celia, dear.'

Winnie was saying, 'I'm so sorry, Ma'am,' while Dorothy stood transfixed, silver tray in hand, only her nose quivering, as she tried to gather herself together.

'Wh-what shall I tell the telegraph boy, Ma'am?' she finally stuttered.

Fighting her growing panic as, in a flash, she saw all the implications of this further death in the family, it was Celia who picked up Edna's telegram from her mother's lap and said swiftly, 'I will come downstairs, and write a reply for him. One of us must meet Edna tomorrow.'

Her mother muttered almost gratefully, 'Thank you, dear.' She had stopped rocking herself when Celia had embraced her, but, sitting on the stiff wooden chair, she looked lost and broken while hopeless tears ran down her face.

Winnie stepped forward and issued an order herself. 'Dorothy, go and get the Master's brandy from the dining-room sideboard, and pour a glass for everyone.' She emphasised the word everyone, to make it clear that she included Mrs Fox, Dorothy and herself.

Clinging to the banister, Celia walked carefully down the long, red-carpeted staircase to deal with the patient telegraph boy.

The youngster was standing in the hall with his hands behind him like a soldier ordered to be at ease. He knew better than to sit down on one of the four red velvet chairs set stiffly against one wall; they were not intended for the lower orders.

He was used to white-faced women with trembling hands, trying to find pencil and paper, and he immediately brought out both from the breast pocket of his grey uniform.

'Oh, thank you,' breathed Celia with relief, as she addressed a loving and sympathetic answer to Edna, care of her father-in-law, and another of condolence to Mr and Mrs Fellowes themselves.

After he had carefully counted the number of words and she had paid him for its transmission, from the change purse in her skirt pocket, the telegraph boy paused and looked hopefully at her.

Celia was puzzled and then realised her omission.

A tip! That was it. She produced another silver threepenny piece and pressed it into his hand. He grinned and picked up his peaked cap from the hall table. She watched him cram it on to his head, as he ran down the steps to his bicycle.

As she slowly closed the heavy front door after the boy, she felt again a terrible sense of despair, made worse by a threepenny piece handed to a patient boy. The small silver coin represented her own inadequacy: her ill-preparedness for dealing with even the smallest problem, never mind coping with a distraught mother and with poor Edna, the loss of her father and her home.

Her father had always done the tipping. A small item in the perplexing world into which she was inexorably being pushed. But she knew it was important if she was to get service. She must remember to take some change with her, if she went to the station to meet Edna. Porters had to be tipped.

As she went back upstairs, her shock gave way to realisation of how much she had been depending upon Paul's arrival. His loss would mean that she and her mother had no one to lean on but Cousin Albert. Edna had, at least, her father-in-law to turn to for advice.

In the bedroom, the baby was crying healthily, Mrs Fox was packing up, after downing a thimble-sized glass of brandy proffered by Dorothy, and Phyllis was lying down again and staring at the ceiling.

'Where's Mother?' Celia inquired of Mrs Fox.

'Your Winnie took her to lie down and drink her brandy in her bedroom.' Mrs Fox glanced in the dressing-table mirror, to make sure that she had pinned her wide-brimmed black hat on straight, and then picked up her shawl to wrap it round her shoulders. 'Mrs Woodcock must sleep now. If she wants the baby by her, make sure you put it back into its cradle when she falls asleep – you don't want to overlie it, do you, Mrs Woodcock?'

Phyllis smiled weakly. 'No, of course not. Dorothy is making me some tea and biscuits – I mustn't have brandy. Then I'll sleep. Celia, you should drink your brandy, though; it's on the dressing table. You must be feeling awful.' She turned to the midwife, to thank her in a weak voice for easing her pains so skilfully.

'You're welcome, Ma'am. It wasn't a difficult birth, was it, Ma'am? I'll come back this evening to take a look at you. If you don't feel right, Miss Gilmore'll phone me, won't you, Miss? I've left me number on the chest of drawers – it's really the chemist next door. He'll send his boy to tell me quick enough, though.'

Celia had no idea where she was going to find a phone from which to make such a call, but hoped her mother might know of one. And there was always Ethel – she loved being sent out with a message. She nodded agreement, and, with a smile and a half-bob, Mrs Fox departed.

Immediately she could be heard going lightly down the stairs, Phyllis said, 'Bring Timothy to me, dear. Poor little thing, crying his head off!'

Very carefully, Celia did as she was told, and then sank down on the bedside chair. With his head on his mother's breast, the baby was comforted and fell asleep. The room was at last quiet.

Though she was crooning softly to young Timothy, Phyllis saw that Celia was trembling almost uncontrollably. She repeated to her, 'Drink your brandy, Celia.'

Celia got up and, while still standing, she gulped it down. It made her splutter, and Phyllis laughed. 'Not as fast as that!' she said. 'Slowly!'

Feeling even more stupid, Celia nodded and sat quickly down on the chair again.

After a few quiet minutes, she asked, 'When will Arthur come to see you, do you think?'

'About five o'clock, I expect – when he's finished work. He'll probably get a carriage or a taxi to take me home.'

Celia was shocked. 'Surely you shouldn't be moved yet? I'm sure Mother wouldn't mind if you did your whole ten days' lying-in here. We're not going to move yet.'

'Oh, I'll be all right. I only stayed in bed for two days after Eric. Arthur couldn't stand the disruption.'

'He shouldn't give you babies then!'

Phyllis was silent. Celia had accidentally hit squarely on the problem which lay between herself and her husband, a fear of intercourse which seemed to produce babies every year. She did not know how to solve it. She had never heard of birth control.

She swallowed hard and then changed the subject by saying, 'Edna is going to need all your help, Celia – with no child to console her.'

The brandy had helped Celia. She was feeling steadier, and fractionally more optimistic. She said, 'Yes. Yes, she will.' Then she added, with a sigh, 'I hope she will be more of a comfort to Mother than I am.'

Phyllis was too tired to do any comforting herself. Her eyes drooped. Celia gently took Timothy from her. He whimpered, and she instinctively held him close to her and rocked him for a while before putting him down in his improvised cradle. Then, after tucking the bedclothes closer round Phyllis and putting a little more coal on the fire, she went out into the passage, closing the door behind her.

She stood for a moment leaning against the closed door and staring at the rich jewel colours of the carpet. Then she shut her tired eyes.

Poor Paul. To escape the war and yet still be taken. It was true that the Spanish flu had gone through the younger members of the population like some mighty scythe. It had killed the remains of the same age group which had died as a result of battle. You only had to look at the crowds in the streets of Liverpool, she thought helplessly; there were lamentably few male faces between the ages of, say, sixteen and forty, and not that many young women – Celia had been luckier than two of her women friends, in that she herself had survived an attack of it.

She shifted her feet uneasily. In the richly furnished, silent hall, she had a dreadful feeling of being quite alone, and she wondered why she should be alive when all her potential friends, never mind the ones she actually had had, were dead.

She shivered with sudden cold, and straightened herself up. Then slowly, with dragging footsteps, she went along the hall to her mother's bedroom, and tapped on the door.

Chapter Fourteen

☙

Impeccably neat in a black jacket and pinstriped trousers, Arthur Woodcock arrived on foot precisely as the Gilmores' grandfather clock in the hall struck a quarter past five. He had taken his usual bus from town.

He handed his black bowler hat to Dorothy and asked to see his wife. Dorothy showed him into the sitting room. It was her own decision; she did not want dear Mrs Woodcock made unhappy by an unfeeling husband, she told herself. She smiled at Arthur, and said politely, 'I'll get Miss Gilmore. The Missus is a bit upset.'

'Humph.' He did not inquire why Louise was upset – he presumed it was from the disorganisation of her day. Well, she wasn't the only one – he would be late for his tea, thanks to his wife's stupidity.

When Celia came into the room, he rose from his chair. Celia looked even more lachrymose than she usually did. Her nose was red, as were her eyes, her hair was disarranged – and she still had on her apron.

She tried to be cheerful for him. 'You've a lovely new son,' she told him, as she held out her hand to him. 'And Phyllis is fine – she's sleeping at the moment.'

'Good.' He shook her hand. 'I'm sorry that you have been so inconvenienced. I've ordered a taxi to come here at half past five to take us home.'

Celia's eyes widened. 'Oh, you can't move her yet. She must rest – and it's not wise to take the baby out. Mama would be quite happy for her to have her ten days' lying-in with us. We

91

would see that she had complete rest. Mama says it is vital for her health that she rest,' she finished eagerly.

'That's most kind of you. She can, however, rest at home. May I go up to see her?'

Confused by his arbitrariness, Celia said, 'Yes, of course.' She wished her mother was with her to insist on Phyllis's staying. Her mother was, however, still on her bed, weeping to Winnie that she could not go on.

As Celia led the way up the stairs, Dorothy again answered the front doorbell. On the step stood a heavily moustached male, wearing a stiff peaked cap. He was wrapped in an old overcoat and innumerable scarves.

'Taxicab for Woodcock,' he announced. Behind him stood one of the new-fangled hackney carriages; as Dorothy told Winnie afterwards, 'making a noise somethin' awful'. In fact, the vehicle was the pride of the cab driver; its boxlike body, its engine gently pulsating under a brass-trimmed hood, were the latest in rapid local travel. It bore no comparison to the old hackney carriages drawn by horses, and the driver did not want it to be kept waiting. 'Now, 'urry up,' he admonished Dorothy. ''Aven't got all day.'

Dorothy told him primly to wait in the hall, while she told the Mistress of his arrival. The man took off his hat to expose a very grubby-looking bald head and stepped inside.

Meanwhile Celia quietly opened the bedroom door for Arthur.

Arthur marched straight over to his sleeping wife. He shook her shoulder, and announced that he had come to take her home.

As Phyllis stirred and opened her eyes, Celia said anxiously, 'I've told Arthur that we all hope you will spend your lying-in with us – it would be a pleasure to us.'

'I am afraid that will not do,' Arthur said primly. 'The other children need you.'

'Lily can . . .' Phyllis began rather desperately, but nothing she or Celia could say would move him. And the decision was precipitated by the arrival of the taxi. 'I've no clothes to put on,' was her last protest.

Arthur lost his temper. 'Did you walk round here like Lady Godiva?' he asked.

Shocked, Celia interrupted to say that Phyllis's clothes were in the wash.

When he asked what had happened to them, neither woman answered him. If, after three other children, he did not understand childbirth, they were much too shy to explain it to him.

He asked if he might borrow the blankets off the bed to wrap her in, and added sarcastically, 'I suppose her shoes are fit to wear?'

Totally out of her depth, Celia rang the bell for Dorothy, who fumed as she clumped upstairs again, past the waiting taxi driver who was muttering in the hall because he was being kept waiting, and the taxi outside was consuming petrol at an awful rate. She was sent for Phyllis's shoes, at that moment lying in the kitchen hearth to dry. Her dress and a black petticoat had been hung to dry over a clothes horse by the same fire. Her underwear had been put in the wash house in the back garden, ready for the attention of the washerwoman when she came on Monday.

Celia glanced around her desperately, unwilling to enter the argument going on between man and wife. 'I'll get Mother,' she said and ran down the passage to Louise's bedroom.

Her mother was lying quietly on the bed, and Winnie was seated beside her gently patting her hand, and saying that everything would get sorted out after a while and then she would feel better. The cook looked up as Celia ran in.

Celia told her that she could not cope with Arthur, who was insisting on moving his wife. 'Please come, Mama,' she pleaded.

Winnie interrupted to suggest that Arthur could come to Louise. When Louise protested that she could not receive a man in her bedroom, the cook pulled another quilt over her.

A furious Arthur was brought in and was amazed to see her recumbent. The surprise cooled him down sufficiently for him to ask, 'Are you well, Mrs Gilmore?'

Louise said, 'I've just heard that Edna has lost her husband. I am afraid it caught me at a weak moment.'

'My condolences. In that case you will be thankful to hear that I am taking Phyllis home in a taxi, which has' – he looked at his watch – 'already been waiting for nearly ten minutes. So much

93

expense! So much bother, simply because Phyllis did not stay at home as she should have done.'

Louise immediately forced herself to sit up and say that having Phyllis in the house was no bother at all. She should stay.

While Louise did her best to persuade the irritable young man to give his wife time to recover, Celia went back to Phyllis, who was sitting on the side of the bed in her bloodstained nightgown.

Horrified, she ran to her. 'Phyl! You're bleeding!'

Phyllis smiled weakly and asked for a fresh napkin of some kind. 'It's all right, dear. Don't be afraid of the blood. I shall be bleeding off and on for a while yet.'

'I'm sure you should rest, Phyl. Tell him to go to blazes!'

'I have to live with him all my life, Seelee.'

It sounded like a death sentence to Celia, as she delved into a chest of drawers to get yet another clean nightgown, a winter vest to go under it and a winter woollen shawl, and then went to the airing cupboard for a clean towel to stem the blood. She did, however, understand Phyllis's remark. It did not do to quarrel with men. They held the purse strings.

Silent and disapproving, Louise, Celia and Winnie eased the drooping little mother into the taxi. Dorothy held the baby, swathed in towels and shawls contributed by Louise and Celia, and then laid him in his father's arms. It was the first glimpse of his father the child had had. He opened his tiny mouth and howled. It did not endear him to his angry parent.

Chapter Fifteen

That evening, though an exhausted Louise was reluctant to discuss their position, Celia insisted that they go through her list, which had lain neglected in her skirt pocket all through the momentous day of little Timothy's birth.

'Everything is too, too awful, Celia,' the older woman sobbed.

Celia really pitied her mother. But fear of the future outweighed pity, and she said firmly, 'I'm so very sorry to bother you, Mama, but if we can get ourselves a little organised, we may feel better.' She did not mention that she was afraid that, tomorrow, Edna might bring with her a whole host of additional difficulties for them to cope with.

Still lying on her bed, Louise pleaded, 'Let me rest for a little longer. We could talk after dinner.' She looked appealingly at Celia, and begged, 'I don't know how to bear it all, Celia.'

'Of course you don't, Mama. It is all so heartbreaking for you. Rest a little longer. I'll get Dorothy to bring some wine up with your dinner.'

She herself felt she had been so racked that she had no more strength. She arranged the warm quilt over her mother and kissed her gently. Then she went down to the kitchen to arrange for dinner on a tray to be sent up.

Celia snatched a quick meal in the dining room, and, later on mother and daughter went painstakingly through Celia's list of the things they had to do. It was obvious that Louise was doing her best to cooperate.

Celia felt that she was being quite brutal in her treatment of her mother and she herself longed to go to bed, but she knew that there was nobody else to take charge of the situation. There was a limit to what she could achieve in one day, she thought wearily, and tomorrow Edna would have to be met and comforted and her plans inquired about.

Edna and Paul had never had a home in England. At the time of their marriage, Paul had been preparing to go to Brazil. They had stayed in Southampton, therefore, with his parents during the months of preparation that were necessary, before his company finally sent him out to supervise a seven-year contract to provide electricity for a rapidly increasing population in Salvador and its environs. As a result, Edna had no house of her own to return to, and Celia wondered if, now she was widowed, she expected to live with her mother. She did not bother Louise with this likely problem. Louise was already distressed enough.

After some persuasion, Louise tremulously agreed that she could, the following day, manage to go, alone, to see the bank manager, the bank being only a short distance away. She would pay in Mr Billings' cheque and inquire exactly how much money she had. She would also ask Mr Carruthers about getting a solicitor of her own; they had agreed that they did not want Mr Barnett to look after them. Meanwhile, Celia would take Dorothy out to the cottage and get her started on cleaning it. She would then go into Hoylake village to see Ben Aspen, the building contractor recommended by Mr Billings, about repairs and redecoration. She would take a train direct from Hoylake to Liverpool to meet Edna.

'Whatever will poor Edna think, if I don't meet her, Celia?' Louise asked in dismay.

'The trouble is, Mama, that we don't know exactly how much time we have, before we have to move – Cousin Albert said the estate agent believed he could sell this house quite quickly, and neither of us has any idea what he means by quite quickly. It could be next week.' She sighed. 'And the expense of running this house is very great – coal, gas, servants, gardener, not to speak of feeding the five us. I doubt if we can last for a month financially, unless Mr Carruthers can spring some nice surprise on you.'

'I know, dear.'

'I'm sorry that I can't go to the bank for you. It is not my account – it is yours, and I imagine they will surely need your signature on something. If you don't go tomorrow, everything will have to wait until Monday – and we will have lost a whole weekend.'

'It really is too bad. Are you sure, Celia?'

'I am sure.' She would go insane, she thought, if she did not reduce the number of things on her list – the load was too great. 'Until we know exactly what money we have, Mother, we can't even buy a new broom.' Her nerves were in shreds and she was not being very diplomatic.

Louise burst into tears, as she agreed. 'I wish Tom or George were here,' she cried. 'They would have been such a support.'

At this mention of her strong, laughing younger brother, who had sailed off so lightheartedly to face the German navy, and Tom, big silent Tom, Celia felt a physical pain, a tug at her heartstrings. How could God be so cruel as to take them both? And then, when the slaughter seemed over, it was strange how the Spanish flu epidemic had swept away millions more of the strong, like Paul.

Where was God in all this? As she had done earlier, she felt a terrible sense that she was spinning alone in a great void.

And then there was beautiful Edna. It was really hard on her. No husband, no father, no child.

In response to her mother's cry, Celia said simply, 'Yes, the boys would have helped. They were the nicest brothers any girl could have.' Her small frame trembled with her efforts to contain her own grief, to attend only to what she was doing, and, above all, not to panic.

She decided to leave until the next evening the question of what furniture they should take with them and what should be sold; to go through it all would take hours, possibly days, and she had a feeling that her mother would defend every bit of it from the horrors of its being sent to the auction room; yet much of it was so large that the removal men would never get it through the cottage's front door, never mind up the narrow staircase.

She tucked her grieving mother up in her bed and told her to try not to worry about anything; she would feel stronger in the morning. Then she went slowly down to the basement kitchen.

She found all three servants, themselves tired out by the unusual day, sitting quietly round the fire, drinking cups of cocoa before going to bed. Their conversation stopped immediately she opened the door. They put their mugs down on top of the fender and stood up.

Celia was embarrassed at having intruded on them at an hour in their long day which was one of the few they had of their own. She said shyly, 'I'm sorry to disturb you.'

Then she quickly went on to ask if, the following morning, Winnie and Dorothy would put together some basic cleaning materials that would be needed at the cottage. 'There's an old straw trunk in the attic,' she told Dorothy. 'We could put everything into it. If the leather straps have rotted, you could cord it up.'

Though resentment welled within her, Dorothy said, 'Yes, Miss,' in her usual dull fashion. She did not want to do anything more, once she had cleared Miss Celia's dinner things from the dining room. Now she would have to go all the way up to the top of the house and root around the dusty attics to find the trunk Miss Celia meant – she would never have the time in the morning. Yet Miss Celia looked so ghastly that she could feel only pity for her.

As Dorothy hunted through the contents of the house's enormous attics for the straw trunk, Celia crouched by the dying fire in the morning room, and planned exactly how she would manage the next day. 'To begin with, I'll send Ethel down to the stables to order a taxicab to take us to Central Station to catch the electric train,' she decided. 'Though it will be more expensive, it will be quicker than going by bus.'

'Miss Celia looks real ill,' Dorothy opined to Winnie, as early the next morning, they packed clean rags, a bucket and ewer, soap, scouring powder, rust remover, a bottle of oil for hinges, black lead for the fireplaces, a big black bottle of pine disinfectant, broom heads, and a dustpan with its appropriate hand brushes.

After they had corded up the trunk, they slipped a couple of the brooms' handles under the rope, so that the whole bundle could be carried between them.

'Oh, aye,' Winnie agreed in response to Dorothy's remark. 'It's all too much for her – what with Mrs Woodcock's baby, and now Miss Edna. I'm going to pack you both a lunch and you take care of her, Doll, and make sure she eats.'

She turned to Ethel, who was wearily working her way through the washing up of the breakfast dishes. 'Ethel, luv. Go down to the cellar and look on the tool shelf. I'd better put in a hammer and nails and some screws and screwdrivers – and a pair of pliers. Bring up what you can find.'

'Holy Mary, Winnie! What are we supposed to be doing out there? Rebuilding the place?' Dorothy interjected. 'I'm not going to undo all them knots, so we can add tools to that lot.'

'Don't be daft. I'll put them in the little shopping basket. But a place what has been empty so long is sure to lack a nail or two, and there's no man to be putting them in for her. She'll have to learn to do it herself.'

Celia took her mother's breakfast tray up to her bedroom, since Dorothy was packing the straw trunk.

Immediately she had wakened her and had drawn back the thick velvet curtains, she asked Louise, 'Could I have a little money from the housekeeping, Mama, please? For the fares and anything extra Dorothy may need for the cottage.'

She had never asked her mother for money before and she hardly knew how to phrase the request. She had received three shillings a month as pin money from her father, the same amount as Ethel earned, and she still had the current month's payment in her locked dressing-table drawer. In view of their sudden straitened circumstances, she had earlier been conscience-smitten as to whether she should give it to her mother or keep it. Then she had been caught up in a fear of making a mistake during the difficult days ahead. Suppose I get off at the wrong station, she had agonised – or get on the wrong train. If I have no money of my own, I won't have a hope of sorting myself out, of being able to buy another ticket or take a bus. I'm so stupid.

Her mother rubbed the sleep out of her eyes and looked at her daughter doubtfully. She sighed, as she said, 'Celia, I'm so tired. I hope we'll be able to manage.' Then she looked about her bewilderedly before telling her daughter, 'Bring my cash box to me – it's in the centre cupboard of the dressing table.'

It was quite a heavy seventeenth-century mahogany box, originally meant to house a Bible, and Celia lifted it with care on to her mother's lap. As Louise sleepily fumbled for her keys in her dressing-gown pocket, Celia stroked the polished wood and said, 'I've always thought what a lovely box this is.'

'Humph. I brought it with me when I married your father – like a lot of the furniture in this house, it came from my grandfather's home.'

Her mother paused to yawn, and then realising that Celia was interested, she went on, her voice still heavy with sleep, 'My grandfather was a widower for years. He lived alone, except for a couple of servants to care for him.

'As you may remember, Felicity and I were the only children left, after my brother died in India, so, on my own marriage, my parents, in their turn, were left alone in a large and very empty house. My grandpa was getting very frail by that time, and he gave up his home and came to live with them.'

She yawned again, as she opened the box and scrabbled about in it. 'Grandpa was very fond of me and he told me I could have anything I wanted of his furniture, provided my mother did not want it.' She looked up at her daughter, and smiled at the recollection. 'Mother thought the stuff was dreadfully old-fashioned, but I was young and I thought it was very fine and delicate-looking – and dear Timothy, your father, though he had an excellent pedigree, didn't have much money when we were first married, so we were both grateful for the offer.' Her mouth quivered as she mentioned her late husband. Then she swallowed, and after a moment, continued, 'Later on, we had everything reupholstered and refinished.

'Then when your other grandfather died, he left us his picture collection, as you may possibly remember. I think the pictures are rather gloomy, but your father liked them, so, of course, we found space for them.'

Celia glanced round the bedroom. 'You always did have lovely taste, Mama. And you mean to say that all this stuff goes back to Georgian times – the Regency? That it is all antique?'

Her mother glanced up from her box. She was pleased by Celia's unexpected compliment. 'I suppose it is. It's certainly very old indeed. But it has been well looked after.' She picked out a note. 'Here is a five-pound note, dear. It's a lot of money. Don't lose it, and don't spend what you don't have to. But I imagine you may have to pay Mr Aspen something on account.'

'I'll be careful, Mama.' She folded the note and stowed it in her own deep skirt pocket. 'Do you have any small change, Mama – for tips? For porters. Edna's bound to have a lot of luggage. And Dorothy and I have to carry all the cleaning stuff out to the cottage. I think that, at Meols Station, I will have to get a porter to help.'

'Yes.' Her mother took her change purse from under her pillow; Celia had crocheted it for her as a Christmas present, because one could no longer buy such a purse in the shops – housewives now used leather ones. She pulled back the rings of it, to delve amid the sovereigns in the pocket at each end, and finally gave Celia some silver sixpences.

Celia's hand automatically closed on the coins, but she did not thank her mother. Her mind was elsewhere. 'You know, Mama,' she said thoughtfully, 'we shall have to sell a lot of furniture, because we have far too much for the cottage.'

'I know. Don't remind me.' Louise's voice was suddenly full of reproach, as if it were Celia's fault that her well-kept furniture would have to go.

'Some of it may be more valuable than we know. Do you know anybody who could say what it is worth?'

'Celia, you really do have the most dreadful ideas. How can I take someone I know round the house to ask them that?' There was a hint of a sob in her voice, as she complained, 'It is bad

101

enough that I will have to let that dreadful estate agent take perfect strangers round the house.'

'Sorry, Mama.' Celia was too exhausted to follow up the subject further. She herself longed to crawl back into bed and simply rest. But then there would be nobody to look after Mama or Edna.

She lifted the cash box off her mother's knees and put it back where she had found it. Then she said, 'Perhaps, tomorrow, Mama, when you are less tired, you could look round the house and see what you want to keep. Remember how small the rooms of the cottage are.'

Louise lay back on her pillows and pulled the bedding up round her chin. 'I'm not likely to forget it,' she responded huffily.

Celia bent and kissed her and went thoughtfully downstairs to have her breakfast. For the first time in years, she really looked at the furnishings of the upper and lower halls and the staircase. Two huge chests of drawers on the first-floor landing, each with an oil painting carefully centred above it; three charming water-colours on the staircase wall; and, in the front hall, two Russell engravings, six chairs, a large hall table, two occasional tables, a hope chest, a barometer, a large hat stand, innumerable vases, candlesticks, trays, a fireplace complete with brass pokers, in one corner a huge china pot with drooping dyed seed pods in it, a brass gong on a stand – and, near the front door, a grandfather clock, which showed the times of sunrise and sunset, and struck the quarter-hours as well as the hours. And of course the carpets – they, also, were probably valuable.

There was enough furniture in the halls alone to fill the biggest room in the cottage chock-a-block, she realised with a sense of shock.

Before entering the dining room to ring the bell for her break-fast to be brought up, she paused and smiled at the beautiful old face of the clock. It had been her friend ever since she could remember; its firm sprightly striking had comforted her through nights when she had lain terrified in her bed or had been shut in her room by angry parents; it reminded her when she was supposed to do her routine tasks of the day, and now, suddenly, it reminded her of her stiff, unbending father carefully winding it up each Sunday morning. He, too, had loved that clock, she guessed – the thought made him suddenly more human to her.

She smiled again. She must remember to wind it on Sunday. She would never part with it, she decided. It might just fit into the back of the hall in the cottage. She must take a tape measure to see if there was room. And she had better take pencil and paper to write down the measurements of the rooms. And a big apron to protect her tailored skirt from the dust.

I'll never manage to remember everything, she told herself hopelessly, as she went to the side of the dining-room fireplace to pull the bell rope again. Dorothy was slow in answering this morning.

I've never had to remember so much in my life. I've just done exactly what I was told to do – no more, no less – bits of things, and be reminded about them – like Dorothy. Only, Dorothy knows more than I do.

As Dorothy rushed into the dining room with the breakfast tray, Celia seated herself at the huge table, and the harassed maid dumped the tray in front of her.

Dorothy stood back, panting a little, as she said, 'Ethel didn't have time to light the fire in here this morning, Miss. What with me getting ready to go to Meols, like – and she having to run down to the stables to order the taxicab for you. She done the one in the breakfast room, though – ready for the Missus getting up.'

Celia assured her that it was quite a warm morning, but that she should ask Ethel to have a good fire in Miss Edna's bedroom by evening. 'Could she manage to clean the room?'

'Oh, aye. She's quite smart, is Ethel. Which room would it be, Miss?'

'Of course! You never knew my sister, did you? The back bedroom with the roses on the walls was always her room. The room we put Mr Albert Gilmore in when he was here. Ask Mrs Gilmore what bedding to use.'

'Yes, Miss. I'm to be ready in half an hour, Miss?'

Celia was cracking her boiled egg. She did not want it, but she knew she must eat something. 'Yes, please,' she replied mechanically to Dorothy's question, and then she asked, 'Have you had your breakfast?'

Dorothy was grateful for the unexpected inquiry. 'Oh, aye. Had it an hour ago, at six o'clock.' She smiled, as she went out of the room. She was certain that the Missus would never have bothered to ask such a question.

Chapter Sixteen

❧

Dorothy had been both excited and scared to find herself riding in a taxicab, a mechanically propelled vehicle which actually did not need a horse to pull it! She had seen cars and lorries in the town – but to be really riding in a car was a thrill indeed. She had never crossed the river by anything but a ferryboat before, and it was with similar excitement that she trotted beside Celia down a long passage and steep staircase to the underground electric train. She was glad that she had agreed to accompany Celia. What a wonderful morning!

The guard stored the clumsy trunk in the guard's van at the back of the train, and, when they had to change to the steam train at Birkenhead Park, he called a porter to transfer the trunk to the other guard. Celia shyly parted with sixpences as tips and all the men looked quite happy.

At Meols, the porter was busy with a series of first-class passengers and took no notice of their beckoning fingers. So, between them, they lugged the straw trunk down the long sandy lane from the station to the cottage, and thankfully dropped it on the doorstep. They were giggling and gasping like two schoolgirls who had been racing each other.

'I bet we been quicker than waiting for that porter to finish with the snobs,' Dorothy said unthinkingly, as Celia found the key for the door.

Celia smiled to herself; she had bought third-class tickets for the sake of economy; they had always gone first class when her father was alive. Was one really a snob if one bought first-class tickets? she wondered.

As they inspected the ground floor of the interior of the cottage,

Dorothy followed Celia very closely and very quietly. It was Dorothy's opinion that one should be careful of ghosts in a house left long empty. They did not, however, seem to disturb anybody – or anything.

They slowly climbed the stairs and went into the front bed-room, which was about as big as Louise's dressing room in her present home.

Dorothy folded her arms across her stomach and considered the grubby, forlorn-looking little room. Her nose wrinkled. 'Where'll I start, Miss?'

Celia laughed, but it was not a happy laugh. 'I don't know, Dorothy,' she admitted. 'I must go into the village to see a man who does repairs, and try to find a sweep to sweep the chimneys. So don't bother about cleaning windows today – the sweep is bound to spread soot, no matter how good he is.' She looked around the stuffy room, and said, 'I noticed, as we came in, that Mr Billings has had the glass replaced in the single room over the hall – and he's taken the boarding down from the downstairs windows – so at least you can see to work.'

'Suppose I start with all the hearths, Miss – get them clear so the sweep can work,' Dorothy suggested, as she slowly drew the hatpins out of her big black hat. 'Then I could give the whole place a good sweep with the hard broom we brought. Get rid of the litter, like?'

Celia gratefully agreed to these suggestions. 'The single bed-room doesn't have a fireplace, so you could clean that room thoroughly. If the linoleum on the floor looks very damp, you could pull it up in strips and throw it out; I think we shall have to buy new. Then scrub the wooden floor underneath with disinfectant. When it dries we can see if we have to replace the planking.'

As they moved out of the bedroom and down the precipitous little staircase, Dorothy nodded. 'You said the pump didn't work. Where would I get water, Miss?'

'I'm going to ask Mr Fairbanks, next door, if you could draw a few bucketfuls from his pump.' She sighed. 'That's another person I have to find – someone who will say whether the well is usable – and will mend the pump.'

Since there was no clean place on which to lay it, Dorothy stuck her hat back on her head, rather than putting it on the hall floor while she struggled with the knots of the rope round the trunk. She laid the broom handles on one side, and pulled off the lid. Very carefully, she took out a neat brown paper parcel and handed it to Celia. She smiled up at her, and announced, 'Lunch!'

The deep lid of the trunk made a clean receptacle in which to deposit hats, coats, gloves, purses and the precious food. Both of them shook out the sackcloth aprons, which lay on top of the cleaning materials, and wrapped them round their black skirts.

They looked at each other, and, for no particular reason, they laughed. 'We look as if we're going hop-picking,' remarked Dorothy. She was glad to see Celia laugh, and she said, 'Would you like to go and see the fella next door about water, while I begin on the living-room fireplace?'

Celia agreed.

Feeling very shy, she walked down the tiled path, the sand squeaking under her boots, round the high privet hedge with its new green buds, to Mr Fairbanks' nicely varnished front gate. Before opening it and entering the garden, she hesitated nervously, and then, before her courage failed her, she unlatched it and hurried up the path.

She knocked timidly at his black-enamelled front door. As she looked at it, she wondered if she would ever reduce next door to comparable orderliness.

From his front room window, Eddie Fairbanks had seen her coming, so the door was opened immediately, and she was greeted like an old friend. In her sackcloth apron, she looked even smaller and frailer than when he had first seen her, and he said warmly, 'Come in, Miss. The wind's cold this morning.'

As he led her into the cosy back room which she remembered from her previous visit, and sat her down in the same nursing chair, she was shivering, partly from chill and partly because she had to deal with a man alone in the privacy of his own home.

While she settled herself in the chair, he turned the hob with its black kettle on it over the fire. 'Will you be having some tea with me?' he asked.

His amiability gave her confidence. She smiled quite sweetly at him, and said not just now, because she had to set the maid to work and then go to Hoylake and from there to Liverpool to meet her sister, who was coming up from Southampton. And would he be so kind as to let her maid draw some water from his kitchen?

'Oh, aye. When she's ready for it, she should come and tell me, and I'll carry it in for her. Would she be liking some tea?'

'I'm sure she would. She had her breakfast awfully early.' What an old dear he was, she considered, as he looked kindly down on her. She stopped shivering.

While weighing her up, he rested his shoulder against the mantelpiece and waited for the kettle to start singing. She looked so careworn that he said cautiously, not wanting to offend her, 'I think – I think you'd better have a cuppa before you go to Hoylake, Miss. While I make it, you go and tell your maid what you want done and that she's to come over when she wants some water. Then both of you come and have a quick cup. How about that?'

She hesitated, and then said, 'Very well. You are most kind.' She found it strange to be treated with consideration – only harried Phyllis seemed to treat her similarly – or Winnie, when Louise was out.

When she told Dorothy about the invitation, Dorothy said promptly, as she continued to rake out the cinders and ashes from the front room fireplace, 'That'd be nice. But you open that lunch right now and eat some of it – sandwiches – because otherwise you won't have time.'

It seemed odd to be given an order by the house-parlourmaid; Winnie was the only servant who had ever ventured advice, and she usually addressed herself to Louise.

Celia took out a sandwich and hastily consumed it. As she brushed the crumbs off her black blouse, Dorothy got up from her knees to take the bucket of ashes outside, and said, 'There's a packet of biscuits. You take it and you can eat them on the train, to keep you going. There's lots else for me.'

'Are you sure?'

Dorothy grinned at her. 'Winnie told me that I had to see that you eat – so you better had, or I'll be in trouble.'

'That's very nice of both of you.'

There was something quite different about this morning, she considered, as the pair of them tramped round to Eddie's house. I am not only doing different things, but people are behaving differently, too. This thought stayed with her as, twenty minutes later, she set out for Hoylake.

She had been armed by Eddie Fairbanks with the name of a sweep, which would save her time hunting about when she reached Hoylake village. 'Go and see this chap before you go to see Ben Aspen,' he advised. 'Ben'll keep you talking for hours, if you don't watch. If you tell him you must catch a train, it will help to stop the flow!'

She smiled, as she hurried through the sandy lane and then on to the tarmac main road. Ben Aspen must be quite a well-known character.

Chapter Seventeen

❧

While en route to the sweep's house, she found the notice board of a plumber on a cottage gate. A plumber might know about wells and pumps, she thought, and promptly knocked on his door.

At both his house and that of the sweep she found herself dealing with their wives. Both of them laboriously wrote down with the nub of a pencil on a scrap of paper her name, her address and the address of the cottage.

Once the plumber's wife had taken the address of the cottage, she said, in surprise at Celia's request that her husband should look at a well and a pump, 'There's mains water down there. What you need is to have it connected and turned on, and have a modern set of taps put in. And there was a sewer laid down as well, as I remember.'

Celia was doubtful that a woman would know about waterlines, so she responded, 'Mother only said it had a well.'

'Well, I never! Well, let Billy come and look at it for you. Tomorrow morning, aye?'

As she turned away from the door, Celia was suddenly wild with hope. If the woman was right, a colossal load of work would be saved. With running water, they could have a water closet – if there were drains nearby, of course – and even, perhaps, a bath with taps. That would make Mother happier, though it might cost a great deal.

I don't care what it costs, she thought. I really don't want to spend my life carrying big ewers of water up and down stairs for Mother's bath. I don't want to try to keep a stinking earthen lavatory from smelling because she will perpetually complain about it – or even one with a bucket, which has to be emptied and the contents buried each day; I doubt if I have the strength even to dig a hole.

She had rarely felt such a strong sense of revolt – but as her father's affairs had been dealt with, she had watched with growing apprehension. Because Cousin Albert had left Louise alone, to deal with her domestic affairs, and Louise had done nothing, all the responsibility was being pushed on to herself. There was no one else, now Paul had been taken by the flu – and to the best of her limited ability, partly out of a sense of self-preservation, she was indeed tackling the situation.

As she waited for the sweep's wife to answer her knock, she felt angrily that it was not that her mother was truly incapable – the birth of little Timothy George had proved that she had plenty of energy, despite her bereavement, when she was interested enough to use it.

The sweep's wife, a waif with a baby at her breast, promised that her Henry would be there that afternoon. She kindly directed Celia to Mr Aspen's domain across the railway bridge at Hoylake Station. 'And follow the lane, like you was goin' back to Meols. You can't miss it.'

Hanging on to her hat, Celia battled her way up Market Street against a salt-laden breeze, climbed the pedestrian bridge over the railway, and turned into a country lane where a freshly green hawthorn hedge, curved landwards by the sea winds, sheltered a few violets and one or two primroses.

A few more minutes' walk took her to a fenced compound with two huge gates which were wide open. To her left, just past the open gate, lay a small shed marked OFFICE.

Celia had never in her life faced, alone, so many strangers in one day, and she was surprised and relieved to find herself again talking to a woman instead of to Ben Aspen himself.

Behind the office counter stood a handsome, fair-haired woman about her own age. Her snow-white blouse with its black bow tie made her look plumper than she probably was. Her tanned rosy face was surrounded by carefully arranged tendrils of golden hair; the remainder was swept into a large bun at the nape of her neck and secured by a big black bow of ribbon.

On seeing Celia, a pair of cobalt-blue eyes twinkled amiably, and the woman picked up a pen and dipped it into a bottle of ink. She held the pen poised, ready to write, as she asked, 'Can I help you?'

Celia explained her business, that she had been sent by Mr Billings and needed some painting and small repairs done to a cottage.

'Me dad's got someone with him, but if you'd like to have a seat there, I'll go and tell him you're waiting.'

She went outside, and, as Celia sat gingerly down on a dusty bench, she heard her calling across the yard to her father. Through the office door, she observed stacks of wood in neat piles, wheelbarrows and ladders, sacks and boxes the contents of which she could only guess at, a mountain of discarded old bricks and rolls of tar paper.

Near to the office door stood a car and by it lay a big tarpaulin, as if it had just been removed from the vehicle. Though the car was dusty, the sunlight caught its brass and black enamel and made it look new. A boy about eight years old wandered in through the gate, and surveyed it. With great care, he drew a round smiling face in the dust on the door.

'Alfie! Leave it alone!' shrieked the lady clerk, as she came running back to the office. 'You know you mustn't touch anything in Grandpa's yard. Come here! Better not let Grandpa see you near that.'

She turned to Celia as she came up the office step. 'I'm sorry, Miss. Father won't be a minute. They was just getting the car out of the barn before you came. They want to sell it.' She paused before entering the office, to look at the car, her expression stricken. 'Me hubby built it,' she explained. 'He loved mechanical things.'

Celia nodded and said, 'He must be a brilliant mechanic.' Then she added shyly, 'I'll only take a few minutes of Mr Aspen's time.'

The boy had followed his mother into the office. He paused to stare at Celia. She smiled at him and, after a moment, he grinned back. 'Have you just come from school?' she asked, trying hard to appear friendly.

He nodded. 'I come to have me dinner with Granddad and Mum.'

His mother seemed a little confused by this baring of her domestic arrangements, and said sharply, 'Now, Alfie, don't you go bothering the lady. Go in the back room and start your dinner. I'll be with you in a minute.'

As the boy wandered round the counter and disappeared through a doorway, his mother said to Celia, 'Me dad's short of men at the moment, Miss. So I'm filling in in the office.'

'That's very clever of you,' Celia replied with genuine admiration.

'Well, needs must. I learned a lot from me hubby. He was me dad's clerk of works, and he always kept the books and did the estimating and ordering for Dad – he could estimate, real accurate – he were a first-class builder's clerk. That's how I met him, 'cos he was working for Dad.' She paused, and to Celia she suddenly looked old. She said flatly, 'He died at Messines Ridge in 1917.'

'Oh, how terrible!'

'I thought I'd die myself,' the woman admitted baldly. 'But I'd got young Alfred to think of – and me dad needed help – working for him has kept me going. Dad wants Alfie to have the business when he retires. It does mean that Dad'll have to continue to work a lot longer than he would've done though.'

Celia's heart went out to the woman. She said compassionately, 'You have my deepest sympathy.' Then, feeling that her remark was too formal, she added, 'I think you are being very brave.'

The woman made a wry face. 'There's a lot like me. You're not married?'

'Me? Goodness me, no.' Celia shrugged her shoulders and made a small deprecating gesture with one hand. 'We did lose George, though, at Scapa Flow, and Tom in France – they were my brothers.' She looked down, and then out at Ben Aspen who was coming across the yard. 'I do miss them,' she said sadly. She turned her eyes back to the clerk, who was knocking sheets of paper into a neat pile on the desk. 'But it's not like losing a husband, I am sure.'

'I don't know, Miss. It seems as if everybody lost someone,

doesn't it? And I worry about Alfred growing up without a dad – though his grandpa keeps him in line.'

'I am sure you do worry.' Celia rose from her dusty bench, as Mr Aspen himself came up the step, and took off his bowler hat.

Celia's first thought was that she had never seen quite such a huge white beard – it stuck wildly out in all directions, nearly obliterating the old man's face. A red nose peeped through an unkempt moustache. Huge white eyebrows bristled above eyes identical to those of his daughter. A pair of very red ears made brackets round the whole. He wore a brown velvet waistcoat over a striped shirt, and his baggy trousers were held in at the knee by pieces of string tied round them.

His voice was very deep, like that of a younger man. 'You wanted some repairs, Ma'am? Betty here said Mr Billings sent you?'

Very diffidently, afraid she might make a fool of herself, Celia explained that she needed someone capable to look over the cottage to see what repairs were necessary – chimneys, downpipes, etc. The structure needed its external woodwork painting, and, in addition, she went on bravely, she would like to know what it would cost to paint the interior – just plain white would do – something inexpensive.

Ben scratched his bird's nest of a beard and looked her over. Not much money, he deduced – but a lady. 'You know Eddie Fairbanks, by any chance?' he asked. 'He lives in a cottage, which I think is the one next to yours.'

'He's the tenant of the other house – they are semi-detached. Mama and I met him when we went over our house earlier this week.'

She waited, while he thought. He said finally, 'Oh, aye, I know the property all right, though I've not been down there for a while. Trouble is I'm short of skilled men, especially them as can estimate.' He turned to Betty, who had stood quietly by her counter, while he dealt with Celia. 'Do you think you could take a look, Bet, and do the estimate? I can tell you what to look for.'

Betty's expression which had been rather sombre lifted considerably. She smiled at Celia, and said, 'I think so. When would you like me to come?'

'Tomorrow afternoon? I've a plumber coming in the morning.'

'We're not usually open Saturday afternoon. But in the morning, you could talk to the plumber while I go round the place. I wouldn't be able to give you a price until I've had a chance to work it out, anyway – it would be Monday for that.'

Considering his reputation for talk, Ben Aspen was quite quiet. He confirmed Betty's promise of a price by Monday, and, as Celia left him, politely said good afternoon to her.

As she turned at the bottom of the office steps, she saw him go through the office, presumably to join his grandson for lunch. She heard him say heavily, 'I'm sorry to sell the car, Bet. But we'll never use it – and it'll deteriorate. It's already sat there five years.'

Before she went out through the great gates which opened on to the lane, Celia stopped to put on her gloves, and looked back into the builder's yard. The car gleamed outside the office door, but her eyes were on the barn at the back of the yard.

Its doors had been flung wide open and a boy was slowly sweeping it out – it looked as if it had a stone floor. It must have belonged to a farm at one point, she deduced. It looked weather-beaten, but the car which Betty said had been in it showed no sign of rust, so it must be fairly watertight.

There was plenty of time before the arrival of the train for Liverpool, so she walked leisurely back to the railway station. She found herself enjoying the country view. To her left, she looked out over a small ploughed field. Beyond it was open land, incredibly green already, leading her eyes to misty, low hills. She basked in the quietness, broken only by the distant sound of sawing from the direction of Ben Aspen's yard and the chatter of sparrows in the hedges. She felt relaxed, at peace, for the first time since her father's death.

At the sight of the railway station, she was quickly brought back to the fact that she had another onerous task to fulfil, before she considered anything else, and she dreaded it. She must meet her elder sister at Lime Street Station. More grief. More comforting to be done.

She thrust other considerations out of her mind, while she went into the little red brick station to buy a train ticket to Liverpool.

She and Edna had never been very close. Edna had been sent as a boarder to a finishing school. After she was twelve, Celia had been withdrawn from Miss Ecclestone's Day School for Young Ladies to help her mother at home, her place in life already decided upon by her parents. The explanation given to the little girl was that she could not learn much more at Miss Ecclestone's and that she was too delicate to be sent away from home. The fact that she and Edna had gone through the usual cycles of ill health together did not occur to the child – they both had had chickenpox, measles, mumps and the dreaded scarlet fever at about the same time, when these diseases swept through the neighbourhood. Influenza, colds and gastritis had struck both of them no more than other children.

The very idea that she was delicate, something wrong with her, something that her parents had not divulged to her, still fed her panic attacks as she grew older.

At the finishing school, Edna had learned to dance and to paint with watercolours, to deport herself with dignity and some grace, to play the piano and to make polite conversation. She had learned a smattering of French, and more arithmetic, history and geography than Celia had. She copied the attitude of her mother towards Celia, regarding her as stupid, disobedient to their parents, an irritating younger sister who was always crying about something.

At the coming-out dance which her mother arranged for her, Edna met Paul Fellowes, the son of one of her father's friends. He was a self-assured, handsome man ten years older than she was and already well established in his father's company. Six months later, she became that magical person whom every girl dreamed of, a fiancée with a diamond ring on her finger. She flaunted the ring at every opportunity as a symbol of her supreme success.

After a two-year engagement, which both the Fellowes and the Gilmores felt was a respectable length of time, in 1912 Celia found herself, as chief bridesmaid, walking behind her sister up the aisle of the Church of St Mary the Virgin amid a gaggle of other young women, all giggling behind their bouquets of yellow roses and maidenhair ferns.

She was so consumed by jealousy of her sister's success that she was incapable of enjoying the ceremony or the reception at their house afterwards, and, for some time, she was referred to by those who had been present as 'that sulky sister of Edna Fellowes'.

For months, Celia pestered her mother about when she would give a coming-out party for her. There was, however, always some reason why it could not be done, the final argument being, towards the end of 1914, that so many families were in mourning that it would be inappropriate to give such a party while the war lasted. A crushed Celia conceded defeat.

As she sat in the Liverpool train, Celia remembered all this. She wondered how she would feel when she met her sister. Edna's experiences were so different from her own.

At least I'm not jealous any more, she considered with a faint smile. Edna lost her little Rosemary and now she's lost her husband. I need a sister at the moment and, other than Mother, I must be the only person in the world who really does need her.

She hoped wistfully that sophisticated, elegant Edna would be as brave as Betty appeared to be. It would certainly help.

Chapter Eighteen

When, at Birkenhead Park, Celia changed from the cosy warmth of the steam train to an unheated electric train, she helped a young woman with two tiny children on to the latter, and the shivers of the children led to a polite conversation. The little family reminded her of Phyllis, who was far more of a sister to her than Edna had ever been, and of new-born Timothy George. Her morning had been so full that she had given no thought to the struggle her friend was probably having.

I should go this evening to see how they are, she reminded herself. With Edna to care for, however, and her mother's probable complaints about her desertion of her during the day, it seemed doubtful if she would get the opportunity.

She sighed. Though she felt she had done quite well that morning, it had tired her. She had made an enormous effort to express clearly and concisely to the people she had met exactly what she wanted them to do; now she prayed that the hope of tap water that the plumber's wife had given her would be realised.

I hope everything works, she thought anxiously. That the sweep and the plumber will come, as promised, that Dorothy and Mr Fairbanks got along together, and that Mr Aspen's daughter gives me a modest estimate.

Her eyelids drooped with fatigue and, and as the electric train sped through the tunnel, she began to doze.

She awoke when the train stopped at Central Station with its usual sudden jerk, and the lady with the children smiled and said she hoped she felt better after such a nice nap.

A little bewildered, Celia helped her fellow travellers on to the platform, and then quietly followed them out of the station, up steep stairs and sloping passages until she found herself at street level.

She paused uncertainly at the station gate. Outside it, heavy drays lumbered past her, interspersed with cars driven by chauffeurs. Innumerable cyclists and pedestrians darted in and out between them.

'Are you lost, duck?'

Celia jumped. Leaning against the stone gatepost of the station lounged a woman with a highly painted face beneath a purple veil draped round a purple hat.

A fallen woman! No one, except actresses and fallen women, made up their faces. Disconcerted, Celia simply looked at her.

The woman laughed. 'Are you lost?' she inquired again.

Celia swallowed, and said in a small scared voice. 'I have to go to Lime Street Station, and I am not quite sure where it lies from here.'

The woman took her by the elbow and pointed her in the right direction. 'Go up here and turn left. Five minutes' walk. You'll find it.'

Losing some of her fear, Celia said politely but shyly, 'Thank you very much.'

The woman laughed again. 'Go on with you, luv. You're a nice girl. You shouldn't be hanging around here.' She gave Celia a little push, then leaned back against her pillar again.

Somewhat shaken, Celia took the route indicated. Amid the hurrying, indifferent crowd of pedestrians, she felt vulnerable and afraid. She had never walked alone in the city centre before and the fact that a fallen woman, as she called her, had actually addressed her had unnerved her.

It was with relief that she reached the huge entrance of Lime Street Station. Here she had, once more, to stiffen her resolve before she could waylay a porter to ask which platform the train from London would arrive at.

Without stopping his rapid scuttle towards a train already in, he told her. When she went to the platform that he had indicated, her entrance was barred by a ponderous, bewhiskered ticket inspector, who demanded her ticket.

Flushing nervously, she told him she was meeting her sister travelling on the train.

'You need a platform ticket, Miss – or you could wait here for her.'

'Where would I purchase a ticket?'

The man looked down at her superciliously as if she were sorely lacking mentally, and said, 'At the ticket office, of course – or from the machine over there.' He pointed to a red-painted machine against the far wall.

Confused and flustered, she looked at the machine and decided that modern machinery would be too much to face, and she went to the ticket office, where, for one penny, she received a grubby grey ticket. The porter at the gate gravely punched a hole in it and gave it back to her. She walked through to the platform and began to calm down.

The train was just coming in.

Hoping to find good tippers, porters were running beside the first-class carriages ready to help with luggage. People meeting the train engulfed Celia, who, being small, was soon elbowed away from the train itself. Doors swung open. Men and women descended and were captured by porters, some of whom had trolleys on which to transfer steamer trunks carried in the luggage van at the rear of the train.

At the back of the crowd, Celia sought frantically for Edna, hoping to see her standing in the doorway of one of the carriages. She stood on tiptoe, and a man's voice behind her said, 'Wait for a minute or two, Ma'am, and the crowd will clear.'

She turned, and nearly knocked a man off his crutches. His blue hospital uniform failed to disguise his fragile thinness. Not much taller than she was, incapacitated by his crutches, he certainly did not need to be pushed and shoved by a thoughtless crowd.

Celia conjured up a smile for him, and stepped to the side of him, as she replied. 'That sounds very sensible. I am looking for my sister.'

'I come out to meet me mate. He's bein' discharged from a military hospital in London – they can't do nothing more for him.'

Celia's sympathy was immediately aroused. 'Is he very badly hurt?' she asked.

'Well, they've patched him up, he says. His shoulder were smashed and he lost an ear as well. A bit scarred and his hearing'll never be the same. And he can't use what's left of his right arm.' The man's expression was suddenly bleak, and Celia realised that he was much younger than he had first appeared to be. Eighteen or nineteen, she guessed.

'And you?' Her tone was gentle.

'Me?' He looked down at his crutches. 'I'll be throwing these away soon, I hope. They say I'll limp always. But I'll be able to walk, thanks be.'

'Good. Where did you serve?'

'Messpot, Ma'am.'

Mesopotamia. Another place of death, another name for sorrow nowadays. 'I'm glad you got back here safely,' Celia said with feeling.

'Thank you, Ma'am.'

As the wounded man had forecast, the crowd was, indeed, thinning. When a large trolley of luggage was pushed away by a straining porter, a tall, elegant woman in black with a black veil over her face was suddenly revealed. She gestured imperiously to a porter, who came to her immediately.

Celia had not expected to have difficulty in recognising Edna. It had not occurred to her that almost every woman on the train would be dressed in mourning and that a number of them would be veiled. The gesture to the porter was so completely Edna, however, that she smiled again at the wounded soldier, said she hoped he would find his friend, and pushed her way purposefully through a loose group of children, her normal diffident good manners forgotten, in her fear of missing her sister.

'Edna,' she called and ran the last few steps towards her.

Edna said to the porter, 'I have luggage in the van.' Then, at the sound of Celia's voice, she swung round and said, 'Oh, Celia! Where's Mother?'

Celia stopped. How do you kiss somebody with a thick veil over her face, when no attempt is made to lift it and greet you?

Edna settled it by saying, 'We have to go down to the luggage van. I have three trunks.' The porter turned his trolley and walked briskly towards the end of the train, followed by Edna. Nonplussed, Celia dodged between passengers going the other way, and followed her.

The porter was given Edna's name and climbed into the van to search for her luggage. Edna turned back to Celia. 'You didn't answer me. Where's Mother? Is she ill?'

Bewildered and hurt by her sister's indifference, Celia straightened her hat, which had been knocked awry during her struggle in the crowd. Before she answered, she had to search for words.

'Mother is not feeling very well, as you can imagine,' she managed to say. 'We are having difficulties about Father's estate, and she had to go to the bank this morning. So I volunteered to meet you.' She tried to smile at the veil.

'I see. I would have imagined that a bereaved daughter was more important than a bank.' She called up to the porter in the van. 'Not that one – the green leather one behind it.'

Celia began to tremble. The fear of a panic attack, there on the station, almost brought one on. Edna was right, of course. She was more important – but the situation was hard to explain in one or two words on a busy station.

She took a big breath, while Edna scolded the porter for not lowering the expensive trunk down on to the platform more carefully. Then she said, 'Well, things have been terribly complicated for Mother and me. I'll explain it all when we are in the taxi.' At the same time the train made a big chuffing sound, as it prepared to reverse itself away from the platform.

'What did you say?' Edna asked, her voice like a schoolmistress demanding a response from a mumbling child.

Celia made another effort and repeated her remark. A second and a third trunk were added to the first, with sharp admonitions to the porter to be careful. Then Edna ordered the long-suffering man to find them a taxi, which he did.

After he had heaved two trunks on to the luggage platform beside the taxi driver, the porter pushed the third trunk into the wide passenger section. Because Edna was fiddling for change in her handbag, he gave Edna's hat box and small jewel case to Celia to hold.

Edna pressed some change into his hand. He touched his cap and said resignedly, 'Thank you, Ma'am.' Celia guessed that she had not tipped him enough. He then held the taxi door open so that the ladies could step in.

As the taxi jerked forward, Edna gave the driver her mother's address. Celia closed her tired eyes. She hoped her Mother would not be hurt by Edna's distant manner.

Edna settled herself in her seat and threw back her veil. Celia felt the tiny movement and opened her eyes. She half-turned to look at her sister.

She was shocked.

A gaunt, yellow visage had been revealed. The hazel eyes, though still quite beautiful, were sunken in black sockets, the chin was long and bony, like their father's had been. The skin was yellow and wrinkled, like that of a much older person. Deep lines between the heavy black eyebrows added to the woman's general air of irritability. As Celia stared at her, she sensed, however, a terrible exhaustion behind the irritability.

'What are you staring at?'

'You have changed quite a lot,' Celia replied honestly. 'I suppose I have, too.'

'In the awful climate which I have endured for the last seven years, one expects to change.' Edna drew off her gloves, to reveal hands equally yellow and shrivelled, though still slender and still graced by the magnificent engagement and wedding rings which Celia had, long ago, envied so much. 'One gets fevers so often that they weaken one.'

Edna leaned back in the taxi seat and gazed out at the bustling, black-clad pedestrians in Lime Street, many of them holding black umbrellas to protect themselves from a sudden drizzle of rain. After the brightly clad, motley crowds of Salvador and Rio, they looked liked participants in a huge funeral. Seeing them, Edna felt so filled with anguish that she did not want to face the remainder of her family.

It had been bad enough dealing with Papa and Mama Fellowes' grief at the loss of their only son and their concern for her widowhood. As if she cared a hoot about Paul – a domineering man, a selfish man at best, a bully determined that she should bear more children.

That, she thought, had been a fight to the finish, because, after Rosemary, she was not going to go through the loss of another child; he had been furious and had taken a Brazilian mistress. She had wished him dead many a time, so that she could be free to be honestly and openly in love with his secretary and occasional translator, Vital Oliveira.

Dear patient Vital, a small man, a nobody but infinitely lovable. Her whole body longed for him.

Amongst the Fellowes family, her despondency and tears had been assumed, naturally, to be for Paul, not from having, perforce, to say goodbye to an almost equally distraught Vital. Both were sufficiently realistic to know that it was highly unlikely that they could ever arrange to be together again, and it had hurt – God, how it had hurt – to part, with that feeling of finality.

Paul was for the first part of their residency in Salvador often away from home, as a great dam was built to create power for electricity. Vital coped with his correspondence and records at the city end of his work. For Paul's convenience, he lived in the same great house.

Without any knowledge of Portuguese, Edna had been left in Salvador to run their home as best she could. It was Vital who at first translated her orders to the servants, who saw that they did not cheat her, who found her a doctor to supervise her confinement. He brought her an English/Portuguese dictionary, for which she thanked him gratefully, and he recommended a teacher.

Rosemary died when her father was away from home. It was Vital who, silently in the background of her distress, kept the house servants in order, found a gentle nun to sit with her and himself arranged the funeral.

They became the best of friends, and later, secret, desperate lovers. A scandal would have finished Vital and ruined Edna. Both realised that they were financially dependent upon Paul. And it was a miracle that they were not found out, Edna thought. There must have been suspicions, but intrigue was part of the society, and there were other love affairs which were politely overlooked. And, anyway, Paul and I were English Protestants; there was little understanding of us.

But old Conchita, the housekeeper already installed in the house when she arrived, had known. She had seen Paul strike his wife on one or two occasions, and slowly she had been moved to protect the young mother.

Edna smiled grimly. To protect her, Conchita could lie with incredibly fast ingenuity. Small and modest in her black dresses, she looked the epitome of integrity – but she resented Paul's high-handed manner with his Portuguese staff – and Vital, who also suffered from this, was the son of a friend of hers. She had been a great help to the lovers.

The answer to Edna's passionate prayers had come in Paul's death on the way home. She had had no option but to come home with him. A single word out of place and Vital would have lost his job with the company and his excellent reputation as a reliable and gifted employee.

Be careful what you pray for – prayers are not always answered in the way you imagine they will be, her nanny had always cautioned her.

How right Nanny had been. She was free, but it was unlikely that she and Vital would ever meet again.

Unaware of the turmoil in the mind of her sister, Celia had expected to deal with tears and hopelessness, and anxious questions about her mother's mourning. She had no idea what to say to this wizened shell of a woman. As they edged their way up the hill towards West Derby, however, she felt she should say something about Paul.

'Both Mother and I were so sorry to hear about Paul's sudden passing. We both feel dreadful that you should have lost him. Mother sends her fond love to you.' She paused, and then added, 'And you have my love and sympathy, too.' The last words seemed stiff and formal to her, but she did not know what else to say.

Edna's barely visible lips tightened. 'Thank you,' she said equally formally. 'It was sudden – quite a shock.' She stared woodenly ahead of her. She had managed to contain her feelings in Southampton while the Port Authorities, all male, had discussed over her head her isolation as an influenza contact. She had, later, done her best to comfort Paul's parents.

At Lime Street, she had hoped to be met and comforted by her own mother, even if Louise did not know the exact reason for her grief. Instead, she was face to face with her younger sister, and pride would not permit her to give way in front of her.

'Was it really Spanish flu?' asked Celia.

'The ship's doctor said it was. All the passengers on the liner were terrified that they would get it. I was quarantined in my cabin, and none of them would come near me. The Health Authorities in Southampton would not let us dock until all the passengers had been examined. They wanted to send me to an isolation hospital for a few days.'

'How awful! Did anyone get it?' Celia began to relax.

'Not to my knowledge. I suppose most of the world has already been exposed to it. I told them that. Finally, I asked them to send for my father-in-law – and he came in his car to fetch me. He promised that he would call the family physician before allowing me to mix with anyone – so they let me go.' Edna's voice expressed considerable satisfaction at her winning of the battle with the Health Authorities, and Celia was suitably impressed.

'Why Paul, I wonder?'

'Oh, Paul? He met all kinds of people in his work and socially. He could have caught it anywhere. In Salvador people get a fever and die and nobody knows what it was that took them. Only something like cholera is quickly identified.'

It seemed a step forward to Celia that she was managing to get Edna to talk to her. 'Why didn't you come home from such an unhealthy place?' she inquired.

Edna considered her answer to this query, before slowly replying, 'Well, I did not want to come home alone. Paul was general manager of the whole project, as you know – and my father-in-law is a party in the consortium that did the development. Paul felt he must see the work to an end; and he did finish it to schedule.' Edna absently twiddled her rings round her finger. 'If we had come home before the war ended, he would probably have been conscripted, in spite of his age. And then he would have lost his life, anyway.' She bit her lips, as she condemned herself as a great liar.

'He might have done,' agreed Celia soberly, and then she added, 'Dozens of people died, too, in Liverpool from the flu – and they were often the remaining young people in a family. It was tragic.'

'No doubt.' Edna sounded remote, uninterested.

Celia felt shocked at such an indifferent reply, and then reminded herself, more charitably, that Edna would be as wrapped up in her own grief as their mother was.

It seems that only I don't have that privilege, she considered with pain; I mustn't weep for Tom or George or express the terror I feel at Father's death; I have to keep on going – but going where?

It's like walking into a fog.

She felt her sister sigh, and she glanced at her. On the yellowed cheek lay a solitary tear. Poor Edna! Celia took one of her hands in her own, and was surprised when Edna clasped her hand tightly for the rest of the journey.

Chapter Nineteen

❧

For most of the taxi ride through the crowded streets of Liverpool, they sat silently side by side. The thin yellow hand clutching Celia's told her clearly that Edna was more upset than she appeared, but, as they approached West Derby, Celia felt that she must warn her sister that she was not alone in suffering grief.

'Mama is still dreadfully upset,' she began. 'It is barely a week since Papa passed away, you know.' She wanted to cry out, be gentle with both of us – please. We are suffering like you are. But she was nonplussed by her sister's lack of any kindly demonstration of feeling towards herself, so she said no more.

Did Edna care twopence about her father's death, she puzzled? She had, after all, been separated from her family for seven years, and had been in boarding school before that. Had she, perhaps, forgotten that it was her sister who was sitting beside her, someone to whom she should feel free to express her sorrow for the loss of both father and husband?

In response to Celia's warning, Edna said impatiently, 'Yes, I know. Papa Fellowes told me. And Mother wrote to me at Southampton.' Edna stared out of the taxi window. 'It is difficult for both of us.' That it might be difficult for Celia still did not seem to occur to her, for her next remark was, 'Papa was a very trying man.'

Celia was shaken that her father's favourite daughter should make such a shocking remark, especially when he was dead; it was certainly not the thing to criticise the dead. From Celia's point of view, Papa had provided everything for Edna, good clothes, education, a fine wedding and a dowry – had even introduced her husband to her. What more could he have done? She felt resentfully that she herself would have been grateful if he had done any one of these things for her. 'Whatever do you mean?' she asked.

Edna's answer shocked Celia even more. Her sister said, 'I wondered if she was thankful to be widowed. A lot of women are. And Mother had to manage Father very carefully.'

'Oh, no, Edna! Mama is quite broken-hearted. And even more so because she is going to lose her home.'

'What?' Edna turned so quickly towards Celia that she hit her knees on the trunk which had been heaved into the back of the taxi.

With her right hand, Celia was steadying on her lap Edna's hat box and jewel case, as well as her own heavy handbag. At the explosive query, she shot a startled glance over the pile at her sister. 'Didn't Mama tell you?' she quavered.

'No.'

In a trembling voice, as if her late father's financial position were her fault, Celia explained as best she could.

Edna sniffed. 'Nonsense. I don't believe it. Cousin Albert has made a mistake.'

Not wishing to quarrel in front of a taxi driver, Celia muttered, 'We will talk about it when we get in. I am sure Mama will explain it to you.'

'Indeed, we must talk about it. I have come up here in the expectation of being welcomed home!'

'Well, of course you are welcome. Where else would you go?' Celia responded indignantly. At the same time she wondered what Edna would think of the cottage, and she shuddered.

At the thought that she might have to share the cottage with Edna, as well as with her very critical mother, she felt suddenly sick.

During her long day, she had begun to think of the little house as being the beginning of a more open life for herself, despite the work it represented. She felt that everybody she had met that day had been very nice to her and had treated her as a person in her own right. Putting the cottage in order was proving to be a refreshing experience.

As the taxi drew up, Dorothy opened the front door. Her mother, looking exactly like Queen Victoria in her widowhood, came out on to the top step, and looked down at them, with the same woebegone expression as Queen Victoria exhibited in some of her photographs.

Edna left Celia to deal with the taxi driver and the luggage and ran across the pavement and up the wide, gracious steps. Her mother held out her arms to her and she was embraced. They turned and went inside.

By the time Dorothy, Winnie and Ethel had helped the taxi driver to get the heavy trunks up the steps and into the hall, Celia had taken the boxes that had been on her lap upstairs to Edna's bedroom. She then came down to pay the driver and tip him. She knew from her father that a man who tipped the proper amount received service from the lower classes – woe betide him if he tipped too little. The driver seemed pleased by the amount she gave him, touched his cap to her and went slowly down the steps. She shut the door after him, and, with the other women, surveyed the luggage.

'We'll never get them up the stairs, Miss,' said Winnie, already resentful that she and the other maids had been totally ignored by Edna as, with Louise, she had gone straight into the sitting room to be warmed by the fire and divested of her hat and jacket. Winnie had been the cook in the house when Miss Edna was a girl; unlike Dorothy and Ethel, she knew her. She even knew her favourite desserts, and had, that afternoon, made a magnificent apple pie with egg custard for her.

Celia noticed Winnie's forlorn look and guessed the reason for it. She realised suddenly that Edna had treated her, too, exactly like a bad employer would treat a servant. She was reminded of Edna, as a young woman, ordering her to fetch and carry for her, without thought or thanks – exactly as her mother did.

She took off her own hat and coat, and said wearily, 'Leave the trunks where they are, for the moment, Winnie. If we can't get them up the stairs, they could be unpacked down here. The empty trunks won't be too difficult to move.'

'Thank you, Miss. Shall I send up the tea tray?'

Celia was so demoralised that she felt that she must first ask her mother, so she peeped round the sitting-room door to inquire.

The two women were already deep in conversation, and Louise barely turned her head when she answered, 'Yes, bring the tea.'

The three servants were bunched by the door leading to the basement steps. Older than the other two, Winnie was still panting from her exertions with the trunks, and Dorothy was sullenly silent. Only Ethel's eyes sparkled with interest at the arrival.

Celia passed on her mother's instructions, and then said gently to Dorothy, 'I'll come down later on and hear how you got on in Meols.'

'Yes, Miss.' Dorothy sounded exhausted, and Celia had a sudden desire to hug her and tell her everything would eventually turn out all right. But one did not hug maids, so she turned and went slowly into the sitting room. She shut the door, and then took a seat a little away from the fireplace which was blocked to her by the other two women.

Her mother was weeping softly into her black handkerchief, while Edna lay back in her armchair and listened, with her eyes closed, to the story of the house and how awful the cottage was.

Celia thought of the warm comfort of Eddie Fairbanks' back room, and, when her mother paused to wipe her eyes, she interjected with some determination, 'I think the cottage can be made very pretty – and this morning I learned that piped water is probably available – you know, Mama, we never went into Mr Fairbanks' kitchen – he may already have had his pump replaced by taps.'

'Really?' Her mother looked up from her hanky in surprise.

'I should hope there is at least clean water there.' There was scorn in Edna's voice. 'I've had enough of bad water these past seven years.' She slowly heaved herself upright in her chair as Dorothy knocked on the door, and then brought in a tea tray heavy with scones and homemade cake. 'How many bedrooms has it?'

Edna's question confirmed to Celia that she probably expected to live with them, and the tiny hopes and dreams which had begun to grow while she was in Hoylake fell to ashes. She had a strong suspicion that Edna would never tolerate closeness with humble people like Mr Fairbanks or Betty or Ben Aspen who had been so civil to her; in Celia's mind had been planted a timid hope that these people could become her own kind and helpful friends. She knew her mother would never approve – but she was used to Mama; and her father was no longer there to insist on filial obedience. She feared, however, that Mama, backed up by an imperious elder daughter, would decide with whom they made friends in Meols and Hoylake and with whom they did not. She would again find friends and acquaintances, if any, picked out for her.

With an effort, she answered Edna. 'Three double bedrooms and a little hall bedroom.'

A tired Dorothy had set the tea tray on a small table by Louise's chair. She poured three cups of tea and handed them to the ladies with an embroidered table napkin under each, and then asked, 'Will that be all, Ma'am?'

Louise nodded, and Celia turned to ask the maid eagerly, 'Dorothy, when you were getting water from Mr Fairbanks this morning, you must have seen whether he had a tap or a pump?'

'Oh, aye, Miss. He's got hot and cold taps in the back kitchen. And he's got a water closet what flushes, by the back door.'

Louise forgot her tears immediately, and expressed great delight. She tucked her black hanky back into her sleeve, and said quite briskly to Celia, 'That will solve so many problems.'

'Yes, it will.' Though a good water supply could in future save her a great deal of work, there was doubt in her voice. She feared that there would now be two women leaning on her. As a girl, Edna had always found ways of pushing unpleasant tasks on to Celia, by saying, 'You are at home. It's your job to help Mother.'

Up to now, there had always been servants to do the physically dirty daily tasks, like emptying the slops from the bedrooms and washing out the chamber pots, the latter still used at night despite the advent of water closets. Celia knew that her mother would never do such jobs; she would bully Celia into doing them. She would, very likely, find herself, in addition, washing the dishes, doing the washing, scrubbing the floors and front steps, and Heaven only knew what else.

How much would Louise and Edna do for themselves, she wondered.

She wanted to walk out, run away. In her perturbation, she wished that she never had to face either woman ever again. And then she told herself that she was wicked, sinful, to even contemplate such ideas.

In any case, to whom could she go? She could think of no one who would not simply scold her for being a fool and ship her back to her mother. Only her godmother, Great-aunt Blodwyn in Wales, who had not come to her nephew's funeral on the excuse that it was lambing time, but, in truth, had not come because she cordially detested Louise, a dislike which was heartily reciprocated. Great-aunt Blodwyn's reputation in the family as a battle-axe of the first water had scared Celia as a child, and she did not seem to be the right person to take in a runaway. Anyway, the farm she had inherited from her husband was far away in Pembrokeshire – and how would a penniless woman get there?

Penniless women could become like the harridan who had directed her to Lime Street Station, disgusting untouchables who slowly rotted to death. The idea, strongly held by her elders and whispered amongst the few girls she had known, was terrifying to her.

Louise was saying, 'That will be all, Dorothy,' and Edna announced that she would like to go to her bedroom to wash and change.

Edna asked if the gardener would take her trunks upstairs, to which Celia replied shortly, 'He comes only twice a week.' It took all her patience to persuade her sister that the trunks could be safely unpacked in the hall and the contents carried upstairs.

Louise said, 'Celia, get Ethel to help Edna carry the stuff up. Dorothy will be laying the table for dinner.'

While Edna fumed and fretted in the hall and looked in her handbag for the right keys and demanded a knife to cut the ropes, Celia ran downstairs to the basement kitchen. She was informed that Ethel had gone for an interview for a job as a nursery maid.

'Miss Phyllis's Lily heard about it and told her,' said Winnie, as she basted a capon in the oven.

Celia went slowly back up the stairs to tell her mother this. It immediately sparked an altercation. Edna said sharply that Louise should not allow the servants to go for interviews before she was ready to dismiss them – and, anyway, why wasn't she taking them to Meols? 'Good servants are never easy to find. In Salvador, I turned mine off on the day I was leaving.'

Bewildered, Louise told Celia to help her sister, and turned back into the sitting room, to pour herself another cup of tea and to weep.

The two of them cut the ropes and Edna unlocked the trunks. She then instructed Celia which trunk she should empty first, and went upstairs to her room.

As Celia appeared in the bedroom with a load of clothes and personal possessions, Edna told her which drawers to put them in. She herself took off her dress and went to the bathroom to wash.

Celia plodded wearily up and down stairs with long gowns swathed in tissue paper, with linen walking suits and straw hats, cotton petticoats, boots and shoes, tea gowns and dressing gowns, all finely made and embroidered – but all rather old-fashioned, thought Celia, with surprise. Edna would need to shorten all the skirts; even Celia who was used to looking frumpy had turned up her skirts, despite her mother's protests; they had, for a couple of years now, hung discreetly just above her ankles.

By the time the trunks stood yawning emptily in the hall, the dinner gong was being struck by Dorothy, for dressing, and most of Edna's dresses were still laid across her bed.

Edna hurried back from the bathroom, selected a black gown, shook it out and tutted that it needed pressing. She said to Celia, 'You might ask the maid to press the rest before they are hung up.'

With sudden spirit, Celia replied, 'You will have to do them yourself. Dorothy is coming out to the cottage with me tomorrow morning, to continue the cleaning of it. I have to meet the plumber there – and the building contractor's clerk.' She put down a winter coat, two umbrellas, a parasol and two pairs of walking boots, and added, 'That's everything, I think. I'm going to get washed.' And she went out quickly, before Edna could protest, to scrub her face, while she trembled with defiance.

Dinner was eaten in painful silence. Louise played glumly with the food on her plate. Edna did courteously praise the apple pie to Dorothy, and Dorothy conveyed the information to a depressed Winnie. Otherwise, almost nothing except the barest politenesses passed between them. Celia kept quiet, afraid that if she spoke, her resentment of the other two would show, and bring down upon her from her mother the usual accusations of ingratitude or bad temper.

After they had finished, they went in silent procession into the sitting room to sit by the fire and drink their coffee which Dorothy brought in on a tray.

Edna seated herself gracefully in her father's chair and, after the parlourmaid had left the room, she opened a little black evening purse, which she carried dangling on her wrist. She took out a pretty silver case and a matching silver tube.

As she opened the case, took out a cigarette and fitted it into the silver holder, she asked, 'Do you mind if I smoke, Mama?'

Aroused from her melancholic contemplation of a future without Timothy, Louise stared at her daughter in shocked disgust.

'Edna! You don't mean to say that you smoke?'

'I do, Mama. The doctor in Salvador recommended it when I was so upset at the loss of Rosemary. He said it would soothe my nerves – and it does.'

'The doctor must have been mad! No lady would surely ever smoke!'

'Tush, Mama. A lot of women do nowadays, especially Portuguese and Spanish ladies. I couldn't do without my cigarettes now.' She waved the cigarette holder with its unlit cigarette around, as if to indicate a big crowd of female smokers.

'I will not allow a woman to smoke in my house!' exclaimed an outraged Louise. 'I think it's awful. Even your dear father never smoked here in my sitting room. He smoked in the library or in the garden.'

Celia was both astounded and intrigued by the disagreement. How daring of Edna to do such a thing! With her hands folded neatly in her lap, she forgot her own woes and watched, fascinated.

Edna was nonplussed. Her mother had rarely refused her anything, and, since her Portuguese friends smoked, as did her mother-in-law, she was unprepared for the objection. She had forgotten that the upper classes in the north of England were much more conservative than those in the south.

Edna's lips were trembling. 'I cannot give it up, Mama. It would be quite impossible. I had my last cigarette in the train, and I badly need to smoke now.'

'Then you should confine such an unsociable activity to the garden or your bedroom.' Louise sounded absolutely frigid.

'Very well, Mama.' Edna rose, picked up her coffee cup, and left the room, a picture of offended dignity.

'This is horrible, Celia. Simply horrible.' Louise pulled her handkerchief out of her sleeve, and touched her eyes with it. 'I never dreamed of a daughter of mine smoking! I hope you never indulge in such a shameful practice.'

Celia swallowed. She did not really know what to say. She knew that Phyllis secretly smoked. 'Er – um, Mama. I don't think I would ever want to,' she finally said quite honestly, 'though it is becoming quite common.'

'I would never deny my daughter a home, but I must say I have always disapproved of women smoking. I cannot think what I shall do about it if she stays with us.'

'You could insist that she does the same as Papa did – smoke in the library or in the garden.'

Louise sniffed in disdain. She heaved a great shuddering sigh. 'I don't know, Celia. I really don't know. Our lives are all upside down, and I don't know what to deal with first.'

'I know, Mama. Just don't worry. Try to rest a lot tomorrow. It will help you,' Celia soothed. For a moment she forgot a lifetime of oppression and saw her mother as yet another casualty of the war and of pure bad luck. She felt sorry for the arrogant, selfish woman, suddenly brought low by circumstances which were not her fault. 'You should go to bed now,' she continued. 'I'll ask Dorothy to put a hot water bottle in for you.'

Chapter Twenty

Long before either Louise or Edna had stirred from their beds, Celia and Dorothy had left for Meols. This time, Dorothy carried only a shopping basket containing newspapers and a bottle of vinegar for cleaning the windows. As well as her handbag, Celia carried a neat brown paper parcel tied with string, which Winnie had pressed into her hand, saying, 'It's a lunch for you and Dorothy, Miss.' Dear faithful Winnie, she thought, and she smiled.

The news that Dorothy had given about Mr Fairbanks' water supply had finally lifted her spirits a little, and this morning, after a good night's sleep, she felt much more optimistic about her new home. Perhaps she could persuade her mother and Edna to share the domestic work, once they were in the cottage.

As they sat in the train, Dorothy, usually so silent, became quite talkative. She declared that, yesterday, Mr Fairbanks had been real nice. He had let her use his loo, as well as giving her hot water for her cleaning.

'At the back of his living-room fireplace, he says, he's got a hot-water tank just like we've got in the kitchen of your West Derby house. Hot water made everything easy for me, it did.

'And the sweep was a nice young man. Didn't make too much mess. He left his bill on the mantel shelf for you.' With her red, ungloved hands in her lap, she considered her young mistress, and then added, 'I promised as we would pay today. To tell truth, Miss, I think he's waiting on the money. He's only just set up after coming home from hospital. He says it's proper hard to get started again in civvy street – but his dad were a sweep, so at least he's got a trade.'

Celia promised to go into Hoylake and pay the sweep as soon as she had seen Miss Aspen and the plumber.

The fact that even a maid needed hot water to do her work properly had escaped Celia, and she was thankful for Eddie Fairbanks' consideration.

Feeling relaxed in the unusual situation in which she found herself, Dorothy felt able to advise Celia to order in from Hoylake a couple of hundredweight of coal and some wood chips, so that fires could be lit in the newly cleaned fireplaces. 'To dry the place out, like. Yesterday, it got proper cold what with the wind blowing in from the sea – and the damp.'

Celia agreed, and added a note to her list to find a coal merchant.

As they approached the cottage, they saw that Eddie was trimming his hedge. On seeing them struggling down the sandy lane, he laid his shears on the top of the hedge and came to relieve Dorothy of the basket. She simpered at him, as she handed it over to him. Real nice manners Mr Fairbanks had.

When he greeted Celia, he seemed to her to be an old friend, and she told him without a hint of shyness what Dorothy and she were going to do that day.

'I'll get me ladder and clean the outsides of the windows for you,' he offered. 'It'll be better than trying to reach them from the inside.'

Dorothy did not wait for Celia to answer. She accepted immediately. Then she turned to Celia and said, 'Sash windows, like your mam has got, I can manage, because I can sit on the window-sill and lower the window over me knees to hold me, so I don't fall. These here is casements – they open outwards. Even if I chanced a fall, I couldn't get at them properly.'

Eddie Fairbanks, who had a daughter in service and knew the hazards of window-cleaning, said firmly that the last thing he wanted was someone around with a broken back. The women laughed, as they unlocked and went into the cottage.

'It looks so much better!' exclaimed Celia.

Dorothy beamed with pride. 'This is a first go. You wait till you've had it painted. It'll look real nice.'

Her words were echoed by Betty Aspen, who arrived soon

afterwards and went slowly over the little building. Celia held the other end of her tape measure, as she carefully measured for two new boards for the floor of the small bedroom and suggested a new windowsill and new plaster below it, because the rain had probably got in between the brick and the plaster. She strongly recommended new window frames for the back windows. 'They're rotten,' she said, 'and beginning to let in the rain. Probably because they face the prevailing wind and have been soaked more often.'

When they entered the kitchen, she looked with mock horror at the heavily rusted old range.

'Miss Gilmore,' she exclaimed. 'While you have workmen on the premises, have it removed. It will give you much more wall space. Later on, you might be able to have a gas stove installed.'

Celia's first thought was of how much it would cost. She dithered.

As if reading her thoughts, Betty urged, 'It could be done quite economically – you'll never manage to get it clean and shiny again. It looks as if it has not been used for years and years.'

With visions of spending hours cleaning weighed against being indebted to Aspens' for months, Celia plunged, and ordered, a little breathlessly, 'Yes, please take it out.'

Betty knew Eddie Fairbanks and, next, without hesitation, she asked if she could borrow his ladder. To Celia's astonishment, while Eddie held it for her, she climbed it fearlessly, her black skirt swinging round the calves of her plump legs, as she examined the roof, its gutters and downpipes and the chimneys. She announced, as she came down, after taking a final look at the back half of the roof, that someone had repaired the latter not too long before. 'And they did the gutters and downpipes. The chimney could do with repointing, but it's not too bad.'

'It would be Mr Billings, the agent, who saw to the roof, I think,' Celia told her. She felt glad that Mr Billings had, to a degree, watched over the fabric of the cottage for her mother. It reinforced the idea that he was a man of integrity.

Betty ploughed through overgrown bushes which had taken over the little flowerbed which ran along the walls of the house, to look at something she called the damp courses, and said that they, too, had been kept clear. Flushed and panting, she emerged near the back door.

As she paused to catch her breath, she looked down the length of the garden and spotted the outside lavatory. She sniffed disparagingly at it. 'Your biggest problem is that – and the water supply,' she announced. 'The rest is easy.'

Eddie was standing patiently near them, in case Betty wanted the ladder again, and he interjected with the information that he had his water from the mains and a good flush lavatory outside his back door. 'The earl got it done for me before I moved in,' he said proudly.

'A plumber's coming to look at the pump this morning,' Celia told them. 'I hope he can do the same for us.'

'Me dad could probably do that for you – and give you a better price,' Betty said promptly, as she took out a notebook and pencil and began to add to the notes she had made of her measurements. 'It pays to get more than one price.'

Celia saw the sense of this. In fact, later on, she often recounted the story of Betty's intrepidness at scaling the ladder, and said that Betty had, that very morning, taught her some of the basic principles of business.

While Eddie repositioned his ladder in order to clean the upstairs windows, and Dorothy came to the back door to tell him that she had the necessary paper, rags and vinegar to do the job, Celia was further surprised when Betty went outside the front gate and began to hunt through the foot-high grass and the straggling hedge.

She pulled out a clump of grass, and said with satisfaction, 'There it is.'

Celia squatted down by her, and watched as she cleared earth and roots from round a brass, embossed disc, like a small lid set in a ring of some other metal. 'You've got a water supply this far, anyway,' she said triumphantly. 'They'll know at the Town Hall if there's any piping into the house. I'm surprised whoever lived here wasn't connected at the same time as Mr Fairbanks was.'

'Maybe Aunt Felicity couldn't afford it – or Father wouldn't do it for tenants – he never wanted this house – said it was a nuisance,' Celia explained. 'But Mother can be very wooden when she wants to be, and she wanted it kept in the family. I can remember vaguely Father talking about selling it.'

'Get the water laid on,' advised Betty. She pointed to one of the upstairs windows. 'If you were prepared to sacrifice the back bedroom above the kitchen, Dad could probably put a bathroom and lavatory in it for you. A bathroom would add to the value of the house.' She turned to Eddie Fairbanks and inquired, 'Do you have a cesspool – or are you connected to the main drains somehow?'

'Cesspool. The earl had it dug when the lavatory were put in.'

'So the cesspool belongs to the earl?'

'Oh, aye. It will, no doubt, since he owns the land. He had it cleaned out recently.'

'So Mrs Gilmore would need to have her own dug?'

'Well, a flush lavatory outside, like mine, still has to be connected up to something!' Eddie Fairbanks took off his cap and scratched his head, while he considered this fact. Then he said doubtfully, 'You could ask the earl's agent if Mrs Gilmore's drains could be connected to it for the time being. There's a rumour in the village that some new houses are to be built just by; probably they will be connected with the main drains at the end of the lane – and if that's true, you and the earl could ask that these houses be connected at the same time. In fact, the Town Hall may insist on the connection to a drain. They don't believe in cesspools nowadays.'

'I'll find out from the Town Hall about the drainage and the water for you,' Betty promised.

'Would a loo and bathroom cost very much?'

'It wouldn't be cheap.' Celia's face fell, and Betty said cautiously. 'Me dad might be willing for you to pay by instalments – like monthly, and he might have secondhand bathroom fitments in stock which are still good – that would cut the cost a lot.'

Celia thought about this for a moment, as they walked towards the front door, and then she said, 'Once we sell our big Liverpool house, Mama should be able to pay all of the bill. I'll talk to Father's trustee about it.'

Betty nodded, and then Celia asked her, 'Would he mind telling me what it would cost for a bathroom, separate from the general repairs, even if we didn't have the work done?'

'He wouldn't mind. You don't get all the jobs you tender for. He'd give you two prices, if you like. One for a sink and taps and connections in the kitchen and an outside loo, and one for a complete bathroom with a loo in the house – and the kitchen taps the same.' She smiled, and added, 'And removing the range!'

Though she was worried at the possible cost, Celia was enchanted. 'Ask him, please,' she breathed. Then she inquired, 'Would you mind, since I have a plumber coming, if I got a price from him, too?'

'No. You would be accepting the advice I gave you just now!' She laughed, and Celia, finding her enthusiasm infectious, laughed as she had not done for weeks.

Delighted with themselves, they did some extra measurements and talked about painting the interior economically. Then, as Betty put her notebook back into her big black handbag, Celia told her about her mother's fine early nineteenth-century furniture – and that some of the pieces were too large to go into the cottage. 'Anyway, we have far too much of it – and china and curtains.'

'Will you sell it?'

'We'll have to. At first, I suggested to Mother that we get it auctioned, and she was quite miserable. Basically, I think both of us felt that we would not get good prices for it.' Celia paused to look at Betty's alert, friendly face, and then, gaining confidence, she plunged into a description of an idea she had had when visiting the Aspens' building yard.

'You remember, when I came to see you yesterday, you were cleaning out a kind of barn – where the car had been stored?'

'Yes, indeed,' Betty sounded surprised.

'I was wondering – I thought it might be easier for Mother, if we stored most of the furniture, so that she had a chance to consider what would look best in her new home – we need to

143

vacate our present house fairly soon. I was thinking that we could sell piece by piece what we did not want and get a better price for it.'

Betty grinned, 'And you'd like to put it in our barn?'

'Yes. Do you think that Mr Aspen would rent it? I don't think I can pay very much.'

'I don't think he's any immediate plans to use it, to be honest. It was a matter of cashing in on the car more than anything.' The smile left her face, as, in her turn, she confided, 'Father thought that now is the time to sell it, while there's a possible market and it's still in good shape. He wants me to have the money as a nest egg, seeing as my hubby built it.'

She looked, for a moment, so desolate, that Celia instinctively put her arm round her shoulder to comfort her. 'Never mind,' she said pointlessly.

Betty bit her lip, and then, steadying herself, said, 'I'm so sorry. It comes over me at times.'

Celia smiled and, as if she had known her for years, hugged her gently. 'Of course it does. I do understand.'

'I'll ask me dad for you.'

'Thank you. I haven't talked to Mother yet, because my sister arrived from South America yesterday, and there has not been much opportunity. I believe that the idea would be agreeable to her.'

Betty had gathered up her courage again and had begun to move towards the lane, so Celia let her arm drop. 'And now I think of it, my sister may have stuff coming from Salvador that she may want to store, too.'

Betty paused to look again at Celia. 'My goodness! You'll have enough to stock a shop.'

Celia giggled. 'That'll be the day,' she said disparagingly. 'I'm not trained for anything.'

'Nonsense,' responded Betty with unexpected briskness. 'Women can do lots of things, if they have to. I never saw a woman ploughing, for instance, until the war began and there was no ploughman to do it.'

'That's true. I remember Great-aunt Blodwyn complaining that

144

she had lost her ploughman to the army. His wife ploughed for her.'

'And Dad's training me to be a builder's clerk and maybe run the business one day when he feels too old – because it's going to take time for little Alfred to grow up and be able to do it.'

'Ah, but you're clever, Miss Aspen – and capable.'

'Tush, I didn't know anything much till Dad took me into the office, to fill in until he could get another man – and then found there were almost none left of the right age and experience. You could learn anything, if you set your mind to it.' Her eyes danced as she said this, as if she were suggesting something naughty.

'Well, thank you.' Celia felt hugely gratified at the compliment.

Although the plumber from the village, when he arrived, was shown politely round the cottage and asked for an estimate, Celia knew in her heart that Betty had impressed her so favourably that she would give the work to the Aspens. She already sensed that, in Betty, she had made a real friend.

That night, as they sat round the kitchen fire drinking their bedtime cocoa, Dorothy told Winnie, who was nursing Tommy Atkins on her lap, that she had never before seen Miss Celia look so happy.

'Then why is she up in her bedroom crying her eyes out?' asked Ethel in surprise. 'I saw her, when I went up to put the hot water bottles in the beds, just now. She were lying on her bed. But I could hear her when I were in the passage – and I didn't know what to do.'

'You shouldn't have gone in, Ethel. You should know that by now.'

'I thought maybe she hurt herself. Banged her head on something perhaps. How was I to know?'

'She was probably just tired out. It's not our business, Ethel. In service, you got to keep your eyes down and mind your own business.'

'Yes, Ma'am,' Ethel replied sullenly, and returned to sipping her cocoa.

Dorothy said, 'Maybe her mam or Miss Edna has been at her

again. It's a pity, because, you know, it were as if that Miss Aspen put new life into her,' she said.

'One of the few times she's been out of her mother's sight, I'd say. Most times, she's never had a chance to be herself,' responded Winnie dryly.

Chapter Twenty-One

❧

When Celia and Dorothy had returned from Meols at about five
o'clock, Ethel had told them that the Missus and Miss Edna had
gone to see how Mrs Woodcock was.

While Dorothy clattered downstairs to the basement kitchen,
Celia took off her outer clothes and went into the sitting room,
where a good fire blazed.

Though Celia would herself have enjoyed visiting Phyllis, she
was relieved that her mother had kindly performed this duty,
and that, though she should go soon, it did not have to be that
particular evening. She badly needed time to talk over with her
mother her ideas regarding their new home, and to hear what
the bank manager had said to her.

She was also anxious to know what plans, if any, Edna had for
her future. Would she want to live with her mother and herself?

Celia dreaded the answer to this question. Secretly, she chas-
tised herself for not longing to share her home with her poor
bereaved sister. You are supposed to love your sister – want to
help her whenever she needs help, she told herself again and
again. But, on Lime Street Station, she had felt the sting of Edna's
remarks, though they were not much different from snubs she
had received from Edna ever since she could remember.

Angrily, she asked herself, why doesn't she show me some
affection? And promptly blamed the lack on her own short-
comings, that she was dull and stupid and not worthy of love.
That Edna's attitude towards her might have been automatic,
learned long ago from their mother, did not occur to her. She
tried to comfort herself by remembering how Edna had held her
hand in the taxi.

Without being asked, Winnie sent her up a tray of tea. It was brought upstairs by Ethel, who carefully put it down on a side table within reach of Celia. 'Dorothy's just getting washed and changed into her afternoon uniform, Miss,' she said, as she took the lid off the pot and gave the contents an energetic stir. 'So Winnie said to me to bring it up to you.'

'Thank you, Ethel.' Celia forced her thoughts away from Edna, and inquired, 'How did you get on at your interview yesterday?'

'I won't know for a day or two, Miss. The lady has one or two others to see – before she makes up her mind, like.'

Since Celia seemed interested, she felt encouraged to go on. 'You see, Miss, I haven't any official experience with children – that was the trouble. But I'm the second one in a family of thirteen.' She laughed. 'Coming to work for Mrs Gilmore was the first time I haven't been knee-deep in kids – and truth to tell, it feels lonely without them.'

'It might be a little different dealing with children in a house in West Derby,' Celia warned. It was a wealthy neighbourhood with a very different standard of living from that of Ethel's family in the north end of the city.

'Oh, aye. I'd have to bath the little terrors every night, no doubt – and be for ever changing nappies – much more than me mam and I could do for our kids. It took Mam all her time to feed them, never mind anything else.'

'How many children did this lady have?'

'Just had her second – she's got a two-year-old as well. She's hardly got started yet.

'And, Miss, there's a day nursery and a night nursery. And, you know, Miss, I'd sleep in the same room as the babies and it would be warm because there'd be a fire to keep the babies warm. And I wouldn't have to clean – other help is kept.' She paused for breath, and finished up by saying wistfully, 'I hope I get it, Miss.'

Suddenly aware, from Ethel's remark, that there was no heating in the bedrooms of the Gilmore servants, Celia said, 'I hope you do, Ethel. I am sure Mother will give you an excellent reference.'

Through the open door into the hall, Celia glimpsed a neatly uniformed Dorothy run to answer the front door. As soon as she opened it, there was a flurry of wet umbrellas being shaken and voices protesting a sudden shower.

Ethel turned guiltily.

'The Missus! And me talking like this!' She slipped out of the room as quietly as a cat, and Celia doubted if Louise even noticed her as she passed through to the basement stairs.

Celia smiled as she poured out her tea. She took a quick sip, and then went into the hall to greet her mother.

Both ladies were struggling out of damp jackets and hats; Edna was saying that the veiling and satin trimmings of their hats were ruined by spots of rain. Dorothy was putting their umbrellas into the umbrella stand. She promised, at the same time, to take the hats and coats downstairs to be dried in the kitchen. But Edna handed Celia her hat, and said, 'Put this somewhere to dry. Lay it on its crown to keep the crown flat.'

Celia looked at it, and said, 'I'd better take the veiling off and spread it out. I think it will have to be restiffened with a little gum water.' Her response to her sister's request had been automatic, and she immediately regretted it. She wanted to say, 'Do it yourself, when you are pressing your dresses.' But her courage failed her.

'I don't know how to do it,' Edna was continuing to Celia.

Her unthinking mother chimed in, 'Oh, Celia is very good at such things. Would you iron mine at the same time, dear?'

The memory of her interesting and satisfying day was wiped out. Seething with indignation, she obediently took her mother's bonnet as well as Edna's hat, and said, 'I'll put them in the laundry room downstairs, and deal with them tomorrow.' And I'll deliberately forget about them, she thought angrily.

In the unlit laundry room, however, she stood and cried. Then she blew her nose and went back upstairs, to find her mother demanding more tea from Dorothy, and Edna saying that it had been a horrible visit; Phyllis's house looked positively unkempt and it stank of babies.

In the middle of the chaos, Phyllis had been lying on her

unmade bed with a baby at her breast and a little boy howling beside her.

'And she didn't even get Lily to make a cup of tea for us,' added Louise. 'It's a good thing her mother is arriving tomorrow to help her.'

Celia was outraged. She forgot her tears, and said maliciously to Edna, 'I hope that you took little Eric up and comforted him and, at least, made her bed comfortable for her.'

Edna was seating herself by the fire and spreading out her damp skirt round her to dry. She froze for a moment, and then, as if she had not heard Celia's remark, she said, 'I think I had better go up and change immediately we have had tea.'

'Celia!' Her mother's voice held a warning note. 'If Phyllis needs more help, it is up to Arthur to provide it. It is not for us to imply criticism of the family's arrangements by offering to help.'

'But, Mama . . .'

'That's quite enough. I don't want to hear any more about it.'

'Very well, Mama.' Though the tea tray that Ethel had brought her had been removed, her full cup still stood on the table next to Edna's chair. With trembling hands, she picked it up and walked over to the window, to stare at the rain-dashed panes while she drank the cold tea.

As she slowly put the cup and saucer down on a table crowded with family photographs in silver frames, Dorothy arrived with a larger tray, which she laid on the tea table beside Louise, and all three women remained quiet until she had left the room. Celia wondered if Louise and Edna had made up their quarrel over smoking the previous evening.

In the same strained silence the women sipped tea and nibbled scones, until Louise, anxious that her girls should not quarrel, introduced the reason for their visit to Phyllis, which was not really to inquire how the new mother fared.

'That awful estate agent man called this morning, to say he was bringing a lady from Manchester, who had need of a large house in which to set up a nursing home. He apologised for rushing us, but he wanted to add this house to the list of those he proposed to show her this afternoon.' Louise fumbled for her black handkerchief again. 'Of course, I said no. It was too sudden.'

'He's not a very easy man to deny,' interjected Edna reflectively. 'I didn't like him.' She ached to smoke, and wondered how soon she could run up to her bedroom for a quick puff.

As if they had never had a cross word between them, Louise turned to her gratefully, 'Neither do I, dear. He's too forward.' She turned back to Celia. 'He said, however, that your father's lawyer had impressed on him the need for speed. And he insisted that time and tide wait for no man – and that the lady was a very likely purchaser. But she had to return to Manchester tonight.' She dabbed her eyes with her handkerchief. 'So I gave in.'

'And we went to see your friend, to get out of his way.' Edna's expression as she looked into her empty teacup was sour, as if something unpleasant was passing under her nose.

'And because it was my duty to visit Phyllis, particularly as she is calling the baby after dear Timothy,' added Louise virtuously.

Celia realised that her mother was doing her best to keep the peace between Edna and herself, just as if they were still small girls quarrelling in the nursery. She picked up the olive branch. 'You were enormously kind to her, Mama, when the baby came so unexpectedly. I am sure she will feel a lifelong obligation to you.'

Louise actually smiled at her younger daughter. She said primly, 'I don't know what else we could have done.'

'Well, you did everything so graciously.' Celia felt she could say this honestly; and then she asked, 'When will the estate agent let you know what the result of the visit was?'

'He left his card with a note on it to say he would call on us tomorrow afternoon, just to give us the Manchester lady's reactions.' She sighed. 'On a Sunday afternoon!'

'It's not very nice, is it?' This from Edna, who had not enjoyed her practically smokeless day while enduring her mother's fairly constant laments.

'We shall have returned from church, at least,' said Celia, trying to comfort her mother about using the Lord's day for selling houses. She decided that the estate agent's insistence on speed opened the way for her to tell her mother about her discussions with Betty Aspen and the plumber. This she did, while Edna listened with some interest.

'A real bathroom? Like we have here?' exclaimed her mother. 'That would be wonderful. Oh, what a relief!'

'Well, perhaps not quite as grand as we have here, Mother. But Miss Aspen – I keep forgetting that she's a widow and her real name is Mrs Houghton – assured me that it would be quite nice-looking. And less likely to freeze up in winter than an outside water closet would. She has promised an estimate on Monday – she'll leave it at the cottage.'

'How shall we pay for it?' Louise asked helplessly.

'If Cousin Albert agrees, we might pay for it out of the money we'll get from this house. Otherwise, Mrs Houghton suggested that we could pay monthly to her father until we have paid it off.'

Edna opened her mouth to say kindly that she had a little ready money, but Celia cut her off by telling Louise about the barn, the rent of which Betty would also let her know on Monday.

'You see, Mama, if it does not cost much to store the furniture so close to the cottage, you can take your time in deciding, finally, what you would like to retain – and if something does not fit, we have somewhere to put it until it can be sold.'

Edna interjected that she had furniture coming from Brazil, which would arrive in about three months' time. It would be coming in on a freighter bound for Liverpool. 'I shall need somewhere to store it, if I remain up here – though Papa Fellowes has offered me a home with his family. The barn would be convenient for me, too.'

Louise leaned across the fireplace to take Edna's hand and squeeze it. 'My dear,' she said, 'you know that I would wish you to be with us.'

Celia dutifully echoed this, though she felt that life with Edna could be miserable. Her hands were clasped tightly in her lap, as she sought to control her feelings. She had, of course, no inkling of the turmoil of emotion through which Edna was going.

'Perhaps you and Mama could share the rent of the barn, and that would make it very inexpensive, I am sure,' she suggested.

While her mother nodded agreement to it, Edna considered the suggestion. Then she said reluctantly, 'I don't think I have to worry about small expenses. Papa Fellowes had the will which Paul made when we were married. He never changed it; he left me everything that he possessed. He was his father's junior partner and it means that money will come to me from the company.'

And thank God for that, she told herself; if she was never able to see Vital again, it was some comfort that she would be financially independent – simply because arrogant, self-centred Paul had never dreamed of dying young; he had made the original will only after his father had suggested it.

Her mother gave a sigh of relief. 'I am so thankful, dear, that Paul took care of you so well. We would have shared what we have with you. But it gives you much more freedom if you are independent.'

Celia opened her mouth to snap that she had absolutely nothing to share. She did not, however, want to upset her mother again, so she compressed her lips, kept her hands in her lap and said no more. A woman can learn, said Betty Houghton, who was well on her way to holding down a man's job. But where could she herself start to learn anything that would give her a chance of freedom?

Edna agreed dully that she was fortunate. She shifted uneasily in her chair, and sighed. She said slowly, 'I have no idea, as yet, what my income will be. Papa Fellowes has promised to send me a cheque each month until Paul's will has been probated. After that, I shall be considered a shareholder in the company, and I will be sent dividends according to the profits made each year.'

Louise nodded. 'It's a very big company,' she remarked. 'You should do well.'

'Papa Fellowes warned me that, though the company is doing extremely well now, sometimes such companies have huge financial losses, and there is no income for a while. He advised that I should save as much as I can in the good years and invest the savings conservatively, so that I will always have some income.'

She thought for a moment, and then added, 'He said that he will be sending me enough until the will is probated for me to live on independently, if I am careful.'

'He really has your interests at heart, doesn't he?' Louise said warmly. 'He must be very fond of you.'

'Both Mama and Papa have always been extremely kind to me,' Edna responded. 'You'll remember them quite well, of course, from when they lived in Liverpool many years ago.' She felt a burst of guilt, as if the failure of her marriage had been her own fault and she was cheating her affectionate in-laws. She wanted to cry. Instead, she turned firmly to her sister, and said through tight lips, 'I would like to see the cottage.'

Celia, who had been listening with envy to the story of Mr Fellowes' generosity and good sense, was immediately alert. The request suggested that Louise had explained, as far as she was able, their financial situation and the grim necessity of selling the house. Edna had, therefore, presumably accepted the fact of her father's bankruptcy.

Celia had begun to think of the cottage as her own domain. But if Edna wanted to live with them, then she would naturally want to see the place. She said reluctantly, 'You could come with me – I shall go out on Monday to see Mrs Houghton and to discuss her estimates – and arrange with her for workmen to be let in. I was hoping you, Mama, would come with me – because you would have to decide if you wished the work to go forward.'

Louise's expression was one of nervous dismay. 'How on earth would I know what should be done – and how much it should cost?'

'Well, Cousin Albert is not here to advise you, so I don't know who else to ask – and it is you who will have to pay for anything which is done.'

Louise clutched at a straw. 'What about Mr Billings?'

'You could, of course, ask him to check the estimates,' Celia responded. Then she added doubtfully, 'I think he might make a charge for doing it – and I can't imagine his turning down estimates from a man he is obviously well acquainted with.'

Louise turned to Edna. 'What do you think, dear?'

Celia waited to be condemned, but Edna said absently, 'Me? I have been out of the country so long that I would not have the least idea. All I know is that everything seems terribly expensive, compared to what it was in 1913. I suppose it's because of the war.'

Celia agreed that her sister's observation was correct. She knew because she kept the housekeeping book for her mother and she had, as the war progressed, watched the butcher's and baker's bills go steadily up. Her mother had had to ask Father a number of times for an increase in housekeeping money. Then she thought suddenly, that's one thing I know. How to keep a simple account book and file all the receipts neatly, so that Father could look at them. She told herself not to be silly – anybody could do that.

Since they seemed to have silently agreed that there was no one to make the decision about repair costs, Celia knew she would have to plunge in and accept Betty Houghton's calculations. She deferred the debate about having a bathroom put in until Betty could tell Louise, on Monday, exactly what she envisaged.

It was agreed that all three ladies would make the journey to Meols on Monday.

Like a good chairwoman of the Knitting Committee they had belonged to during the war, Celia brought up the next subject on her agenda, by asking her mother to tell her what Mr Carruthers at the bank had had to say.

Except for payments to tradesmen, Louise had never discussed money with Celia, and she did not seem to be very keen to do so now. She did not immediately reply.

Celia urged, 'We need to know, Mama, whether we have any immediate money to pay workmen. I still have most of the five pounds you gave me, though I have paid the sweep.' She suddenly remembered the plumber, and told her mother how he had come and had also promised an estimate, on Monday, for the work he could do. 'That would be a way of checking at least part of Betty Houghton's estimate, wouldn't it?'

The information about the plumber was received by Louise with evident relief. In answer to the question, she said that Mr Carruthers had given her so much information about banking that her mind was quite in a tizzy. She was, however, clear that there was at least twenty pounds in her account and, in addition, she had paid in Mr Billings' cheque for nine pounds and eight shillings.

To Celia, nearly thirty pounds, together with the remaining bit of housekeeping Louise still had for the month of March, was a great deal of money, and she said so to Louise. Her own allowance from her father worked out at less than two pounds for an entire year. If there were only the two of them to maintain, and they could move into the cottage, she knew that the money in the bank would go quite a long way.

Edna simply wrinkled her nose and said nothing. She did not want to commit herself to anything much financially, until she knew what amount Papa Fellowes was going to send her.

'And was he able to give you the name of a solicitor?' Celia asked.

'Yes, indeed. He very kindly took me down the street to introduce me.' Louise's voice rang with approbation. 'Mr Little of Hart, Howard and Little. Such a handsome young man. Like George, he served in the navy and was actually once sunk by a submarine. He has only been home for a year. He was most sympathetic about dear George and Tom.'

Celia hoped that the young man's law was as good as his looks. I don't care if he looks like a Gorgon's head, she decided, if only he will keep us from falling into some unexpected abyss.

Her mother continued. 'He says I must never sign anything without first showing it to him.'

'Sensible advice,' remarked Edna to no one in particular.

'What does he charge?' asked Celia.

'Oh, I could never be so vulgar as to ask a gentleman, such as he is, what he charges! He will no doubt send us a bill.'

Though she felt that some snaillike progress had been made, Celia had a strong desire to scream. She was deadly tired from the long day; and her mother's silly attitude towards the lawyer added to her underlying fear that she would never manage to get her safely into a new home.

The silence which fell between the three women was broken

by the sound of Dorothy banging the hall gong, to indicate that it was time to dress for dinner.

Edna rose with obvious relief. She looked down ruefully at her skirt, which, after being so damp, would certainly need pressing. She wondered if she could push her ironing on to the washer-woman, who, she had learned from Ethel, came to the house on Mondays; the woman could do it while they were in Meols. Ethel had murmured shyly that she would probably expect to be paid a bit more for the extra work, and Edna had accepted this suggestion.

Louise looked up at her and then at Celia, who had also risen. 'Will the estate agent expect tea when he comes tomorrow?' she asked, with a quaver in her voice.

'I have no idea,' replied Celia, who felt she could face no more.

Chapter Twenty-Two

Three weeks later, a triumphant Ethel gave three days' notice, packed her small tin suitcase with her few belongings and, on the third day, went home to her mother, to spend a little while with her, before starting her new job as nursemaid.

Louise was very resentful of such short notice. 'Such impudence!' she exclaimed. 'She was smirking all over her face, as she told me. I felt like refusing to pay her her last week's wages!'

Amid the chaos to which the dining room had been reduced, they were carefully wrapping crockery in newspaper before laying it in wooden barrels ready for the movers. Celia paused, a huge gravy boat in one hand. Shocked, she exclaimed, 'You didn't actually do that, did you, Mama?'

Her mother bridled. 'No, but I threatened to – and it frightened her. I can't stand impudence.'

'Her mother depends on her sending most of her wages home,' Celia said unhappily. 'I am sure she was scared.'

'Well, I finally gave it to her. Good riddance to bad rubbish.'

Celia thought of the warm friendly youngster who had cheerfully done all the rough work of a big house. Was that all the thanks you got when people did not want you any more?

She shivered at the idea, and then slowly placed the gravy boat in a barrel, which would be stored in the Aspen barn until its contents were sold. What would three women do with twelve place settings of Crown Derby – in a cottage? she had asked her mother.

'We may have important visitors,' declared Louise loftily.

In despair, Celia expostulated, 'But we are already taking three sets of six with us!'

Louise agreed to the china being stored. 'But not sold, mind you!'

'It's a good thing we've got the barn,' Celia remarked. 'The workmen are still in the cottage, because they've yet to paint the parlour – though Betty persuaded Mr Aspen to do a fast job for us, specially.'

'A fast job sounds most unladylike.'

'That's what Betty called it.' Celia's lips compressed tightly, as she swallowed her irritation.

'And really, dear, I don't think you should be on first-name terms with a workman's daughter.'

Celia longed to snap back that Betty was proving to be an excellent friend, but restrained herself. It was useless to debate the matter; Betty was indisputably working-class.

As they packed, upstairs in her bedroom Edna wrote to her father-in-law in Southampton to notify him of her impending change of address. As she sealed the letter, she thought about writing to Vital. They had said farewell in the belief that they would never get the chance to meet again. It was wiser to leave it thus, she knew; and yet, the real pain inside her swelled at the idea of becoming lost to him for ever if he had no address for her.

She seized another sheet of paper and quickly scribbled a few lines on it to say that she expected to live with her mother for the time being and gave the cottage address. She added that she would be grateful if he would send on any letters addressed to her Brazilian home. That, at least, she thought, was a reasonable request, should anyone else chance to see the letter. She flung herself on to her bed; she did not cry – she was past that. She reached for her cigarettes.

While Celia strove to complete the packing of the best china, her thoughts turned to her old friends in the kitchen. Dorothy would not start her new employment as a cook-general with a family across the road for a day or two, so she had been glad, Celia knew, to stay on. She hoped that Louise would manage to pay any wages due to her, though the woman would probably be thankful enough just to be fed and housed until she started her new job.

It left only Winnie. What was the old cook going to do?

Perhaps she'll stay with one of her sons, Celia thought.

Long before the war, she remembered, Winnie, widowed when young, used to go on her days off to her own mother's house to see her boys. They were being brought up by their grandmother while Winnie went out to work to earn the money to feed them.

Celia made up her mind that when they had completed packing the contents of the china cupboard, which led off the dining room, she would go down to the kitchen to inquire what the elderly cook's plans were.

Winnie had been a tremendous help. She had picked out what she considered to be a reasonable set of kitchenware for a small kitchen, and it had been sent by carrier to the new home, together with boxes of food staples from the pantry. Large pieces of coarse crockery, like bread bowls, had been packed for storage, except for a few utensils for use in their final days of residence.

'Do you know if Winnie has found a position yet, Mama?'

Her mother was lifting a heavy silver basket out of the sideboard drawer. She said, 'I think we should take the silver out to Meols ourselves.' Then, in answer to Celia's question, she replied, 'I don't know. I haven't had time to ask her – I've been quite worn out.'

Though Celia answered in her usual gentle way, 'I know, Mama. The last few weeks have been very stressful,' Louise sensed a lack of sympathy, and, as she put the heavy basket of cutlery on to the table, she looked hard at her daughter.

Ever since dear Timothy had passed away, Celia had definitely not been herself.

Louise decided that the girl was getting above herself. That was it. Without her mother's permission, she had authorised all kinds of repairs to the cottage; she would never have dared to do that, if her dear father had been alive. And she had taken Dorothy down to the cottage for days at a time, so that there had been no one to answer her bell when she rang. Eventually – very eventually – she considered bitterly, Ethel or Winnie had come panting upstairs – but it was not the same. She had also been inconvenienced by the fact that Celia herself had not been in the house to do the innumerable small tasks that were required of her, as cupboards and drawers were cleared out. She had even found herself having to reply to late-arriving condolence letters, which had made her cry. It wasn't fair. And, though she had been told to do it, the girl had done nothing about notifying friends and relations about their change of address.

With the West Derby house not yet sold, the financial worry had been quite appalling – when she had written to Cousin Albert about it, he had replied by return of post that she could probably get a small loan from the bank on the strength of the pending sale of the house.

Ask Mr Carruthers for a loan? It was a shocking thought. Really, Cousin Albert was being no help whatever. What use was he as an executor? Nevertheless, pushed by Celia, she had obtained from Mr Carruthers a loan to help out. Because she trusted him, she had blithely signed for it without first consulting her new solicitor and had never asked about the rate of interest that would be charged.

In her confusion she had no idea that Cousin Albert, terrified of a female invasion of his quiet home, was doing exactly what the law demanded of an executor – attending to the deceased's estate, or lack of it. He was determined not to become involved in Louise's financial troubles. As her husband's cousin, he had, he felt, given her sound advice; it was up to her to take it. He had, out of a sense of duty to his cousin's wife, set in train for her the sale of her house and would see that she bought an annuity from the proceeds. Other than that, he kept his head down and communicated only with Timothy's solicitor, Mr Barnett, and with his elderly clerk, whose salary he was temporarily paying himself, since he had to have someone in Liverpool to help him deal with angry creditors.

On top of Cousin Albert's callousness, here was Celia worrying about servants, thought Louise savagely – when she should have been concerned about her poor mother's dreadful state.

Her feeling of neglect surfaced, and she snapped, 'Servants are supposed to look after themselves. She probably has expectations somewhere.'

'Yes, Mother.'

After seven huge barrels lacking only their tops, which the removal men would nail on, stood in a neat line in front of the divested sideboard and china cupboard, Louise allowed herself to be installed in a chair by the morning-room fire to rest.

A troubled Celia slipped down to the kitchen to see her old friend.

Winnie was preparing dinner and was just putting a chicken into the oven to roast. As Celia edged round the big kitchen table to stand by the fire to warm her hands, grubby from the packing she had done, the cook straightened up and closed the oven door.

'I've got a big beef casserole at the back of the oven,' Winnie said. Her voice was strained and weary. 'It can go over to the cottage with the furniture tomorrow and be a good dinner for you. Your mam won't want to cook on her first day in her new house.'

She turned to the table and sat down by it. Swiftly, she began to peel potatoes which she had already washed.

'You are very kind, Winnie. That's most thoughtful of you.' Inwardly, she wondered if her mother would agree to cook at all. Then she explained the reason for her visit to the kitchen.

'Well, Miss Celia, I haven't got nothing yet. But I'm registered with Grey's Domestic Staff Registry and I've answered a couple of ads in *The Lady*. I'm hoping something will turn up.' She dropped a potato slowly into a pan of cold water, and then picked up another one.

'Do you have anywhere to stay while you're waiting?'

'Not really, Miss.'

'I thought you had sons?'

'Oh, aye, I had two. One emigrated to Canada. He's a miner in a place called Yellowknife. And the other one went to sea as a ship's cook.' She sighed, and her paring knife stopped its rapid run round the potato as she looked up at Celia. 'He married a Corpus Christi girl – an American – and sailed out of there for

162

years. He seemed to forget about his old mam. Then, one day, I got a letter from his wife saying that he had been drowned when the Jerries torpedoed his ship.'

'Oh, how terrible! I never knew that,' Celia exclaimed.

The paring knife was slowly put back to work and another potato plopped into the pan, before Winnie could answer. She said, 'Your mam knew. It were a dreadful shock. I loved my boys and I always hoped he'd bring his girl over here to settle, and that I could live with them when I couldn't work no more.

'A good granny can always make herself useful,' she finished up a little piteously.

'Oh, Winnie. I had no idea! You poor thing.'

'Your mam probably kept it from you, so as not to upset you,' Winnie replied, putting the kindest interpretation she could on Louise's lack of communication.

Celia glanced round the kitchen, as if searching for inspiration. The big underground room already seemed deserted, its shelves practically empty. No Ethel at the kitchen sink patiently washing dishes. No sound of Dorothy's quick feet thudding down the stairs; she was out at the cottage, giving the kitchen a final clean and unpacking kitchenware already sent out. Not even a bell ringing for service upstairs.

'What are you going to do after you've done the final cleaning of the house? Mother said she had asked you and Dorothy to do this. This house'll be empty by tomorrow night, and she assumes you will have everything tidy by the day after – and be on your way.'

'I'll find a room somewhere. The Missus says she'll tell the removal men not to take the beds from me and Dorothy's bedroom – she says they can be abandoned – they're not worth moving. She wants Dorothy and me to clean up down here, after everything that's supposed to be moved is moved. She said that, if necessary, I can stay over a day or two to finish the cleaning. There's food left over for us in the pantry, and she'll pay me by the day.' She dropped another peeled potato into a saucepan. 'Is the house sold yet, Miss?'

'Not yet. There are two people considering it – a man who

wants to make apartments out of it; and you saw the lady who wants to have it as a nursing home – she's still thinking about it. I believe the estate agent is bringing her tomorrow to look at it again – when it's empty.'

'Oh, aye. She can judge better then.' Winnie's voice seemed lacking in real interest. Then she roused herself to say, 'With so many wounded and not having enough hospitals, they got to have places to put them – those as will never get better, I mean.'

'Yes. It's very sad.' Celia paused, and then said wistfully, 'I wish you could come with us, Winnie. But now that Edna has come home, and one of the bedrooms has been made into a bathroom, the cottage won't hold anybody else.'

'I realise that, Miss. Our Dorothy told me all about the cottage.' She smiled slightly, and said formally, 'I hope you'll be happy there, Miss.'

'Thank you, Winnie. Will you write to tell me how you get on? I do hope you find a place soon.'

'Thank you, Miss.' The cook got up and took a small notebook from the mantelpiece. It had a pencil on a piece of string dangling from it. 'Could you write down your address, Miss?' she asked shyly. 'Because I may need to give your mam's name to a new employer. She's given me a good written reference to carry with me, but sometimes they like to write direct to your old employer – to make sure the reference is genuine, like.'

'Of course.' The address was carefully printed out. Then there did not seem to be anything more to say.

Celia put down the pencil, and turned to the cook. She bent over her and kissed her on the cheek. 'Goodbye, Winnie.' Then she put her arms round the old woman's shoulders and hugged her. 'We've been good friends, haven't we?'

Winnie returned the kiss and the hug. 'You take good care of yourself, Miss.'

As she reluctantly let Celia go, the cook felt that they both had their problems. She told herself that she wouldn't, for the world, like to have Miss Celia's worries. What's going to be left for her when she's as old as I am? At least I can cook. Somebody'll be glad of me.

Chapter Twenty-Three

❧

A long empty furniture pantechnicon backed cautiously away from the cottage's new front gate and, after its wheels had flung up a flurry of sand in all directions, it began its journey back to Liverpool to fetch another load which would, this time, be delivered to Aspen's Building Contractors in Hoylake.

In the Liverpool house, Louise and Edna were supervising the dispatch of the furniture, and in the Hoylake cottage Celia and Betty were dealing with its reception and the placing of each piece of furniture. By this time, Celia and Betty were fast friends, and Betty had begged a few hours off from her father, in order to help Celia.

All carpets, pictures and mirrors required in the new home had, two days before, been moved in a smaller van, and the carpets laid by the removal men, as directed by Celia. Much to Louise's horror, Celia had travelled in the van with them to the cottage. Later that day, Louise and Edna had come out to Meols to help to hang curtains and pictures, despite the fact that two men were still working in the bathroom and that the frames of the back windows would not be replaced for another week. A gaping hole where the old kitchen range had been awaited the attention of a plasterer. Such was Celia's fear, however, of the financial drain of the maintenance of the West Derby house that she pressed her mother ruthlessly to move without delay.

None of the women realised how much effort Betty had made to get the work done quickly. She had persuaded her father to give it priority, and had harried the foreman into putting their two best plumbers on the job. It was these two men who, in the late afternoon, came downstairs to say that everything was connected, and that the ladies could now have the water turned on.

This was solemnly done and the taps allowed to run.

As soon as the men had left, there was a rush to use the lavatory.

The plumbers had tidied up, but both sink and bath needed to be scoured.

'What shall we do?' wailed Louise.

'Clean them,' snapped Edna. She immediately went down to the kitchen to find rags and scouring powder and then, rather clumsily, went to work. The result was not very good. Her mother complained, and was met with pained silence.

Supervised by an irate Louise, who refused to actually do anything on the grounds that she was too heartbroken, Celia and Edna had spent the rest of the day inexpertly hammering nails into newly painted walls and hanging the pictures and mirrors wherever they saw fit; their mother, when asked, had gloomily refused to be interested in where they were hung, so, where possible, they hung them in the same rooms that they had been in in the Liverpool house.

Celia had remarked to Edna that it was a relief to be rid of most of the dirty old oil paintings that had graced the walls of the Liverpool house, and have only watercolours to look at. 'Except, of course, for the two oils I've just put here in the living room with the Landseer etching; Mother dotes on them.'

'Well, it's her home,' Edna replied. 'If that's what she wants . . .'

A little stab of fear went through Celia. The cottage belonged, indeed, to her mother – not to either Celia or Edna. She felt that, in future, she should never forget that fact.

Now, as the huge pantechnicon bumped safely on to the main road after delivering the furniture, Celia surveyed the little living room they had created, and declared to Betty, 'I don't think I would have ever been able to achieve this without your support, Betty. You've been such a help.'

Betty was tucking the dining chairs further under the table, to give a little more room for moving about. She made a mock bow.

'My pleasure,' she said. 'It's been the first fun I've had since the war. Even Dad's got interested in it, and he'll see the spare furniture properly stored so that it isn't damaged.'

'He's wonderful – so kind. In fact, everybody I've met in Hoylake has been so nice to me – and patient with Mother.'

'You're a pleasure to deal with – and your mam isn't any different from other women left in the same predicament – there are thousands of them – they just don't know things, that's all. If you can explain simply to them, they usually see the common sense of what you're suggesting. And your mam is no exception.'

'Well, you went far beyond the cause of duty, when you came over to Liverpool and went through the house with her to tell her what would fit here and what would not. She would never have accepted my word for it that you can't get a wardrobe built for crinolines into a cottage!'

Betty laughed. 'And the old-fashioned night commode that she had in her bedroom?'

It was Celia's turn to laugh. 'She only gave in because you could measure that the distance from her new bedroom to her new bathroom was less than walking across her present bedroom to use the awful old thing!'

Her mind turned to the dire need to sell some of the furniture, and she asked, 'Will your father mind, Betty, if I bring prospective purchasers into his barn to show them the pieces for sale?'

'Not him. The gates are open from 7 am to 6.30 pm, anyway; and it will be a bit of an advertisement for him.'

'Let's sit down and have a cup of tea, while we wait for Mother and Edna,' Celia urged. 'They are bringing all the personal luggage that they didn't want to give to the movers.'

'Jewellery?'

'Yes – and furs and silverware.' She remembered something else for which she had to thank Betty. 'Remember sending me to see Mrs Jowett, in Liverpool – the lady with the antique shop?'

'Yes.'

'Well, once she heard your name, she was really helpful about pricing the furniture. At first, she wanted to come out and buy herself. But I did exactly as you advised me – I told her that I

167

wanted to sell it myself, so that I made the most money. She didn't make fun of me – just said it was sensible. She's lent me a pile of magazines, and a list of Victorian furniture and what is a reasonable price for it – if it's in good condition. And two books on eighteenth-century furniture.' She patted the well-worn tomes sitting on the table in front of her. 'She said she was not an expert on eighteenth-century pieces; though since I know their origins – provenance, she called it – she assured me that I can probably get good prices for them.'

She smiled reflectively at the memory of the old Jewess, who had, in the course of an hour, tried to pass on to her a lifetime of experience in the trade. Then she went on, 'She told me that big pieces take time to sell these days – new houses – and flats – are smaller than pre-war ones – and there isn't the space for heavy furniture.

'She also said a lot of well-to-do people are closing their town houses and renting a flat instead, so that's brought more old furniture on to the market. But, you know, Betty, a lot of Mother's furniture is early Georgian and quite dainty.'

Betty nodded agreement. 'She's right. Dad's got one or two jobs where he's making big houses into flats – houses like yours, in Liverpool, and the ones on Meols Drive in Hoylake.'

While the kettle for tea heated on the fire, they went slowly through the lobby and hall, both of which were newly painted cream; and the sunlight caught the glass door which Celia's grandmother had loved so much, and reflected the pretty design on to the wall.

In the hall hung some of her mother's favourite watercolours. Under their feet lay part of the good Brussels stair carpet from the West Derby house. The stone floor of the back room, to which they now slowly returned, boasted the Turkey carpet from the old dining room; it had been cut to fit the smaller room. Louise had said crossly that it was pure sacrilege to hack at such a beautiful carpet, but she had insisted on bringing it, so that was what Celia had arranged.

The red velvet curtains from the same room had been shortened by a local seamstress to fit the little windows. In the struggle to hang both pictures and curtains, the weary sisters had snapped and snarled at each other and argued with their mother.

In one case, Louise had suddenly decided she did not like the curtains in the front bedroom which was to be hers, and they had to take them down and put them in Edna's room. Edna did not like them either, but lost the battle.

It had been the most tiring two days that Celia ever remembered. Her shoulders and back had ached unbearably during the night.

By the time the three women had caught the train back to Liverpool, they were barely on speaking terms. The following morning, however, Edna, usually so silent, had asked Celia if she would rub her back with surgical spirit because it ached so badly. Celia agreed.

When she lifted her sister's shift in order to apply the embrocation, she had been shocked at the incredible thinness of her. Her shoulder blades stuck out and her backbone looked like a knotted cord.

As she banged the cork back into the surgical spirit bottle, Celia asked, 'Are you well, Edna? You are too thin.'

'I am perfectly well, thank you. I am simply unused to having to work like a servant.' The tone did not brook a response, so Celia turned away; she herself had, in the previous month, done much more than either of the other two women, but she had not lost weight.

Now a fire, built by Celia according to Dorothy's careful instruction, blazed in the old-fashioned cottage grate which had been well burnished with black lead.

Dorothy is a professional when it comes to cleaning, thought Celia with a sigh, as she set out teacups on the table, and I will never be as good.

The division of domestic responsibilities had yet to be discussed, and Celia had automatically assumed that most of the work would be piled on to her shoulders.

'Dorothy's going to come in some time tomorrow, to clean out the garden shed,' she told Betty. 'It's got shelves on which we can store all the trunks.'

'That'll be a help,' Betty replied. She wondered grimly who would be the first woman to get up the following morning and make the living-room fire. Probably poor old Celia, she decided.

At that moment, Dorothy was busy cleaning the rapidly emptying house in West Derby, and Winnie was supervising the removers, while she also wielded a broom. Dorothy was not very happy about her new job as the only servant in a home, but she reckoned it would do until she got something better.

She had leaped at the chance of coming out to the cottage once more. She had always prided herself on knowing a good man when she saw one, and she had welcomed the possibility of meeting Eddie again. She had told Winnie that he was elderly – but not old – and a real nice fella.

Winnie wished her well, and wondered if the Missus would mind if she herself continued to sleep for a few extra days in her attic bedroom. After some thought, she decided that Mrs G. would probably never find out that she was there. If the estate agent called, she could always tell him that, in order to deter vandals, Mrs G. wanted her to stay until the house was sold. As she stolidly swept bare boards, ready for Dorothy to scrub them, she felt some relief at the idea of gaining a few more days' respite from wandering the streets looking for cheap accommodation while she continued her hunt for a job.

To this end, when packing up the contents of the pantry ready for transfer to the cottage, she had carefully segregated some of the large store of dry goods and hidden them in one of the cellars, where also lay at least a couple of hundredweight of coal which was not worth moving. If absolutely necessary, and if the house took time to sell, she could exist for a number of weeks, she planned, on porridge, potatoes, a little barrel of eggs preserved in isinglass, on bread she would bake for herself and on any scraps left over after the family had left.

Winnie had dealt honestly with the Gilmores during all the years she had been with them. But now, deeply resentful of Louise's indifference to the plight of her servants, she knew she must secure her own survival. If she could not get a job, her only resource would be the workhouse, and she shuddered at the very idea of being reduced to that.

In the Gilmores' new home, the removal men had placed the furniture under Celia's direction. It still needed a little adjustment, but the general effect was so friendly that Betty sank into a chair with a contented sigh, and said, 'It looks lovely, doesn't it?'

'Yes!' Celia did a small dancelike twirl round the centre table, and came to rest by Betty. 'And you did it!' She put her arms round her new friend and kissed her.

Betty said firmly, 'No. I didn't. I simply encouraged you and Mrs Gilmore.' She smiled up at Celia. 'All the pair of you needed was confidence. Between the two of you, you put it all together; and Dad won't send his bill until the end of the month – I'll see to that!'

Celia laughed; she was worried about money, but was sure that, once the Liverpool house was sold, everything would be all right.

Betty asked, 'What about Mrs Fellowes?'

Celia sighed. Before she answered, she took the lid off the teapot and took down a tea caddy from the mantelpiece. As she carefully measured the tea into the pot, she said slowly, 'Well, Mother has encouraged Edna to come to live with us. So she's going to have the back bedroom, next to the bathroom – and we have put into it most of the furniture from the bedroom she had as a girl. Her own furniture will arrive eventually from South America – all beautiful and hand-turned, according to her – so, if Mr Aspen is agreeable, we'll put that into your barn until she is certain about where she will live.' She reached for the kettle which had come to the boil and poured the water on to the tea. Then, as she stirred it, she considered her sister.

She glanced at Betty, and went on, 'Edna's really very odd, Betty, and I worry about her sometimes. It is almost as if she is on the edge of a complete breakdown – and she's no flesh on her at all. I don't know whether she talks to Mother when I'm not with them, but I find it very strange that she never talks about

Paul – or even generally about her life in Brazil. You would think that she would be eager to tell us all about it – because it would be very interesting – but she never says a word to me. It is almost as if it defeated her – if one can be defeated by a country.'

'Perhaps her loss is too great, Celia. Perhaps it is too painful to talk about it. Not only has she lost her husband, but she has lost a country – which she may well have loved. And you said that her little girl was buried in Brazil?'

Celia nodded. She poured the tea and sat down opposite Betty. She offered her a plate of biscuits, and Betty took one. After they had eaten their biscuits, Celia continued her line of thought about Edna. 'I keep getting the feeling that she really didn't care much about Paul. He was a good match and she never complains about him – she just doesn't say anything about him. She's like someone patiently sitting in a railway station, waiting for a train to arrive.

'It puzzles me. It's as if his memory simply does not exist in her mind. Your David's always in your mind. I know, because you mention him with such love all the time, that I wish I had an equivalent memory to sustain me.' The last words were said with real longing.

Betty nodded, and then said lightly, 'You're young enough yet to meet someone.' She pushed her cup across the table, and asked, with the freedom of a friend, if she could have more tea. Celia quickly picked up the teapot and refilled the cup. She then pressed more biscuits on her.

As she settled in her chair again, Celia said, 'I don't have a chance, you know that. Besides, who will look after Mama?'

'She'll be young enough to look after herself for a very long time,' responded Betty a little tartly. She reverted to their discussion of Edna, and said, 'This little house will, unavoidably, make you and Edna live very close to each other – and she may open up, when she gets really used to you – and you to her. Be patient with her. She's obviously not well.'

'Betty, you're a saint, which I am not. But I'll try.'

Suddenly, Louise's voice could be heard raised high in complaint, as the new gate squeaked open. Behind her, Edna gave sharp orders to someone. A heavy weight was dumped at the open front door. There was a sound of men's voices, as Louise came down the passageway and into the little room.

'Oh, tea!' she exclaimed thankfully, and plunked down on a straight chair beside the table. The table had a plum-coloured velvet cloth on it and the pompoms which trimmed its edge got entangled in her handbag. She threatened to drag the cloth and the tea tray off the table. Celia sprang to her aid.

'Good afternoon, Miss Aspen,' she greeted Betty. 'Dear me! What a knot I'm in. No place to lay down a handbag in that poky little hall. I really don't know how we shall manage.'

Betty ignored her complaint. 'I'm Mrs Houghton,' she corrected her rather sharply.

'Of course. I am so sorry, Mrs Houghton.'

As her daughter untangled her handbag from the tablecloth, Louise ordered, 'Make a big fresh pot, Celia. We're exhausted!'

Outside, men gasped, and shouted encouragement to each other to 'Heave!' and Edna admonished them to be careful of her trunks, and told them to carry them straight upstairs.

One of them stepped inside to take a look at the extremely steep staircase, and there was a stubborn male refusal, the excuse being that they would scratch the obviously newly painted walls.

'Unpack 'em first, Ma'am. Then you can ease 'em up more careful,' they advised in chorus.

True Merseysiders who felt they were being pushed too hard, thought Celia with a smile. She herself had come up against such an attitude more than once during the previous month, and had discovered that the working class, no matter how poor it was, had a strong sense of self-preservation. She had learned to respect it.

Edna said something in Portuguese which sounded derogatory, and the indignant men answered her in a united rumble of defence.

Celia, having unravelled her mother from the tablecloth, ignored her request for tea, and went to see what was happening outside.

Betty rose and said she must go back to work. She wished

Louise happiness in her new home, and received a tired, resigned smile in return.

Outside stood a big railway station handcart with two trunks and a large suitcase still on it. Beside the cart lay three huge steamer trunks and a couple of packing cases. Edna was carrying, one in each hand, two large travelling jewellery cases.

Celia faced two red-faced porters standing by the trunks on the path, and a very cross Edna. She said placatingly, 'Don't worry, Edna. We'll manage. The trunks will have to be stored in the garden shed anyway.'

'I won't have handmade leather trunks stored in a place which is probably damp!' snapped Edna in response.

Behind Celia, Betty, trying to get out, edged round another big trunk which had already been dumped in the lobby. 'Hello, Freddy – George,' she greeted both men. 'Good afternoon, Mrs Fellowes.' She cast a critical glance over the trunks and said, 'With respect, Mrs Fellowes, the size of these really is too big for you to get them up the stairs, I am sure. They may get wedged – and almost certainly the staircase wall will be scratched. The men are simply being careful.'

The porters immediately relaxed and looked very self-righteous.

Edna had already met Betty on several occasions and had learned to respect her quick mind. She therefore accepted this professional estimate of size, and, with an effort, controlled her irritation. She said politely, 'Thank you, Mrs Houghton.'

She made way for Betty to get on to the pathway, and then stepped round the trunks and into the house. Betty gravely winked at the porters and touched Celia's arm gently in acknowledgement, as the younger woman whispered a heartfelt 'Thank you.'

After Betty had marched down the red-tiled garden path, her black skirt swinging, her sensible shoes crunching the ever-present sand, the porters lifted the remaining luggage off their handcart. An unsmiling Edna thrust a sovereign into the hand of one of the men, and said, 'You may go.'

Without thanking her, the porters, wooden-faced, pushed the

clumsy vehicle into the lane. After struggling in a muddy puddle, they managed to turn the handcart round. Celia watched them, as they followed Betty towards the main road.

Their good neighbour, Eddie Fairbanks, had cut the front hedge for them, and the cottage now had a view of a patch of rough green grass with a few trees and, at some distance, the thatched roof of the cottage where the fishing family lived. The whole area was so quiet that Celia concluded that the tide must be out. She had not yet had time to walk down to the sea.

The tiny front garden was a trampled mess after the constant comings and goings of workmen and movers, but, in an untouched corner, a rambler rose which Eddie had left unsnipped clung to the hedge and was putting out leaves.

Comforted by the sight of it and by a warm sun, Celia reluctantly turned to face the problems within the house.

Chapter Twenty-Four

The first evening of the family's residence in their new home began peacefully, despite the muddle of clothes hastily unpacked from the trunks and dumped on to beds, and an argument about what to do with the trunks themselves. The trunks were eventually left by the front steps because no one could suggest where to put them, except in the garden shed, which was still awaiting Dorothy's ministrations. Tired out and aching everywhere, Edna mentally abandoned them; what were trunks anyway?

Since Edna and Louise both declared themselves exhausted, Celia laid the table for dinner. She had, some hours earlier, placed the casserole, which Winnie had made for them, in the oven of the range in the living room, to heat up. Now, she put out some bread and butter and made a pot of coffee.

Louise, who had given little thought to the need to eat that evening, looked at the single big dish in the middle of the table, and asked, 'Is that all that Winnie prepared? She said she was going to make dinner for us.'

'She put everything in one big dish, Mama – for simplicity.'

'No soup? No dessert?'

Celia pulled out a chair and sat down; Edna was already seated. She unfolded her linen table napkin and laid it across her lap.

'No, Mama. She simply made lots of meat and vegetables.'

Since her mother made no move to serve, though Celia had set three plates in front of her, she asked, 'Shall I serve?'

'Please.' The reality of her new life struck Louise forcibly. No one was going to cook for them or serve them; they would have to do everything themselves. She sulkily passed the little pile of plates to Celia.

Edna inquired, 'Shall I cut some bread, Mama?'

'Please.' Louise's little mouth was clamped closed. What had she come to? Looking round the cosy little room and then at the sparsely laid table, she again wondered bitterly why Timothy had had to die in the prime of his life – and leave her to rot in a place like this.

Edna sawed three thick slices of bread from the last loaf Winnie would bake for them, and then lifted up the wooden bread board with both hands, to offer pieces to her companions.

As she took a slice, Celia cast a quick, thankful glance at her sister. Now she was installed in the cottage, would she help her?

Louise ate slowly. The casserole was delicious. Celia knew it, but Louise grumbled throughout the meal. She felt terribly confined in the tiny room, she said – they could barely move around in it. She had banged her leg on the metal corner of one of her trunks and it was hurting. Going up and down stairs into freezing bedrooms had given her a chill, she was sure of it – everything was so draughty. 'Perhaps one of you girls would make a fire up there for me?' she whined hopefully.

Neither daughter answered because neither of them wanted to set a precedent. Most people managed without them – with hot water bottles in their beds, Celia finally reminded her.

Edna said wearily that she had a hot water bottle with her, and that perhaps dear Mother would like to borrow it tonight. She could buy one for herself tomorrow in the village.

Louise responded savagely that, somewhere amid the furniture on its way to Aspen's there were probably umpteen hot water bottles. If not, she doubted if she could afford a new one after all the expense of setting up the cottage and moving into it.

Celia said soothingly that she would look for an old brick or a stone to put in the back of the oven to heat for her – wrapped in a towel, it would keep her feet warm in bed. 'Winnie used to have bricks in the back of the oven all the time, to heat the servants' beds,' she informed her mother.

'Servants!' exclaimed Louise. 'They take all kinds of liberties!'

'Well, you will be saved from that in future!' remarked Edna with unexpected acidity.

Louise's answer was icy. 'I am aware of it,' she almost snarled.

Edna helped herself to butter, and Celia asked if anyone was ready for coffee.

'We could have coffee in the front room,' Louise pointed out.

'There isn't a fire there, Mama. It may be rather chilly. And, as yet, there are heaps of boxes piled up in the middle of it. We have to get it tidied up by tomorrow, so that Mr Aspen's man can finish painting it.'

Celia hastily poured the coffee and handed her mother a cup, before she could reply. 'Would you like to sit closer to the fire, in here?' She pointed to her mother's favourite easy chair, carefully installed at the side of the fireplace so that she would be warm, and yet leave a little space to walk round the table. Louise squeezed round Edna's chair and plunked herself down in it.

She waited for Celia to hand her her coffee and then complained that she had nowhere to set it down.

'Mr Fairbanks always puts his cup down on the flat top of his brass fender,' Celia told her with determined cheerfulness.

'Humph.' Louise's grunt conveyed all too well her opinion of Mr Fairbanks' habits.

Louise's remark that she probably could not afford a hot water bottle had reminded Celia that they had to discuss money matters, and also domestic duties. And who was to care for the garden?

At the thought, she felt a little sick inside, but after she had served coffee for Edna and herself, she turned her chair so that she could see the faces of both the other women, and bravely opened up the subject, by saying, 'I imagine, Mama, that you and Edna have discussed what she should contribute as her share of the expenses?'

Without waiting for a reply, she added to Edna, 'When we were talking about your furniture being put in the barn, you told us that you will be receiving funds from Paul's company, so I imagine you will be able to help Mama – at least a little bit. Especially until the house is sold and Cousin Albert has arranged for Mother to have an annuity from that.'

Up to that moment, Louise had not thought that Edna should

contribute to the household; she still thought of her as the dependent young girl she had been before her marriage.

'She's my daughter!' she exclaimed. 'I don't expect any money from her! Any more than I do from you.'

Celia's pale face flushed. She wanted to say indignantly, 'But I earn my food by running after you like a slave. And mighty little thanks, never mind money, I get for it. And ever since she came home, I've been at Edna's beck and call, too.' But wisdom prevailed, and she simply hung her head.

Edna stirred sugar into her coffee. 'Of course I shall contribute a share to the housekeeping, as long as I am living here,' she said indignantly. 'Now we're settled in the cottage, I would myself have brought the matter up tomorrow. I got a letter from Papa Fellowes yesterday, and he has arranged to send me a cheque each month. He has advised me to open a bank account nearby. The first cheque should arrive in a day or two.' She glanced resentfully at her mother. 'Up to now I have had only the money which Paul and I were carrying with us and a little which Papa Fellowes gave me – to help. He is very kind.'

She looked suddenly very forlorn. To comfort her, Celia impulsively put out her hand to cover her sister's shrivelled yellow one. She was rewarded by a wry smile, as Edna withdrew her hand to pick up her coffee cup and sip the cooling drink.

After she had dabbed her lips with her table napkin, Edna went on, 'There is also a thing called a letter of credit, which Paul used to transfer his savings from Salvador – but that's part of his estate, Papa Fellowes said, and it will be some time before that money comes to me. He recommends that, when he is able to cash it for me, I should bank it for emergencies.'

Louise had listened with rapt attention. 'It sounds as if you will be quite well off.'

'I don't know yet. I certainly won't starve.' Edna moved uneasily in her chair, as if agitated by the comment, and then added with real bitterness, 'As yet, I have no idea what I shall be able to do.' How could she say to this self-centred mother of hers that all she wanted to do was to be with Vital. Yet, if she went back to Brazil and married him, people would immediately begin to gossip – and they could both be ruined socially, even if they could find enough money to live on.

Louise was contrite. 'I'm sorry, dear. I should not have asked about your affairs. It is kind of you to offer to contribute to the housekeeping – and I must say that I shall be very grateful for it, since I have to keep two people.' She glanced towards Celia.

Celia flushed even more deeply with embarrassment. She summoned up a smile for Edna, however, and echoed Louise's thanks.

Louise heaved herself out of her chair, leaving her coffee cup resting on the flat surface of the brass fender. 'Well, I suppose I must go upstairs and put away my clothes,' she said wearily. 'It is going to be terribly cold up there. I must put on my velvet jacket.'

Celia got up, too, and mechanically went into the hall to find the velvet jacket and help her mother into it. As the cold silk lining touched her, Louise shivered dramatically, and said, 'Really, Celia, I think you should have lit more fires.'

'It has been a very busy day, Mama, and it *is* the end of April!' Dear God, how am I ever going to cope? she asked herself, and went back into the living room.

Edna had already piled the dishes together, and she said, 'You wash and I'll dry.'

Celia's spirits rose a little. She had earlier put the kettle on the fire, and when it had boiled, had set it on the hob to keep warm for washing dishes.

When she poured the water into the kitchen wash basin, set in a brand-new sink, she suddenly realised that it had two taps. She put down the kettle on the draining board, and there was an immediate hiss as its hot bottom scorched the wood. She snatched it off before it did any real damage, and with a laugh, said to Edna, 'I'd forgotten that, when Mr Aspen put the boiler in, it would be linked to the kitchen sink as well as the bathroom! Like an idiot, I've been running upstairs when I wanted hot water or I've been boiling it. Isn't it wonderful – we've got hot water upstairs and downstairs!'

'It will be a real help,' agreed Edna. 'Where are the tea towels?'

'I suppose Dorothy put them in one of the drawers.'

Though Edna was not very cheerful, she was at least company, thought Celia, and she had volunteered to help. As she inexpertly washed the dishes and handed them to Edna to dry, she ventured a question.

'Did you have many servants in Brazil?'

'I had six indoor ones, and two peons for the garden – and a housekeeper called Conchita.'

'That must have been nice.'

'It was in a way – but it could be terribly boring; they often quarrelled amongst themselves, and then I had to sort them out. And that wasn't everybody. Paul had a Brazilian live-in male secretary, Mr Vital Oliveira; he was very helpful, particularly when I first arrived and could not speak any Portuguese. He would translate for me, and he explained about local customs.' At the latter recollection, she smiled softly down at the saucer she was drying. 'Then there was a chauffeur who lived over the garage – there was a car for city use – these two men were company employees, not mine.'

She put the saucer carefully down on a side table, and took another one from Celia. She continued, 'Paul was away quite a lot of the time, up in the hills to see how the dam was going on – that's how they were going to get electricity, though I must say I don't understand these things. His senior works people and a translator – and the chauffeur – went with him. The chauffeur was in charge of the horses and stores that they had to take along.'

In the weeks that Edna had been at home, this was the longest response that Celia had got to a question, and she realised that it was the first time that she had been alone with Edna. Quite often, after a meal, Edna would vanish off to smoke in her bedroom or, if the weather was fine, into the narrow town garden behind the house. Conversational exchanges, when they occurred, had been between Louise and Edna; if Celia had been in the room, she had been ignored or sent away to do some errand for one of them. And, of course, she told herself, she had been away at the cottage much of the time.

'How did you fill your time?' she asked Edna, and Edna

described a round of visits to other English women – and some Brazilians. 'When I first arrived, I had a Portuguese lesson each morning.'

'Can you speak it?'

'Yes – I think reasonably well now.'

'How clever of you!' Celia's admiration was genuine. 'What else did you do?'

'Sometimes there were festivals, like Christmas and Easter. And they were rather keen on saints' days. The churches had processions, which we used to watch from somebody's balcony. And there were musical evenings . . .' Her voice trailed off. 'I was ill a great deal – I seemed to catch every germ you can imagine, especially after little Rosemary died.'

'That must have grieved you very much.'

'It did. I refused to have any more children until we returned here.'

'How could you refuse? Phyllis says they come every year, once you're married.'

'There are ways.' Edna laughed a little cynically. 'And I just said no.'

The implications of the latter remark were lost on Celia, but she said, 'I wish you would explain that to Phyllis. She has already four little ones, and she looks so ill because the strain of it all is too much for her. I worry a lot about her – I simply must go to see her again soon.'

'Hasn't she ever heard of Margaret Sanger? She wrote a book at the beginning of the war on the need to limit families – and before her, there was, for years, a Malthusian League which spread information about how to do it. Really, Celia! English women should come into the twentieth century.'

Celia emptied and rinsed the washing-up basin. Then she sought a towel in the same drawer that had yielded the tea cloth, and slowly wiped her hands. She was blushing, as she admitted, 'I've never heard of any such thing. And I don't think Phyllis has.'

'Humph. A couple of years ago, a lady called Marie Carmichael Stopes wrote a very clear book about it. I am sure it must be available in Liverpool. Poor Phyllis should read it – she doesn't need to tell her husband!'

While Celia slowly digested this information, Edna folded the cloth she had been using, then realised that it was very wet and shook it out and draped it over the side of the sink to dry. With reference to Phyllis, Edna suggested diffidently, 'It might be a good idea if she first talked to her husband!'

'Him?' Celia's laugh was scornful. 'He's the most thoughtless man you can imagine.' Then she added anxiously, 'I've only seen Phyllis once since little Timothy was born. I wonder if Mother and you could manage, if I went over to Liverpool to see her tomorrow afternoon? I could tell her then. As you know, Dorothy will be here for a few hours to help you. And I should really go and see if the furniture has been put into the barn – and that it's all there.' Her voice was heavy with anxiety. 'And whether Winnie and Dorothy have cleaned the house properly, so that it is ready to be shown to the nursing home lady.'

'You had better ask Mother.' Edna relapsed into her usual melancholy silence, and wandered out of the kitchen and went upstairs, presumably to smoke and to put away the clothes lying on her bed.

Though Celia felt relieved that she had made some headway with Edna, she was overwhelmed with the work which would have to be done on the morrow. Could she, somehow, persuade her mother to go into Hoylake to buy food? The shops would surely send anything she chose – she had seen errand boys trailing around on their delivery bikes when she had been in the village before. And then someone must at least make the living-room fire and keep it up, so that they could cook, someone would have to wipe the mud from the lobby and sweep up the kitchen, make the beds; perhaps Dorothy would do those jobs just for tomorrow.

And we must decide what to do about the garden.

Every time she mentally went through the list and considered its long-term implications, however, the jobs came back to her.

Already tired to death with the effort of the previous few weeks, she wanted to scream.

Impulsively she yanked open the back kitchen door, stiff from new paint, and stared into the wilderness of the back garden.

Fresh sea air blew in upon her, making her skirt and apron billow. It caught at tendrils of her hair and blew them out of their confining pins. She thankfully lifted her tired face to it. A full moon in a sky empty of cloud gave good illumination.

In all her visits to the cottage, she had always walked towards Hoylake, never towards the sea – she had simply been too busy. And it was not cold this evening, she thought. Spring is here.

Left on the back of a chair was a shawl, discarded by her mother in favour of her heavy velvet house jacket. She snatched it up and whipped it round her shoulders. Her outdoor shoes lay, waiting to be cleaned, on a piece of newspaper by the kitchen door. She kicked off her house slippers and slid her little feet into them. Not bothering to tie the laces, she stepped out of the house and closed the kitchen door softly behind her. There was no back gate, so she ran round the side of the house.

When she reached the front gate, she turned right and right again, so that she faced the sea. A narrower lane continued before her. Bending to the wind, she joyfully took it.

Chapter Twenty-Five

Half stumbling over her loose shoelaces, she ran down towards the sea wall.

Between the cottage and the ocean, a huge dyke guarded the common land from the inroads of the remorseless sea, and she could hear the gentle slap of the waves rippling against the other side of this concrete embankment. The tide must be nearly full, she thought with sudden happiness.

Before climbing the embankment, she paused to catch her breath.

The moon lit up the coarse grass of the common and the rough surface of the dyke. A pair of oystercatchers, disturbed by her hurrying footsteps, fluttered out of the grass, to rise and then settle a little further away, to await the turn of the tide, when they would go hunting over the bare damp sand.

Faintly she could hear young voices calling to each other. It sounded as if a party had come out to enjoy a swim in the moonlit sea.

Feeling a little envious, she hitched up her skirt and climbed the steep land side of the embankment. The tide was coming in quite fast, she noted. Further out, towards the horizon, great waves foamed over the Hoyle sandbank.

She glanced to her right, where in the near distance, the Leasowe lighthouse, long disused, stood like a ghostly monument to forgotten seamen. The old castle beyond it was invisible, as was the new clutter of makeshift shacks, bereft of water or sanitation, which had, during the past year or two, been built by poverty-stricken homeless people on what was common land. A faint glow on the horizon marked where Liverpool lay on the other side of the Mersey Estuary.

About thirty feet out, a dozen or more people were cavorting in the water and splashing each other.

Holding down her skirts with one hand against the whipping wind and clutching her shawl with the other, she glanced to her left. Far on the horizon lay the dark hump of Wales pinpricked by an occasional light. Between it and her, she knew, lay the treacherous mouth of the River Dee with its infamous shifting sands waiting to drown the unwary.

A sharp shout from the water drew her eyes back to the bathers, and she was startled to realise that they were all naked.

She was immediately shocked and disapproving. She had swum many times herself at Rhyl, but always garbed, like other bathers, in a black woollen bathing costume, which, though it showed her figure, certainly covered her from neck to knee. And in Rhyl there were always bathing machines, drawn by horses a few feet into the sea itself, where one could change one's clothes and then slip discreetly into the water. Here, she could clearly see in the moonlight the bouncing breasts of women and the flash of male buttocks as men dived under the waves to tease the women.

'Come on, girl! Hurry up. Take your clothes off and come in,' said a male voice behind her, and someone gave her bottom a playful smack as if to encourage her to go down to the water.

She spun round.

A totally nude man was rocking on his heels in front of her. She was appalled, and her mouth fell open in a gasp.

She had never seen a naked man before, and his hairiness revolted her. A shock of black hair, a huge black moustache, a black doormat on the chest which tapered down over a protruding stomach to a bunch of hair out of which dangled, instead of the fig leaf on statues, the appendage which Phyllis had once tried to describe to her. Heavy hairy legs and huge ugly feet reminded her of an ape in the zoo.

As he snatched merrily at her shawl, he became, suddenly, a menace. 'Come on, now. Don't be shy,' he urged, breathing the smell of beer into her face, as he danced lightly in front of her to keep himself warm. 'All the other girls are in already.'

'How dare you!' she hissed frigidly, clutching her shawl close to her neck.

He was a little nonplussed. 'Well, what are you here for? You don't have to be such a prude. Come in and have some fun. Don't be silly.'

But, in panic, she dodged round him and was gone, slipping and sliding down the concrete slope towards the cottage, regardless of torn stockings or loose shoelaces, running along the shadowed lane, panting with fear.

For a moment, he stood watching her while he shivered slightly in the wind. Then he shrieked, 'Tally-ho! Tally-ho!' and, with arms waving, ran sure-footed down the slope after her.

His hunter's cry was apparently heard by other males, who answered promptly from the water side of the embankment. Two more men scrambled, dripping, to the top.

Regardless of the sudden cold of the wind on their bare skins, all three followed the fleeing figure down the lane, whooping joyfully as they went.

Celia glanced back and screamed in pure terror, her belief in the friendliness of her new neighbours gone.

O Lord! No back gate to the cottage garden. She shot round to the front, straight into the arms of another man.

In pure hysteria, she screamed again and again and struggled in a pair of strong arms, while her shocked mother, who had heard her, pushed hard in order to open her bedroom window, stiff from its new paint.

Suddenly the window gave, and Louise was nearly precipitated out of it. 'Celia,' she shrieked. 'What on earth's going on?'

Chapter Twenty-Six

❧

Strolling up and down in front of the cottages while he enjoyed a last smoke before bedtime, Eddie Fairbanks had hardly time to stuff his pipe into his jacket pocket before he caught the fleeing young woman in his arms.

'Jesus! What's up, luv?' he gasped, as three satyrs came tearing round the hedge, shrieking, 'View halloo!' as if they had sighted a hunted fox, to resolve themselves in seconds into three slightly shamefaced young men stopped in their tracks.

They shivered in the wind.

'What the hell are you doing?' Eddie demanded furiously of them over Celia's shoulder. 'Get out of here, you stupid bastards. Frightening a decent young woman to death!' He glanced down at Celia. 'It's all right, luv. It's all right.' He glared again at the young men fidgeting uncertainly before him. 'Now you get going and get yourselves covered, or I'll call the military police, I will.'

An exclamation from the bedroom window caused the men to look up. They were being viewed with horror by a portly lady in a nightgown and frilly bedcap. Behind her loomed another female, who was tittering loudly.

The titters did it. They turned and fled as quickly as they had come, while Celia clung to Eddie, her face buried in his shoulder as if he were her father. At the sound of his voice, she had ceased to scream, but she was still shaking with fright.

'Come on, luv. They've gone.' He felt behind his back, to open the Gilmore front gate. 'I'll take you in to your mam. She'll make some tea for you. The boys don't mean no harm – they was just teasing you, I bet.' Holding her firmly, in case she fainted, he eased her up the garden path.

It was Edna, in a dressing gown, who opened the door to him, while Louise, wrapped in a quilt, stumped slowly down the staircase, saying crossly, as she descended, 'Celia! What are you doing outside at this time of night?'

Eddie ignored the older woman and said to Edna, 'She's had a proper scare, Ma'am. Take care of her.'

'Who were they?' Edna asked, as quite gently, she helped a weeping Celia across the threshold, and passed her to her scolding mother.

'They're probably ex-servicemen, Ma'am. There is a number of big houses round here as is nursing homes, so to speak – there's one full of blind, waiting to get into St Dunstan's. This lot was probably mostly shell-shocked or in for treatment for illness or gas in the trenches.' He sighed heavily. 'There's so many of them that it's easy for them to get out at night, and they come out to the pubs – and people stand them drinks – and they pick up the local girls.' He looked at the shrewd brown eyes before him, lit up by the oil lamp hanging in the hall. 'You know how it is.'

'I do have some idea,' Edna responded dryly. 'Though I cannot imagine what made Celia go out.' She gathered her dressing gown more tightly round her thin figure, and Eddie stepped back down the step. Then he hesitated, and said, 'Be careful of Miss Celia – she's gone through a lot lately. And done a lot.'

'It has been a difficult time for all of us, Mr Fairbanks.'

He was dismissed. He absently took his pipe out of his pocket, and looked at it. 'Oh, aye. It's a hard time for everybody. Good night.'

He plodded slowly down the path, carefully shutting the gate after him and went back to his empty house.

As he knocked the dottle out of his pipe on the top bar of the fireplace and then refilled it with fresh tobacco, he thought of the silly naked youngsters he had just told off.

'Half crazy with what they've been through,' he considered. 'Under twenty-five, I bet, but with four years of bloody war already behind them. Hell-bent because life don't mean much to them any more. Nerves shot; lungs ruined.'

As he tamped down the tobacco in his pipe, he sank slowly into his easy chair.

He was reminded suddenly of the earl in whose gardens he had served so faithfully. With three sons killed, when the old man died the earldom would probably die out – or go to some far-distant cousin safe in the Colonies. Proper cut up, the old earl had been. But maybe it was better than having them come back as crazy as the lads who had chased Miss Celia.

You could hate the aristocracy and the middle classes as much as you liked, he pondered sadly, but you had to admit that their families had paid a frightful price in the war – if you thought of the losses in proportion to numbers. And they were the educated, the future leaders – Eddie was very feudal in his outlook. In his book, rank had its obligation to provide leaders, as it had done since time began, and keep in line young louts like the men who had chased poor Celia.

There were thousands of working-class lads who never saw a battlefield, he ruminated – and thank goodness for that – safe in factories and works, they had been. And a tremendous number had been turned down by the army doctors as being physically unfit for service; rotten food, rotten housing, polluted rivers and air had wreaked havoc on the health of those who lived in the slums of the cities – and yet that very bad health had actually saved them from being flung into the furnace – it was strange how bad luck could become good luck, he mused.

But as long as he could stand up and walk, there was no excuse for an earl's son not to fight – or, come to that, for the boys who volunteered from Liverpool offices – the work they did in banks and insurance offices, shops and professions could be done by women. Likewise, the work of men on the farms. Boys like them simply answered the call to the colours and joined the Liverpool Pals – and knew they were going out to die, like Mrs Gilmore's boys next door, though one of them hadn't gone to France – he'd been drowned with Lord Kitchener, Miss Celia had told him.

The thought of young George Gilmore's drowning reminded him of the lads like his own son, merchant seamen who had drowned in thousands, sent to the bottom by submersibles – submarines, they called them now – the devil's work.

As he remembered the expressions on the faces of the scandalous young men he had chastised, his mood lightened and he chuckled. They had looked such utter fools. How Miss Celia had panicked – and her a brave little thing if ever there was one.

Then he told himself that it was no laughing matter; despite the cold wind on their damp naked bodies, they might have managed to rape her. They'd probably leave a few babies in the district before the military got round to putting them back into barracks or into better treatment in military hospitals.

But barracks and hospitals, wherever nurses and doctors could be found, were still full of the terribly wounded, unlikely to get better – or, if they did, with lives foreshortened by years in the trenches.

And their womenfolk – how were they managing? He knew a number of mothers and wives already harried to death by the need to care for helpless, crippled servicemen – and on miserably small pensions, to boot. Or widowed with young children and no man to help to look after them. Betty Houghton was lucky that she had her father, Ben Aspen, to keep a hold on young Alfie.

He pulled himself up. 'Tush, man. You're getting morbid – it's too much being by yourself,' he chided himself. 'Maybe it's good that you've got some neighbours at last.'

He heaved himself out of his chair and went across the room to find his bottle of rum.

Chapter Twenty-Seven

Followed by her mother, Celia stumbled into the living room and collapsed. She put her head down on her knees and sobbed helplessly, while Louise stood over her and continued to storm about stupid girls who went out at night and brought all kinds of trouble down on themselves.

When Edna entered the little room, she hesitated. The oil lamp on the mantelpiece still burned, but the fire had gone out and it would take time to rebuild it in order to boil water to make tea. She went to the sideboard and, with difficulty because of lack of space, opened the cupboard door and pulled out the first bottle she could reach. She managed, also, to open the matching cupboard on the other side sufficiently to get out a teacup. She had no idea where Dorothy had put the wine glasses.

With a little shrug, she filled the richly decorated cup with white wine.

She had almost to push Louise out of the way before she could kneel down by her sister. 'Have some wine,' she urged. 'It will help you.' She put her free arm round Celia's shoulders and pulled her a little upright.

Edna's touch was kind and Celia made an effort to stop sobbing, as she thankfully turned towards her. She obediently swallowed some of the wine, which was pleasantly sweet. Then she pulled her handkerchief out from her sleeve and blew her nose.

'I'm so sorry,' she gasped, and took the little cup and finished its contents. 'I was just so frightened. They were naked. Lots of them, men and women in the sea!'

While Edna laughed at this, Louise stopped in the middle of

her tirade, and exclaimed, 'Women?' Then she turned on Edna, and snapped, 'This is no laughing matter!'

Edna giggled. 'The men looked so funny!'

Celia put down the empty cup on the floor beside her feet. Still sobbing, she said defensively, 'They looked horrible to me. I was frightened to death.' She turned back to her sister, in whose eyes humour still twinkled.

'Haven't you ever seen a naked man before?' Edna asked.

'No! Of course not!'

'Really, Edna!' This was from Louise.

'Well, Mother, very few men look good in their skins.'

Louise's voice was icy. 'This is not a suitable subject for discussion. You are not to go out alone at night in future, Celia. You would never have done it in Liverpool, and why you should do so here is beyond me.'

Celia sighed, and continued to sniffle. 'I wanted to see the tide coming in.'

'Well, do it in the daytime – there are two tides a day on this part of the coast. Use your common sense, girl, if you have any.'

Louise pulled the trailing quilt closer round her shoulders. 'Now, let's get back into bed.'

Edna got slowly to her feet. She was taller than the other two women, and suddenly, although garbed only in a dressing gown, she seemed authoritative, as she said sharply to Louise, 'You are being too hard on poor Celia, Mother. It is not her fault if she doesn't understand much about men. I would myself have assumed that out here in the country I would be quite safe, even at night.'

Louise was shocked at being chided by a daughter. She opened her mouth to answer indignantly, and then thought better of it; as a result of their earlier discussion that evening, it seemed Edna was likely to be a source of much needed funds. She clamped her lips tightly. The quilt swished round her as she stalked out of the room and up the stairs.

Celia was dumbfounded at the sudden defence offered on her behalf. With her mouth half open in surprise, she slowly wiped her eyes and then rose from the sofa.

Edna said, 'I'll come up with you and see you into bed. You'll be fine in the morning. You don't have to be so frightened. I am sure they were only teasing you.'

At Edna's unexpected kindness, Celia wanted to cry again. Instead, she took Edna's outstretched hand and allowed herself to be led upstairs. Though the comfortable warmth of the wine was slowly spreading through her, her breath still came in small shuddering sobs.

In the bedroom, Edna quickly struck a match and lit the bedside candle. Then she shook out Celia's cotton nightgown from the small embroidered nightie case laid on her bed, and held it while Celia shyly undressed. As soon as she had taken off her camisole and eased the straps of her vest off her shoulders, she slipped the gown over herself and modestly completed her undressing under its voluminous folds.

Edna sat down on the end of the bed, and said quite crossly, 'I am not sure who annoys me most – Mother or my mother-in-law.'

Celia sat down by her, in order to peel off her black cotton stockings. She said in amazement, 'But I thought you loved Mother?'

'Well, of course I do – she's my mother. But that doesn't mean that she isn't infuriating. She forgets that I'm a grown woman married for years and used to my own household. She treats me like a little girl, and you like a companion-help, who must do what she's told or she'll lose her job.' As she shook her head in annoyance, her black plaits hanging over her breast swayed slightly as if they were in total agreement with her remarks. 'Although Mother has had enough grief to last her a lifetime, she is a very capable woman, and I'm fed up with her constant complaints; she isn't suffering any more than millions of other women. And she hasn't done anything much towards this move to the cottage. I am nearly as bad, because I've tended to sit and listen to her, partly because I am quite bewildered by my own problems and the strangeness of England. You've done all the work.'

Celia did not reply. She got up slowly and hung her stockings on the back of a chair with her other clothes. Edna, she thought, had been very kind this evening. As she pulled back the bed-clothes, she said, 'Perhaps Mother will change, as she gets used to having you near her again as an adult.'

'I doubt it,' replied Edna gloomily. She rose from the narrow single bed, so that Celia could get into it. Her hands were clasped tightly in front of her, as she added, as if forcing herself, 'I am sorry I haven't been much help to you. I've also had a great deal to do which has involved a lot of correspondence with Papa Fellowes – and all the time I've had to think carefully what I am to do – because my life, like Mother's, has been reduced to chaos. There is nothing left of my married life – no home, no servants; and a very difficult change of country, with no one here to depend upon except Papa Fellowes – he really is doing his best to order my financial affairs for me.'

Her face pinched and white against her pillow, her fright forgotten, Celia was astounded as Edna looked down at her and asked, 'Do you think you will be all right now?'

'I think so,' Celia replied. She snuggled down under the bed-clothes. 'Thank you, Edna. I'm so grateful. We'll talk some more tomorrow. I tend to forget your loss, but I am sorry about it; you must be feeling absolutely awful. And Mother is still very upset after losing Father – it takes time.'

Edna's responding smile was a little grim, but she bent down to kiss Celia on her forehead. 'Shall I blow out the candle?'

'Yes, please. And I'm sorry, Edna, that I was such an idiot.'

Unexpectedly Edna laughed. 'It is not you who are the idiot,' she assured her, and went quietly to her own room, leaving a bewildered, but not unhappy, Celia to a night of disordered dreams.

Chapter Twenty-Eight

Celia had forgotten to set her alarm clock and when, the next morning, she dragged herself out of bed, put on her grey woollen dressing gown and went downstairs, she found Edna ineffectually trying to build the living-room fire.

She was not having much success because she had not yet shovelled out yesterday's ashes from underneath the grate. Celia went through to the kitchen and brought a bucket and shovel and an old newspaper.

Still in their dressing gowns, they spread the newspaper over the hearth rug and side by side they kneeled down before the cold hearth, while Celia passed on the lessons on fire-making given her by Dorothy.

They sat back on their heels to watch the wood begin to crackle under the coal. Then, covered with dust from the removal of the ashes, they finally got up triumphantly, as the coal caught and began to blaze.

Celia went to fill the kettle. 'Better take Mother up some tea,' she said, as she turned the hob over the lighted coals and laid the kettle on it.

Though she agreed, Edna's voice held doubt. She said, 'Be careful what you do today, because you'll set the pattern for the future.' She paused, while, with her hands, she brushed down the front of her dressing gown. Then she went on firmly, 'Don't take Mother's breakfast up to her, for example. She's not an invalid, and there is no reason why she should stay in bed for breakfast.'

Weary as she was from her adventure of the previous night, Celia had taken it for granted that carrying her mother's breakfast up to her bed was precisely what she would have to do every day of her life. At her sister's advice, she gulped. 'I'm sure Mama will be awfully cross,' she said apprehensively.

'If you've any sense, Celia, she's going to be a lot angrier before you've finished.' Edna paused to look her sister up and down, and then went on, 'You look just about as ill as anyone could look and still be on their feet. You should see a doctor. I never could understand why you let Mother walk all over you.' Her voice rose. 'Your life isn't worth living – and it won't ever be unless you do something about it.'

This sudden outburst from her strong-minded sister surprised and confused Celia so much that she could not reply. She was trembling as she went back into the little kitchen to wash her hands again under the kitchen tap, before laying the table for breakfast.

Edna followed her, her own grubby hands held loosely in front of her, while she awaited her turn at the tap. She went on, 'Since coming home, I've been so upset myself that I've tried to keep out of things between you and Mother. But after being away for seven years and then seeing you, it hit me like a hammer. Though you're a grown woman, you still fawn around her – and cringe when she shouts at you. I know I'm tactless, and I've found myself ordering you around just as she does; then I feel so cross when you obey me, instead of telling me to get up and do it myself. But, as I said last night, my own life has been torn apart – and I'm not finding widowhood very easy.' Her lips quivered, and she sounded suddenly tired and dispirited.

'Even my servants aren't around me any more,' she continued. 'I've been used to having servants at my beck and call all the time – and I tend to expect somebody else to do everything for me. I don't even have a home of my own,' she finished up unhappily. She stood chewing her lower lip, as if she might say more about her predicament, but had thought better of it and remained silent.

Celia slowly dried her hands on the towel, while Edna washed hers. She was suddenly frightened by Edna's reference to seeing a doctor, but there was no doubt that her sister meant well.

Finally, she responded timidly, 'You're being so thoughtful of me, Edna, that I almost want to cry. Until last night, I had no idea that you felt like that. And the loss of Paul must be dreadful. I am so sorry – I've thought only of Mother, and not much about you.'

She handed the towel to Edna. At the same time, her old terror surfaced, that she was in some way physically handicapped or mentally ill and had never been told about it. 'Do you really think I'm ill?' she asked anxiously.

'I think you are probably very run-down – you look it. I think you need a good holiday – away from Mother.'

Celia laughed. 'That's impossible. Mother would never allow it – she would say she could not spare me.'

'Well, I'm here for the time being. And we could get a woman to come to clean the floors, to help out. I think it could be done.'

Celia sighed. 'I don't have any money to see a doctor – or go on a holiday.'

'Really?'

'Of course not.'

'I assumed Father had made you a reasonable allowance, since he kept you at home. Or had, at least, made some financial arrangement, like insurance, an annuity, or something – kept separate from his business debts – to cover you when he and Mother died. He must surely have thought about you.'

'He gave me pin money – the same amount as he paid Ethel.'

'The skivvy?' Edna asked, as they moved slowly back into the living room.

'Yes. Mother always bought my clothes – out of her dowry money.'

Edna made a face. 'They look like it!' she replied.

As she picked up a teapot and went to make her mother's tea, Celia glanced down at her old-fashioned black skirt, which lay on the back of a dining chair. She had brought it downstairs to sponge and press it. It was good wool and warm, she had always told herself. She had had it since before the war; it would never wear out.

While Celia made the tea, Edna laid the table, her mouth clamped shut very like her mother in a temper.

'I'll put some water on to boil eggs, and I'll make some toast,' she said. 'It's an easy breakfast.' And, as Celia carefully carried a cup of tea towards the hall and staircase, she added, 'And don't say anything to Mother about what we're going to do today.'

Celia paused. Mystified, she asked, 'Why not?'

'Because I'll make sure that Mother shops for food and cooks the dinner. It won't hurt her; she won't have to carry anything – the shops will deliver. She has to wake up and begin living again.' She shrugged a little hopelessly. 'You and I can't do everything. And it'll give you a chance to go this afternoon to see Phyllis.'

'Oh, Edna! Could you arrange that? I do want to see Phyllis. I must also go to Hoylake to see that the furniture in Mr Aspen's barn is all right. Betty says I should advertise it in the local paper.'

Edna said grimly, 'Betty's right. Getting all that collection sold is going to take time, too. You leave Mother to me.'

It was a fairly silent breakfast, except for a monologue delivered by Louise. When Edna had called up the stairs to say that breakfast was ready, Louise had descended slowly. She was still dressed in a bedcap and dressing gown, and her first complaint was that there was no hot water coming out of the bathroom tap. How was she to have a bath? And she felt almost too tired to get up for breakfast, she announced dolefully; Celia should know very well that she had to eat before she got out of bed.

A little scared, and anxious to placate her, Celia swallowed a spoonful of egg, and ignored the complaint about breakfast. She told her, 'The fire takes some time to heat the water in the big boiler behind the fireplace, Mama. In about an hour, you should be able to bath.'

'It was always hot when I was ready to get up in the old house.'

Before Celia could reply to this, Edna said smartly, 'And Ethel got up at five thirty to make sure that it was hot for you.'

'Humph.' Louise could not answer the implied reproof, so she ignored it. 'The toast is burned round the edge and you haven't trimmed the crust off it,' she fretted as she looked at it with disgust.

Edna picked up the toasting fork, and stuck a slice of bread on to its prongs. She handed the fork to Louise, and said with glacial sweetness, 'Make another slice yourself, Mother, and then you can be sure it is exactly as you like it.'

Celia closed her eyes in anticipation of an explosion, but her mother stared at Edna with shocked amazement and then, when she found her voice, responded with resignation. 'I suppose this will do.' She ate the offending toast with every indication of acute distaste. She then asked for another cup of tea and, with this in hand, once again retired to her bedroom.

As soon as her back was turned, Edna gravely winked at her sister.

'Oh, Edna, you are cruel!'

'Cruel to be kind,' was the unrepentant response.

When the sound of their mother's footsteps on the stairs had died away, Edna said, 'You go and get washed quickly before she gets into the bathroom. And go to Hoylake. You could go straight from there to Liverpool to see Phyllis, if you like.'

'Would it be all right?'

'Of course it would, you idiot. These things have to be done.' Edna looked around the little room, which, by this time, was rather untidy. 'I'll wash up and make this room respectable, and each of us can keep our own bedrooms clean and tidy.'

Celia leaned back in her chair. 'You're wonderful,' she said. 'I wouldn't dare suggest that to Mother.'

'Well, if her room becomes a mess, that's her headache. I'm not going to make her bed or clean the room for her – and neither should you have to.'

Celia hastily wiped her mouth with her serviette, folded it and put it into the silver ring her Great-aunt Blodwyn had given to her at her christening. Then she eased herself round the table, planted a shy kiss on Edna's cheek and fled quietly upstairs, to get washed and to count her last remaining bit of pocket money to see if she had the train fare to Liverpool and then enough for a tram out to West Derby. She still had a couple of pounds given to her by Louise, to cover her various expenses while she had been travelling backwards and forwards from West Derby to the cottage; it never occurred to her to use any of it for a personal expedition, like going to see Phyllis.

She was so filled with hope and her wonderment at Edna's outburst that she forgot, for the moment, the sickeningly unpleasant encounter of the previous evening. As she quickly combed her hair into a neat bun at the back of her head, she said, in astonishment, to her reflection, 'Edna cares about you. I really believe she does.'

Less than an hour later, she was greeted enthusiastically by Betty Houghton, who slid down from her high stool behind the rough wooden counter of her father's office. She closed an account book, before she took Celia's hand, and said, 'Everything looks all right. I don't think any of the furniture was damaged. The movers had it all wrapped in padded quilts. Come and have a look.'

She took down a key from amongst a number hanging near her desk, and together they walked briskly across the yard. It was busy, and Betty explained that her father had recently acquired a good sub-contract to build city housing in Birkenhead that summer.

'He's looking for skilled craftsmen, but they're hard to find. There's a lot of men looking for jobs, but they're not skilled – and it looks to me as if a lot of them ought to be in hospital still. He wants at least four brickies and some hod carriers.'

'Brickies?'

Betty laughed at her bewilderment. 'Bricklayers. He'd a nice young man here today, but he looked like a ghost. Though he said he'd done six months of bricklaying, before he joined the army. Dad couldn't even offer him a labouring job – he said he'd never stay the course, he was too run down.'

'Poor soul.'

'And as for hod carriers – you've got to be as strong as an ox to carry hods of bricks and mortar up to a brickie all day,' Betty informed her, as she unlocked the great barn.

The residue of Celia's home looked very forlorn. All the

piled-up furniture had a veil of dust on it. Dismantled bed frames from the guest rooms had been leaned against the walls; their horsehair mattresses had been laid on the tops of tables and sideboards and against the fronts of chests of drawers to protect them from being scratched. Pictures of all kinds had been laid face to face on top of the mattresses. Rolls of rugs, barrels of china and ornaments and packing cases of unwanted kitchen equipment lay, as yet unopened, along the back wall.

Celia looked at the mighty pile in some despair, and exclaimed, 'Phew! I'll never manage to sort it all out, never mind sell it.'

'I think you will sell it and at decent prices, if you advertise it in the Hoylake paper – and, say, in the *Evening Express*.' With a chuckle, Betty flung out her arms as if to a waiting audience and declaimed, '"For Sale. Handsome fruitwood furnishings, many Georgian pieces. Sale includes fine china, ornaments, carpets, etc., also some kitchen equipment." That should do it.' She drew a happy face in the dust on what had been Timothy Gilmore's desk. 'What bothers me is how you are going to price it – I'm sure some of it is valuable – and I've no idea about the pictures, for example. Have you?'

'I've been worrying about that. Your friend Mrs Jowett helped me a lot – she was really sweet – but I'll still be guessing. I thought the first thing I could do would be to look in the very good furniture shops in Liverpool and see their prices for new things. I'm going over to Liverpool to see Phyllis Woodcock this afternoon. I could take a quick peep in that nice furniture shop in Bold Street, before catching the tram out to West Derby.'

'Well, at least you'll know that your price should be lower than theirs – though I'm not even very certain about that – those chairs are very fine; if they are antiques they may be worth more,' Betty replied, pointing to a neat line of refugees from the Gilmore dining room. She turned and smiled a little wryly at her friend. 'We're both out of our depths on this.'

'I have the books, of course, that Mrs Jowett lent me, as a rough guide to the age of what I have. She said to set the price at the most you feel you can get, and come down very slowly if someone is interested in a piece.'

'She would know.' Betty stared at the wild conglomeration before her. She herself did not know how to advise her friend. She suggested, 'I think there are one or two second-hand furniture shops in Berry Street, at the top of Bold Street. You could go in and ask the price of anything that looks familiar to you. You might get some ideas.'

Celia agreed and, almost reluctantly, they locked up and went back to the office.

Celia looked worried. 'I could always get an auctioneer, I suppose,' she said.

Betty tried to cheer her up. 'An auctioneer will just get what he can for you. Out here, where there are so many high-class homes, such auctions always draw antique dealers and they bid low. Unless you're desperate for money, don't try to hurry the selling. Learn a bit first.'

'Mother is sure that we are poor as church mice, Betty. But Cousin Albert believes that we shall manage quite well once the house is sold. And I must say that I have been agreeably surprised at how much we have managed to do with what little money Mother had. And Edna has promised to help.' She stopped, and then said with a rueful grin, 'I'm the only one who doesn't have a bean.'

'Perhaps you could get a job.'

'Me? How could I? I don't know anything. Anyway, Mother wouldn't let me – I've got to sell that barnful first, because Mother's not going to stir a finger, as far as I can see. And it can't stay here for ever.'

'I don't see why your mother can't help you.'

'You have to remember that she's bereaved.'

'So is everybody,' responded Betty a little sharply, as she thought of her husband lying in a mass grave at Messines Ridge.

Celia bit her lower lip. 'Of course. I know, Betty.' Betty was so brave, she thought wistfully. She sighed, and said that she would come over in a couple of days, to make an inventory of the furniture, before pricing it. 'If I've got everything listed in a notebook I can put a likely price by each piece. So that I don't get flummoxed.'

Betty tried to pull herself together by concentrating on Celia's problems. Before she replied, she told herself for the umpteenth time that it was no good moping about David; it wouldn't bring him back. With forced gaiety, she teased, 'A notebook sounds most professional. We'll make a businesswoman of you yet!'

Celia laughed, and they stood talking for a few minutes amid the busy whirl of the yard, before Celia reluctantly said goodbye.

Chapter Twenty-Nine

Holding young Timothy George against her shoulder, Phyllis answered her front door herself. Two-year-old Eric, his cheeks stained by recent tears, clung to her skirt. Phyllis's careworn face lit up as she saw Celia, and she stepped back to make way for her friend to enter the narrow malodorous hall. 'Come in – come in, dear,' she said. 'How nice of you to come such a long way. How are you?'

She opened the door of a tiny front sitting room, which had the dank airlessness of a room not much used, and, as Celia responded politely to her inquiry, she led the way in.

'Do sit down, Seelee. I'll ask Lily to make some tea for us.'

She hastened kitchenwards, while Eric, with his finger in his mouth, stood in the doorway and stared at the visitor.

Prior to taking a tram out to West Derby, Celia had walked rapidly down Lord Street, Church Street and Bold Street to take a quick look in the windows of the one or two furniture shops that she found; as she went along, she jotted down prices in her notebook.

Near St Luke's Church, she had found two second-hand furniture shops. She ventured shyly into both, and even more shyly asked the prices of one or two pieces amid their dusty stock, which were similar to those her mother owned; they had little of the quality of her mother's furnishings or of the style of Mrs Jowett's stock. She stored away the information that second-hand shop owners did not seem to mind if you just wandered round and looked at what they had. Her inspection made her realise that there was quite a difference between second-hand and antique shops.

She was both tired and late by the time she arrived at Phyllis's house, and she sat down thankfully in a pretty Victorian armchair. The room was familiar to her from many visits, when the friends had often shared their doubts and unhappinesses with each other – not many happinesses, thought Celia a little sadly.

She smiled at Eric and invited him to come to sit on her lap.

Eric refused to budge from the doorway until his mother returned to sit opposite her guest. As he moved close to Phyllis and rested his head against her arm, she laid Timothy George in her lap. He was awake, so Celia asked if she might nurse him.

'Of course you can,' Phyllis said and carefully laid the child in Celia's arms. 'And how is dear Mrs Gilmore?' she asked with brittle brightness.

Celia chucked little Timothy George under his chin and he kicked his tiny feet quite happily at the attention. Celia sighed at the thought of her mother. She replied, 'She's a little depressed at leaving her old home – and she misses Papa very much.'

'Naturally,' Phyllis responded politely, though she could not imagine that one would miss a husband very much.

The conversation threatened to languish. It was disappointing to Celia, who was used to Phyllis's pouring out the latest news about the small ills of her brood or about her husband's complaints. She never knew how to deal with the latter, but, in talking the matter out comfortably with Celia, Phyllis had always seemed to gain fresh courage. Today, however, she seemed absent-minded, as if she could not bring her thoughts to bear on what her visitor was saying.

Celia smiled down at the baby and inserted a finger into his tiny hand. The child grasped it, and Celia laughed. Before the organisation of the move to the cottage had fallen on to her shoulders and absorbed most of her time, she had managed to run over to see the new baby only once. It did not seem to have grown much so she now asked, 'Is he gaining weight all right?'

'I think so. My milk isn't coming in as well as it should, and he doesn't like the cow's milk with which I supplement it.'

Celia made a face at the baby. 'Poor Timothy George!' Her

eyes were on the child, and she did not see the fleeting despair of his mother's expression.

Lily, the Woodcocks' cook-general, pushed the door open with her backside. She eased Eric out of the way with a nudge from her bent knee, and set the tea tray down on a small table in front of his mother. The maid's apron was crumpled and grubby, and, as she straightened up, she pushed untidy bits of hair back off her face with her forearm. 'Will I be cutting the bread and butter for Christopher and Alison's tea now?' she asked, her accent sounding thick and ugly as if she had a cold. 'They'll be coming in from school soon.'

Phyllis replied mechanically. 'Yes, please. Open the new pot of plum jam for them.'

'When can Eric go to school?' Celia asked.

'When he is three – in September.'

'That should give you a little more time to yourself, with only baby Timothy at home.'

'I suppose.'

Celia wanted to bring up Edna's advice that it was not necessary to have babies one after the other. Though she felt that it was momentous news, she did not know how to open the subject; it was not something for a single lady to talk about. It savoured of wicked private subjects.

Instead, she said brightly, 'During the school holidays, you should bring the children out to visit us. We could have a picnic on the shore, and they could paddle.' Maybe Edna could talk more frankly to Phyllis and tell her exactly how a steady flow of infants could be brought to a halt.

Phyllis said, 'Thank you,' without expressing any particular enthusiasm for seaside picnics.

Celia looked at her friend uneasily. 'Are you all right, Phyllis? Do you feel recovered from having Timothy?'

Phyllis smiled slightly. 'Not quite. I am rather tired, Seelee dear. Timothy has not yet learned to sleep the night through, and Arthur gets so cross when I have to keep getting up to attend to the child.'

Celia knew only too well Arthur Woodcock's cold, whining

voice. She had always wondered what had attracted Phyllis to him – and, in fact, Phyllis herself did not seem to know.

Celia had often thought that, fearing being single all her life, Phyllis had done what most girls did and had accepted the first offer of matrimony which she had received from a man with prospects. According to his wife, bearing in mind the number of bank staff who had been killed in the war, Arthur certainly had reasonable prospects of promotion. She had remarked, 'He was fortunate that his weak chest kept him out of the army.'

Phyllis had, during an earlier visit, mentioned that women who had served as bank clerks during the conflict were not being encouraged to stay on. 'I expect they will be glad to be at home again,' she had said idly.

It was a most unsatisfactory visit. Celia was unable to re-establish their usual freedom together. She told Phyllis how pretty the cottage looked and how kind Betty Houghton and Mr Fairbanks had been to her, about the shocking naked swimmers in the sea, and the putting in of a bathroom and hot water. It all came out higgledy-piggledy, and Phyllis listened politely and said, 'Indeed?' or 'How dreadful!' or 'How wonderful!' in all the right places, but there was no true reciprocation.

After twenty minutes and a cup of tea, a puzzled Celia gave up. She kissed the baby and carefully handed him back to his mother. She bent down to kiss a reluctant Eric, who turned his face away and clung to Phyllis.

'I must go. Goodbye, dear. Don't get up. I'll see myself out.' She put her arms round the little mother, and kissed her on the cheek. 'I'll come again soon.'

She was thankful to be out in the fresh air. During the train journey back to Meols, however, she worried about her old friend. That she herself had changed greatly since her father's death did not occur to her.

When she had gone, Phyllis leaned back in her chair and burst into tears. She was in a state of numb terror that she might be pregnant again. Arthur was not a patient man and he had forced himself upon her nightly for the past two weeks. It had hurt her physically; her pleas for a little longer to rest between babies had been ignored. His lack of consideration had hurt even more.

At home, Celia found Edna peacefully reading a novel in front of the living-room fire. The room looked tidy; the table was already laid for the evening meal. There was no sign of her mother, and as she took off her jacket, she inquired where she was.

Edna looked up with a grin. 'She's resting. She's had a busy day.'

Celia's conscience smote her.

'What happened?'

'Well, I persuaded her to go to the village and order some groceries and buy some meat, and so on. She was most put out, because she was refused credit – she's used to having weekly bills from the butcher and grocer, as you know.'

'Oh, dear! Didn't she have any money with her?'

'Yes, I gave her some – she would not believe me that, as a stranger, they wouldn't trust her. I told her, also, that she must get her bank account transferred from Liverpool to the local branch here, so that she can easily draw money when she wants it. She didn't like the idea of having a strange bank manager to deal with – said she would prefer to go to Liverpool each time she needed money.'

'What did you say?'

'I didn't say anything. Let her learn how inconvenient it is going to be.' She saw the shocked look on Celia's face at this remark, and she sounded defensive as she added, 'It's no good, Celia, she simply has to change her ideas – we all have to. We are facing a new world, and we've nobody to help us, except ourselves.'

A sharp lance of fear of the unknown, the unpredictable, shot through poor Celia. She had already had too much of having to make decisions, of treading nervously along unknown paths, as she arranged for the cottage to be made habitable.

It had been a tremendous struggle for her. Her life had always been ordered by her parents, her slightest suggestion immediately crushed, and she had learned early to accept numbly all that they decided. Now her father was not there to order – and her mother had become a lamenting, pitiful heap.

She glanced round the cosy, crowded room as she sank down into her mother's easy chair. Suddenly, the room seemed to spread out its arms and offer her sanctuary – and she realised that she had organised it all herself. She had created this sense of comfort. A good odour of cooking had now been added to it by someone else.

Swallowing her fears, she said to her sister, with a nervous laugh, 'It smells as if everything fell out all right.'

'It did. The stuff she bought was delivered this afternoon by various errand boys, and she made a chicken pie – which is in the oven. And I managed to make a bread and butter pudding, which is also in the oven.'

Celia was dumbfounded. 'I would never have had the courage to push Mother into doing anything she didn't want to do,' she said flatly. 'Quite frankly, I took it for granted that I would have to do everything, now that we have no servants.'

Edna patted her knee. 'Oh, no. We'll try to share the work fairly. I've had enough of that kind of nonsense. I enjoyed tidying up this morning, and talking to Dorothy and to Mr Fairbanks when I saw him in his front garden. He inquired how you were, by the way. And Dorothy did, too. She made a good job of the shed, though I saw her hanging around talking over the hedge to Eddie Fairbanks for quite a while.'

At the mention of Mr Fairbanks, Celia felt a small twinge of jealousy. He was her friend, not Edna's or Dorothy's. She managed to respond by saying politely, 'That was very kind of him to inquire about me.' Her mind, however, quickly reverted to her mother, and she suggested that they must see that Louise got a rest each afternoon.

'Of course. But the busier she is, the less time she has to grieve.'

Edna put down her book and stood up. She took down a small brown business envelope from the mantelpiece, and dropped the missive into Celia's lap. 'Mr Aspen's yard boy came down on his bike to deliver this to you,' she said.

As she picked up the letter and looked at her name on it, Celia felt her nervousness return; nobody ever wrote to her except Great-aunt Blodwyn, who wrote meticulously at Christmas, Easter and on Celia's birthday.

Celia wondered why Betty could possibly need to write to her. She had seen her only that morning, and she had already received a statement from her with regard to the work done on the cottage; though the sum involved had seemed reasonable to her and there was a note on the bill that arrangements could be made to pay by monthly instalments, she had not yet had the courage to give the account to her mother.

She fumbled as she tore open the envelope.

Chapter Thirty

❧

As she read her letter, Celia's expression changed from trepidation to pleasure. She looked up at Edna, who was peeking into the oven at the side of the fire to see how dinner was progressing, and announced, 'A friend of Betty's, a cabinetmaker, has asked to see our furniture – he came in after I left this morning, and Betty mentioned it to him. She says he's interested in pieces that are dilapidated but made of good woods.' Celia's voice squeaked with excitement. 'He has a little furniture repair business – and she says he is knowledgeable about antiques because he does restoration work. He can alter heavy furniture to make it fit into a smaller home, and she thinks he might be interested in some of our heavier stuff.'

'That sounds very interesting.' Edna closed the oven door and turned round to face her sister, as she added, 'Not much of Mother's furniture is in need of repair, though.'

'Betty thinks that his knowledge of old furniture might be helpful to me.' Celia smiled down at the letter. 'In her PS she says he's a friendly type and that she's known him for years. She's arranged for him to come to their yard at eleven o'clock tomorrow morning, and she hopes this is convenient.'

Edna straightened herself up. 'It certainly is convenient. Away you go tomorrow morning.'

'What about Mother? She's not yet made up her mind about what she wants to sell.'

'Just tell her that someone is coming to look at it all. If they make an offer, she can then decide if she wishes to accept it.'

Though Celia nodded, her face fell. 'You know, Edna, it's going to take a terrible lot of time and running about, if I have to negotiate backwards and forwards between Mother and a buyer for every piece. Unless you want to help, I don't think I could do it. I imagine that people would want to take away immediately anything they decided to buy, wouldn't they?'

'They will, of course,' Edna agreed. She hung the oven cloth on its hook by the fireplace.

'And there's so much else to be done. The garden is a shocking mess – and just keeping the house going from day to day without servants will keep us all quite busy – I'm tired out already.'

Edna was suddenly curious. 'Is Mother going to give you anything for all the work you've done on the cottage? And for selling the furniture?' she asked.

'Give me something? What do you mean?'

'Well, er – um – pay you or buy you something?'

'I'm her daughter. She expects me to do what she wants – for love.'

'Look here, Celia. With a lot of work and a bit of luck, you're going to make hundreds of pounds out of that mighty pile of furniture, and you could find it less wearying, if you received a little money for the effort involved.

'If it were auctioned, she would have to pay the auctioneer, wouldn't she? Or if she asked a second-hand furniture shop to dispose of it for her, the shop would charge her a percentage on everything sold, probably a large percentage.'

Celia looked dumbfounded. 'I couldn't ask Mother for money!'

Edna could look quite ferocious at times. Now she did, as she snapped sharply, 'Are you going to be her slave for ever – until she dies? Well, I'm not and neither should you be.

'And another thing, Celia. As I said, times have changed. I don't have to worry, because Paul left me provided for. But you would be wise to learn how to earn a living.

'I know a lot of women are giving up their jobs to go home and be housewives again, now that the war is over. On the other hand, for a lot of us there is no chance of marriage – because the men who could have married us are dead, all the young businessmen, the professional men, the sons of county people – all gone!' She sounded bitter, as she went on, 'I'm told that, in the north-west here, there are whole villages without a single man left between the ages of seventeen and fifty. Do you know a single aristocratic or middle-class family without someone dead or dreadfully hurt?'

Celia looked at her, appalled. Her lower lip trembled as, in answer to her last question, she agreed. 'I don't know anyone, not that I ever had any hope of marriage. Even in Phyllis's husband's family, they lost two boys – Andrew had just qualified in law and the other one was an actuary in an insurance company.'

'That's exactly what I mean. There's hardly anybody left. We have to look after ourselves, particularly because Father left you nothing.'

Celia was silenced and filled with fear, as, with sudden perception, she looked down the years and saw herself, after Louise's death, an ageing, unpaid companion at the beck and call of some lady like her mother, not much better than a slave working for roof and food – because she did not know any other way of staying alive.

She was not given to self-pity, but, in her sense of shock, a tear ran down her face, and Edna said crossly, 'Don't start to cry – start to plan. Look, if Mother gave you ten per cent of everything you get from the furniture, it might be enough to pay for some training, though I can't suggest what for – and, at twenty-four, you are rather old to start.'

Celia was so agitated that at first she could not reply. Then she blurted out, 'I couldn't ask her, Edna. And, anyway, she needs me at home.'

'Rubbish. She's a perfectly capable woman, not quite fifty years old yet. I could broach the subject for you – or perhaps Cousin Albert could talk some sense into her next time he comes up to Liverpool.' Edna's expression relaxed, as she saw Celia's eyes fill. 'Cheer up, sweetie. You have to be at your best tomorrow – a business lady with something to sell.'

'It's almost too much for me, Edna – to face all at once, I mean.' She could feel panic beginning to overwhelm her again.

Edna sensed her real distress, and said firmly, 'Face one thing at a time. Go to Betty's yard tomorrow and if this man wants to buy something, simply set the best price you can and sell it to him – and don't worry about anything else. I'll keep the house going. And Mother has to learn that if she doesn't help you to sell the wretched stuff, she has to take the consequences. You are quite right that you cannot run backwards and forwards to consult her all the time.'

Celia got up wearily, Betty's letter still in her hand. 'Yes,' she agreed, and summoning up a smile, she added, 'It's good of you to care.' Then she said automatically, 'I'd better make a cup of tea for Mother and wake her up.'

Edna opened her mouth to object, and then thought better of it. 'That would be kind,' she replied. 'I've just to wash some lettuce which Mr Fairbanks gave me this morning, and dinner will be ready.'

Though still resentful at her elder daughter's sudden insistence, that morning, that she must actually contribute some effort to the establishment of their new life, Louise felt better after her nap, and accepted the cup of tea which Celia brought upstairs to her. After she had taken a few sips and Celia had drawn back the curtains from the bedroom window, she inquired, quite amiably, how Phyllis was.

Celia expressed her unease at Phyllis's fatigue, and her mother responded that having one's family was the most fatiguing period of any woman's life, particularly if the household did not include a nanny.

Celia felt suddenly that she would rather have her own life than the hopeless one of trying to please Arthur. She did not think that it was the moment to broach the subject of her own future, so she said simply that Edna was making a salad and that dinner would be ready in a few minutes.

She left Louise drinking her tea, and went into their brand-new bathroom to bathe her face and tidy her windblown hair. The water ran hot, and she breathed a thankful prayer for such a luxury.

She felt refreshed after washing herself. As she ran downstairs, she began to anticipate with pleasure seeing Betty again.

*   *   *

Edna had refilled the kettle and put it on the hob. On the table steamed the chicken pie and by it lay a bowl of crisp green young lettuce.

The two young women sat down opposite each other and waited patiently as their mother plodded slowly down the narrow staircase and came to the table. Before sitting down, she gazed gloomily at the meal awaiting her, and sighed. Celia jumped up and pulled out her chair for her. Without thanking her, Louise sat down, and without a word proceeded to serve the pie. Obviously Edna was not yet forgiven for so ruthlessly driving her to action through the day.

Celia told her about the note from Betty.

'A strange man? How will you receive him?'

'In the barn,' replied Celia.

'By yourself?'

'I will have to, Mother, unless you want to come along.'

Louise looked very disapproving, so her daughter hastily added, 'Betty will be there. Would you like to come to meet him?'

'Certainly not. I don't want to have to talk to a workman, while I'm still in mourning.'

Edna interjected sharply, 'We are all in mourning. But you can leave it to Celia and Betty Aspen – I mean Betty Houghton – I keep forgetting that she was married; they seem to get along splendidly – and they are both very sensible.'

Then, without warning to Celia, she changed the subject, and said, 'Celia is going to have to work very hard to sell the furniture, Mother. I think she should have something for doing it. I would suggest fifteen per cent of all the money she manages to collect.'

At this suggestion, Louise's look of alarm was almost comical, her fork with a piece of chicken poised on it halfway to her mouth. But Edna went on ruthlessly, 'You are still very upset, I know – and naturally so. So I feel you should leave it all entirely to Celia how she does dispose of the stuff. It will all have to go – there's simply no more room in this cottage to put anything more.'

The silence grew and Celia's face flushed with embarrassment. Finally, Louise asked, 'But what does she need money for?'

She sounded genuinely puzzled. 'I keep her – and she will have her usual pocket money, as soon as Cousin Albert arranges my financial affairs.'

Celia opened her mouth to say that she should not worry about paying her. She felt she was simply being helpful to dear Mother.

Edna sensed this and quickly broke in again.

Her tone was sharp, as she said, 'I don't think, Mother, that you quite realise what a difficult position Celia is in, now that Father is no longer with us and has left her unprovided for.

'In the nature of things, she will not always be able to depend upon you. She needs to learn a way to earn her own living, as many other women out there will have to do.'

Louise looked bewilderedly at her elder daughter, as she slowly put the piece of chicken into her mouth. Then she said disparagingly, 'What can a girl like Celia do? She is not a working girl – she is a refined upper middle-class girl.'

'What do you expect her to do, when you die?' asked Edna icily, while Celia, shocked, murmured, 'Edna!'

'Well, I haven't thought about it. I have had enough to cope with since your father's sad passing, without thinking about Celia when I die.' She slowly put down her fork, and added with more certainty, 'I would have thought she could live with you. And she would have half the Birkenhead property from me, which would give her pin money. The other half would, naturally, go to you.'

'I certainly would not let her starve,' responded Edna tartly. 'But she does need a life of her own – as do I.'

The idea that Edna wanted to do anything other than stay with her shook Louise. She had just picked up her fork again and now she dropped it on to her plate with an alarming clatter. 'What are you thinking of doing?'

Edna found herself facing the surprised gaze of both Louise and Celia, and she said, 'I do not yet know.' Her voice was calm, but her eyes spoke of despair.

Since that seemed all that she would say, Louise, after a pause, chided her. 'I thought we would all live together?'

'Oh, Mother! We probably will. But you forget that I have

been bereaved, too. I am simply in no state to make up my mind what I want to do. And Papa Fellowes has not yet settled Paul's estate. When he has done so, I must think what I am going to do for the rest of my life.' She sighed. 'With no children, I feel I need to plan. But not yet. In the meantime, I want to see you and Celia happily settled.'

Celia smiled at her sister. She was afraid to say anything, and she watched with some anxiety as Louise pushed her plate away, got up from the table, and marched back upstairs.

Chapter Thirty-One

❦

That night, Louise lay on her bed and cried helplessly. She cried because her small safe world had already fallen apart and it appeared as if it might disintegrate even further. She had, she told herself, no one with any sense to turn to for help.

Even Mr Carruthers, her bank manager, was miles away. And cruel Edna had said that she must find a new bank in Hoylake, which meant dealing with a stranger. It was all too much for her.

Immediately after Timothy's death, she had assumed that Cousin Albert would secure a continuation of her life as she had always known it. She expected that widowhood would be very sad; she would grieve for the loss of her husband. But the pain would lessen with time, as had the agony of losing both her boys. Safe in her lovely home with familiar servants, in her usual circle of friends and acquaintances, with Celia to organise her social life, existence as a widow would be bearable. She had realised, a little guiltily, that it would also give her a certain amount of freedom to do as she pleased; she would not have to consult Timothy all the time.

Cousin Albert had soon disabused her of those expectations. Her cosy, wealthy world of 1914 would never return, just as her sons never would either. She and Celia would be lucky if they could make ends meet in this dreadful little cottage, round which the sea wind roared relentlessly.

The arrival of Edna, particularly an Edna with money, had cheered her up. If Edna's income was considerable, perhaps jointly they could afford a better house. With two daughters at home, she would not miss the servants so much; they could run the house between them.

But Edna seemed to be coming out of her own grief now and was proving to be quite awkward; she did not seem to be at all certain that she would continue to live with her mother. She was also putting ideas into Celia's head. Celia was a fool, but she might, with training, find a way to earn her own living – and leave home. A single woman living alone? She would be labelled a fast woman – a shocking idea.

At the latter thought, Louise cried harder. She herself could be left alone in this cottage, with very little money, with no friends nearby, no daughter or servant to make fires, do the washing, clean the house. For the first time in her life, she was terrified.

Loneliness gaped at her like a great, deep cavern, a future completely soundless, except for the remorseless crying wind. Not even the mewing of the cats would break the silence.

Celia had protested at Louise's abandonment of the household cats; Louise had simply shooed the animals out of the back door.

'They'll starve,' Celia had lamented.

'With all the mice and rats in Liverpool?' Louise had responded scornfully. 'They can hunt. They won't starve. And, sooner or later, someone will find them on their doorstep and take them in. That's how we acquired them originally. Don't you remember? They just arrived, at different times, at the back door, and Winnie took them in to deal with the mice.'

Louise was right. Celia, already disorientated, accepted their loss as yet another misery to be endured, and said no more.

Wrapped in her fine feather eiderdown on her bed in her new home, Louise cried on. Nobody cared about her. Nobody understood her. She admitted that even to have Tommy Atkins to cuddle would have been comforting. But big black Tommy Atkins was probably stalking mice down the narrow back alleys of Liverpool or learning to tip the lid off a dustbin to get at the contents.

Even cats knew everything about taking care of themselves, thought Louise angrily, as helpless grief gave way to rage at her predicament. Well-born women were not expected to be capable of facing the world outside the home.

Celia, left to herself, even if she could earn a living, might get entangled with a man – though she was, of course, quite old and plain – and make a fine mess of her life. Louise remembered the soldiers playing in the sea and had a horrifying thought of facing an illegitimate grandchild, if Celia was ever let off the leash. At all costs she must remain with her mother, no matter what Edna said.

With this determination and the justification that only Celia knew her taste in library books or could do all the mending and darning thrown at her, Louise stopped crying and, shortly after, fell asleep, exhausted.

It seemed no time at all before her younger daughter was gently shaking her awake and presenting her with early morning tea.

As Louise struggled to sit up, she noted that Celia was already dressed to go out, her hat pinned on her head. She lacked only her outdoor jacket.

As she took the teacup from Celia, she asked sulkily, 'Are you going to Hoylake to see Miss Aspen's man friend?'

'Mrs Houghton's,' corrected Celia nervously. 'She's a widow.'

'Humph.' Louise sipped her tea.

'Yes, Mother. I have to be there for eleven o'clock. I thought I might walk over, because I haven't had any fresh air for days.' She stood uneasily by the bed watching her mother sip her tea, and then said anxiously, 'If he wants to buy something, I think I must agree immediately, don't you? If the price seems reasonable? I can't very well come all the way back here to ask you if you are agreeable to it.'

'No. You can't. I can see that. I am not stupid.'

Celia sighed, and assured Louise that she was far from stupid.

'How will you know what to charge people? We can use every penny, in case you've forgotten.'

'I do have some idea about prices, Mother.' Celia's voice held no hint of the indignation that she felt, and she continued firmly, 'You remember that I went to see a friend of Mrs Houghton's who owns an antique shop in Liverpool, and she gave me quite a lot of information on antique furniture and showed me round her shop and told me the prices she expected for each article. She was tremendously kind and gave me some idea of the likely value of our dining-room furniture, for instance.'

Louise was draining her cup and did not reply, so with a gulp, Celia added, 'Edna says that you do not have to shop for food today – there's enough in the house. And Mr Fairbanks is going to ask the fish and chicken lady to call on us every week – to save our having to go to the shops all the time – he says her stuff is very fresh – better than the shops'. Are you sure you don't want to come with me to Betty's office?'

Louise sniffed. 'I could not bear to,' she asserted forcefully. 'All my lovely things in a dusty barn!'

Celia's face softened, and she said with contrition, 'I'm sorry, Mother. It must be very hard for you to face.' She took her mother's empty cup from her. Then she leaned forward to kiss her cheek. 'I hope to be back by lunch time, but don't wait for me.' In a more cheerful tone, she said, 'I've had my breakfast, but Edna will have hers with you.'

Celia waited for an answer, but none came. She slipped nervously out of the room.

Downstairs, Edna, still in a dressing gown, was warming her backside by the fire which she had made. She inclined her head towards the staircase. 'How are things up there?'

'Not too good.'

'I can cope with her. You go now. Don't walk. Take the train to Hoylake Station – I think it puts you down quite close to Betty's place, doesn't it? Then you'll have time to take a quiet look at the furniture before he comes.'

Celia reluctantly agreed.

When she arrived, the builder's yard seemed full of lorries, two belonging to Mr Aspen; one was being loaded with bricks and another with lumber. A third vehicle was delivering large boxes. There was no sign of the car which Betty's husband had built. Celia presumed that it had been sold.

Celia now had her own key to the barn and she walked straight over to it and opened it up. She decided on a number of pieces which might benefit from being made smaller. Then she walked leisurely back to the gate and Betty's office. Betty was at her desk and looked up with a cheerful grin. 'Good morning, Miss Gilmore,' she said teasingly.

In a shadowy corner a man rose and, tweed cap in hand, emerged into the sunlight pouring through the doorway.

Nervously, Celia turned towards him.

He was much more gentlemanly-looking than she had expected. His black hair was neatly cut and, under heavy brows, eyes as blue-grey as the sea weighed her up. He was short, though heavy-set. Betty introduced him formally to her as Mr John Philpotts, repairer of fine furniture. Celia put out her hand and it was shaken firmly by a very strong one.

In a voice with a tinge of Welsh in it, he announced that he was pleased to meet her.

After a few pleasantries, the three of them went over to the barn. The building did not have any lighting, so they pulled the doors open as wide as they would go. The contents could then be seen clearly in the daylight.

'Phew!' exclaimed Mr Philpotts, his face breaking into a smile as he viewed the cornucopia within. He turned to Celia, and said, 'To look at this will take some time. Do you mind if I go through it rather carefully?'

With her hands clasped tightly in front of her, Celia assured him that he could take all the time in the world, if he was interested, and Betty said that, in that case, she would go and make some coffee and bring it over.

At Betty's request, the furniture removers had banked as much furniture as possible against the walls and then made a pile in the centre, leaving a narrow passageway through which Celia and John Philpotts slowly made their way.

The furniture repairer had brought a notebook and pencil, and after asking permission, he paused, from time to time, to carefully turn a chair upside down to examine it, or open drawers and cupboard doors, to gaze at finishings and joints and hinges or knobs. Once or twice, he asked the origins of a piece, and all the time he made notes. When he wanted to handle a piece, he tucked the pencil behind his ear and put his notebook into his side pocket, so that he did not mislay either of them amid the jungle of furniture. Celia kept her usual silence; she was anxious not to offend him in any way.

When Betty brought a tray of coffee, she suggested that they should all sit down and drink it while it was hot. Mr Philpotts gallantly undertook to lift down three chairs for them, so they sat in the sun in the doorway and watched the busy builder's yard. When they were settled and the women were politely sipping their coffee, Mr Philpotts sat down, and, cup in hand, chewed the end of his pencil as if it were a cigar which had gone out. He seemed deep in thought, but occasionally he would get up and go back down the passage to look again at something. Celia noted that he dragged one foot, as if he lacked strength to put it down straight on the ground.

Though Celia maintained her nervous silence bordering on reverence in the presence of a man, his old friend, Betty, asked him, after a minute or two, whether he had seen anything he was interested in. He replied unexpectedly promptly that he was interested in a lot of it, and he named several of the big pieces which Celia had earlier earmarked. He turned to Celia, and assuming that she was basically a dealer, remarked, 'You have a beautiful stock, Miss Gilmore.'

Celia smiled and replied, 'Didn't Mrs Houghton tell you? It's all from my parents' home.'

The man's rather grim, deeply seamed face broke into a surprisingly cheerful grin. 'Betty did say that, but looking at it, I didn't think it could have all come from one family home. There's enough to stock a shop.'

He went on to tell her that much of it was rather big for apartments and the smaller, lower-ceilinged houses of the present day. He could, however, often make sideboards, like the three she had, smaller by taking out the centre cupboard. 'And, of course, tables like the big dining table at the back can have all their extra extensions taken out and be shown as much smaller. I would like to buy the extension pieces and make them into hall tables, parsons' tables, et cetera. And there's another sideboard there that does not seem to match anything else – the big one made of oak. I could take out the centre cupboard and make a useful cupboard for odds and ends, and then join the two ends together to make a handsome, but small, sideboard again. I am sure I could find markets for them.'

'How clever of you!' exclaimed Celia.

'Oh, you'd be surprised what you could do with this lot. Betty said that you had some china, too?'

'Seven barrels of it.'

'Complete sets?'

'Oh, yes, Mr Philpotts. There is one service with twelve settings and all the bread and butter plates and vegetable dishes – and three different sizes of meat dishes. It's Crown Derby.'

'Well, well!' He surreptitiously rubbed his left thigh, as if it hurt – and, indeed, it did hurt. With an effort, he got up again, and asked of Celia if he might look further.

'Of course you may. Take all the time you want.'

Betty gathered up the cups and said she must go back to the office. Her father's lorries, gears grinding, went out of the gate, and suddenly the place was quieter. Celia continued to sit in the sunshine. She was excited, but tried not to show it. Mr Philpotts looked so respectable and the sunshine was so pleasant that she wished her mother had come with her. But Mother would have condescended so much to a tradesman that she would probably have offended him, so perhaps it was as well that she was alone, despite the awful responsibility.

Still carrying his empty coffee cup, Mr Philpotts eventually returned and sat down in front of her. He laid the coffee cup under his chair, and then took his notebook out of his pocket and laid it on his knee.

After a minute or two, he began, 'Before I make an offer for the articles I mentioned, may I ask you a personal question, Miss Gilmore?'

Celia nodded nervous acquiescence.

'Are you simply disposing of this surplus furniture because, perhaps, you have no room for it in your new house? Or do you need to really make a solid sum of money out of it? Or are you thinking, perhaps, that you will begin a business buying and selling second-hand furniture, with this as your first stock?'

Celia's surprise at the last question was apparent to the man before her. He said hastily, 'I hope you're not offended?'

'Oh, no. The idea of a business had not occurred to me.' She went on to tell him that the furniture was her mother's, and she was sure Mother would be grateful for as much as she could obtain for it. 'As for my running a business,' she finished up with a shy laugh, 'I have no experience at all – of anything.'

He smiled slightly, and then asked, 'May I tell you what struck me when I saw some of the pieces that you have?'

'Certainly.'

'They are beautiful,' he said flatly. 'But they will take time to sell. And those that are big will have to be shown in a way to indicate that they would fit into a modern home. Hence my interest in making small pieces out of larger ones.'

Celia nodded, and waited for him to explain further. Before he did so, he shifted uneasily in his chair, and inquired, 'Did Betty tell you anything about me – or my business?'

'Only that you repaired furniture.'

'Well. I've only recently been demobbed after serving for four years, and I don't have much of a business yet. But I did finish my time as a journeyman – and I worked for furniture makers subsequently. I always did furniture repairs at home on the side, even tackling antiques, which demands a fair knowledge.

'When I came home six months ago, I began to do repairs again, and I'm earning fairly steadily – but I've no capital.'

He looked at Celia slantwise. She was all attention. He said, 'I'm telling you this because I have an idea which may benefit both of us. But you should know my background first. I should mention, too, that I am still under treatment for the wound in my leg – and I can't stand for long. So I have to find ways to supplement what I can manage to earn at my old trade by selling pieces like parsons' tables which don't have an immense amount of work in them.'

Celia was suffering from nervous strain. Please, Lord, she prayed, let him come to the point. Aloud, she said with real sympathy, 'I hope your leg doesn't hurt very much.'

He shrugged. 'I have my good days and my bad days,' he told her with a grin. 'Do you want to know what I'm thinking?'

'Oh, indeed I do.'

'Well, you have a lot of fine furniture and need some money. I'm a skilled craftsman with a tiny shop just off Market Street – it's got a nice front window facing Market Street. Though I don't need the shop, except to show my tables occasionally, I need the work rooms behind it. I want to suggest to you that we team up. You have the shop and I'll continue in the back. We share the rent. It will mean that we both have low overheads.'

Celia's expression was rapt, as if she had suddenly seen sunlight after days of storm, but the word 'overheads' puzzled her and she frowned.

'Overheads means rent, taxes, lighting. Things like that.'

The frown cleared, and she nodded.

Emboldened, he went on. 'To give you some money to begin with, I would like to suggest that we sort out all the workaday stuff you've got in there – kitchen tables, older beds – anything that is not of much real value. Send the lot to a saleroom. An auctioneer will at least get something for it.'

'Yes?'

'The rest we move into the shed at the back of my shop. We put together sets and show them in the front window as complete rooms, as far as we can. I'll reduce the size of all the cabinets, sideboards, bookcases – the latter are too high to fit under the eight-foot ceilings in modern houses. Two of the five wardrobes you've got could have the drawers on which they stand removed and small feet put on instead – they're mahogany – lovely wood – only need polishing. I could probably make hope chests out of the drawers.'

Celia was thrilled. She forgot about her mother. She had her hands clasped together as if in prayer, as she said impulsively, 'What a wonderful idea!'

He laughed. He said, 'There's a catch in it.'

Her face fell.

'Anything that I've altered or refinished, you pay me half of what you get.'

She was silent, and he added persuasively, 'My work is very skilled work.'

'I do understand that, Mr Philpotts. I'll have to ask Mother,' she said with some anxiety, and then she asked him, 'Do you really think I can sell anything?'

'With your nice manners, Miss? With the kind of clientele I have, why you could sell anything with patience. You'd soon learn a trick or two for selling. With a bit of luck, you'd be dealing with high-class buyers.'

She smiled prettily. 'Thank you,' she said. 'I think that's the first compliment I've had in my life.' Then again anxiety clouded over. 'I've no idea what Mother will say about it.'

'Well, you should explain to her that, this way, she'll probably get the best return, although it'll be slow. There's a clientele round here who know good furniture when they see it. In addition, you should advertise as far as Chester and suchlike places. When they come to me for repairs, they'll see what you've got. And you could have your tables laid with your Crown Derby dinner services – it would look good.'

'What about the pictures? We seem to have quite a lot of them.'

'Now that's something I don't pretend to know anything about. You could get an art dealer to look at them, if you think they're good.'

Celia abandoned thought of the paintings, for the moment. She was more worried about her mother's reactions. It would not be the thought of selling the furniture that would strike her, but the dreadful indignity of a daughter, granddaughter of a baronet, becoming a shopkeeper. She would be horrified at the very idea.

Louise had always referred to Celia's father as being in commerce – not trade. Trade was vulgar. Celia wondered how she could even broach to her the subject of owning a shop.

Celia's sudden hope died. 'Mother will never agree to it – she'll send it all to an auctioneer first.'

Mr Philpotts rose slowly and stretched his sturdy form to its full height. 'Go – ask her,' he said. 'Nothing try, nothing have. I've a good name in this village – I'll not cheat her.'

'Oh, I'm sure you wouldn't. Betty would not have introduced us, if she had not felt that you would really help us.'

'Aye, I've known Betty and her dad – and her mam – since I was a little lad. Will you ask your mam?'

'I will,' Celia replied slowly, though the thought of doing so filled her with nameless terror. She put out her hand to shake Mr Philpotts' hand in farewell. He held it tightly for a moment, and then said, 'Don't be scared – I think we'll both benefit. Let me know how you get on.'

She licked her lips, and nodded agreement. Through her hand he could feel her trembling before he slowly dropped it.

She stood, framed by the open barn doors, and watched him drag his way across the yard, to pause a moment to look in at the office door. She saw him wave to Betty and then continue out of the yard. Then she sat down suddenly on one of the chairs and cried from sheer nervous tension.

Chapter Thirty-Two

❧

When Celia arrived back at the cottage, Edna was seated by the living-room fire. She had a black skirt on her knee and a mouth full of pins. As Celia took off her hat and laid it on the table, she greeted her through her clenched teeth by saying, 'You are just in time to pin up this hem for me. All my skirts are too long for English fashions.' Then, after hastily removing the pins from her mouth, she inquired sharply, 'Have you been crying?'

'Yes, I did have a little weep.' Celia pulled her cotton handkerchief out of her sleeve and quickly wiped her eyes. Then she sat down opposite Edna, her hands clenched on her knees, and burst forth, 'I'm so scared of what Mother is going to say, Edna. I don't know how to ask her.'

Edna dropped the skirt off her lap and on to the floor and laid the pin cushion on it. 'What on earth do you mean? What now? Was the Philpotts man rude to you?' she asked.

'Oh, no, Edna. He was very nice indeed. He's not a gentleman; he's a skilled artisan. But I think you might like him.' She poured out the details of Mr Philpotts' offer.

'He's offered me a partnership in a little business, in effect, Edna,' she finished up. 'But it is Mother who will have to be the partner – because it's her furniture. But you know Mother. She'd burst into tears every time she looked at her furniture, and she'd be horrified at the idea of serving in a shop, and she won't want me there, either.' She shrugged her shoulders helplessly. 'Even if she agrees, she'll never do a stroke to help. It is I who will have to be at the shop all day, every day. And I can't do that and be here to look after her and help you with the house and the washing and the cooking and the cleaning – and do the garden.'

She wrung her hands in despair. 'What shall I do? I hardly know how to even begin with Mother.'

At that moment, the back door opened and Eddie Fairbanks called, 'Anybody home?'

Edna responded immediately that he was to come in. They heard his boots clomp as he kicked them off by the door and then he walked in in his socks. Celia's first thought was to thank heaven that Mother was not there to see a next-door neighbour in her living room without shoes on.

He beamed cheerfully at both sisters. He had been thinning out his seedlings and was carrying tiny fresh lettuces and some spring onions on a piece of newspaper.

'Thought you might like these,' he said. 'They're a bit muddy with the rain we had in the night, but they're real crisp. Where will I put them?'

He gazed at the two women seated by the fire, and realised that he had walked in at a difficult moment. Miss Celia looked as if she had been crying. Eyes and nose were red.

'I'll put them on the draining board,' he said hastily and prepared to retreat to the kitchen.

It was quick-witted Edna who insisted he stay and have a cup of tea. So the lettuces were disposed of in the kitchen, and Celia pushed a dining chair round so that he could join them by the fire.

Following her sister's lead, Celia said sweetly, 'Do sit down, Mr Fairbanks.' Then she turned to push the hob with the kettle on it over the blazing fire.

Edna was already getting teacups out of the small sideboard. She inquired brightly, 'Do you know a man called John Philpotts – lives in Hoylake?'

Eddie looked surprised. 'Sure I do – cabinetmaker and French polisher? Nice lad. Lost his fiancée in France – she was an ambulance driver or similar. He came back wounded, to be told about her death, poor lad. How is he – and how did you come to meet him?'

Celia answered him shyly. 'I was talking to him today, Mr Fairbanks. About Mother's furniture.'

'Oh, aye?'

Celia glanced at Edna inquiringly, and Edna said, 'Tell Mr Fairbanks about his suggestion. If he knows the man he can give an opinion.' She came, teapot in hand, to sit down until the kettle boiled.

Eddie nodded, and wondered what John Philpotts had been up to.

Celia's agreement sounded doubtful, and she evaded the issue by inquiring where Louise was. 'Is she napping?'

'No. She was complaining that she was completely fed up, so I suggested a walk on the promenade at Hoylake. She was going to take the train to Hoylake Station. I thought the fresh air would help her.'

Celia swallowed. She was going to have to go through her story three times, she realised. She sat slowly down on her chair and looked shyly up at the old man. He was smiling at her, so she went on to tell him about her morning interview.

She finished up by saying, 'Betty said it might lead to a very nice occupation for me – as an antique dealer.'

While Eddie stirred his cup of tea, he considered the matter carefully. Finally, he said, 'It depends what your mam thinks, doesn't it?

'The only piece of advice I would like to give you is to have a written agreement with John as to exactly what each of you is going to do and how the money will be split. The family solicitor nearest to here is, I think, in West Kirby – but that's only the next station after Hoylake – it's not far. He'd make it right for you. And being local, Miss Celia, he won't charge as much as a big Liverpool man might; it could save you a pile of trouble later on.' He wiped his mouth with the back of his hand, and then assured her, 'It's not that you can't trust John – he's a decent fella – but, as time passes, you tend to forget exactly what you agreed – or change things without thinking, like. Then you might quarrel. It's human nature.'

'Would you like to do what this Philpotts man suggests, Celia?' Edna asked with real curiosity.

Celia hesitated, and then said, 'Well, I don't know. I suppose

I would learn how to sell things – and that might help me to get another job – though what Mother would say if I worked in a shop, I shudder to think.

'I can't do what Mr Philpotts suggests – that is, use our furniture as a basis on which to launch a continuing business – because I won't have the money, will I? It will be Mother's.'

Eddie had not worked for forty years for a lord without understanding to perfection the social gradations of his society. He said cautiously, 'It's no disgrace to work for a living, love, if that's what you want to do. And your mam might be prepared to share the proceeds of the sales with you – so you could save most of it and buy more furniture to sell. You'd never make a fortune, but there's others as make a living that way.'

Edna said, 'My furniture will arrive from South America in about two months' time. I shall not need all of it, even if I set up a home of my own. I'll give you what I don't need for your shop. It is handmade and carved very nicely.'

Celia looked at her open-mouthed. 'Would you really?'

'Well, of course I would. I don't have to worry about every penny, and you haven't a cent to bless yourself with. And, if truth were told, it wouldn't hurt Mother to let you have the proceeds of the furniture sale.'

Eddie studied a tea leaf floating around in his cup. And these people think they're hard up, he considered. They don't know they're born. Miss Celia was unlucky, now. He'd seen such women before. He'd heard that a lot of them like her, when their family didn't want them any more, had been shipped off to Canada or Australia to marry pioneers they'd never seen.

He felt very sorry for her, and there she was, looking at him with wide scared blue eyes as if she knew already what life had in store for her, poor little lass. Even her sister's kind offer did not seem to have taken the fear out of her.

Regardless of speaking in front of their plebeian visitor, Edna was continuing her tirade about her mother. She went on, 'If you are earning, you can eventually contribute to the household – so Mother will not have to keep you.'

'Oh, aye. That's true,' interjected Eddie. He took Celia's hand

and said, as if to his own daughter, 'Don't be so frightened, luv. Your mam may be quite pleased at the idea.'

Celia seriously felt that her mother would never be pleased at anything she did or said. But this was her own special friend speaking, a friend she had made by herself, and she gained a little courage from him.

Edna smiled at the pair of them. She hoped that Eddie Fairbanks would still be with them when her mother returned. Louise was more likely to keep her temper, if an acquaintance were present. To that end, she asked him to give her his cup so that she could refill it.

Chapter Thirty-Three

❧

Louise walked slowly down King's Gap towards the sea. Though the tide was ebbing, there was still enough water on which the spring sunshine could dance, and a light breeze caught playfully at her widow's veil; the wind did not roar at her as it had done round the cottage.

She felt lonely and depressed. She had intended to call on Lady Tremaine, the widow of one of her husband's business friends, who lived in Meols Drive, Hoylake. She was one of the few women she was acquainted with on this side of the Mersey. When she went to the house, however, the lady was not at home, and she had had to content herself with leaving her card with the parlourmaid.

She could not immediately recall the address of anyone else in Hoylake with whom she could claim acquaintance, and she wished that she had, after all, accompanied Celia to her appointment with Mr Philpotts. She could not, she thought savagely, even go into a village shop to amuse herself by trying on hats. For a lady wearing a mourning bonnet to indulge in such frivolity would not be considered good conduct.

She turned along the promenade, and paused, one hand on the iron railing at the edge of the pavement, to look down at two children, as they sought sea shells on the shore. They reminded her of Tom and George when they were boys, and, also, that they had left no grandchildren to console her. What did widows do? she wondered. Nobody seemed to need them nowadays, perhaps because there were so many.

Except that she was temporarily drained by the stress of Timothy's untimely death and the consequential money shortage, she was a woman of excellent health and she had always kept herself busy, apart from running her home most efficiently, by planning elaborate dinners or soirées for Timothy's friends; she was well known as a hostess, and such efforts were very helpful to Timothy in keeping in touch with other businessmen; there was a point in arranging them. But such entertaining would not be possible on the small income she would have in future, even if it were a suitable occupation for a widowed lady. Aimless afternoon teas for other widows would be about the limit she could afford.

As she began to recover from the shock of bereavement, her sense of frustration was making her increasingly restless, and, in consequence, she continued her wanderings along the promenade until she was quite tired. Then she turned round to walk back the way she had come.

I can't live like I have been doing these past few weeks, she considered fretfully, as she watched the sea birds hunting over the wet sands.

Still deep in thought, she reached a bench on which, at the very end, sat a man. He held a walking stick clasped upright between his knees. He had rested his chin on his hands and looked as if he were searching the horizon for something. He wore a peaked tweed cap and a belted macintosh.

He looked respectable enough, so Louise sat quietly down on the far end of the bench to rest her feet. She nodded absently to the man as she passed him and said politely, 'Good morning.'

He ignored her.

She did not accept the rebuff kindly. As she arranged her skirts around her, she thought crossly that this was not Liverpool where you would not talk to strangers. Hoylake was still small enough to be considered a village. Almost everyone would know everyone else, and she herself wanted to become casually acquainted with the local inhabitants. Once she knew the social standing of people, she would, as a result of moving so far away from her old home, have to make new, suitable friends from amongst them.

Really, some people were awfully rude.

While she rested her feet, her mind fretted on. She had received that morning a troublesome letter from Cousin Albert saying that he had had an offer for her house and that the price was being negotiated by the estate agent. He expected to be in Meols in the course of the next week or two.

'And where does he think he is going to sleep in a three-bedroomed cottage?' she asked herself crossly. Celia would simply have to give up her room and share Edna's bed. A male guest would be under one's feet the whole time. And such a lot of work.

There was also the dreadful finality of the sale. How was she going to face the fact that strangers would now have the right to live in her home? It was certain that Albert would not understand her grief over it. In fact it seemed to her that nobody, including Edna, herself a widow, understood what she was going through without dear Timothy to lean on and his needs to think about.

Her reverie was interrupted by a hoarse voice from the other end of the bench. It asked, 'Is someone there?' The accent was a Lancashire one.

The oddness of the question made Louise jump. She replied tartly, 'Yes. There is.'

It was as if the man had not heard her, because he went straight on speaking to her, and what he said shook her out of her irritation at Cousin Albert, out of her personal misery.

She turned to stare at him, her mouth open in disbelieving shock.

In a voice which seemed weakened by illness, he said, 'I hope I'm not disturbing you, but I get very bored sitting here. I'm deaf and blind. I can talk to you, but you can't talk to me – unless you would be kind enough to sit close to me and touch my hand once for yes and twice for no. Then, at least, you can say yes or no to me.'

She was alarmed by the unexpectedness of the request. She had been taught in childhood that nice women didn't touch strange men, unless they were first introduced – when a lady could politely allow her hand to be shaken.

For a second or two, she stared at the bent figure at the other

237

end of the bench. Under the long, belted macintosh, she noticed that his trousers were hospital blue.

An ex-serviceman. Dear God! What dreadful thing had happened to him?

She knew from the newspapers about the number of blinded soldiers, who had, somehow, to be taught to read Braille and manage for themselves; she understood that the existing facilities were overwhelmed by their dire need. But that a man could be blinded and deafened had never occurred to her.

She was revolted at the idea. It was a revulsion equivalent to finding one of Tommy Atkins' half-dead mice in the drawing room, when her first instinct had been to call someone else to remove it – and dispose of it out of her sight.

But she was not without feeling. This was a young man, like Tom or George. A real man – not a mouse to be shovelled into the rubbish bin. Poor soul!

She swallowed nervously. Supposing George or Tom had returned to her smitten like that? What would she have done? How could she have coped with someone that helpless? How would she communicate with them? How could she convey to this man that she was grateful to him for going out to fight – sacrificing himself for king and country, as army generals were fond of saying.

The man had fallen silent, as she stared at him. She was suddenly filled with an immense pity, and what few motherly instincts she had ever had came to the fore. He didn't look more than thirty. Now that the war was over, how would he earn a living? Would he get a decent pension? Would his wife nurse him?

She forgot about Cousin Albert and all her other worries. Plucking up courage, she rose from her end of the bench, and bashfully reseated herself close to him. He felt the swish of her skirts against his leg, and asked, 'Are you a lady?'

She lifted his left hand from the walking stick, and he allowed her to turn it and open the palm. Very gently she touched his palm once. She saw him smile.

'Do you live here?'

Again she signalled yes. She allowed him to rest his hand, palm upwards, on her lap, while he told her how he had, in France, been blinded, deafened and wounded in the back. 'I'm with a lot of other lads in one of the houses facing the sea – I know by the smell of the wind that it faces the sea. All the lads are blind, but I believe only two of us are blind and deaf – and I don't think the army doctors know what to do with us.' His laugh was very cynical. 'If I had a family, I suspect they would just send me home and make the family work it out. But I have no close kin – which is why I joined the army in the first place.'

Louise was so shaken at the idea of such a decent-looking man, no gentleman but nevertheless very respectable-looking, being abandoned that she found herself trying to hold back tears, and one dropped on to his hand.

He felt it, and shifted round to face her. Very carefully, with two fingers he followed the line of her arm from his hand, up to the fur collar of her coat and then almost poked her chin as he found her face.

'Don't cry,' he said, as he felt the dampness on her cheek. 'It doesn't help.' He sighed, and then asked, 'Can I feel your face, so that I will know what you look like?' He felt her nod agreement.

As the fingers went gently over her skin, Louise was shocked to find herself sexually stirred. It was impossible with a strange man – indecent. But it was there, roused by a man young enough to be her son. Did he feel the same? She was a little frightened.

She held herself rigid, while the exploring fingers ventured over her curled fringe and then her bonnet and the veil thrown back over it.

If he felt anything, he gave no indication of it. He checked the veil again, and again he sighed.

'Forgive my asking, but are you a widow?'

She tapped yes.

'The war?'

She tapped no.

'Natural?'

He felt her sigh in her turn, and he did not probe further. A natural death made sense. The feel of the loose skin under her eyes told him that she was not young. And most war widows would be young and less likely to wear a veil.

He had held his stick between his knees, and after he had steadied it, he dropped his hands in his lap and tried another tack.

'I'm Sergeant Richard Williamson, 5th South Lancashire Regiment, and I was born in St Helens. I've been all over the world with the regular army. It's a miracle that I'm still alive, I suppose. What's your name?' He smiled suddenly, 'You could try spelling it out on the palm of my hand, if you like.'

Poor boy, she thought. Still so young, despite his rank – and trying so hard to communicate.

Totally absorbed by his terrible predicament, she ignored her own feelings, and again picked up his left hand. Very carefully she traced L, which he got immediately, and, after a couple of tries, he managed O and U. The rest of her name defeated him.

She saw the frustration on his face, and she squeezed his hand in the hope of conveying her understanding. Without thinking, she said to him, 'It doesn't matter. Louise is not a very common name.' Then she remembered that he could not hear.

He turned his hand round and clasped hers. 'Mrs Lou!'

She lifted his hand to her mouth, so that he could feel her laugh, and it made him chuckle, like a finger game would amuse a small child.

Their laughter ceased abruptly, as they were interrupted by the sound of footsteps behind them. Richard felt Louise freeze and then turn to see who was approaching.

He sat absolutely still, wary as a disturbed rabbit.

'Oh, Ma'am, I hope Mr Williamson is not being a nuisance to you?' A young woman in a nurse's cap and apron stood behind the bench. 'Sometimes they can be a pest – and that stupid.'

Louise rose. She noticed that the woman did not wear a nurse's pin. A servant dressed as a nurse did not impress her. She said frigidly, 'Certainly not. I am horrified by his predicament – and I was happy to try to communicate with him.'

The girl shrugged. 'Oh, aye. It's proper sad. Bad enough when they're blind. There's two of 'em here as is blind and deaf. Proper difficult it is looking after them.' She turned to Richard and tapped him on the shoulder.

He rose immediately, and held out his hand to where he thought Louise might be. She turned back to him and shook his hand. 'Goodbye, Mrs Lou,' he said, his voice formal.

Louise did not know what made her continue to hold his hand, but she did, while she asked the young woman, 'Where is he staying?'

The answer sounded a little impatient, 'In Mon Repos. That's the house across the road. It's a nursing home now. Holds thirty men.' She put her hand firmly under Richard's arm and began to turn him away from Louise.

'Wait a minute,' Louise interrupted. 'May I come with you to the house? I should like to arrange to see Sergeant Williamson again. He tells me he has no relations – on whom he could call for help or advice. He might be glad to know a local family.'

Louise could appear very formidable when she chose. The girl hesitated. She looked carefully at her. Sealskin collar to her well-cut black coat, real kid gloves clasped in one hand, a hand with a huge diamond ring. A widow's bonnet and veil. A rich widow?

She smirked almost insolently, and Louise could have hit her. Then the girl shrugged. 'Very well, Ma'am. But I tell you, he's got a mind of his own, he has.' There was more than a hint of resentment at a man who would not do what he was told, because he could not hear, and therefore, instead, did what seemed to him to be best in the circumstances. She added reluctantly, 'You could talk to Matron if you want. He's got to come in now – it's lunch time.'

Still holding Richard's hand firmly, so that he would know that she was going with him, Louise repositioned herself, in order that the girl could guide him. Slowly, the three of them crossed the road, and Louise had to relinquish Richard's hand, so that he could use his stick to feel his way up a flight of steps to a lawn, where a number of abandoned lawn chairs suggested the existence of other residents in the fine, big house before them.

As they progressed, Louise's dislike of the young woman faded, to be replaced by some apprehension of the quandary in which

241

she had suddenly placed herself. She knew nothing about the care or training of the blind or, even worse, the deaf and blind. She was about to offer help to a man who would surely be under doctors who, she presumed, already knew what to do for him. Or did they? That was a question to be asked.

But it might have been my George or Tom in such a desperate situation, she told herself passionately. In need of all the help they could get. At least I might be able to offer some entertainment to alleviate his boredom. Richard Williamson must be nearly out of his mind with simple, excruciating boredom.

And just what do you think you can do for this man, a working-class man? she asked herself.

The answer was that she had not the faintest idea, but she would try. It would give her something challenging to do.

She forgot her horrid cottage and her irritating daughters, as her far from stupid mind ground rustily into gear after weeks of disuse, and she began to think constructively of means of communication, of how to give Sergeant Williamson something to do other than sit on a bench.

Swept forward on a tide of overwhelming compassion and not a little of her own need, Louise entered the hall of the nursing home. She heard, in the distance, the rumble of young male voices and the clatter of knives and forks. Thirty of them, the maid had told her. How cruel war was.

It was the idea of two of them being both deaf and blind, however, which drove her upstairs to see an irate matron.

Matron was fed up with volunteers and other do-gooders whose enthusiasm, now that the war was over, waned within weeks; with a government which was simply muddling through and wished heartily that wounded soldiers would go home and get on with their lives; with a nursing staff with a marked tendency to get married and depart.

At first, Louise had some difficulty in persuading the matron, a very experienced army nurse who had seen more medical horrors than she cared to remember, that something more should be done for Sergeant Richard Williamson and his similarly afflicted comrade.

If Louise felt like doing something, she could be very stubborn. She was not stupid. She had some idea of planning and organisation. Her home and entertaining for her husband had both been well run. During the war, she had worked steadily for the Red Cross, and she understood the need to raise funds for charity.

But the dire need of an ordinary Lancashire man sitting on a seaside bench and an unknown number of others like him carried her far beyond the idea of charity. She sensed that it would take long-term dedication and, like the raising of Red Cross funds, endless patience. And, as she talked to the disillusioned matron, she realised that she herself would need to encourage others to help, just as she had when interesting herself in various charities.

A couple of hours later, when she finally left the nursing home, a bewildered matron, though very hungry for her forgotten lunch, had promised her cooperation in a scheme to find help for Sergeant Williamson and his fellow sufferer.

'As far as I know, there's nothing to help people like Richard, except I did hear that an American lady was once able to help a young deaf-blind girl,' Matron said flatly. Her grim middle-aged face was heavy with melancholy. 'The blind will be taught Braille, as soon as we've found teachers for them – the usual places are full, and the boys are having to wait. But I don't see how they can teach anyone blind and deaf.'

For the moment, Louise could not see a way out of Sergeant Williamson's dilemma either. She pushed the problem away for the moment, and inquired, 'Will they get a pension?'

'I suppose they will. There's supposed to be a bill going before Parliament this year, which, if it passes, will make the government responsible for all legally blind people. But you know government – they're as slow as snails.'

Louise nodded. 'Is Braille difficult to learn?' she asked. 'If we could find a way to teach him, we could communicate with Sergeant Williamson.'

'We could – Braille in itself is not that difficult – but the nurses and aides here are run off their feet. I don't think there is one of them who has the tenacity to learn something which won't be of much use when they return to general nursing. Braille would not be much needed by a civilian nurse.'

'I have time – I've all the time in the world,' replied Louise with a certain amount of bitterness in her voice. 'I wonder if I could learn it.'

It did not occur to her that her daughters would be thankful if she would use some of her time to help them. They did not need to earn a living like men did.

The matron smiled. 'You really want to help them, don't you?'

'I do,' Louise responded, with the same commitment with which she had said the same words when she had married dear Timothy.

Let her try, decided the matron; something good may eventually come out of it. But she had not much hope. Once a war was over, governments were not very interested in soldiers.

Nevertheless, she shook Louise's hand and assured her that she could visit at any time. 'The blind boys would probably be grateful if you could read to them occasionally – something light that would amuse them.'

Louise picked up her handbag. She rose and thanked Matron for her time. 'I'll most certainly come to read to them,' she promised. 'Do you think they'd like *Three Men in a Boat*?'

'I'm sure it would make them laugh – and that would be good for them,' Matron said.

Louise trudged slowly up to the station. She had felt drained and tired when she sat down beside Sergeant Williamson. Then she had been shocked out of her fatigue and her grief. Now she felt suddenly worn out, maddeningly frustrated because her tired mind simply would not work. Reading would help the blind boys, but it would not help Sergeant Williamson. And it was his predicament which touched her heart.

Chapter Thirty-Four

❦

After three cups of tea, the conversation between Eddie, Edna and Celia languished, and he announced his departure because he had to cut his hedge.

Both ladies rose and ushered him out of the back door, with many thanks for the lettuce and spring onions. Just as he was about to vanish round the side of their house, however, Edna called him back to ask if he knew a young man who would clear their back garden and dig it over for them.

Eddie paused and scratched the back of his head. 'Do you mind a lad who's not all there?' he asked tentatively, while Celia tugged at her sister's sleeve and whispered that it would cost too much.

'Shush, Celia, it won't be that much.' Then she replied to Eddie. 'We don't mind who does it, as long as it gets tidied up,' she assured him.

'Well, I'll ask young Ethelred's mam if he could do it. He's a strong lad, though he's lost a few marbles.'

'That would be most kind of you.' She pushed a quietly protesting Celia back into the kitchen.

'We can't afford these things, Edna,' Celia argued. 'I was going to do it bit by bit.'

'Don't be a duffer, Celia. It needs real muscle, and you are not going to undertake it. I can manage the few shillings it will cost.' As they re-entered the living room, she added playfully, 'I have high ambitions for you. I'm very keen that you work with this Philpotts man and that it grows into a proper business and is a success.'

Celia smiled a little ruefully. She collected the tea things to take them to the kitchen sink. She said, 'It all depends on Mother.

And she's going to be furious at the very idea.' She opened the back door and emptied the tea leaves round an anaemic-looking fern growing near the door. 'Edna, it is ferns that like tea leaves, isn't it?'

Edna came out to view the slightly yellow-tinged plant. 'I've no idea. I think we'd better buy a gardening book.'

Unexpectedly, Celia chuckled. 'What a useless pair we are! We don't know anything, do we?'

'Not much. I could try addressing it in Portuguese to find out if it likes tea leaves. It may not know English.'

Laughing, they turned, to face Louise, who had come silently through the front door and was astonished to see such levity in a house of mourning.

They greeted her, and Edna said she hoped she had enjoyed her walk.

Louise drew off her gloves and took out her hatpins. 'Well, yes and no,' she replied grudgingly. 'Have either of you done anything about dinner?'

Celia and Edna looked guiltily at each other. In one shot, their mother had put them in the wrong. 'No,' they admitted in chorus. When they followed Louise into the living room, Celia surreptitiously leaned over towards the fire and pulled out the oven damper, so that the oven would be hot if they needed it.

'I might have known it,' their mother said dolefully. Then, as she went to hang up her coat and hat, she asked Celia to make some tea and put some cheese and biscuits on a plate for her.

'I haven't had any lunch,' she explained. She made her request mechanically, however, as if her thoughts were elsewhere. 'I think I'll lie down for a little while. Bring it upstairs.'

'Yes, Mother.' Celia's response was equally mechanical. She had been gritting her teeth to keep down her sense of panic. She had been certain that her mother would open the subject of the furniture by asking how she had got on with Mr Philpotts. But she appeared to have forgotten all about him.

Celia was disappointed. The problem was weighing so heavily upon her that she was anxious to discuss it as soon as possible. Now it seemed that she herself would have to broach the subject, and she had no idea how to do it without, straight away, bringing Louise's wrath down on her head. She wished suddenly that Mr Philpotts could be with her to support her when she did so. He seemed such a calm, sensible person.

Chapter Thirty-Five

❦

Muttering irritably under her breath that she was old enough to know, roughly, what time dinner should arrive, Edna retired to the kitchen, to open the meat safe hanging on the wall and take out the remains of yesterday's chicken and see if she could make another dinner out of it. Celia pushed past her to fill the tea kettle at the tap.

Edna looked gloomily at the dried-out chicken remains. 'Better take Mother a lot of biscuits with her tea,' she advised. 'This bird is going to take some resurrecting.'

In spite of her inward qualms about facing her mother, Celia smiled. 'Cut lots of veggies up small, parboil them and then mix the chicken scraps with them,' she suggested. 'You can thicken it with a bit of flour mixed with water.'

'Aha! Wonderful! You can take over the cooking. Do you know how to make dumplings? They'd fill it out, too.'

'No. You could get down the cookery book which Winnie packed for us,' Celia suggested, and whipped the kettle away to put it on the fire.

After ladling tea leaves into the pot and putting it to warm by the fire, she returned to the kitchen.

'I wonder what has happened to Winnie. Has Mother said anything to you about her?'

'No.'

'Do you know if anyone has asked for confirmation of the written reference Mother gave her?'

'I don't think so.'

'I hope she has found a place. She was going to find a room to live in, while she kept on looking. I'd write to her, except that

248

I don't have an address. I gave her our address, because she told me that sometimes a new mistress likes to write directly to the old employer, in case the reference the servant is carrying is a forgery.'

With her finger poised over a recipe for dumplings, Edna asked idly, 'Did Mother do anything about trying to get her a position? She was with us a long time – since before I was married.'

'Not to my knowledge.'

Edna put down the cookery book slowly and said, 'I hope she did. I know I turned off my servants the day I left – but at least I knew that the next company man to be the tenant of the house would probably rehire them – and they knew it.' She shrugged. 'I expect she's OK. A good cook shouldn't have much difficulty in getting a place.'

Celia sighed. 'She was a good friend to me.'

'Was she? You knew her much longer than I did.'

Upstairs, Louise had taken off her dress and put on her brown velvet dressing gown. She had propped herself up on her bed with her writing case on her lap. She was chewing the end of a pencil, as Celia carefully edged the tea tray round the door. She looked up and inquired, 'Celia, do we have the address of the School for the Blind – I'm sure there is one in Liverpool?'

Astonished at such an odd remark, Celia put the tray down on the bedside table, and responded that she was sure they did not have it. 'I would have kept a record of the address, if you had ever contributed to it, Mama – but I don't think they ever solicited funds from us.'

'Hmm, I wonder how I can get it?'

Celia straightened up and winced as an unaccustomed pain shot up her back; carrying buckets of coal from the coal shed outside the back door was not very kind to backs, she decided.

In answer to Louise's query, she said, 'I'm not sure, Mama.' She stood staring at her mother's lap desk for a moment, and then said thoughtfully, 'I remember that I once got an address for you from the library – they have a number of reference books.'

'Is there a library in Hoylake?'

'Yes. I passed it yesterday.'

'Well, you can walk along to it tomorrow and see if the librarian can find the address. And also the address of St Dunstan's.' She added testily, 'Don't dawdle there. Pour the tea.'

Celia swallowed uneasily; it seemed as if her mother had revived the almost feverish activity which had always been a prelude to giving a party or organising the removal of the family to Rhyl for its annual holiday. She asked, 'Are you having trouble with your eyes, Mother?'

'No. But I want to learn Braille.'

Very puzzled, Celia exclaimed in surprise, 'But Braille is for blind people.'

'I know that.' Louise turned herself to face her daughter. She said, 'Do you know, Celia, in Hoylake there is a house full of blind soldiers waiting to learn it before being discharged. If I can learn it quickly I can help to teach them.' She sighed and turned to stare across at the open window. 'Even worse, Celia, two of them are both blind and deaf – and the matron says that no one really knows how to communicate with them at all.'

Celia handed her mother tea and biscuits and then sank down on the side of the bed. 'How dreadful. Poor things!' She was honestly shocked, and looked at her mother as if she had never seen her before, while Louise jotted something down on a list she appeared to be compiling. When her mother began to compile a list, it was certain that she was about to embark on, what was to her, a serious undertaking.

Louise flung her pencil down on the bed. 'Yes, Celia. Poor things indeed. Can you imagine what it would be like if one of your dear brothers had been sent home to us in such a state? Where would we begin? What could we do?'

'I don't know, Mother. It would be terrible. How did you stumble on these soldiers?'

Eagerly now, Louise described her morning. She finished up by saying, 'I feel an urgent need to help if I can.'

Celia nodded. She did understand. It was yet another shocking revelation of young men's suffering in a merciless war.

She sat quietly for a moment or two. It looked as if her mother might be in the process of casting off the role of impoverished widow, which Celia had imagined she would play for the rest of her life. Was she reverting to that of a society woman who knew that rank had its obligations, a person who knew exactly how to plan a charity ball or banquet and had the strength to do it? Perhaps it would not be the best of roles, but at least it might put some life back into her. Most of her mother's acquaintances in Liverpool had a pet charity to which they contributed money or voluntary work.

Celia recalled that when Phyllis's baby had arrived so precipitously it had revived her; she had become the domineering matron who had been the scourge of less efficient Red Cross volunteers during the war. More shrewd than Celia, Edna had remarked only a few days earlier that their mother was a perfectly capable woman if she would only bestir herself.

And here she was, trying to bestir herself to some purpose on behalf of two ordinary soldiers, as if they were her own sons.

As she remembered her two brothers, Celia wanted to burst into tears. She had always recognised her mother's grief over the loss of them.

She made herself smile at Louise. Wounded soldiers in their helplessness could, indeed, be cared for as if they were Tom and George. At least it was worthwhile giving them a hand, if it could be done; it would also make her mother focus on a definite goal instead of drifting miserably from day to day. Celia forgot, for the moment, her own problems, the greatest of which was the unexpectedly dedicated lady reclining beside her, and said with real enthusiasm, 'Mother, I think you're wonderful! I believe the library is open in the evenings. I can try to get those addresses tonight.'

Her mother's face glowed at the unexpected praise.

'May I tell Edna?' Celia asked. 'I should go downstairs to help her.'

'Of course.'

Chapter Thirty-Six

Downstairs in the living room, Edna received the information with a very startled expression.

She slowly dropped a handful of chopped carrots into a saucepan on the fire. Then she grinned mischievously and gave a derisive hoot, as she stirred the mixture of vegetables and leftover chicken.

'You mean to say that Mother has found a cause, a real honest-to-goodness cause?'

'It looks like it.'

Wooden spoon poised over the pan, Edna stood rubbing her chin thoughtfully with her other hand, and left a long smudge of flour on her face. Then she said slowly, 'It'll be the making of her, if she can do it. I wonder if she realises what a huge undertaking it will be?' She looked disparagingly down at the chicken stew she had concocted, and added ruefully, 'She'll have no time for matters domestic – we'll get that job.' With a dripping wooden spoon, she gestured round the little room. Gravy flew from it and hissed as the liquid hit the hot range. The smell of burning was added to the stuffy atmosphere.

Celia laughed a little helplessly. 'I suppose we'll manage somehow. She doesn't do anything much now. Frankly, I think we should encourage her as much as possible – because it is a very real cause, Edna,' she said, and went to wash the lettuce brought in by their neighbour.

She felt very tired and wondered how many more responsibilities she could undertake. Edna had said that she would try to get the garden cleared of its overgrowth for her – but that was only the beginning. It had to be planted, weeded, raked, hedges cut.

How could she do it? Tend a shop? Help Edna with the washing, ironing, cleaning, shopping, cooking, et cetera, and, on top of all that, do all the errands that Louise would now expect her to do in connection with this new interest. Edna could not do everything at home – and, in any case, Edna had hinted that she might set up a home of her own, once Paul's will had been probated. If she did that, the work for Celia would be overwhelming.

As she spread the cloth on the table, she wondered wistfully if she would ever have any leisure, even for a walk or to read a book. Or to visit Phyllis Woodcock.

It was almost certain that Louise would, indeed, use her as her secretary in her new endeavours, much as she had done during her father's lifetime – and how could she refuse when the need of the men her mother had met was so acute?

As promised, Celia went to the library that evening, and came home with a number of addresses of organisations which might help the deaf and another list of charities interested in the blind, but nothing in connection with those doubly handicapped.

Within the next two days, Louise wrote letters of inquiry to all the addresses provided by the librarian, seeking a clue to any charity which might know how the deaf-blind could be helped. Was there a form of signing, she inquired, for the deaf-blind, similar in principle to that used by the deaf?

She also received a further letter from Cousin Albert to say that he would arrive at the cottage on the following Monday and would stay at least three days, while he dealt with the estate agent selling her house and with the affairs of Timothy's estate.

It caused no little turmoil in the cottage, when Louise insisted that Celia double up with Edna. She was to remove her clothes from the small wardrobe in the hall bedroom and see that everything was clean for her second cousin.

'Mother!' wailed Edna. 'Can't he stay in a hotel in Liverpool?'

'Apparently not,' Louise snapped back. 'He's probably trying to save himself expense.'

Celia did not say anything. She did not want to offend her mother before discussing Mr Philpotts' offer with her.

She had not yet found an opportunity to broach the subject; it seemed as if Louise was either closeted in the tiny front sitting room writing, or had gone to Hoylake.

Much to Edna's annoyance, and adding to Celia's sense of being besieged by work, Louise had demanded that a fire be lit in the, as yet unused, front room, and that her lap desk be brought down and put on the tea table there.

Edna fought a noisy battle about the cost and work of making two fires each day – and lost. Louise was adamant that the work she was about to do was a priority over everything else.

Even Edna never considered telling her that if she wanted a fire in the room, she should make it and clear it up herself. Neither sister could visualise Louise doing such a menial task.

The same postal delivery that brought Cousin Albert's letter also brought two letters from Brazil for Edna.

Louise picked them up from the hall floor as she came down for breakfast, and she scanned the envelopes with some curiosity before handing them to Edna.

She seated herself at the table and began to open Cousin Albert's letter. 'Who are your letters from?' she asked. 'This one is from Albert.'

'Just friends,' Edna replied and slipped them both, unopened, into her skirt pocket. Inwardly, she steamed with irritation. Mother had no right to inquire who her correspondents were. She was a widow and entitled to her privacy. Celia was still a spinster and subject to her mother, but not Edna.

The inference of Edna's casual reply was not lost on Celia, who was quickly eating her breakfast egg, and she felt a pang of envy. It must be wonderful to be free, she thought.

'Edna, you'd better see that we have enough food in the house to feed Albert, in addition to us,' Louise ordered, as she put Albert's letter back into its envelope.

'Do you have any money?' Edna inquired quietly.

Louise looked startled. 'I think so,' she said. 'I've a little left over from the rents which Mr Billings sent me.'

Since moving into the cottage Edna had found herself paying for almost all their day-to-day needs and she felt that this was the moment to bring it home to Louise that she must pay her share. Her inquiry made Louise bite her lip and then promise to give her something for groceries.

The discovery that it would probably cost all Louise had in her purse to feed an extra mouth strengthened Celia's idea that, if permitted, she should try to earn enough to contribute to the housekeeping. She would delay no longer. She would, that evening, talk to Mother about it.

Chapter Thirty-Seven

❧

Carrying a brass coal hod of additional coal for her mother's fire, Celia knocked tentatively at the sitting-room door and was told in a querulous voice to come in.

Louise was running her hand along the large bookcase which took up one wall of the tiny room. She glanced round at her whey-faced daughter, and asked, 'Do you know where your father's books by Philip Oppenheim are? The boys apparently like his novels.'

'Yes, Mother. They're in a box in Betty's barn. We decided we would never read them again.' She squatted down on the hearth rug and, with the aid of a pair of tongs, added a few lumps of coal to the fire.

'Well, bring them back. I need them.'

'Yes, Mother.' The thought of carrying baskets full of books back from Hoylake made her back ache even more; Oppenheim was a very prolific writer.

As Celia rose stiffly from the hearth rug, Louise returned to the littered tea table. She sat down in front of it and scanned the list of things she felt she had to do, which seemed to be constantly beside her and never to grow any smaller. She did, however, now cross off Oppenheim.

Celia carefully placed the coal hod beside the end of the fender, clasped her hands tightly in front of her over her grubby apron and turned towards Louise.

'Mother, I need to talk to you about Mr Philpotts and the furniture.'

'Now?'

'Yes, Mother. I must let Mr Philpotts have an answer to a

suggestion he has made.' Celia stood woodenly before her, hoping that she herself wouldn't break down with sheer fright. Two days' contemplation of Mr Philpotts' offer had convinced her of the common sense of it. And with a little money, she could be independent, even if she was a spinster.

Louise asked impatiently, 'Well?'

Celia had rehearsed very carefully what she would say, and she explained quite clearly what the idea was. She finished up by saying, 'The crux is that all the furniture is yours, not mine, and if we go into a modest partnership, such as Mr Philpotts has suggested, there should be some kind of written agreement that I may act for you – unless you would like to start a business yourself, of course.'

'Tut! I shall be much too busy. In any case it would be totally infra dig.'

Celia gritted her teeth. 'Very well, Mother. When I spoke to Edna about it, she suggested that you might allow me to own the furniture – as the capital, so to speak, to start a business in antiques and collectibles. I would hope, Mama, to make enough, in the long term, so that you did not have to keep me; I could contribute regularly to the household, and then you would reap a financial benefit from the investment.'

Too terrified to go on for the moment, she paused as she saw the gathering storm in Louise's expression. Then she added uncomfortably, 'Edna says it is essential that I learn to earn my living – because I shall be alone when you ... er ... pass on.'

'Keep a shop!' Louise was trembling with affronted dignity – and with an underlying fear that she would lose her hold over Celia, who would be most useful, not only at home, but as a general runabout in connection with the work Louise was undertaking. 'How insulting that this man should suggest it – and who is he, anyway, to interfere in our affairs?'

'He's just a small businessman. Basically, he has floor space to let in front of his workshop – and he'd like to share the rent with someone.'

Inwardly Celia prayed, God don't let me panic until I'm through this. She took a big breath, and went on determinedly,

'As I said, he's a furniture repairer and French polisher, and his kind of clients are likely to be people who appreciate good furniture; they may be interested in what we have for sale.'

Louise's chest swelled with indignation. She slammed down her pen and a blot of ink flew on to the carpet. She replied furiously, 'I'm surprised that you did not dismiss him on the spot. I won't hear of it. My good name – your father's good name – on a shop? A most repellent idea!'

Patiently Celia fought back. 'The shop does not have to have our name on it, Mother. We could call it something neutral, like Hoylake Fine Furniture.'

'I won't have it. Edna is quite wrong to encourage you. No girl of mine is going to serve in a shop. Anyway, you aren't capable of running anything.'

The latter remark stung.

The insult quelled Celia's panic. It was replaced by honest rage.

'Mother! You're most unfair,' she almost shouted. 'Who fixed up this cottage? Who found workmen and made it habitable? Who arranged the removal – and did most of the packing?

'I did, without much help from you. Who is going to have to plant the garden and make it decent? I shall – because you won't.' Her voice rose to a shriek. 'I know that the ex-soldiers need your help – but I need an atom of help, too. I know you're in mourning – and Edna and I have done our best to help you. But there's a limit.' She unclasped her hands and banged them flat on the table. 'You'd like to keep me tied to your apron strings until you die – and then you won't care what happens to me because you'll be dead and won't have need of me any more. Mr Philpotts and Edna have suggested a future for me and an investment of your discarded furniture – that's all.'

More shattered by this unexpected explosion than she liked to admit, Louise sat up straight and glared at the girl.

'Be quiet! You're behaving like a silly child. This idea of a shop is lunatic. I have no doubt that Edna will look after you when I'm gone – you're not capable of looking after yourself.'

At her last words, Celia's temper died. Reimplanted in her was the haunting fear that there was something the matter with her, that she was not normal in some way and was, therefore, incapable – and had been kept at home because of it. Since her father's death, she had done her utmost to cope with the many problems it had presented, and she had considered that she had, in the circumstances, done rather well, but perhaps other people would have done much better. She had no yardstick by which to measure her performance.

Now, she went a ghastly white, and clutched her arms across her waist as if she had been struck in the stomach. Then with bent head she stumbled to the door, opened it and went out into the hall. She hooked her toe in the door and slammed it behind her.

She nearly ran into Edna, hurrying from the living room.

'Hello,' Edna greeted her, obviously relieved to see Celia on her feet. 'I heard you shriek – thought you'd fallen down the stairs. Are you hurt?' She touched Celia's white cheek. 'You look absolutely awful!'

Celia looked into her sister's concerned face. She mourned, 'Oh, Edna, help me,' as she fell into her arms.

Edna gripped her stricken sister firmly, and said, 'Come into the living room and lie on the old settee. Shall I call Mother?'

'No,' Celia gasped, and stumbled to the settee, where she collapsed and curled herself into a tight knot.

Puzzled, Edna took one of Celia's clenched hands and chafed it, while she glanced over her face for bruises or some other injury. Then she pulled a knitted blanket down from the back of the settee and covered her. She turned and ran to the back kitchen for a glass of water.

'Here, sip this,' she ordered Celia and lifted her head so that she could do so. She eased the glass between Celia's chattering teeth, and water slopped over her. The shock of its icy coldness soaking through her black blouse seemed to ease the poor girl's rigor, and she gasped, 'Thanks.' Then she whispered pitifully, 'I'm so frightened, Edna. Mother's so angry.'

'Were you asking her about Mr Philpotts?'

'Yes. About my having the furniture. I don't think she cares very much whether or not I have the furniture – but she was so

259

put out at the suggestion that we could start a shop, and that I should work in it. She was really shocked.'

'That's just like Mother.' Edna sounded slightly amused, as she leaned over to put the water glass down on the table. 'But that shouldn't throw you into a panic, dear. It could make you angry, of course – but you shouldn't be so upset just by that.'

Celia gave a big sobbing sigh. Through her chattering teeth, she said, 'It was what she said at the end that hit me – and she's said it so many times in my life – that I'm not capable of doing anything. And I wondered again if I'm kept at home because I'm mentally lacking – or because I've got tuberculosis – or something.'

'Ridiculous! Ever since I came home, you have steadily proved it. The only thing that is the matter with you is that you have never been taught anything, except to say, "Yes, Papa" and "Yes, Mama" like a talking doll. I am sure you could do very well, with Mr Philpotts to help you out to begin with.'

She still had her arm round her tiny sister. Now she hugged her close, while she considered the situation. Then she said, 'I think you need to be reassured by somebody outside the family. I noticed, when I was out, that there is a lady doctor who practises in Hoylake. You could tell a lady everything that has happened to you – much more easily than you could a male doctor. I think another woman would understand.' She smiled and hugged her sister closer. 'I am sure that she would reassure you that you are sane, though I don't think you're very well physically – we've all been under great strain and you have had to do a great deal – I simply don't know how Mother can say that you're incapable.'

She smiled down at Celia, and she could feel the younger woman's body beginning to relax. 'Let's go to see the doctor tomorrow,' she soothed. 'She probably has a morning surgery.'

'I can't pay her.'

'I know that – but I can. Between us, in case of emergency, Paul and I were carrying a fair amount of cash with us when we left Brazil. I changed it into English sovereigns when I arrived, and, thanks to Papa Fellowes, I have not had to spend much of it, except to help Mother out with her housekeeping. I can certainly afford a few shillings to pay for a doctor for you.'

As Celia began to protest, Edna stifled her objections by saying that she could accept the fee as an advance birthday present. 'Don't worry,' she added. 'My income will be quite adequate as soon as the will business is settled. If a doctor can lift this cloud from your mind, I think it will be the best birthday present I can give you.'

'It would, Edna. It really would. Do you think the doctor could? Could we go to her without telling Mother?'

'Certainly. She's going to read to her boys tomorrow morning and then help to take the two deaf-blind ones for a walk.' Edna laughed softly. 'We'll leave the housework – just forget about it.'

Celia struggled to sit up, and Edna loosened her hold on her. 'What am I going to do about Mr Philpotts?'

'Well, I think we should talk to Cousin Albert, when he comes on Monday. He may see how sensible John Philpotts' suggestion is – and understand that in the end Mother won't lose financially. If anyone can talk sense into her, I think he can.

'She has to realise that you're a human being, her daughter as much as I am. She must consider your future.'

'I never thought of Cousin Albert.'

'Well, at least he's a man, and Mother may listen to a man.'

'You're being wonderfully kind, Edna,' Celia said gently. 'I'm so grateful.'

Edna made a face. 'I'm making up for past sins. I never realised until recently what was happening to you. I was at school for years and you were just the younger sister at home. Quite honestly, I thought you liked helping Mother, and I was dreadfully self-centred anyway. For myself, I knew that to please Father I had to net a husband – a suitably well-off one. Then I was all excitement about meeting Paul – and then I went to Brazil. And, frankly, when I came back, I was quite distraught myself – my whole life seems to have gone to pieces, and England seems so different.'

Celia swung her feet carefully to the floor. She put one hand gently on Edna's shoulder. 'It must be dreadful for you, you poor dear,' she said with sympathy. Then she went on dejectedly, 'We didn't really see much of each other, did we?' She sat looking down at her slippered feet, and then, after reflection, said, 'I always thought Mother would bring me out and arrange for me to meet someone to marry, like you, as soon as I was old enough. Then the war came and both Mother and Father kept putting me off – and Father wouldn't hear of my becoming a nurse or anything. And that further convinced me that there must be something wrong with me, because a lot of untrained girls went to nurse the wounded.'

She looked up at Edna. 'You know, he threatened that if I left home, he would cut me off without a penny. And in the end, it was so ironical – he never did make any provision for me.'

'I think that was awful.'

Celia reverted to the question of her physical health. 'I've never seen a doctor in my life, not even when I caught Spanish flu,' she confided. Then she glanced apprehensively at the door into the hall. 'I'm so scared, Edna. I thought Mother would come after me – but she hasn't.'

'She must have thought that she has settled the matter with her refusal – and that you just had a childish tantrum which you will have forgotten by morning.' She began to laugh, and soon Celia was giggling, too.

In perfect imitation of their old nanny, Edna said reprovingly, '"Now, Miss Celia, no lady allows her temper to get the better of her. A gentle answer turneth away wrath, remember."' Then she added in her own voice, 'It can also make people think you are a doormat. Now, off you go to bed before she wipes her feet on you again.'

Chapter Thirty-Eight

After spending the tumultuous years of the war in a London hospital constantly full of wounded, Edith Mason came home to the village where she was born, to practise medicine with her father, who had had a family practice there for many years.

Though it was extremely difficult for a woman to obtain training as a doctor, old Dr Mason had given his only child every support and encouragement, and he was happy to welcome her home and to have such an experienced physician as his junior partner. Like many other medical students of the time, she had faced a constant flow of terribly wounded or very sick men, and, perforce, her experience during training had been much wider than it would have been in peacetime.

With her father as her partner, his patients tolerated her, though men often specified that they wanted to see old Dr Mason. When, in January 1920, he died, however, the old, ugly prejudice against women doctors surfaced and patients tended to drift away to any physician who wore a pair of trousers.

To Edith's relief, however, it became evident that women were glad to discuss their more intimate problems with her, and, at the time of Celia's visit, she was beginning to rebuild the practice, though she was still far from busy. Edna knew of her only from her business plate bolted to her front gate.

Edna felt that Celia would simply freeze in front of a male doctor and that what her sister needed most was reassurance. Dr Mason seemed to her a sensible choice.

When the two young women arrived at the doctor's front door, they obeyed a cardboard notice hung on the door handle and entered her hallway. A further notice by an open doorway instructed them to Please Take a Seat, so in they went and shyly sat down.

Dr Mason's waiting room held only one middle-aged lady, who sat primly upright in a corner. In response to a small ting-ting of a bell, she immediately rose and went into an inner room to see the doctor. The sisters heard her being greeted with a cheerful good morning, and then the door was closed.

When Edna and a very timid Celia answered the bell and went in to face her, Dr Mason was able to give them plenty of time.

At first Edna did the talking, but when finally her description of her sister's fears about her health became clear, the doctor turned to Celia.

Celia said baldly, 'I want to know, Doctor, if I am quite normal and sane in my mind and that I am not physically ill in any way. My parents have always kept me at home and consistently said that I am incapable of looking after myself.'

Edith Mason saw much more in this request than Celia realised. She knew the type quite well. A daughter kept as a superior servant, no social life, no sex life, little education, few friends. Queen Victoria had set the fashion for this misuse of a daughter, and Dr Mason had seen a number like her, and, indeed, wives with the same crushed passive look. She knew that, in the case of the latter, sometimes their only escape was into a form of semi-invalidism which had little to do with real illness.

She suggested, first, that she take Celia's medical history and then give her a thorough physical examination.

Celia said she did not have any medical history. She had never been to a doctor before.

The doctor laughed and, after questioning her, ended up with a long list of childhood illnesses and, as an adult, recurring coughs, colds, unknown fevers, and Spanish flu.

When Edith saw the fear in her patient's eyes at the length of the list, she assured her that it was quite an ordinary list. Most people went through all these illnesses.

Celia agreed. 'It must be so, I suppose. Mother never called the doctor for any of them.'

Dr Mason took Celia behind a screen in a far corner of the

spacious room, and asked her to undress and wrap herself in a white sheet lying on an examination table. While she did so, the doctor went to check that there was no one else in the waiting room.

Edna remained in the consulting room as chaperone. She was, however, seated at the furthest possible distance from the screen, and could reasonably be expected not to hear the doctor's quiet conversation with her patient.

It was Celia's first medical examination and her face went pink with embarrassment. While she was seated on the examination table, the doctor put her stethoscope to her chest and listened to her heart, turned her around and knocked carefully on her back, peered down her throat and down her ears, examined her throat and tongue and turned down her lower eyelids to check for anaemia. She took a little hammer and tapped her knees for reflexes. Then she laid Celia out on her back and took a good look at her, stark naked. She saw a short, small-breasted, perfectly formed, very white, reasonably nourished body that had obviously never been exposed to sunlight, hips of a normal width for her height. She was probably perfectly capable of bearing children and of feeding them. There was no apparent sign of malformation or ill health.

Anxious not to discommode a patient who, she guessed, had probably never been stripped in front of anyone, never mind a doctor, she did not feel for breast cancer.

She gently covered the little body with the sheet, and pulled a swivel chair up close to the table and sat down herself, picked up her clipboard from under the table and began to make some notes.

'I should take your pulse,' she said, her worn face breaking into a smile. 'I forgot.' And, looking at her closely, Celia realised, with surprise, that this self-possessed, careful lady was not much older than Edna.

Celia returned the smile. She felt perfect confidence in the physician, and answered as carefully as she could the questions she was then asked. No aches? No bad accidents at any time? No pains? Headaches? Menses regular? Celia had to have the word 'menses' explained to her, having previously only heard polite euphemisms, including the curse, for the menstrual cycle. Her last curse had been two weeks before.

Dr Mason sat back and looked at the prematurely sad face before her, and said that she appeared to have normal health, except that she was a little anaemic, for which she would prescribe a tonic. 'And much more fresh air,' she suggested. 'Do you walk?' Yes. 'Can you swim?' No. 'Play tennis?' No. 'Ride a bicycle?' No. 'Church?' No. 'Mother goes, but I have not had time for months.'

The doctor leaned back in her swivel chair. 'What do you do with your day?' she asked in a friendly, conversational way.

Under the sheet, Celia squirmed uneasily. 'Usually I do whatever Mother wants doing. But now she's widowed, I have had to do all kinds of things.' Her voice sounded flat and tired.

'What kind of things?' The doctor's voice was soft and amiable.

The story of her father's bankruptcy and having to move to the cottage came out, at first diffidently, and then in a rush. 'Mother is so upset that she is not able to do much,' she finished up in polite defence of her surviving parent. 'So I had to make all the arrangements.'

'And what do you personally hope to do in the future?'

And Celia replied dully, 'Look after Mother and the house and the garden – and . . .' She tailed off.

'And?' The doctor prompted.

Celia looked her squarely in the eye. 'Do you really want to know?'

'Well, it is natural that you might want to do something you enjoy in your spare time. You don't have to tell me, but the more I know about you, the better I will be able to advise you. Did you lose someone in the war, my dear?'

'Both my brothers. There is just Edna, Mother and I left now – Edna's husband died of the Spanish flu.'

'No sweetheart?'

Celia laughed disparagingly. 'Me? I'm far too plain to have a sweetheart.'

Edith smiled inwardly. This, she thought, is where I begin the healing. 'I don't think you're too plain,' she assured her. 'You have a pretty, healthy body, and you are not at all ugly.'

'Really?' Celia had never in her life received a compliment regarding her appearance.

'Of course.' No need to tell her that most of the males of her generation were dead.

'Is there nothing that you would like to do, if you had time? Your mother is not going to live for ever. You need to have something else to do.'

Celia propped herself up on one elbow, and said almost eagerly, 'Well, yes, there is. But Mother has always assured me that I am totally incapable of doing anything. My father, too. That's why I came to you – to find out if I am sick in some way – or if I am mentally deficient. You see I get so frightened that I curl up into a ball and I can't do anything for hours until it passes.' Her voice faded into despair. 'You must think I'm awfully stupid.'

Panic attacks. 'You poor child. Because of these episodes you think you are mentally deficient?'

'I fear so. Edna doesn't think I am, but she doesn't know me very well. She's been in South America for years and has only just recently come home.'

The doctor again put her fingers round Celia's wrist. The girl's pulse was now racing. She grasped her hand and squeezed it. She smiled, and said, 'You strike me as a perfectly normal person, perhaps a little too dutiful a daughter, but, nevertheless, perfectly normal. Now, tell me what it was you wanted to do – it must be important since it apparently drove you to come to see me.' She laughed. 'Nobody knows better than a woman physician how difficult it is to become a professional – or do anything the least unusual.'

And while Edna fidgeted her way through a couple of magazines, Celia told Edith Mason about Mr Philpotts and the proposed furniture shop.

Edith Mason smiled. She said easily, 'People said things like that to me when I announced that I was going to be a doctor. Women are incapable, they told me, besides which it is vulgar – I might have to look at blood – and at naked men – shocking!'

Celia giggled nervously. Then she remembered the revolting characters who had chased her when she walked on the sea wall, and she felt slightly nauseated.

Her new-found doctor continued, 'Fortunately, my father was there to encourage me.'

'My father wasn't like that.' Celia's golden eyelashes closed over her tired eyes, as she remembered her dread of her father. The tiny movement was observed by Dr Mason. A lot of pain there, she considered. Had the man used her sexually?

She decided that it would only frighten her more if she inquired. Instead, she said briskly, 'Perhaps you would like to dress, while I go to my desk and write this up. And then I hope I can suggest a few things to improve your health.'

She removed herself and went over to exchange a few pleasantries with Edna. She had noted Edna's mourning dress, but assumed that, like her sister's, it was worn because of her father's death. She sat down by her, and told her that Celia did not seem to have anything wrong with her, but she should get out and about, enjoy herself in the fresh air and get more sleep.

Edna's deeply lined, yellowed face broke into an unexpectedly pretty smile. 'I told her so.' She fidgeted with her black leather gloves, and then added, 'She's had a rotten life at home, and she's coped marvellously since Father died. But Mother keeps telling her she's a fool – and she isn't. She's just crushed.'

'I couldn't express it better myself,' Edith Mason replied softly, not wishing to have Celia hear herself discussed. 'You will know more about this business she wants to start than I do; but if it is worthwhile, it could be the making of her. A real interest.'

'And a way of maintaining herself after Mother dies,' replied Edna a little sharply.

'Oh, she didn't mention that. It must be an underlying fear, however.' She hesitated, and then said tentatively, 'She tells me that you have also lost your husband, and it must be trying for you to have to cope with Miss Gilmore's ills at such a time. Please accept my condolences.'

'Thank you,' Edna said. Then she heaved a big sigh. 'It's good for me to have Celia in whom to take an interest, since I have no children.'

The doctor took one of Edna's hands in both of hers, and said, 'Though you have not consulted me, the advice I am going to give Miss Celia may help you, too.'

She wrote a prescription for a tonic for Celia. 'Three times a day after meals. And I'd like to see both of you again in two weeks' time.' Then she advised them to take a long walk together every day or, better still, buy bicycles and go out and explore the Wirral. 'It's lovely at this time of year,' she said.

'Cycling in mourning? Mother will have a fit. She'll never permit it,' Celia protested.

'Tell her doctor's orders. Try to persuade her to ride with you,' suggested the indomitable doctor, and sent them home laughing at the idea of their mother in her long gowns riding a bicycle.

Laughing herself, Edith Mason went back to her desk, to write up her notes. Afterwards, she leaned back to stretch, and considered idly all the so-called stupid daughters and dumb maidservants who had hung up their aprons and gone out during the war to replace men on farms, in factories, in banks and offices. In France, she had seen them driving ambulances and nursing dreadfully hurt men in first aid stations on the front lines of battle. She hoped that now the war was over they would refuse to be treated ever again as nonentities, especially now that they had the vote – provided they were aged over thirty.

'Up with women,' she muttered with a grim smile, and went to put on her coat and hat and do her house calls – on a bicycle.

Chapter Thirty-Nine

❧

As they went out of the doctor's front gate, Edna said with a gleam in her eye, 'I told you so, Celia. Nothing to worry about.'

Celia laughed a little shakily, and agreed. 'How kind she was,' she said warmly. 'I never thought of going to a lady doctor – and I simply couldn't have talked to a man – I don't think a man would have had much sympathy for me.'

Edna said, 'I think she understood the kind of life you have had, and that she really wanted to help. I liked her enormously; I'd enjoy having her as a friend.' She stopped, to fumble in her pocket for her handkerchief with which to dab her nose. Then she said, 'I don't really know anyone on Merseyside any more – and I miss my Portuguese friends in Brazil – and not having a place of my own.'

As they crossed Market Street, Celia replied with quick sympathy, 'I'm sure you do. I hope you'll make some new friends here, in time. I've already made a friend of Betty Houghton, though Mother thinks she's far too common.' She grinned mischievously as she said this, and then, as they regained the safety of the pavement, she asked, 'Would you like to meet Mr Philpotts? His workshop is somewhere near here.'

'Yes, I would.'

As they slowly made their way down the street, Edna went on, 'You know, Britain has changed so much in the years I've been away that I feel at a loss how to proceed in quite ordinary situations. Or perhaps I am so used to Brazil that I have forgotten what England is really like.'

Celia considered this for a moment, before replying. Then she said, 'Everything had to change because of the war. But we all thought that, once the war finished, we would go back to our old life – as it was in 1914.

'But we haven't been able to, Edna. Nothing is the same. The war's been over for nearly eighteen months, and we still seem to be in chaos. People are still distraught, still struggling because one of their number is either dead or wounded, and they have to make do in some new way. And when I do get a chance to read the newspaper, it is frightening: reports of unemployment and lack of housing – and huge war debts – and strikes threatening.'

They paused at the edge of the pavement, to allow a donkey cart out of a side alley, and the driver tipped his cap as he drove past them. Celia smiled at him, in response.

'I've felt the change myself,' Celia continued, as they crossed the alley. 'Mother was always saying that, when the boys came home, we would be busy again, as they established careers, got married, and she had grandchildren; it seemed as if life would be more normal.' Her voice faltered, when she went on, 'But Tom and George never will come home, so she won't have any grand-children – she grieved over Rosemary, you know, and so did I – poor little lamb. I would have so enjoyed her.'

As she mentioned Edna's daughter, she glanced at her sister. But Edna's expression was quite blank, as if she had retreated, once more, into herself.

Poor Edna, Celia thought contritely. She's had a rotten time, too. I shouldn't have mentioned Rosemary.

Anxious to keep the conversation going in spite of her blunder, she changed the subject. She said, 'Although Mother has, I believe, left a few cards with distant acquaintances round here, she hasn't had one response, not even an invitation to an at home or morning coffee.' She stood aside to let an old crone wrapped in a shawl get by, and then said, 'I've come to the conclusion that ladies simply haven't the energy to re-establish their social life. Or perhaps, now she is a widow – not a couple – Mother will have to find entirely new friends amongst other widows.'

As a swarm of morning shoppers pushed between them, she paused in her chatter, and then said with a deprecating laugh, 'I doubt if anyone is interested in three impoverished ladies living together; no hostess would want to make the awful effort of finding three matching men for her dinner table.'

Edna bestirred herself to answer. Her mind had been diverted by thoughts of little Rosemary's lonely grave in far-away Brazil. At Celia's mention of the probable shortage of males at a formal dinner, she was reminded of quiet, cultivated Vital; he would be a pleasant addition to any dinner table; he belonged to a society where there was often a shortage of women, because they died young in childbirth. She wanted to whimper with the pain of it all.

Instead, she turned her attention firmly to Celia, and said, with a slight shrug, 'Our family is all upside down because we've had so many losses, and, as well, we've had to move. But you are right, dear. There are so many like us that I don't think home life will ever be the same again.'

As they walked slowly along, Edna lapsed into silence. Then she said suddenly, 'Eddie Fairbanks was telling me that the young men and women whom you saw cavorting in the sea with – er – nothing on – are not exceptional. He says that there is a lot of wild gaiety in London – even in Liverpool. Night clubs, drunkenness, and shocking things going on between the sexes. Not our kind of life at all. He says it's people trying to make up for their lost youth.' She smiled grimly. 'I don't seem to remember having much youth to lose myself. I was a mother at twenty-two.'

They had to stop to allow a flotilla of perambulators to pass them, and Edna made a small gesture towards the women hurrying towards them. 'So many people are still in mourning – it's all blacks and greys – you can see it. So many widows' weeds.' She moved swiftly aside again to avoid being bumped by a pram, and added, 'And an astonishing number of babies. Breeding troops for the next war?'

Celia was shocked. She stopped dead. 'Edna! How can you say such a dreadful thing – there will never be another war. It's too terrible to contemplate. We've finished with wars.' She did, however, see what Edna had pointed out. Not only were the women in mourning, but they looked carelessly dressed; they did not look elegant in their blacks and greys. There was a general air of dowdiness which, at this time of year in such a well-to-do district, would have been alleviated by the sight of new spring costumes in the latest fashion, and pretty hats trimmed with bows and flowers. Some of the few men about were still in uniform, and those in civilian dress looked generally older and wore unrelieved black, including black bowler hats.

Celia sighed, and eased her sister round a corner. 'Mr Philpotts' workshop is just here, I think,' she said.

The corner itself was occupied by an empty shop with windows facing both Market Street and the side road. Beyond the shop, on the side road, was a brick wall broken only by a single board door painted a dingy green.

The two women approached it doubtfully, but were reassured by a black notice board screwed to the adjoining wall, which stated in faded gold letters

J.D. PHILPOTTS, UPHOLSTERER & FRENCH POLISHER.
COMPLETE RESTORATIONS UNDERTAKEN.

Celia swallowed nervously. 'I hope he doesn't mind our calling on him.'

'You're probably more important to him than he is to you at the moment,' Edna responded quickly, determined that the doctor's reassurance should not go down the drain immediately.

Celia's eyebrows shot up in surprise. 'I must say I never thought of it in that way.'

She smiled, and knocked at the door.

There was no response.

'Try again,' encouraged Edna.

There was a sound of slow movement within. 'Coming.'

The door swung open to reveal Mr Philpotts, looking rather different from his last meeting with Celia. He wore patched and stained overalls and his shirtsleeves were rolled up to the elbows to expose muscular forearms thatched with black hair. His wrists and hands were stained with a reddish-brown dye and he carried a grubby rag. On his head he wore an ancient peaked cap, and his face carried traces of the same stain as that on his hands.

He looked nonplussed for a moment – his clients usually sent for him rather than themselves descending on his smelly workshop, and he looked at the two women as if they were strangers. Then recollection dawned.

'Miss Gilmore!' he exclaimed.

Celia found her voice. She said apologetically, 'I'm afraid we have disturbed you when you are busy. Perhaps we can come another time. I wanted to have a look at the shop and to talk to you about one or two things.'

'Oh, that's all right, Miss. Come in. But mind your skirts don't brush anything. I've a grand piano drying out here. Follow me closely.' He dragged himself slowly down the side of the workshop.

The place was lit by skylights and was less dark than they had expected. The grand piano shone like a new one, and Edna, who played, looked at it enviously. They followed the polisher carefully, their eyes beginning to run from the sting of the rich mixed fumes of linseed oil, varnish, furniture polish and male sweat which assailed them.

He led them across a narrow corridor into another room, carefully closing each door after they had entered. Here lay the bones of a set of dining chairs, their seats and padded backs ripped out. Rolls of material filled shelves along one wall. Beneath them were bales of cotton and horsehair, their contents protruding slightly along the seams of the sacks. A heavy-duty sewing machine and a large cutting-out table, with a pair of shears lying on it, occupied the centre of the room. Another set of shelves held what Celia supposed were woodworker's tools. On a wall hung several handsaws, two of them gleaming, the rest obviously rusty with neglect. A high old-fashioned bookkeeper's desk with a matching chair stood against a wall. Above it was a small shelf holding files and account books. On the desk itself stood a spike with bills or receipts impaled upon it.

In the middle of the workroom, Mr Philpotts turned towards them. 'I'm sorry I've only one chair at the moment. I'm really only just getting started again.' He pulled the bookkeeper's chair out from beside the desk. 'The place was locked up for the duration when I went away – me uncle owns the property, you know. He didn't charge me nothing in rent while I was serving. But now I'm trying to get everything on a proper footing again.' He glanced from Celia to Edna. 'Have a seat, Miss.'

Celia told him not to worry, that they had come only for a few minutes. As the elder sister, Edna automatically perched on the uncomfortably high chair. Celia then introduced her to him.

He immediately responded, 'Pleased to meet you, Ma'am.' Then he turned to Celia and asked, 'What was it, Miss, that you came about?'

She apologised for not giving him a quicker decision regarding a possible partnership, but said that she was waiting for her father's trustee to visit them on the following Monday. 'My mother, Mrs Gilmore, will naturally want to consult him first.'

'That'll be OK. And you wanted to see the shop?'

They both smiled and nodded, and he led them back through the workshops, again shutting doors carefully after him. 'I have to keep the furniture I'm finishing as dust free as I can,' he explained. 'If I keep the doors shut, I don't get much draught blowing it around.'

The shop was thoroughly neglected, dusty and badly in need of repainting, but it was quite large, stretching back a fair distance. It had very nice corner windows.

Mr Philpotts explained his idea of showing the furniture in the window as if it were in a room. 'Inspire them, like,' he said.

Celia remarked that she would not be able to show all the furniture at once.

'Oh, aye,' he agreed. 'There's some old stables at the back, though, with a good stone floor – and one wide double door. If you send some of the poorer pieces, like the iron bedsteads, to the salerooms, I think there'll be space for most of the good pieces, between the shop and the shed. Old Aspen may not mind if you continue to rent his barn for a bit, anyway. He's a very decent fella.'

In her mind's eye Celia saw the shop glittering with new paint and all her mother's best pieces set out to catch the eye of the passing shoppers. She saw herself receiving customers like honoured guests, and letting them admire the furniture even if they did not buy. Life suddenly seemed to be opening out.

'I been thinking about your safety in the shop by yourself, Miss. But I'll be on the premises most of the time, and you could have a little handbell to press if you were uneasy. And I'd be with you as quick as I could.'

Personal safety had not occurred to her. She had simply felt shy at being in the company of Mr Philpotts all day. Total plainness and self-effacement had meant that no man had ever approached her, except with distant politeness. And no self-respecting upper-class girl considered working-class men as anything but people who did the work you told them to do. So, in her view, poor Mr Philpotts was perfectly safe to be with. The idea of other threats to her person disturbed her; she recollected with nervous fright her encounter on the great dyke.

'Surely I would be all right, wouldn't I, Mr Philpotts? There are always lots of people in Market Street.'

'On the whole, I would say yes, Miss. I'd like to suggest that you keep the silver locked in some of the cabinets at the back of the shop though. Small valuable things, like silver, would attract shoplifters.'

'Oh, dear. Yes, we can certainly do that.'

'In fact, I was thinking, Miss, that if the silver is high quality, you might like to put it up for auction with a real classy auctioneer, like Sotheby's. And the same the oil paintings.' He stopped to rub his face wearily and left another brown smear on it, as he thought for a minute.

Then he went on, 'I got a client who might come and look at the pictures for you, if you would like. He's a teacher at the art school in Liverpool. I done some work on frames for him, and just yesterday, he brought a couple of real nice gilt frames to me, to ask if I could clean them. Which I'll do, of course. Now, he'd have some idea if the paintings were worth anything much.'

Edna had kept silent during the conversation, because she wished Celia to handle it, but she had paid attention. She said to Celia, 'I think it would be a good idea to let experts see both silver and paintings. Mother inherited nearly all of them from her grandfather, when he gave up his home – and he had an even nicer home than we did. Some of the paintings came from Father's boyhood home.'

Celia looked at Mr Philpotts, and said, 'We'll arrange it, as soon as we have Mrs Gilmore's permission. Thank you for the suggestion.' Then, remembering Eddie Fairbanks' advice, she said a little gaily, 'We have to find ourselves a solicitor to help us arrange a simple partnership with each other – just so that we are clear what we are doing.'

'I suppose you're right, Miss. I hope it doesn't cost much.'

She laughed. 'Me, too,' she agreed.

She thanked Mr Philpotts, and Edna rose. Neither lady offered her hand to be shaken; although he had dropped his dirty rag in the workshop, Mr Philpotts' hands looked too messy to shake.

He grinned cheerfully at them as he unlocked the shop door into the street, and let them out. She was a proper little sweetie, she was, and her sister seemed a nice lady – no side.

'See you next week,' he said. For a second or two, he watched them wistfully, as they paused to put on their gloves before proceeding down the street. Thanks to the bloody Huns, he was never going to be any use to a woman again, he told himself bitterly. Perhaps it was a good thing that Alison had died in France, because he would not have been able to marry her, anyway.

At the thought of Alison, he heaved a great sob which stuck in his throat until he thought he would choke. Sometimes life dealt you some rotten cards.

Chapter Forty

❧

Cousin Albert descended on the little house by the sea like a slowly rolling avalanche. None of Louise's excuses that she had to read to blind soldiers and go to Liverpool to talk to the director of the School for the Blind worked with Timothy's stout trustee. Albert was determined to wind up her husband's and her affairs without any unnecessary delays. He wanted to go back to his own gentle retirement of fishing in the Trent, painting water colours and being spoiled by his eager servant and friend who looked after him.

The problem had been in dealing with Timothy's debts, and making sure that no claims were made on his wife's income. This had not been as difficult as he had at first imagined. Louise's marriage contract made it quite clear that most of the contents of the house were part of her dowry, as well as the cottages in Birkenhead. And, in addition, when the house itself had long since been put in her name by Timothy, he had specified that he was transferring both house and contents to her, so that left no doubt as to her ownership of all the contents. He must have seen, over a number of years, the financial clouds gathering.

'The house is as good as sold,' Albert told her, 'although it will be a few weeks before the legal aspects are completed. The lady wanting to start a nursing home has made a reasonable offer. She wants immediate possession.'

'When shall I get some money?' Louise asked anxiously.

'Before the end of the summer,' promised Albert. 'As soon as I know the exact sum we shall have to invest, I will look for the best annuity I can get for you.'

On the principle of pressing him to waste no time in doing

this, Louise said, 'Humph. I don't know how I shall manage until then.'

'Just have to manage on your rents,' Albert told her blithely. He was not going to offer to lend her anything; he had already paid his cousin's funeral expenses, and his expenses in dealing with the will were a loss to him – and that was enough.

Louise wept a little. She was lucky that neither of her daughters had yet had a private session with Albert; otherwise, she would have had the question of the shop unloaded on her that same evening.

As it was, she declared that life was too, too utterly hard, and took to her bed with a request that hot cocoa – and a glass of brandy, if they had any – be brought up to her.

Later, she also asked for her dinner to be brought up. Celia understood the considerable load of grief opened up by Cousin Albert, so she kissed her and promised to do this.

Her absence from the dinner table gave her daughters the opportunity to talk freely with Cousin Albert, as he sat, white linen table napkin tucked into his stiff, winged collar, and devoured the steak and kidney pie which Louise had prepared – like most middle-class women of her generation, she had, in her youth, been taught how to cook on the principle that, even if she employed a cook, the mistress of the house should be thoroughly conversant with all aspects of catering for a large family. Unfortunately, the custom had not continued into Edna and Celia's generation; more of their youth had been spent practising on the piano, or on reading, painting or embroidery or writing letters, rather than toiling in the kitchen. In school, Edna had also learned to play tennis and lacrosse and to ballroom dance, while Celia danced attendance on Louise.

It was Edna who now, almost gleefully, opened up the question of how to dispose of a barnful of furniture.

Despite the doctor's reassurance that she was quite well and capable, poor Celia was still scared, and she kept quiet.

As he wiped his mouth and leaned back to await dessert, Cousin Albert saw the common sense of Celia's attempting to earn a living. He was perfectly aware, from Louise's grumbling letters to him, what the young woman had, since Timothy's death, already achieved on her mother's behalf. In the back of his mind, he had been haunted by an uncomfortable premonition that, if he outlived Louise, he could, in his old age, have to maintain a penniless Celia in his contented male household. Here was a chance to lay at least that ghost to rest.

So Edna found the proposition received with rapt attention. Cousin Albert even smiled at silent Celia.

Just like the Cheshire Cat, thought Celia, though she did not understand the reasons behind his instant approval of the scheme.

As a dish of rice pudding and stewed prunes was set before him, he said, 'As I see it, there are two problems which must be clarified before you can do anything. One, the furniture belongs not to Celia, but to her mother. I presume, also, that the business, at least in its early years, would not produce enough return to pay Celia an adequate recompense for her work and at the same time show a profit which Louise could enjoy?'

'Exactly,' Celia blurted out, with her mouth full. 'If the furniture were mine, even from a small profit, I could give Mother something for my keep – I wouldn't cost her so much.' She swallowed, and went on more clearly, 'Of course, every time I sold a piece, I would have to save some of the money so that I could buy new stock, wouldn't I?'

Cousin Albert beamed. 'Yes,' he agreed. 'We'll make a business lady of you, I can see that.'

He was fortunately unaware that, because of his patronising tone, Edna felt a strong desire to tread hard on his toes under the table. She forbore, however, and instead smiled sweetly at him.

He carefully spat a prune stone out into his spoon and placed it on the edge of his dish. Then he went on. 'Two, you also need an agreement between yourself and this Mr Philpotts regarding rent and any repairs he may do for you. What do you know of this gentleman?'

They told him that he was well known locally as a decent, honest tradesman, who had recently been demobilised, wounded, from the army, and had just started up his business again. At this, Cousin Albert had a sudden hope that he might see Celia married off to such a person, which, from his own point of view, seemed even better.

'Obvious solution. Louise should give you the furniture, dear Celia. She won't ever need it again. The annuity I shall arrange for her, together with her rents, will give her an adequate income. She owns this house. Not bad at all.' He emptied his plate, put down his spoon and heaved a sigh of satisfaction. He beamed, and helped himself to a piece of cheese from a board proffered by Edna, while he continued to address Celia. 'Exactly what does the furniture consist of, my dear?'

Celia told him, and then added, 'There is some good china and her silver tea service, silver serving dishes and cake baskets, stacks of it – and all the old pictures that used to hang in the hall and in Father's study. Mother chose the nice ones she wanted to hang in this house.' She gestured vaguely towards the mantelpiece, over which hung an etching of Landseer's *A Stag at Bay*.

Cousin Albert glanced at the stag and grunted, 'Humph.' He looked round the room and found a couple of works featuring shaggy highland cattle standing in front of purple mountains. 'I imagine that you could sell the ones in the barn to local people.' he suggested.

'I expect so.'

'I wonder if dear Louise would, perhaps, like to have the silver auctioned by a good Liverpool auctioneer. It would give her some money to carry her through until I have bought the annuity. If you think she would like that, I am sure that it can be arranged.' He looked down at his dessert spoon and cheese knife. 'I see she has retained her tableware.'

Edna turned to Celia, and said, 'That's exactly what Mr Philpotts suggested; with regard to the silver he mentioned Sotheby's. I think it's a very good idea, Celia. The silver is probably the most valuable part of the whole collection. It may be out of date in design – but it is good – I seem to remember that it was very heavy.'

Celia agreed. She said shyly, 'I don't want Mother to give me

281

anything terribly valuable – only the furniture she doesn't want. I would be very happy if the silver raised enough money to help her now.' She laughed a little ruefully, when she added, 'I doubt if Mama ever thought about its value. She's always had it – the same as her friends had silverware. To her, it was simply too much clutter to store in this cottage.'

Edna interjected that Mr Philpotts felt that the silver in the little shop might attract thieves.

'He's right,' agreed Cousin Albert. 'I presume it is still packed up?'

'Yes, in barrels.'

'I'll talk to Louise about it.'

'Can you persuade her that it would be no disgrace for Celia to run her own shop?' Edna asked. 'I believe that her main objection is that it is improper for a lady to be in trade. And I also think she is shocked that Mr Philpotts, poor soul, will be in the same premises.' She suppressed a small chuckle behind her table napkin. The gesture, however, was not missed by Cousin Albert; he saw her twinkling eyes and then Celia's blush.

He replied carefully, 'Men and women are beginning to work together – in fact, they had to do so throughout the war. However much one may disapprove of it, a dignified young woman like Celia should have no problems.'

'Dear Cousin Albert,' Edna responded. 'You really are so wise and sensible. I hope you can convince Mother.'

The stout old gentleman beamed at her. He patted her hand and promised to do his best, as soon as Louise felt rested enough to receive him.

Because she was stifling a laugh, Celia kept her eyes down. Really Edna was without shame!

Chapter Forty-One

It took time. But then women were so difficult to deal with.

With grinding patience, the following morning, Cousin Albert agreed to visit the nursing home full of blind soldiers and listened to Louise's belief that she should try, at least, to help them, particularly the two deaf-blind men.

Safe in his personal cocoon, the war had, largely, passed Albert Gilmore by. With no sons to worry about, his worst anxieties were concerned with the steady rise of prices. It was almost as much of a shock to him to see the young men in whom Louise was interested as it had been to Louise herself. He was not an unkind man and was genuinely touched at the sight of the helpless men.

In a vague way, he also understood her need for a reason to live, some honourable cause to work for in her lonely widowhood, and here were substitutes for her dead sons. The hugeness of her undertaking made him feel guilty that he had done nothing about the war, except be thankful not to be involved.

That evening, he sat with her in the front sitting room and after discussing the visit to the nursing home, he turned the conversation to Celia and the need for single women to work nowadays. He mentioned a well-educated young woman cashier in his bank, who had, throughout the war, dealt with his banking needs.

'Now, with demobilisation, of course, the men are returning, and poor Celia would not stand a chance of such employment. In fact, she will have the greatest difficulty in maintaining herself once you are gone. And I believe she is now at least twenty-four so she has not much chance of matrimony. A tiny business of her own, however, could make all the difference.' He paused to sniff appreciatively at a glass of Timothy's brandy, thoughtfully provided by Edna. Then he continued, 'Beginning it in a very small way, with a small businessman to guide her while she learns to buy and sell, should mean that she won't make any major mistakes.'

He saw Louise stiffen in her chair, and before continuing in that vein, he said he wanted to speak to her about the silver.

'Silver?'

She listened open-mouthed while he suggested the plan he had already discussed with her daughters. Then she said, 'We could simply send everything for auction.'

'And spoil dear Celia's chance? No, Louise. You don't really need the furniture or the pictures or the china, or what they would bring in a sale. They would not fetch that much at auction anyway.

'Now the silverware is different. From what I remember, the silver is outstanding in workmanship and weight. It is probably worth much, much more. Give Celia the chance with the furniture. Let her try at least. She may, at worst, learn something which will prepare her for the new world we are facing – and it will have cost you very little. Since, after a while, she may be earning quite well, she can help you with the upkeep of the home.' He did not mention that he hoped she might marry – he considered that the idea of an artisan as a son-in-law would probably send Louise through the ceiling with an explosion of rage.

It wasn't that easy. Her old excuses that she needed Celia at home nearly defeated him. But he remembered that his own house was run by one manservant and a charwoman, so he suggested the employment of a daily woman to come in – that should be enough to keep a cottage going. Edna would have hugged him, had she heard him go on to suggest that she probably needed one anyway; Edna had for several days been putting off scrubbing the very dirty kitchen floor because she simply had not much idea of how to go about the job.

Afterwards, Cousin Albert felt that he had come through the

equivalent of negotiating the post-war international peace proposals – but with greater success. He hoped that he had removed for ever the chance of having to endure women relatives in his home.

He stayed an extra week while he did his best to arrange everything so that Celia got legal ownership of the contents of Ben Aspen's barn and a shop sublet to her by John Philpotts. He also got the couple to sign a simple agreement regarding any repairs and refurbishing John did on the furniture for her; it was not perfect, but he thought that it would be workable.

He then took Louise to Liverpool to see her husband's solicitor regarding the legal details of the house sale and to meet the purchaser of her home, Mrs Dora Johnson, and the estate agent. Carried along by Cousin Albert's male self-confidence and the sense that he understood the sale of a house, she forgot completely Celia's warnings about her need for a solicitor to look after her own interests, and the charming Mr Little, to whom Mr Carruthers had sent her.

As she followed the grim-faced purchaser and the agent into Mr Barnett's office, she whispered to Albert that she hated selling the house to such a common woman.

Fearing she would make a fuss in the lawyer's office, Cousin Albert hastily whispered assurances into her ear that, though the lady did not sound her aitches, she was a very worthy, experienced nurse and one could respect the work she proposed to do.

Chapter Forty-Two

✿

A veiled Louise and a businesslike Mrs Johnson signed their way through a sheaf of papers laid before them by Mr Barnett. Firmly guided by him, Louise put her name to every page without reading it or raising a single objection, exactly as Cousin Albert had taken for granted she would do.

The two ladies afterwards politely shook hands, and Cousin Albert shook the solicitor's hand. He breathed a sigh of relief that he would shortly have Louise off his hands. The house was sold.

Mr Barnett got up from his desk and bowed everyone out of his office.

In the outer office, Mrs Johnson paused, and said hesitantly to the other three that, if Mrs Gilmore could kindly spare the time, she would very much like to go over the house with Louise, while they were both in Liverpool. 'And you could tell me which chimneys smoke at times, like, and how long the hot water boiler takes to heat and how much water it holds – maybe I should have a bigger one installed. I am sure you could make some very useful suggestions regarding the adaptation of the house to nursing.'

Louise turned to Albert. 'Oh, Albert,' she wailed, 'I couldn't bear to look at the house.'

Over her head, Mrs Johnson mouthed, 'It would save me a lot of time if she would.'

Albert sighed, and said to the black veil, 'I know it would be difficult for you, my dear Louise. We have to remember, however, that Mrs Johnson hopes to help men who have been badly wounded and need care until they can be admitted to a more permanent military institution. She naturally wants them to be as comfortable as possible.'

Mrs Johnson beamed at him. A sob came from under the veil.

He looked desperately round at the agent for inspiration, but before they could think of any way to persuade Louise, Mrs Johnson, a nurse with long experience, chimed in, in dulcet tones, to suggest that poor Mrs Gilmore might feel a bit easier if she had a nice hot cup of tea and a little rest in the tea shop across the road, before going to the house. 'It would set her up like nothing else would.' She smiled at the veil, and then added persuasively, 'I wouldn't keep her long at the house, but it would help to speed things up if Mrs G. would tell me a few details about it.'

Cousin Albert had put his arm round Louise's shoulders, and he could feel her cringe at being referred to as Mrs G. He felt that he should refuse and should take her home. But Louise, suddenly aware of cohorts of wounded in dire need of comfort, said, with a sniff, that if advising about chimneys would help our dear wounded, she would certainly make the trip.

Hugely relieved, Cousin Albert swept them into the lift. They were propelled down to the ground floor by an elderly, uniformed, one-armed lift man who, seeing yet another forlorn, veiled widow, leaning on Albert's arm, pulled the lift's ropes with care and brought them to a particularly gentle stop at street level. 'Poor dear!' he said to Albert. 'Lost 'er boys? I see 'em nearly every day.'

Slightly annoyed at this very personal remark, Albert merely nodded his head, and then eased the ladies out of the lift.

In the café, Louise lifted her veil back and silently ate a petit four and drank a luke-warm cup of tea, while the philistine opposite her downed a rum baba and an equally chilled cup of tea. Cousin Albert, refusing tea, went to get a taxicab. The estate agent elected to go with him.

A widow herself, Mrs Johnson felt very sorry about Louise's grief, but did not know what to say. She rather wished, after all, she had not asked her to visit the house.

Finally, when she could endure the silence no longer, she asked tentatively if Louise would be kind enough to furnish her with the names of reliable local workmen.

Louise swallowed the last of the petit four, looked up and stared blankly at her.

'You see, Mrs Gilmore, I'm from Manchester, where I'm already running one little nursing home. I don't know Liverpool very well, so I'm anxious to know who to turn to. I also want to get reliable staff.'

Louise nodded, and Mrs Johnson, feeling the need of some further explanation, went on, 'Me hubby left me a thriving grocery shop and I ran it for a bit. But I'm no grocer. I'm a good nurse though, even if I says it myself – and I never gave it up altogether, even when I was married – so I sold the business and bought the Manchester nursing home – and it's done real well. A Liverpool doctor came to see one of my patients, and he gave me the idea that I could start another one here.'

She put down her cup and leaned back from the table. 'So here I am.'

By this time, Louise was diverted. She managed to remark, 'How interesting. How will you run them both?'

'Well, there's lots of army nurses out of work at present – and there's a real shortage of men for them to marry, so they've got to find work. I've a couple of real experienced nursing sisters workin' for me in Manchester – and the visiting doctors trust them. I can spend some time getting your house ready – and I'll see how we go.'

Haltingly, Louise began to tell her of her own work amongst the deaf-blind. By the time Albert, puffing from his exertions, returned to tell them that a taxi awaited them and that the estate agent was already ensconced in it they were deeply engaged in conversation, and Louise was enduring the dropped aitches of Mrs Johnson with considerable fortitude.

Women! He would never understand them, Albert thought, as he paid the bill.

As they trailed up the unwashed front steps of the empty house and then waited while the estate agent, using his own key, unlocked the dusty front door, Louise wanted to cry. She was further distressed when they entered the vast emptiness of the hall.

'I thought I'd divide the hall up into me office and a reception area,' remarked Mrs Johnson prosaically as she looked slowly round it.

From behind the veil came a heavy sigh, and then a sudden shriek.

The service door at the back of the hall had opened silently, and, like a ghost, a white-haired woman clad in black stood before them. Her mouth agape with consternation, the woman stood transfixed as she faced the little group by the front door.

'Oh, Ma'am!' she gasped.

An astonished Louise flung back her veil with an angry gesture. 'Winnie! What on earth are you doing here?'

Albert was equally surprised. The estate agent, who had been putting his key chain back into his waistcoat pocket, looked up in absolute bewilderment. Both Mrs Johnson and he knew Winnie as the temporary caretaker of the house and neither could understand the fuss.

Sudden tears were running down Winnie's face. She glanced desperately to either side, as if trying to escape.

Louise repeated her question.

Winnie licked her lips. She hung her head and said sullenly, 'When you left, I'd got nowhere to go – though I tried hard to get a job.'

'So?' Louise forgot her sorrow at having to look once more at her empty home. Her property had been violated, taken advantage of, and she was very annoyed.

'I thought you wouldn't mind, Ma'am. You never moved the furniture out of my room – wasn't worth it, you said. Likewise, the coal in the cellar.' She twisted a grubby handkerchief in her hands. 'I thought it would be useful to you if someone were in the house. It'd keep vandals from smashing the winders or even getting into the place. Till I got a live-in place, like.'

She fell silent.

The estate agent said hastily that he had been under the impression that that was exactly what Mrs Gilmore had intended. He had felt it was an extremely good idea. He had met Winnie on his first inspection of the home. She had said then that she was the cook and had served Mrs Gilmore for many years, and she had showed him round the kitchens and cellars. Mrs Gilmore might possibly recall that she was out when he came.

Mrs Gilmore did recall her unhappy visit to Phyllis's house on that day. She sniffed. It may very well have been a sensible idea, but Winnie had no right to take advantage of her like that.

'I still feel that her presence is very reprehensible. You had decent notice, Winnie, and you should have left on the day agreed as soon as the cleaning was completed.'

Winnie said shamefacedly, 'Yes, Ma'am.'

'You are to pack your bag and go, before we leave this house. You are trespassing.'

'Yes, Ma'am.'

Mrs Johnson had watched the exchange with fascination. The woman had held her temper admirably in the face of her employer's anger. And she was the cook? On her previous visits, Winnie had always discreetly withdrawn to her attic bedroom, and Mrs Johnson had thought her to be an old, trusted nanny, and had never really talked to her. The estate agent had explained that she was temporarily caretaking the house, which was the explanation of her presence given to him by Winnie.

Winnie slowly turned and went back down the kitchen staircase, where her straw trunk lay in a cupboard. It held everything she owned, and she had kept it downstairs so that she could move out quickly when the house changed hands.

In the vast, practically empty kitchen, she sat down on a solitary straight chair, put her hands over her face and sobbed aloud. She felt she had no friend in the world who could help her. Mrs Gilmore was a soulless bitch.

Meanwhile, Louise and Mrs Johnson went slowly round the house. Much of the curtaining had been included in the price of the house, and Mrs Johnson assured Louise that it would be a comfort to 'the boys' because it would keep out both cold in the winter and too much light in the summer.

In the bathroom, Mrs Johnson explained that each ward would have its own washstands, chamber pots and bedpans, and the invalids would mostly need bed baths. So one bathroom would probably be enough.

They discussed plumbers and painters and gas men and gardeners, until Louise became quite absorbed in the project, and Albert, finding an abandoned chair in a front bedroom, decided resignedly that he would sit there until they had finished.

As they descended to the basement kitchens, Mrs Johnson said she would make the servants' sitting room into another ward. It looked out on to the brick-lined area, a sunken yard alongside the basement which allowed light into the room. 'I could put some pots of geraniums out there, and it would be a nice place for men who can be lifted out of bed to sit in the fresh air. I believe in fresh air.'

'There is a large garden,' Louise reminded her.

'Oh, I'll grow a pile of fresh vegetables in that, though I'll keep a tiny lawn with flowers for the boys.'

Winnie heard the conversation as they came down the stairs, and she hastily wiped her face and picked up her hat from the cupboard. As they entered, she jabbed in her hatpins, and then glanced sulkily up at the ladies.

Mrs Johnson smiled kindly at her, and said, 'Oh, Winnie. I would like to have a word with you before you go.'

'Yes, Ma'am. Shall I wait here?'

'Please do.'

In that second, Louise realised that the house was truly not hers any more, and that Mrs Johnson now had every right to give orders in it. She wanted to expostulate, however, that Winnie was her servant and that she would say what she was to do. But she equally suddenly realised that this was no longer so; she had, long since, dismissed her.

She thought she would choke, as Winnie smiled suddenly at the new owner. Winnie sensed that she had just found herself a new job.

They inspected the area and the steps that led from it up to the garden.

Louise felt she had had enough. She pulled her veil over her face and said she must go home. They rejoined the estate agent patiently standing in the hall. He gave the entire collection of keys to the house to the new owner, with the remark that Winnie had additional keys to the back door and the back garden gate.

'I'll get them from her,' replied Mrs Johnson placidly.

Hearing the sounds of departure, Albert came slowly down the stairs. Farewells were said, and he escorted a very frustrated Louise down the steps to the waiting taxi.

'Tell the taxi driver to come back for me, when he's finished with you,' Mrs Johnson shouted after them.

The taxi driver heard and tipped his hat in acknowledgement. Albert merely nodded.

In the cab, Louise exploded. 'So that's how Winnie was able to come and go. Celia never collected her house keys from her. Stupid girl!'

Albert sighed, and began the slow task of calming her down. To divert her attention, he spoke of the impending sale of the silverware which would, he was sure, do much to alleviate her present impoverished situation.

That evening, Celia got a resounding scolding for forgetting to collect all the keys of the old house, and subsequently wept silently in her bedroom.

A few days later, the silver was valued and a reserve price put on it prior to auction. Once it was sold, Louise had a respectable bank account – in a local bank, with a charming young manager, Mr Gwynn-Jones, who quite put Mr Carruthers in the shade – and Edna got her charwoman.

With regard to the proposed antique shop, Celia was, at first, frightened to death at the sudden realisation of the responsibilities she was taking on.

Supported by Edna's, Betty Houghton's and John Philpotts' encouragement, however, and a second visit to see Dr Mason to have her prescription of Dr Parrish's Food renewed, she began slowly to bloom. Dr Mason did not fail to notice a certain new liveliness in her, and took the time to discover the source of it.

She sat back in her chair, and told Celia, 'I know you can do it!' And privately hoped to God that she was right.

Chapter Forty-Three

❧

'Mr Fairbanks says to come to dig your garden – a shillin' for three hours.'

As Edna faced the blond giant standing on the back step, she dried her hands on her apron and stared at him – white knights sometimes arrive in strange disguises.

Absolutely calm pale-blue eyes stared amiably back at her. 'It's a right mess!' He gestured over his shoulder with a huge, grubby thumb. 'I looked at it. Want the bushes took out as well?'

Edna swallowed, and found her voice. 'Yes, please. And your name is . . . ?'

'Ethelred. What's yours?'

Though she was shaken by his impudence, she answered him, 'Mrs Fellowes.'

· Ethelred smiled hugely and stuck his thumbs in his leather belt. 'Now we know each other, like me mam told me we would.'

Edna smiled a little stiffly, and asked, 'Do you have a spade, Ethelred?' She knew that some gardening tools had accidentally been sent to the barn instead of to the cottage. They had yet to be retrieved.

Ethelred's face crumpled up like a baby's about to cry. 'No,' he said sadly. Then he brightened as if enlightenment had dawned. 'Mam said if you didn't have one, Mr Fairbanks would lend us one.'

'Good,' said Edna, whipping off her apron. 'Let's go next door and ask him.' She walked round the outside of their cottage, Ethelred ambling behind her, like a friendly dog being taken for a walk. She thankfully handed him over to Eddie, who offered to instruct the boy in exactly what should be done.

Since Edna had no ideas about the garden, she readily accepted the offer.

Ethelred was not the fastest worker, but once a job was explained to him, he went at it steadily. He received with excessive pleasure a large mug of cocoa at mid-morning and quaffed it happily as he stood in the sunshine. Then he handed the mug back to Edna, and announced, 'I'm goin' to pee,' and strode straight through the wild hedge at the bottom of the garden on to the common behind it. Still buttoning his fly, he returned to removing the sod and bushes off the original garden beds before actually turning the soil over. At the very bottom of the garden a pile of rubbish began to grow.

'When I'm done I'll make a good bonfire of it,' he promised Edna cheerfully. 'We can roast some potatoes in it.'

Edna prayed that he would not accidentally set the house on fire.

Though Ethelred's mind might lack a tack or two, he proved to be wonderfully helpful when the two women began to fix up the shop. He was a gentle creature and became very fond of Edna. When she handed him a yard broom, to sweep out the shop, he kept on going right into John Philpotts' workshop and Edna had to persuade him that it was not her domain. She suggested that, perhaps, he would kindly sweep the pavement round the corner shop and also the front doorstep. This latter job took rather longer, since he knew absolutely everybody passing by, and some of them stopped to ask him what he was doing. He had a very sociable morning.

Urged on by Betty, Ben Aspen quoted Celia a very small sum for lending one of his labourers for a couple of mornings to paint the interior of the shop. The price of the white paint was included. Since Celia did not as yet have any money, Betty simply added the charge to what the Gilmores owed for work on the cottage.

Ethelred helped to sort out from the barn the shabbier furniture which was to be sent for auction, and the auctioneer took it away in a lorry. After a closed van came from Liverpool to collect the barrels of silver, Celia was able to retrieve a couple of carpets which had been stacked at the back of the barn. She laid them on the newly scrubbed shop floor.

Edna and Celia had never been so tired in their lives. They found they worked quite well together, though they often disagreed about detail. As promised, Edna paid Ethelred for his work in the garden, and then lent Celia enough to pay him for his help in connection with the shop.

'We simply cannot function without him,' she said flatly.

Celia was glad to see Edna's complexion improve in the fresh sea air, which was inescapable in blustery Hoylake. She was naturally a dark woman, but she lost much of the unhealthy yellow look which life in the Tropics had given her. Because she smoked less, she was also eating better and her figure filled out. She seemed to enjoy helping Celia set up her little shop, and spent more and more time there.

She got on very well with John Philpotts, and sometimes talked to him about her life in Brazil.

Because Edna had been married, John felt more at ease talking to her, rather than to Celia, and, from a number of small hints, Edna guessed that he was impotent as a result of his wounds.

Neither woman would allow John to move furniture; they feared that he would damage his already wounded leg.

'I have to move pieces in the course of my own work,' he protested. But they laughed and told him they were not going to make a beast of burden of him. They did, however, borrow a small trolley cart, which he himself used for moving furniture round his workshop, and, since Ethelred had obviously become their devoted slave, John left the lifting to him.

Having Edna with her eased Celia's first days with John Philpotts, and her shyness slowly ebbed away. With regard to Ethelred, his almost childlike attitude made her protective of him; she never considered him as an adult male. He had, however, tremendous physical strength and was a real asset. He could lift almost anything.

Celia chose with care the first stock she wanted to show in her shop. When a small furniture remover from the village moved it over to the new premises for her, she got him to bring as much of the rest as could be squashed into the storage shed at the back of John's yard without damaging it.

There was still an alarming amount left in the barn, so she asked the furniture remover to stack it neatly to one side, and then went to see Betty about keeping it there.

Betty laughed, and said, 'Leave Father to me. It'll be all right for a while.' Then she recommended a sign writer to paint the name of the shop on the front of it. It was christened by the three of them, Celia's Antiques and Collectibles.

With over twenty-five pounds from the auction of the mass of everyday furniture from the maids' bedrooms, the kitchen, the servants' sitting room in the basement, the back hall and the back staircase, not to speak of a hefty stone angel which had stood in the back garden for years, she was able to pay for the remover and for the sign.

'I still owe you an awful lot, Edna,' she wailed. Then she added, 'You know, the angel drew the best bids.'

'Most appropriate, and don't worry about the money – I don't have many expenses. I can wait,' replied Edna cheerfully. 'Papa Fellowes sent me a cheque for this month.'

The outside of the shop got a good hose down from Ethelred and, when it was dry, Celia polished the front door and Edna cleaned the windows.

The day before she was to open, Eddie Fairbanks brought her, on a little trailer attached to his bicycle, two heavy white flower-pots crowded with red geraniums. He placed one on either side of the front door.

The whole place looked very pretty in the early summer sunshine.

Celia was overwhelmed when she saw the flowers. She thanked Eddie and then impulsively gave him a big hug. 'Everybody's been so kind,' she said, and took out her handkerchief and blew her nose hard.

Cousin Albert had also helped her with advice regarding a business licence, for which Edna had loaned her the money until the auctioneer paid her.

Altogether, Celia found herself surrounded by helpful friends and, in some wonderment, she said to Edna, 'I've never before had friends – or anybody – who did things for me; even Phyllis wasn't like this.'

Edna laughed. 'It's overdue,' she said. 'I don't think you've ever been out without Mother before. No chance to make any real friends of your own.'

Louise did not come to look at the shop. She said rightly that it would be too painful to see the contents of her old home up for sale. Though her visits to the soldiers in the nursing home often took her into Market Street, she always avoided passing the shop by crossing to the other side of the road.

Celia understood, and she sympathised. Because she was not so much under her mother's thumb, she was able to understand more fully her mother's efforts to come out of her grief and create a new life for herself.

One evening, after she had closed the shop for the night, she went over to the Aspens' yard, to rummage in the barn for more of the Philip Oppenheim books which her mother wanted. While doing so, she came across a little trunk of her own personal possessions.

Kneeling on the stone floor, she unstrapped it and looked at the curious collection of oddments which she had kept over the years. Wrapped in tissue paper and laid on the top was the dress she had worn for her Confirmation, together with the prayer book given her by Great-aunt Blodwyn. She smiled at the recollection of the excited fourteen-year-old who had worn it; she had felt like a bride. Underneath were letters, which she had lovingly tied together with blue baby ribbon, letters from both her brothers while at boarding school, and, later, when they went to war.

In the failing shaft of light from the setting sun through the great door of the barn, she held them in her hands and bowed her head and cried.

They had thought about their little sister consistently throughout their short lives, she realised. Perhaps, if there had been no war, they would have found amongst their friends some decent young man to marry her. At least she would never have had to worry about her future; one or the other of them would certainly have given her a home – and affection.

Outside, she heard Ben Aspen's workmen shouting good night to each other, and she hastily put down the letters and delved in the bottom of the box. Two battered dolls, some children's books, and at the very bottom the only toy which she knew had been given to her by her paternal grandmother, a wooden box of hand-made building bricks. She had no real memory of her grand-mother, but she lifted the box out and opened it.

Each little cube was about two inches in size and was grubby from much play. On all six sides of each brick, a letter of the alphabet had been carefully carved in relief, so that the letter stood out. She ran her fingers gently along the bricks, and remembered how her nanny had taught her the alphabet from them and how to spell simple words.

At the thought of Nanny kneeling on the floor with her and patiently spelling out words, she had a sudden inspiration about how her mother could, perhaps, communicate with the two poor deaf-blind servicemen about whom she was so concerned.

She bundled her other treasures back into the trunk and closed it. She would ask Ethelred, some time, to carry the trunk to the cottage. Her personal grief forgotten, she hurriedly pushed the barn doors closed and locked the padlock. She ran across the deserted yard to Betty's office to say good night before she left.

Betty had on her coat and hat, ready to go home. Her father was with her, so Celia simply paused to say that she had locked the barn up and wished them both good night. Then, clutching her box of bricks, she ran for the train to Meols.

Chapter Forty-Four

Celia sat behind a little table which Ethelred had set across a corner at the back of the shop for her. It had a drawer in it in which to keep money, and, in that position, it would be difficult for a customer to ease round the table and open it. She had a brand-new account book in front of her, so that each day she could enter the transactions which had taken place. She also had a receipt book; a pen; a pencil box holding a pencil, India rubber and extra pen nibs; a piece of blotting paper and a cut-glass inkwell. On a corner of the table lay a number of books on antiques, which she was reading her way through very carefully.

All she needed was customers. Though a number of people walked in and looked round, nobody bought anything.

Occasionally, someone asked a price, and she would get up and walk round to them to tell them, and, perhaps, open a drawer to show the fine dovetailing of the piece's interior or remark that the wood was the finest mahogany and that the piece was over a hundred years old and, therefore, an antique. They invariably remarked that things were too expensive, but she refused to reduce the price.

She was very despondent, and made still more so when she discovered that some of the china ornaments she had put out for display had been stolen.

'It must have been when I was showing a dressing table to a woman, you know, John,' she lamented. 'Her friend was strolling round looking at things. I got distracted. Two really pretty shepherdesses and a pin tray just gone like that,' and she snapped her fingers to illustrate the rapidity of the theft.

'Oh, aye, it's a common enough ploy – two friends work

together – and you'd better watch out if a woman comes in with children – the kids'll clear a display case while you're dealing with the mother at the counter.'

'The children would steal?' Celia was shocked.

'Yes.' John sighed and sat himself down on a wooden rocking chair. He was dressed in a suit and had a heavy portfolio of upholstery samples, which he laid carefully on the floor beside him; he had just returned from seeing a customer in her home. She wanted all her drawing-room furniture re-covered and repolished, a nice job which would help his finances.

He looked round the shop, and suggested, 'You could put your knick-knacks and – them four mantel clocks – in the big glass cabinet over there and lock it – I see it has a key. Keep the key in your pocket. And keep your eyes open, luv.'

She nodded, and sadly did as he advised.

'I must go and write up me estimate,' he said, and heaved the heavy samples into his workshop.

A week later, he knocked on the intervening door between his workshop and the shop, and, as usual, came in without waiting for her answer. He had brought her a rather grubby mug of tea, which he set before her on top of the closed receipt book. She thanked him shyly and put her cold hands round the mug to warm them, before drinking the tea.

He again sat down on the rocking chair, and said, 'I talked to Alec Tremaine last night. Met him in the Ship Inn. He's the teacher at the art school that I told you about. If it's all right with you, he'll come in on Saturday to look at your paintings. He says he's no expert, but he'd have a shrewd idea whether they were good or not.'

Acutely aware that the money left over from the auction was being rapidly eroded by the need to pay her rent and Ethelred's wages, she inquired anxiously, 'What would he charge?'

'Oh, he's not going to charge you; he's quite interested in old paintings. Paints himself, as well as teaching.'

'That's most awfully kind of you and of him. I shall be here all day, needless to say.'

As if he hadn't heard her last remark, he went on heavily, 'Him being a teacher and not owning a gallery, I think you're not likely to be cheated by him in any way – if there is something fairly valuable amongst them, like. A gallery might say they were not worth much and offer to buy them as a job lot very cheap. You could lose a lot of money that way.'

Celia sipped her tea and smiled, 'Oh, I'm sure you wouldn't recommend anybody who would be likely to cheat. And would a gallery really cheat?'

'Well, it can happen in any business, and more than anywhere in the antique trade. You can be had quick enough by anybody. When you need to buy stock, you ought to remember to decry whatever's up for sale, so that you give the lowest possible price for it.' He grinned slyly at her.

She knew that he was right. Her father's business adage, often repeated when his wife had been extravagant, had been buy low, sell high. And the value of second-hand furniture was, at best, uncertain; she was sure of that.

John got up and stretched himself. 'Haven't seen Miss Edna for a couple of days. Is she well?'

'Oh, yes, thank you. She's just catching up in the house. We've all been out so much that it's a mess.' She looked ruefully round the shop, and said, 'She can't do much here, at the moment – I'm not exactly busy.'

'No, that's for sure, luv.'

'Do you think I've priced stuff too high for people?'

'I doubt it. I think you're not getting the right kind of people into the shop. You need to do some advertising – and I need to do some, too – we could do it together, if you like. Let's talk about it when Miss Edna comes. Or Betty Houghton might have some ideas – there's a smart lady if ever there was. Maybe get a little article into the Hoylake paper or, better still, the Chester paper, about the opening of the shop.'

Although she had no idea what either Edna or Betty could contribute, Celia agreed enthusiastically, and John went back to his workshop.

The little bell on the front door tinged as someone entered. Celia turned towards it.

'Oh,' she exclaimed. 'Dr Mason! How nice to see you.'

Chapter Forty-Five

Edith Mason came swiftly in, and looked round. 'How pretty it all looks,' she said, her eyes twinkling merrily behind gold-rimmed spectacles. 'Do you mind if I have a look?'

'Please do.'

Edith put down her doctor's bag by Celia's work table, took off her gloves and loosened a blue silk scarf which she was wearing. She proceeded to circle round, occasionally pausing to stare at a particular piece. She stopped in front of a bookcase in which Celia was displaying a collection of Victorian and Edwardian novels, many of them beautifully bound in leather, their titles in gilt. She laughed, and remarked, 'I see many old friends amongst these.'

'Are you looking for anything special?'

'I actually wanted a really large desk for my consulting room. But you don't seem to have one.'

'Oh, but I do. I have Father's desk. It's in the back shed, however. Would you mind coming through to the back?'

'Not at all.'

Celia shot the inside bolt on the front door, and then led her client through the back passage to the rear door.

'Phew!' exclaimed the doctor, as they passed the closed door of John's workshop.

Celia laughed. 'It's Mr Philpotts with his French polishing. I'm sorry – it makes an awful smell.'

'It can't be very good for him. I hope he has his workroom well ventilated.'

'Well, there are windows.'

They crossed the yard, and Celia unlocked and opened the

double doors of the shed. In the poor light, she pointed out the desk.

It was rather dusty, so Celia pulled her little yellow duster from her pocket and ran it over the wood. She pointed out that it was double pillared with seven drawers, all with dovetailed corners. The pillars and the fronts of the drawers were elaborately carved. Round the top surface it was inlaid with mother-of-pearl in a pattern of lotuses. The writing area was covered in fine green leather embossed with a leaf-patterned edging in gold.

The drawer pulls were heavy brass, and Edith ran her fingers round one of them. 'Hand thrown?' she inquired.

'Yes. It is certainly beautifully made, although I don't think it is quite old enough to be classed as an antique,' Celia said honestly. 'My paternal grandfather brought it from Malaya.'

'How much do you want for it?'

'I am asking twenty-five pounds.' She knew that a cheap new desk could be bought for about five pounds, and she held her breath, while Edith considered it.

'It's rather expensive,' Edith said, running her fingers longingly over the exquisite mahogany. She sighed. 'I would like to see it in a better light, before I decide.'

'That could be arranged. If you would like to step in again tomorrow, I'll ask Ethelred to move it into the shop. You would be able to see it in a good light there.'

'Thank you. I would like that.' She shrugged, and confided, 'As you can imagine, I never know exactly when I will be free, but some time before you close, I'll come over.' She smiled at Celia, and added, 'I love beautiful things round me. I'm using Father's old desk at present. All the drawers keep sticking, and the surface is stained beyond redemption. It doesn't give a good impression – besides which,' she said ruefully, 'I have to see an awful lot of it, and I would like to have something good. You know, Father never cared about possessions, and with no mother in the house, there was no one to suggest anything better.'

Celia laughed. 'People make do every day with things they don't like, don't they? And keep in store the really beautiful

305

things they should be enjoying. Don't worry, I'll keep it for you until you come.'

The hint that it could be sold quite quickly was not lost on Edith. She thought that Celia was learning fast. She noted with some relief that the girl had lost the look of absolute despair which she had exhibited in her office.

The next day, the desk, in all its well-polished glory, stood in the window, its rich wood catching the afternoon sun, and when Edith saw it through the window, she knew that she wanted it very much, a fitting memento of a month when her practice had shown real growth. She dickered over the price, and Celia brought it down slowly to twenty pounds, agreeing reluctantly to a payment of ten pounds that day and ten pounds in fourteen days.

'You don't have to deliver it until I've paid the second instalment,' Edith said encouragingly.

Celia looked at this lady who had, she felt, given her new life, and had a strong inclination to give her the desk. Common sense won, however, when she remembered that she had obligations herself. She responded by saying that she was sure she could trust Edith to pay, and that Ethelred would deliver it on a handcart the next day. 'I'll wrap it well in a quilt so that it doesn't get scratched,' she promised.

The doctor gave her a cheque for ten pounds, and Celia carefully wrote her first receipt. For years afterwards, she said that this was the most exciting moment she could remember in all her life – with one exception.

After she had seen the doctor out, she ran through the shop, cheque in hand, to tell John Philpotts the good news.

Chapter Forty-Six

❦

After Ethelred had delivered the desk and while he still had the rented handcart, she closed the shop a little early, and together they walked over to the Aspens' yard, to collect all the pictures that she had. As Ethelred lifted them out of the barn, she arranged them carefully, back to back, on the old quilt which she had spread over the handcart. Betty came over from her office to look at some of them, and heard about the impending visit of Alec Tremaine.

'That's just like John,' she said. 'He'd help anyone struggling.'

'I hope his friend won't mind helping me.'

'I'm sure he won't. He'll probably be quite interested, if he's an artist, as you say. I wonder if he's Lady Tremaine's son back from the war at last.'

'I've no idea,' replied Celia. Then she said slowly, 'I believe that Mother is acquainted with a Lady Tremaine.'

It took three patient journeys with the handcart to transfer all the pictures to the shop, after which she sent Ethelred home and herself dusted them lightly with a feather duster, as she had seen Dorothy do, and then propped them up all round the shop, wherever they could be placed.

In order to save the train fare, she walked home.

As she crossed the road just before reaching Meols Station, she was nearly run down by a young woman on a bicycle. The woman swerved to avoid her, flung a laughing apology over her shoulder and continued merrily pedalling towards Hoylake.

Safely on the other side of the road, Celia, who had never ridden a bicycle in her life because her mother thought they were vulgar, watched her enviously.

307

With some of Dr Mason's money, I'll buy a second-hand bike, she promised herself. She said I should cycle. I won't tell Mother. I'll ask Eddie about it. She felt very bold and daring.

At home, Louise and Edna had already begun to eat dinner. They were both a little worried about her being late. 'You should tell us when you expect to be late,' her mother scolded.

'Yes, Mama,' she agreed, as she ran upstairs to wash her hands and tidy her hair before coming to the table.

As she snatched up her comb, she noticed the box of bricks she had earlier brought from her old trunk, and she picked up the box and took it down to the living room. She put it on the sideboard, and slid, breathless, into her chair.

She did not tell her mother about the sale. She thought it might distress her to know that her husband's desk had gone for ever. Nor did she mention the impending visit of Alec Tremaine to see the pictures. She had begun to feel strongly that it was her shop and her business, and was nothing to do with her mother, who would, anyway, only criticise anything she did.

While they were drinking an after-dinner cup of tea fairly sociably round the fire, she told Louise about the box of bricks. She got up, put down her cup, and then emptied the bricks on to the tablecloth.

'I thought, Mama, that you could spell a word or two by putting the bricks in a row, and then guide the men's hands round the letters.' She spoke eagerly, anxious to help.

'Both of them must be able to read already, and if their fingers were sensitive enough, they could recognise the letters. For instance, you could spell WALK, and they would possibly get the idea that they were going to go for a walk.

'You said that you had been able to tell them a few things by outlining letters on the palms of their hands – but the bricks would be steadier, and they could run their fingers over them more than once, if they were in doubt.'

She turned the bricks over quickly, and said, 'I don't think there is a question mark – or an exclamation mark – but somebody who could whittle could make two bricks with them on. Then you could ask a question, like WALK? and they could say yes or no.'

She stopped and looked triumphantly at Louise.

It was Edna who realised the possibilities first. She said, 'Celia! It's wonderful – it would be a crack in a wall of silence for them.' She stood looking at the little blocks, and then added thoughtfully, 'You could get them to identify the letter on a block and then guide their fingers to the same letter in Braille – and with a bit of luck they would understand the connection. You could really teach them, Mama.'

Celia nodded quick agreement. 'It would be awfully slow, I am sure. But, Mama, you could communicate quite a lot, if they can manage to read the letters.'

Louise was very tired; she was still shaky from the loss of Timothy and Paul. She did not answer immediately.

In addition, she had had an uncomfortable afternoon with the army doctor, when he had visited the nursing home. She had suggested that the two deaf-blind could be taken swimming, if an orderly who could swim went with each of them.

The doctor did not want to be bothered with wild ideas put forward by a stupid elderly widow, and had rudely quashed her suggestion as nonsense. He argued that all the men would then want to swim – and it would be impossible to ensure their safety in the water.

She had swallowed her anger, and had taken Richard and Charlie out for a walk on the seashore. As the tide retreated it left firm, damp sand on which they were not likely to trip up, and they walked quite steadily, one on either side of her, arms linked with hers. They seemed to enjoy it.

If only the pair could have read Braille, she thought, their own ideas on swimming might have been conveyed to the doctor and helped to win the battle. A knowledge of how to read and write Braille was, she knew, the first essential. Edna and Celia did not need to remind her.

Cup in hand, she turned wearily and without hope.

Her mouth fell open. She put down her cup and got up to look at the bricks. She realised immediately that here at last was a simple way to communicate with young Richard and Charlie until they could learn Braille. As Edna had said, it could form the actual link which would enable them to do so.

Through trembling lips, she said, 'Spell a word for me, Celia, and I'll close my eyes and see if I can read it.'

Celia arranged the bricks to read BLIND, and with closed eyes Louise allowed her hand to be guided to them. At first she spelled it out as BLINO, but Celia shook her hand and took her fingers back to the beginning again, and the second time she read it correctly.

Mrs Lou stood looking at the word and then she cried, and they laughed and cried together.

'I bet Eddie can carve you a question mark and an exclamation mark,' Edna assured her mother. Like Celia, she had a blissful belief that Eddie Fairbanks could do anything.

Chapter Forty-Seven

When a very fit-looking man, trilby hat in hand, entered the shop, he found Celia on her knees sorting her mother's Crown Derby dinner service for twelve into two sets for six. She had noticed that, in the hardware store down the road, china services were being sold in sixes, and she thought it might be easier to dispose of smaller sets. She had come in early to do this, and now she rose hastily from the floor, undoing her apron as she turned to her visitor.

She smiled, and said, 'Good morning, Sir.'

'Alec Tremaine, Ma'am, John Philpotts' friend.'

'How nice of you to come,' she said, and held out her hand to be shaken. He took it carefully and shook it.

John Philpotts had told him, 'She's a little pet. So fresh and innocent. I don't want her to be cheated, if she has something good to show you. Take care of her.' And holding her hand and looking into a gentle pale face, Alec felt suddenly that he was going to enjoy helping her with her pictures very much. John was right – she looked like a real old-fashioned girl, and he astonished himself by thinking immediately that his mother was certain to approve of her. It was some time before he realised how quick a mind lay behind the calm blue eyes.

Unmarried, battle-scarred and weary after four years in the army, he had been thankful, at the age of thirty-three, to find a post teaching commercial art in a Liverpool college; it was a fairly new discipline. Before the war, he had been quite successful as a watercolour artist and book illustrator.

Now, he began to fret that his knowledge might not be adequate to judge Celia's collection of paintings. A quick glance round her showroom had told him that the contents were certainly not those of the usual second-hand shop, and this quiet little gentlewoman was certainly no ordinary second-hand shop owner.

Celia was equally unsure of herself. She turned a dining chair round for him to sit on, and then asked if he would like to take off his macintosh, since he was likely to be with her for some time.

He slowly divested himself of the garment and she fluttered to the back of the store to hang it up, nearly knocking over a pile of Crown Derby dinner plates. Then she realised that he would not sit down until she did, so she hastily got out another chair and sat on it.

Her hands modestly folded in her lap, she smiled shyly at him. He was a stolid, pleasant-faced man. His brown hair was close-clipped and had a few white hairs glinting in it. His face was clean shaven, deeply lined and ruddy from exposure. Military service had, presumably, given him his very upright posture. He spoke with the perfect pronunciation of a public school man.

She thought he was wonderful, a returned hero. As she carefully weighed him up, a wave of very odd sensations went through her. Though these made her feel a little unsteady, she led off the conversation like a good hostess, by inquiring how he would like to proceed.

Wrenching himself back from thoughts far removed from paintings, he said he would, first, like to walk round slowly and take a general look at the collection.

Not wishing to embarrass him by hovering behind him, she said she would finish sorting out the dinner service and put it away. He nodded, and, with hands clasped behind his back, he went slowly round the collection of paintings, most of which were oils in heavily carved gold frames. Occasionally, he took a picture down and carried it to the window to take a particular look at it. Despite his solid weight, he walked lightly, she noticed.

After half an hour, she brought him a cup of tea. She boiled the water on a gas ring in a tiny washroom at the back of the shop. He thanked her absently, and continued his promenade, teacup in hand. While she waited, she sat down at her corner table to drink her own cup of tea and draw faces on the blotting paper.

She did not know how to bear the suspense in silence, and was thankful when a girl of about fifteen entered and began to look round.

Celia put down her cup, and went forward to ask her if she needed help.

'I want a present for me mam,' was the reply. 'I thought you might have a nice ornament.'

Celia immediately opened the china cabinet and brought down a series of vases and small figurines. At two shillings each, the girl said they were too expensive. She could get similar ones down the road for sixpence.

'Well, this one and this one are early Royal Doulton,' Celia defended. But Royal Doulton meant nothing to the girl, and, after looking disparagingly at the various clocks in the shop, she walked out looking quite huffy.

A small burst of laughter from behind Celia, as she shut the door, lifted her low spirits.

Alec ventured a comment. 'Bravo,' he said. 'I can see from your stock that you don't need that kind of clientele. You need real collectors.' Then he immediately regretted his impolite intrusion into what was essentially her business, not his.

Unruffled, she smilingly agreed with him. His comments made him suddenly more human to her. 'I know, Mr Tremaine. You are quite correct. But I'm not sure how to let them know I am here!'

'Ah, well, if you would like to, we'll talk about that another time. I would be happy to make some suggestions, if you would permit it. Are you ready to talk about pictures?'

'Indeed, yes.' She went towards him eagerly, and they circled the shop together.

'Some of the paintings have been done by amateurs and I suggest that they were, perhaps, framed as gifts to loved ones. I think you could sell them for a guinea or two, to people who want good frames, say, for mirrors or other pictures.' He paused to look down at her, and asked, 'Shall I put them on one side for you?'

Fearing that she herself might make an error in sorting the pictures, if she did it when he was gone, she agreed, and he stacked them neatly against the back wall.

When that was done, he told her, 'Most of the others were done by local nineteenth-century artists – I recognise the names of some of them. They are not great paintings, but they were commissioned by someone with taste, and they are pleasant to look at. They are quite valuable, I think. Look at this one.' He lifted one down to show her. It was a peaceful scene of Raby Mere, which had hung in the dining room of her old home.

'It is nice, isn't it? Father was rather fond of it.'

He carefully put it on one side, and picked up the next one, which was painted in the style of the Impressionists.

'That's called *Sunday Afternoon*,' Celia offered. 'I can't think why. It's mostly blurred.'

He smiled down at her. 'It is, I think, quite good.'

They spent over an hour slowly going through the collection, until there were only two left. So that it could be seen particularly clearly, he propped up near the window the portrait of a young woman.

'I may be wrong,' he cautioned, 'but I have an idea that this is a Ramsay, though the frame seems to cover the signature.'

'Ramsay?'

'He was an eighteenth-century Scottish artist, noted for his portraits of Scottish gentlefolk. If I am right, it might fetch a fair sum, particularly if it were shown in Edinburgh.'

'Really? I think it's a painting of one of my ancestors.' Her pale-blue eyes had widened with astonishment. 'That would be a wonderful help! Cousin Albert says I must accumulate capital, so that I can buy good replacement stock when it is offered. At the moment I couldn't possibly buy anything.'

Alec murmured absently something about her having only just started out. Then he picked up the last painting, a seascape. 'I kept this one until last, because I am almost afraid to raise your hopes too much.'

314

Celia's heart gave a frightened thump. Then she realised what it was he was holding, and she said carelessly, 'Oh, that's the Turner. It's awfully dirty, isn't it? It's called *Hoylake Sands*.'

Alec was so stunned at her remark that he nearly dropped the precious work.

'You mean that you know it is a Turner?'

Fearful that she had said something wrong, she backed down and replied cautiously, 'Well, that's what I've always been told.'

Alec gasped. 'By Jove! I couldn't believe my eyes when I looked at it; I thought it must be simply a good copy.'

He went to the window and laid it in a clear shaft of light. Then he took a magnifying glass out of his pocket and studied it carefully.

Celia watched him, totally bewildered. She said, 'Mother didn't think much of it, but it fitted in in a spot by the breakfast room fireplace, and there it hung for years and years. That's why it's so dirty – from smoke and soot.'

Alec began to whistle under his breath. Then he asked, 'Have you any idea how it came into the family?'

'Well, when Great-aunt Blodwyn, my grandfather's sister, came from Wales to my sister Edna's wedding – she dislikes Mother, you must understand – I remember their quarrelling in the quiet, acid way that ladies sometimes do.'

Her laugh was rueful, as she glanced up at him. 'They were sitting in the breakfast room having a morning glass of sherry.' She stopped, and then said blankly, 'I remember the day so well. Great-aunt Blodwyn had her arm round my waist as I stood by her chair.'

Alec Tremaine looked at the small, dainty person in front of him, and remembered some of John's casual remarks about her. John had said cynically that she had probably been kept single so that she could care for her parents in their old age. It was a well-known custom much decried by the new Suffragette movement.

Celia realised that she had strayed a little from the question she was supposed to be answering, and went on quickly, 'Anyway, I remember Great-aunt Blodwyn baiting Mother by saying that

315

such a good painting should not be left where it would gather soot.'

It was Alec's turn to chuckle softly, but he did not otherwise break into her story. In his mind's eye, he saw the kind of petty cattiness that occurs between women with not enough to do to really occupy themselves.

'Mother said it was a grubby old thing and she thought it was time it was thrown out and they bought something new. She never would throw it out, though, because Father was stuffy about these things – he liked old paintings and old furniture.

'Then Great-aunt Blodwyn flared up and said it was treasured by her grandfather as the gem of his collection of paintings. It had been painted by a man called Joseph Turner – she said that her grandfather had commissioned it, when he went to visit his friend, Mr Fawkes of Farnley Hall in Yorkshire. The artist was also staying with Mr Fawkes, and he did the painting while they were both there. Simple as that.'

Alec Tremaine plonked himself down on his dining chair. 'Well, I'm damned!' he exclaimed, and then immediately apologised for his bad language. With a sudden thought, he asked, 'Do you know who Joseph Turner was?'

'Not really. He must have been an artist. According to Great-aunt Blodwyn, her grandfather was always buying pictures from artists whom he had met – it was his interest – the artist could have been anybody.'

'Turner was simply one of the greatest artists Britain has ever produced,' Alec told her. 'When I was studying, I spent a good deal of time examining his watercolours and engravings of them. I've seen many of his oils, too, of course.'

'Good heavens!' She hung her head and looked a little shame-faced. 'I'm so terribly ignorant,' she burst out. 'Edna might have known who he was – she went to school and learned to paint.' He sensed a bitterness in her tone.

He had noticed the pile of books on antiques amid the things lying on her work table. To comfort her, he made a slight gesture towards them and said, 'By the look of your desk, you seem to be making up for lost time now.'

She nodded, her face sad. 'I'm trying to.'

She looked so downcast that he said, 'Don't worry, Miss Gilmore. Both John Philpotts and I think the shop will be a success.'

What John had actually said was that the two sisters were unexpectedly enterprising. 'They know they don't know nothing, but they've got the guts to admit it – and they'll learn; they don't waste their time like so many are doing.'

'I'm sure I'm making all sorts of mistakes,' Celia said, almost as if she had read his mind.

He grinned, and got up briskly. 'We all have to learn,' he replied. 'I never thought of teaching until this year.' Then he gestured to the two paintings which he had specially picked out, and suggested, 'If you would allow me to show these two to the head of my college, he might be able to suggest what their worth is, and the best way to dispose of them.'

She nodded, and smiled politely. 'Please do.' Despite the hopes he had raised of making some badly needed capital, all she could think of was that her ignorance had shamed her before this lovely man. After he had left, she spent some time sitting at her desk and going wistfully over every word he had said.

Also deep in thought, Alec walked over to his home in nearby Meols Drive to eat his lunch with his widowed mother. In the trenches, he and his fellow officers used to talk occasionally about being at home at their own fireside. Some of the men already had wives and small children, and they spoke longingly of the comfort of decent meals, warmth and affection. When they were very hungry, which was quite often, they planned their favourite meals, each man grinning and adding a bit to the feast until it became one enormous joke – and it was always homely meals that they longed for and for women, like wives, whom they knew well.

Lady Tremaine and her companion doted on Alec and were bent on 'feeding him up'. They were also bent on his paying court to his cousin, Daphne, a nice enough young woman, who would, they felt, be a suitable wife for a younger son who had not inherited much from his father. Alec had dutifully inspected the lady and played a few games of tennis with her. But that morning Alec had suddenly glimpsed something better, not just a woman who attracted him but a whole peaceful, orderly way of life, and his mother found him unusually silent at lunch time. She suggested a game of golf, but he said he felt like a stroll round the Liverpool Art Gallery, which he had not visited since he returned home, and took himself off to the railway station to catch a train to the city.

Chapter Forty-Eight

❧

At home that night, Louise retired reluctantly to the sitting room to write a reference for Winnie, in reply to an inquiry from Mrs Johnson who was considering her for the post of cook in her new nursing home. Though still annoyed that a servant of hers should go so far as to trespass on her property, she had strict instructions from both her daughters that the reference should be an excellent one. Determined that her old friend should get the position, Celia reiterated to her mother Winnie's great ability to cook everything, from dinners for large parties to wine jelly for an invalid. 'Make it a really nice reference, Mama. Winnie is quite a wonderful cook.'

Being fundamentally a conscientious woman, Louise knew that Celia was correct, and in her best copperplate, she assured Mrs Johnson of Winnie's capabilities and her honesty. In her secret heart, she admitted that she wished she still had Winnie with her, and she quite envied Mrs Johnson her ability to employ a cook.

While Louise was safely occupied, Celia poured out to Edna the story of Alec Tremaine's visit and the Turner painting and her own dreadful ignorance.

Edna remembered the painting and said she had always known it as 'the Turner'. 'There were so many paintings of one sort or another in the house,' she said apologetically, 'I never thought of it as anything special. They all seemed to have been handed down to us from the year dot.'

'I felt such a fool, Edna, and he's what Winnie would have called a loovelly man.' There was a yearning in her voice.

'You are smitten!' Edna teased.

319

Celia shrugged helplessly. 'Cats can look at kings.'

Edna smiled. 'Cheer up. What's he going to do with the two paintings?'

'We packed them up carefully and he's taking them to show the principal of his college.

'It was funny, Edna. He actually insisted on giving me a receipt for both the Turner and the Ramsay, and he promised not to let them out of his sight.' She sighed. 'Frankly, I thought he was overreacting.'

'Oh, no. They are probably valuable. It looks as if he will really take care of your interests.'

'Not mine. Mother's.'

'What do you mean?'

'Well, Mother let me have the pictures, because she thought they were old-fashioned and of no value. Morally, if I get any real money for them, I should hand it to her.'

Edna exploded. 'What utter nonsense! The paintings, the furniture and the china are all yours. Cousin Albert arranged it legally. And over the years, believe me, you've earned every cent of anything you get for them.'

She was truly angry. She got up off her chair, and spun round to walk up and down in the narrow space of the living room. 'I won't hear of it!' she almost shouted. 'It's absurd.'

She looked so like her mother in one of her rages that Celia quailed for a moment. Then she laughed. 'You're so good, Edna. I feel conscience-stricken, that's all.'

'Forget it. Mother's doing very nicely, what with the money from the silver and the annuity, which Cousin Albert is now arranging for her. Most of the time she's so absorbed with her boys that she forgets we exist, except to keep the house going.'

'Mother's certainly got a hold on life again,' Celia admitted. 'She's trying to get a committee together.'

'She is. She's already learning Braille and is beginning to get a grasp of it, and the Liverpool School for the Blind has been quite helpful with advice. Of course, they deal with civilians, whereas Mother's young men are still in the army. You forget her. She's fairly happy, and you enjoy whatever comes your way,' she ordered. 'Alec Tremaine sounds a dear. Be nice to him.'

'Yes, Edna,' Celia replied in mock submission.

Two days later, on his way home from the station, Alec dropped into the shop just as she was about to close up.

He whipped off his hat and told her in haste that her pictures were stored in his principal's office safe, until the principal could give more time to examining them. 'We're short of staff,' he explained apologetically. 'And there is a real rush of older students returning from the war. We are nearly run off our feet.'

She assured him shyly that neither he nor his principal should go to too much trouble for her. There was no hurry.

They stood looking at each other uncertainly, and then he said, smiling ruefully, that he must not be late for dinner – his mother didn't like it.

'My mother doesn't like it either,' she said with a small chuckle, and she held out her hand to be shaken.

He grasped it firmly, and said, 'I'll keep in touch. Goodbye.'

The feel of the warmth of his hand stayed with Celia, even after he had let himself out. As the sound of his footsteps on the pavement diminished with distance, she was flooded by feelings never before experienced. They seemed, somehow, to be connected with small unexpressed, unexplained longings that she had sometimes felt before; longings that no one else seemed to mention in conversation and which she had assumed, therefore, were vulgar, like talking about having the stomach ache or wanting to vomit.

Now, for a moment, she felt unsteady enough to think that she might faint, and she sat down suddenly in the nearest chair until it eased.

When finally she did lock the front door after herself, she walked home in an almost dreamlike state.

Some weeks elapsed without a word from Alec Tremaine and Celia began to think sadly that he had lost interest.

He'll post the paintings back to me, some time or other – with polite regrets that they are worthless, she told herself.

With a neat energetic Welsh woman as daily cleaning lady, Edna had more time to spare and she began to take a solid interest in the shop.

Small advertisements were put in local papers and in the *Liverpool Echo* and the *Evening Express*, which were read quite widely. Aided by Betty Houghton and John Philpotts, the two women emphasised the first-class quality of their stock and the fact that a French polisher and upholsterer was on the premises.

Betty also sent to see them an aggressive young woman who said she was the social reporter of the local paper, and that she would like to do a small article on the opening of the shop. Later, Celia described her to Edna as looking just like a ferret in a smart hat.

Notebook in hand, she breezed round the shop, admiring this and that, while John and Celia watched her as anxiously as if she were a ferret very liable to bite.

Behind her back, John quietly asked for the key to the china cabinet and a puzzled Celia gave it to him, eyebrows raised in silent question. 'Small gift,' he hissed. 'To mark the happy occasion of her visit.'

Celia was quite bewildered but she gave him the key. He quietly picked out a pretty cup and saucer and wrapped them in tissue paper. After about ten minutes and a few questions addressed to Celia, the lady announced that she had all the information she needed. Celia thanked her for coming, and John saw her to the door. As he opened the door, he handed her the parcel, and said they had enjoyed her visit and would like her to have the enclosed little memento of it.

All coyness and blushes, she accepted the present and they saw her lay it carefully in the basket attached to the handlebars of her bicycle.

John turned and laughed at Celia. He said, 'Write its value off in your account book as business expenses. It will be some of the best money you ever spent.'

He was correct. A very enthusiastic little article graced the column, next to a report of a local wedding. A number of ladies came to see this interesting new arrival on Market Street. They were a different breed from those who had come and gone at other times, and, as a result, Celia sold a pair of side chairs to one, and a number of delicate glass specimen vases to a collector. There was also an elderly man who bought a pair of pictures by a nineteenth-century local artist, whose work he admired.

Edna's furniture had arrived some weeks before from South America, and Celia began to show in her shop some pieces of it which Edna had given her when they first unpacked it and put it in the barn. It was very unusual to English eyes, and attracted a fair amount of attention. She wanted to give to Edna the money she received for it, but Edna would not hear of it.

She said, 'Celia, I am not sure how much I shall receive from the company, but I do know that I shall be quite a well-to-do woman. I don't even spend half of what Papa Fellowes sends me at present. Except for a few pieces, you can have it. I'm getting a lot of fun out of the shop – and that is enough for me.' She did not say that the furniture reminded her too much of great unhappiness for her to ever want to use it again.

'Have you decided about making a home of your own yet, Edna? You might need the furniture, after all.'

Edna thought of the tender letters going back and forth to Brazil. Because the liaison had originally been an illicit one, she had said nothing about Vital to either Celia or Louise. She sighed, 'Quite honestly, Celia, I don't know yet what to do. But you are not to worry. Let's get you launched first.'

Celia had almost given up hope of seeing Alec again, when he suddenly dropped into the shop late one afternoon, to tell her that examination of her pictures had been delayed, because the college principal was in hospital having further surgery on an old wound in his back.

'I'm so sorry for the long delay, but it cannot be helped, Miss Gilmore.'

'It doesn't matter,' Celia assured him. 'Is it very serious surgery?'

'Well, back surgery, I am told, is difficult, and he will need some time for recovery. But they hope to alleviate the nagging pain he has been enduring.' Alec frowned, and then added, 'They should never have called up men of his age.'

Celia sighed. 'I expect they were getting short of young ones.'

'They were indeed, Miss Gilmore.'

They spent a little time chatting about the war, and then a customer came in. Alec said shyly that he would be in touch with her, smiled and left.

With an inward sense of pure happiness, Celia reluctantly turned her attention to the lady who had entered.

Efforts at publicity drew other dealers to view their stock. They offered to buy pieces for ridiculously small prices. Both sisters quickly recognised them for what they were and sent them on their way.

It was not long, however, before more bona fide customers began to stroll in. Unlike many second-hand and antique stores, Celia and Edna took a lot of trouble to make the shop pretty and show off what they had in a good light. Everything shone with polish and the place smelled sweet with bowls of dried lavender.

It had been John's opinion that the hardest things to sell would be the beds, despite the fact that they were in good condition and had fine, carved bed heads.

'It's because folk are afraid of vermin,' he explained.

Undeterred, Edna got Ethelred to bring them, one at a time, from the barn, and, using some of the enormous amount of bed linen they had, she made them up as if ready to get into. She decked them out with a bunch of flowers or an old shawl or, in one case, a rose-trimmed summer hat laid on the counterpane, as if the owner had just come into the house.

In six months they had not a bed left. In two cases they had sold them complete with the bedding on them. They disposed of some of the others by agreeing to keep the bed until the cost was paid by weekly instalments.

'I suspect that couples setting up house are buying new furniture for the living rooms and economising when it comes to the bedrooms,' said Edna shrewdly.

A trip to buy furniture in Liverpool or Birkenhead involved either taking the electric train, which to many was quite expensive, or a complicated journey by bus and ferry. Celia undoubtedly benefited from the fact that hers was the only shop selling furniture between Hoylake and Birkenhead, at a time when private cars were few and there was, anyway, no tunnel under the Mersey through which to drive to Liverpool. She soon learned to stock some old, but good, furniture which was not as expensive as her genuine antiques, and this gave her a steady turnover.

They began early to look for advertisements of estate sales, where they might purchase new stock. 'Before we buy, we'd better attend some sales,' Celia suggested. 'So that we understand what to do.'

They temporarily formed the habit of shutting the shop on Mondays and Tuesdays, days which seemed to bring the smallest number of clients. And off they went to country estate sales on bicycles which Eddie had obtained for them from a local repair shop.

It was as well they did go, because they learned how professional dealers joined up to keep the prices low at auctions, and yet outbid them. They also learned, sometimes by bitter experience, to examine with care every piece they wanted to buy, and not to be carried away by claims of antiquity.

Though Celia was learning fast, Edna was by far the more astute buyer. She had had much experience in South America of bargaining for everything, and she would pile in with great gusto, when Celia was far too polite to question an offer and would simply refuse it.

It was Celia, however, who really studied furniture as a subject. She read widely, and would shyly stand by a dealer at the showing before an auction and summon up courage to ask questions – and learn how to identify the work of famous furniture makers.

She found that there were second-hand dealers and antique dealers, and a third group which catered for collectors, mostly small things, like china, medals, coins or old toys.

'You'd be amazed what people collect,' one lady told her. 'I've a chap on my list who does nothing but collect corsets, the older the better.' She laughed. 'He's not perverted. He dresses exhibitions in museums, and to make the garments hang right, he needs proper underwear under them.'

Celia looked so innocent that, at first, it was apparent that the dealers assumed she attended sales for amusement rather than to buy. Until they began to know her face and heard her bid, they would talk quite frankly about fake antiques and cheap copies of better quality furniture.

She accepted any bit of information she could pick up, though she and Edna had had the advantage of living in a circle of people whose homes were invariably beautifully furnished, and had acquired, without realising it, an eye for fine design and finish. As a result, they could make a reasonable guess at the probable age of a piece.

After a while, the two women found themselves part of a fraternity of dealers, who, though often hostile to each other, tended to hang together at estate sales. As time went on, more than one client of Celia's Antiques turned out to be a person sent to them by another dealer, who did not have in stock what the client wanted. She took care to reciprocate.

While she waited with what patience she could muster for word from Alec regarding the two paintings he had taken away, Celia announced an art sale, everything one guinea, to get rid of those paintings which he had said were done by amateurs. She kept on the walls of her shop those which John had told her were done by local professionals.

On a fine October day, she set out the amateur efforts along the frontage of the shop. She herself sat in the doorway.

She discovered that pictures of flowers went very quickly, and two framed samplers were snapped up by an elderly lady who said she collected them. One street scene was stolen. Anything dark and gloomy failed to move.

John advised her to enter the stolen painting in her account book as one guinea lost by theft. 'It's an expense of doing business,' he explained calmly. Celia, who was learning about life almost too quickly, ruefully followed his advice.

It was news to her that people collected old samplers, and she decided regretfully that she had probably sold her samplers far too low.

As soon as it was fairly apparent that the business was beginning to thrive, John also advised her to take out fire insurance, which she did. 'Fire's what I fear most,' John told her. 'It can wipe you out.'

Both Edna and Celia had begun to doubt that they would ever receive an opinion on the painting of Hoylake Sands, but, totally unexpectedly one Saturday afternoon, Alec came hurrying into the shop.

Celia was seated behind her little counter table and he saw how her face lit up at the sight of him.

Hat in hand, he bowed, and apologised. 'I am sorry to have left you so long in suspense. Getting the college back to a peace-time footing without our principal has taken up more time than we expected.'

Celia was so pleased to see him that the paintings seemed suddenly unimportant. She smiled, and said, as she pointed to a chair conveniently set near her, 'It doesn't matter. Do sit down and tell me what happened and how your principal is. Would you like a cup of tea?'

He refused the tea, as he seated himself and laid his hat on a sideboard at the back of him. Then he turned to grin at her cheerfully. The smile made her heart jump.

'Well, good news and bad news. The old boy is fine and was very interested, once he had a chance to really examine them. When I told him where I had got them from, he was cautious, however. He thinks they may be genuine, that is to say, not good copies, but is not sure. He has suggested I show them to an art expert.'

'Where do we find one?'

'I thought, first, of the Walker Art Gallery in Liverpool, and then I thought we might as well go to the Turner specialists and take them to London to the Tate Gallery. They have a whole Turner collection. And, in addition, they would probably know a Ramsay if they saw one. I am sure someone there would be kind enough to look at both of them.'

'Would they really bother with us?'

'I think so. After all, it was Tate of Tate and Lyle, the sugar people, in Liverpool, who founded the gallery. They owe something to Liverpudlians like us.'

Celia laughed. She was so happy, so glad to see him. 'Of course. Do whatever you think fit. It is most kind of you to be so interested.'

'Well, I spent the summer helping to plan a new curriculum and special extra lectures for ex-servicemen; and I never got an autumn break because of the absence of our principal – we're still so short of staff. But, as soon as the exams are finished, I'll get a few days' holiday – before Christmas – and I would be very glad to take them to London – if you'll trust me with them a little longer.'

'Of course, I trust you.'

By God, she really does, he thought, and he enjoyed the feeling it gave him.

Then he said, 'Well, you know, Miss Gilmore, it would be wonderful if we could announce the discovery of another Turner painting. If it happens to be true, it will give you enough capital to assure the continuation of the business, and enough to invest elsewhere for future use. I can tell you that it will put Celia's Antiques on the map.'

'Would it really? The lack of ready money to replace our stock has worried both Edna and me. And, by the way, do please call me Celia – John always does.'

His eyes twinkled, as he replied, his voice holding a little surprise. 'Well, thank you – I'm Alec. Now, keep your fingers crossed, Celia,' he teased. 'The Ramsay will be a nice find, too, if it is genuine.'

As he picked up his hat from the sideboard, he paused and, almost diffidently, asked her if, on the following Friday evening, she would like to go with him to the cinema to see a motion picture.

She blushed to the roots of her hair, and said she had never seen a film. He assured her that they were the coming thing in entertainment. '*The Birth of a Nation* isn't a new film, but I am sure you would find it interesting,' he urged.

As a result, Celia entered a new magical world. She also enjoyed having her hand held during the more exciting scenes.

She did not tell her mother that she had sat in the dark holding the hand of a man she barely knew. She accounted for being so late home by saying she had spent the time rearranging the books in the shop for a sale the following week.

She decided that she would certainly never ever mention to Louise that, after the cinema show was over, they had walked along the shore and he had put his arm round her waist, while they watched the waves breaking on the distant sandbanks. And he had kissed her goodbye at the top of King's Gap, before they ran laughing across the road to the railway station and he had put her on the train for Meols. And she was going out with him again next week.

Sometimes you have to lie for peace, she decided after much quiet thought on the subject, and she felt so wonderful that she could not bear to have the feeling shattered by an angry parent. Nobody in the whole world, she knew for certain, had ever felt like she did; she was in love.

Edna laughed, when she confessed this to her, and said she was delighted. She had to have Alec described in detail to her, because she had, as yet, not met him. Celia spent about half an hour on the subject, without even stopping for breath.

Edna said wistfully that she wished she was as lucky as her sister. And Celia realised that the tables had indeed turned; Edna must be envious, much as she had been on her sister's wedding day.

She gave Edna a big hug, and said with conviction that Edna's time would come.

Edna nodded with a quiet smile, and went upstairs to her bedroom to smoke and to write to Vital.

Chapter Forty-Nine

As winter crept on, the shop became quite busy, with fur-clad customers in search of ornaments, pictures and books for Christmas gifts. It was clear that Edna, just as much as Celia, had become a part of Celia's Antiques and Collectibles. She obviously enjoyed the battle of wits as they bought and sold, whereas Celia found it difficult to maintain a firm stance in the face of some clients who tried to force her prices down. It was Celia, however, who kept carefully the proof of the provenance of particularly good antiques, and, when they were occasionally asked to sell pieces on commission, it was she who kept note of the furniture's ownership. She also cleaned the store, polished the furniture and kept the accounts.

Despite her fear of bargain-hunting clients, she spent more and more time in the shop, while Edna bought at estate sales. If driven into a corner on the subject of price, Celia would say that she must consult her partner before agreeing to bring it down by more than ten per cent.

On occasions, clients would criticise a piece of furniture because it had minor scratches or chips or the upholstery was shabby. This gave the young women a chance to bring John Philpotts to the fore on the subject of repairs, and his salesmanship often clinched a deal.

They also went half shares with John in the purchase of a handcart and a better trolley to facilitate the movement of both his repairs and their stock. 'One day,' John promised, 'we'll buy our own van for deliveries.'

'Will you teach me how to drive?' Edna teased.

John was unexpectedly silent. Then he said reluctantly, 'We'll see when the time comes.'

It was only later that Edna was told by Eddie Fairbanks that John blamed himself for the death of his fiancée while driving an ambulance in France.

'You see, love, if he hadn't taught her, she'd probably never have gone to war. Not that the poor girl would have got much comfort from him if she'd stayed at home waiting for him.'

'Why not?'

'Didn't you know? The poor lad's so wounded he'll never be any use to a woman. You don't have to tell every Tom, Dick and Harry, of course.'

Edna nodded her head slowly. 'I suspected it from a few hints he dropped, though, naturally, I would never actually ask him straight out,' she said. 'But you do hear of men coming home disabled in every way, and their wives and fiancées stay with them and care for them.' She looked thoughtfully down at her feet, as if shy at discussing such a delicate matter, and then she suggested, 'I think, at times, that love can be an all-encompassing and forgiving emotion. And his fiancée might well have stood by him, even if the marriage could not have been consummated. He's a very nice man.'

'Oh, aye. It's possible.'

'Well, anyway, he's an excellent friend to both Celia and me – like you are.'

'Well, thank you, Miss Edna.' The old man grinned and returned to picking rosehips off the bushes in his front garden. What a fine, understanding lady Miss Edna was. He hoped she would find a nice man some day. He snipped three particularly lovely Christmas roses, and then called her back to give them to her.

Without Ethelred, the women admitted, they would have been lost. Much of the furniture was heavy, and, before it was sold, often had to be moved more than once. Eventually he became their full-time employee, at a very modest weekly wage, and he divided his time between their garden and the shop. As the newspapers reported an increased number of unemployed, his mother, knowing his limitations, was pitifully grateful.

'You've given him pride in himself, like nobody else would have bothered to do,' she told Celia almost tearfully, as one day she brought in the sandwich lunch which he had forgotten to bring with him to work.

'Well, he's the sweetest person to work with,' Celia replied. 'And he is so honest – I never have to worry about that. Of course, the shop isn't making very much yet – but we hope to improve his wages as time goes on.'

Alec Tremaine did not bother Celia with details of the convoluted situation he found himself in, as he sought to prove the origins of the two paintings he had taken away. Because he would not entrust them to anyone else, he had to wait for opportunities such as his pre-Christmas holiday to take them personally to show to various experts to hum and haw over.

The Ramsay was indeed a Ramsay, he was assured at the Tate, and the two women agreed, when asked, that it should be auctioned in Edinburgh.

During a weekend when Alec begged a Friday off he took the train to Scotland. He was armed with an introduction to the Director of the art gallery in Edinburgh. He was agreeably surprised when the gallery itself made an offer for it.

He made a long-distance call on a crackling telephone to his new-found friend at the Tate. His friend pointed out that the price seemed a little low. If he wanted to try for a better price, the gallery could bid at an auction.

Thoroughly out of his depth, Alec said he would consult the owner, and went back to Hoylake.

'Take it,' said Edna. 'We could get the finding of it written up in the Chester newspaper and even in the *Scotsman*, perhaps. It would give us wonderful publicity, that we made a find like that – and anyway, we need the capital.'

And so it was arranged. She was right about the publicity.

Instead of using the money for the Ramsay to buy stock,

Alec suggested that it would probably more than pay a first-class specialist to clean the Turner.

'It would have to be done by a most reputable firm,' Alec warned. 'Because it could be easily damaged – it would have to be taken out of its frame, which nobody has tried to do up to now.'

He looked at Celia, and said, 'As I told you, the chap at the Tate is dead sure it is genuine. But he did say that to sell it on the international market – and it would be international – you'd do better if you had provenance to support the claim that it is a real Turner; otherwise, it is going to cost you a lot, with insurance and transport, while other experts nod their heads over it.' He paused to whistle under his breath, and then added, 'I suspect that, if it were cleaned, all the glorious Turner colours would come up and it would look more convincing.'

Celia was loath to chance losing what they had gained. She protested gently that they needed the money so badly.

'Tush, Celia. We take chances every day,' responded Edna. 'We make all kinds of blunders when we're buying and selling. Let's take this one big chance. It could be the best investment we ever made.'

Finally, they all crossed their fingers, and, once more, Celia packed the painting up very carefully.

The decision entailed two more visits to London, the first, a day or two later, to deliver the painting to an art restorer recommended by the Tate. The second, for which he took a day's leave one Friday some three months later, was to collect it after the cleaning was completed. Alec began to think that he was buying the London, Midland and Scottish Railway Company with his own small salary. 'The things I do for love.' He smiled at his predicament, and began to give earnest thought to engagement rings and to introducing Celia to his mother.

When the picture was finally returned to its owner, it glowed with colour. The man who had so painstakingly cleaned it had raved over it, and for the first time Alec was himself completely convinced that it was a genuine Turner.

While all three of them were in doubt as to what they should do next, Great-aunt Blodwyn became the unexpected source of confirmation of the picture's origins. When Celia wrote to her aunt for her birthday at the end of March, she mentioned her adventures with the shop and the good news about the portrait by Ramsay. She also said how much she wished the Turner was a real one.

She received by return of post a registered letter.

'I have preserved a lot of my grandfather's letters and papers, because he was an interesting man,' her godmother wrote. 'He did a considerable amount of writing about the state of the arts in his day. I always knew that Turner painted that picture – only Louise never seemed to realise that it was valuable and should be taken care of. I am glad you have more sense.

'Grandpa loved the picture – he said Turner did it from memory. I believe it was my grandfather's single biggest investment in a painting, though, as you know, he had quite a collection, some of which ended up in your house.'

Attached to her letter was another, rather crumpled epistle, in which in faded copperplate Joseph Turner acknowledged the safe receipt of a bank draft from Sir Thomas Gilmore in full settlement for an oil painting called *Hoylake Sands*.

Alec looked stupefied when he was shown the letter.

'Well, I'll be damned!' he exclaimed, and sat down, so flabbergasted that he forgot to apologise for using a swear word.

'This will do it,' he said with a satisfied grin. 'It will do it! You'll have plenty of capital to do whatever you want.'

Deeply moved, he got up and put his arms round Edna and hugged her, kissing her on either cheek. Then he smiled down at her little sister, and took her in his arms and did the same.

She blushed profusely as he held her for a moment before releasing her, and Edna decided that it would be very nice to have a brother again. As they discussed the moves they must make to put the painting on the market, she lit a cigarette and longed for Vital.

EPILOGUE

Timothy George stowed his godmother's wheelchair in the back of his van, and drove her and her thin graceful companion, Rosemary, back home from the ceremony at the cenotaph to Celia's old-fashioned house in Hoylake.

All three of them were cold and rather dispirited.

Timothy George went straight upstairs to his apartment on the second floor. He thankfully turned on the electric fire in his bedroom and changed out of his uniform, which was a little tight around his waist. He hung the garments on hangers, and unpinned his medals and laid them carefully on the dressing table. He stood, for a moment, frowning down at them, and wondered if his son, a pillar of a London bank, would keep them after he himself was gone. He doubted it.

He went slowly downstairs to join Celia.

Celia's house, which she and Alec had bought on their marriage, had seen many changes.

After Celia's marriage, Louise and Edna had continued to live in the cottage at Meols, until, one day without warning, a glowing Edna had calmly introduced to Louise a small, neat stranger with charming manners. His name was Vital Oliveira, who had just arrived from Brazil to work as a translator for a big Liverpool fruit importer.

During the long correspondence with his beloved, he had not been idle; he had sought assiduously a post in England, by writing to every British company he had ever been in touch with. It was Edna who had suggested the Liverpool Fruit Exchange as a possible source of work, and through them he had finally reached a

335

company which bought and sold fruit in Spanish and Portuguese-speaking countries. His excellent references, some of them from British companies, finally got him a decent post as translator. He would have to travel from time to time, but his base would be in Liverpool.

He had been in England two months, when he and Edna had announced to a startled Louise that they were to be quietly married within a month.

Since the couple wished to live in Liverpool in order to be near Vital's place of work, Louise had been thrown into a panic at the idea of being left alone in the Meols cottage.

Celia had wanted to offer Louise a home in her new house, but Edna would not hear of it. 'She'll start to bully you again, Celia, like she did when you were young,' she said forcefully. 'She could ruin your marriage. And, if I had her, she would probably ruin mine. Better by far that she should remain in the cottage.'

Through an employment agency, they found a penniless, culti-vated lady to be a companion-help to Louise. Though Louise complained steadily about her, the arrangement actually suited them both very well. They lived out quite productive lives in the cottage by continuing Louise's interest in the fate of deaf-blind veterans.

In later years, as she began to interest others in the desperate plight of these unfortunate men, Cousin Albert became a fund-raiser for her, and did much to provide Braille lessons and teachers for them. Their joint compassion was a first step in a journey lasting nearly thirty years, to keep the deaf-blind army privates from being put into mental asylums and conveniently forgotten. Dear Mrs Lou won some battles, but lost many others. She became known to many of the men as a tender presence who smelled of lavender and was not afraid to hug them. She was a much loved lady.

Warned by the startling sensations caused by Sergeant Richard Williamson's gentle fingers on her face when she had first met him, she kept her personal feelings rigidly to herself, though, in her heart, she knew that probably the kindest thing she could do for any one of them would be to take him to bed. Upheld by Victorian principles of the nobility of self-abnegation, however, she never took advantage of their loneliness, and simply hoped they might find their own compassionate young women. And a few of them did. For herself, it was a bitter inward battle.

Louise made generous use of the cottage's spare bedroom by offering free seaside holidays for anyone who was both deaf and blind. They were specially good about this when they received requests to accommodate tiny tots who were so afflicted. At Mrs Lou's, a number of children, for the first time, explored the feel of sand in their hands and waves breaking over their tiny feet, and the lovely cosy lavender-scented comfort of being rocked in Mrs Lou's lap.

While she had the physical strength, Louise worked steadily to try to improve the lives of deaf-blind servicemen. In a country exhausted by the greatest war in history, however, there was a tendency to deal, first, with the greater number of men who were blinded but not deafened.

Over many years, poor Louise was to have considerable problems with the military's medical community, as she struggled to give a better life to her doubly disabled boys. Steeped in nineteenth-century attitudes towards medicine, abominably snobbish, they might bestir themselves for officers, but, as far as they were concerned, too often the other ranks were born unto trouble, as the sparks fly upwards, and must, like Job, patiently endure their suffering. She had discovered to her horror that the usual way of disposing of them, if they were deaf-blind and had no family to whom they could be sent, was to put them into lunatic asylums. If they were not insane when they went in, they frequently soon became so in their desperate confusion. This tragic information fired her with even greater determination to help them.

It was only years later, after another war, that she came into touch with the Perkins Institution for the Blind in Boston, Massachusetts, and was able to suggest to others interested that there should be special training for teachers to work with the deaf-blind, particularly in military hospitals. The names of Helen Adams

Keller and her wonderful teacher, Anne Sullivan, became an inspiration.

Celia and Edna ran the antique business until Edna's marriage, after which Alec and Celia, helped by Ethelred and John and an art student or two, managed to run it, while, in quick succession, Celia gave birth to three healthy, mischievous boys, Peter, Paul and Bertram. They finally sold out in the second year of the Second World War.

The Second World War had brought them little but grief. When their last-remaining, third son, Bertram, was killed in Sicily, Celia and Alec offered part of their house as a home for his young widow, Margaret, and her twin boys. The second and third floors were made into a self-contained apartment for them. Celia and Alec occupied the ground floor, and, in later years, after Alec's death, the basement had been made into a living room and bedroom for a carer for Celia.

The grandsons were a consolation to Alec and Celia, as well as to Margaret. Alec had done his best to be a helpful grandfather to them, though he had not lived to see them grow into adulthood.

They were a cheery pair of young scamps, not in any way scholarly, and, in a country where jobs had become difficult to find, they had, after they left school, both joined the Navy.

To mitigate her loneliness after their departure, their mother continued to share Celia's house. Celia, desperately lonely after her own widowhood, was very glad to have her continued company. It was the merest chance that both lads happened to be on the same ship when, while serving in the Falklands, it was hit by a missile and sank.

Although they were not the only family to suffer losses in all three wars, Celia had, at first, thought that both she and their mother would go mad with the remorseless grief which seemed to stalk the family. 'It's so often the same families who serve,' she cried out in her sorrow.

Though friends were kind, and Margaret's mother left the hotel she owned in Devon and came north to comfort her daughter, the two women could find no relief.

Celia felt suddenly very old and weak. She said to Margaret

one day, 'My dear, you are still fairly young. On the other hand, I won't last long. You could make a new life. What about going to help your mother with her hotel? You would meet people. Begin a new life.'

So Margaret found Rosemary, an unemployed Trinidadian, to come to live with Celia, and then went down to Devon.

Unable to move around very much or go out without help, Celia thought she would die of boredom, never mind grief, though Rosemary became devoted to her and was happy in the small, private domain she had in the basement.

Then Timothy George was widowed. After his Royal Air Force service in the Second World War, he had run a small engineering firm in Birkenhead, and he and his wife used periodically to come out to Hoylake to visit his godmother. After his wife's death, he turned to Celia for comfort, the one person who had consistently shown him affection since the day he was born in her mother's house.

She persuaded him to move into the upstairs apartment.

'I shall leave the house to you, anyway,' she told him. 'I haven't anyone else to leave it to.

'Rosemary could look after both of us – she's a cheerful person to live with. And here, in Hoylake, you would have one of the best golf courses nearby – lots of male company.' She had chuckled mischievously, as she added, 'And I wouldn't complain if you found a nice lady to share the flat.'

Though Timothy George doubted he would ever find another female companion, even if he wanted one, he felt that the arrangement would, at least, relieve him of the bother of housekeeping. He had, also, a great affection for Celia; he had, since boyhood, frankly shared his troubles with her, because she had often had more time for him than his own frail, harassed mother. She was not nosy, either – she wouldn't want to know every detail of where he had been or what he had been doing.

So he agreed.

Rosemary was consulted, and for a much bigger wage, she was willing to look after them both. It was a strange little household, but it worked extremely well.

This afternoon, the three of them were to share a cold lunch in Celia's apartment, and Timothy, with the familiarity of a son, knocked and then entered her room.

Before going to attend to the lunch, Rosemary had helped Celia into an easy chair. She was napping, and her new white wig was a little awry on her head. He went over to a side table, and poured himself a whisky and soda. The clink of glasses woke Celia and, as she straightened her wig, she demanded one, too.

As she watched him pour the whisky, she remembered the baby put into her arms so many years ago. It seemed fitting that, in lieu of her own darlings, this child should be her final consolation, and she smiled faintly.

Her hand was surprisingly steady as she took the glass from him, and he sat down beside her. She held the glass so that a stray ray of sunlight lit up its rich amber colour.

She was silent for a little while, twiddling the glass between her fingers. Then she said, 'You know, Timmy, what with an Empire and two World Wars plus the Korean War – and the Falklands – this old country of ours has been drained of male brains for a couple of hundred years.'

Timothy snorted. After all, he thought, he himself was still here.

To humour her, however, he agreed. 'Administering an Empire must have been pretty draining,' he said lightly. 'All the hundreds of bright young sparks serving from India to the Caribbean who got killed off by yellow fever, malaria, cholera – and the Khyber Pass.' He grinned, as he mentioned the famous Pass. 'When I was a lad, if you didn't have a great-uncle killed at Rorke's Drift, you almost certainly lost one defending the Khyber Pass.'

'True,' agreed Celia. 'My mother's brother was killed in India.' She sipped her whisky, letting it slide around her mouth to savour it. 'At the service this morning, I was thinking what a different place Britain would be, today, if we hadn't lost those men – and then two consecutive generations in the wars. So many of them were well educated or highly skilled. Just think, we might even have had a government of men and women who knew what they were doing!'

This was so close to what he himself had been thinking after the service that he burst into sardonic laughter.

'Well, we did produce Margaret Thatcher,' he reminded her.

'She came too late, and she wasn't clever enough to keep us out of the Falklands,' Celia replied, her eyes suddenly full of tears for the third generation. 'Poor Mike and Dave.' She held out her glass to him. 'Would you get me another glass of whisky please, dear? I feel a little low today.'

He was immediately contrite, and poured another drink for her.

She took the glass from him and stared absently into it, as if she saw in its golden depths the long procession of lost legions, taking away with them their own, unused, individual brilliance, their skills and their seed. Then she sighed; she knew that she would soon join them.

As she lifted her glass, she suggested, with forced cheerfulness, 'To all our beloved absent friends. May they rest in peace.'

He turned to look down at her. So tiny, so old, he thought, yet so indomitable. He touched her glass with his.

'Amen to that, my dear,' he said very gently. 'Amen.'